Praise for *The Villa Triste*

"This novel has such a marvellous setting and great historical drama that it hardly needs a murder to get the action moving. [. . .] Grindle mixes a modern murder mystery with a clever historical one and both work beautifully. Readers who have no idea of the horrors the Italian partisans (many of whom were women) suffered will find the war story riveting, but the whodunit works as well." *The Globe and Mail*

"With convincing characters set against a nuanced plot, *The Villa Triste* is a fine, layered novel that perfectly captures the moral ambiguities of war." Jim Napier, *The Sherbrooke Record*

"A present-day murder investigation drags history back into focus as policeman Alessandro Palliotti races against time to unlock the past. Settle down for the long haul with this complex, involving read." *My Weekly*

"The women in the Italian Partisans finally get their due in fiction [. . .] Markedly more at ease in the contemporary chapters than in the past, one of Grindle's distinguishing skills is characterisation and dialogue. And although for some the denouement may not come as a great surprise, this story overall is exhilarating. It is also, of course, profoundly sad – or triste, as they say in Florence." *Herald Scotland*

"A beautiful evocation of those dangerous times, this subtly drawn thriller then jumps forward to the present day and a murder in 2006, which seems to have connections to the partisans. Delicate and with a narrative style that deserves the greatest respect, there are echoes of Michael Dibdin in Grindle's second book, and I can think of no higher praise" *Daily Mail*

"Here is the perfect summer holiday read. Long, gripping and beautifully written." *Literary Review*

"Away from such tranquil, bucolic scenes Lucretia Grindle has explored Tuscany's dark, disturbing soul and delved into an equally foreboding chapter of its history to distil a complex, enthralling thriller. . . Carefully crafted with an authentic and compelling dialogue, Grindle saves her best story-weaving to the thrilling denouement that creates a surprise as unexpected and delicious as the finest Florentine cuisine." *Daily Express*

"Using the smallest of detail – a reflection in a mirror, the light shining on a ring, the heat haze hanging over the river – she brings to life a city and its people. Exhilarating, emotional and enthralling, this is a story that lingers in the mind long after the last page has turned. . ." *Lancashire Evening Post*

Also by Lucretia Grindle

The Villa Triste

LUCRETIA GRINDLE

McArthur & Company
Toronto

This paperback edition published in 2011 by
McArthur & Company
322 King Street West, Suite 402
Toronto, Ontario
M5V 1J2
www.mcarthur-co.com

First published in Canada in 2010 by
McArthur & Company

Library and Archives Canada Cataloguing in Publication

Grindle, Lucretia W.
    The villa triste / Lucretia Grindle.

ISBN 978-1-55278-969-8

    I. Title.

PS3557.R552V54 2011   813'.54   C2011-904478-1

Cover illustration by Mel Curtis/Getty Images
Printed and bound in Canada by Webcom

10 9 8 7 6 5 4 3 2 1

For Susan and Darci,
my own Isabellas

Author's Note

Although the characters in this book are fictional, they are inspired by the lives of real people and the events of 1943–1945 that are described are true. By the end of the war, over 200,000 Italians were formally recognized as members of The Resistance. Some 55,000 of those were women, 35,000 of whom were named as *Partigiane Combattente*, Partisan Fighters. This is only a tiny portion of their story.

PART ONE

—◦◦◦—

FLORENCE

8 September 1943

My wedding dress slid over my head, the ivory satin cool and slippery. The day was hot. It was barely noon, and already a blanket of stuffy air hung over the city, turning the sky a pale dirty blue. I could feel my hair wilting, loosening from its hairpins and sticking to the back of my neck as the seamstress's assistants, a cadre of silent young girls in pink pinafores, fastened me into the dress, their deft fingers working the rows and rows of tiny buttons. When they were finished they took me by each arm, like an invalid, and stood me on a stool, ready for the final fitting.

I could hear a clock ticking in the front of the salon, loud and slow, marking the time in thick syrupy drops. I tried not to count in my head. Crazy people count in their heads. Hysterics and lunatics. Thirty-two seconds passed before the Signora herself came into the fitting room. She looked at me and made a clicking sound with her teeth. Then she went to work. With every tuck and pinprick the dress tightened, until I began to wonder if this was how a snake felt just before it shed its skin.

My sister, Isabella, had vanished. She had put in a brief appearance at the salon but now, through the fitting room's half-open door, I could see her hat, abandoned on a pink tufted settee.

3

The hat was ugly, and had been insisted upon by our mother. It was Mama's fiftieth birthday today, and instead of coming with me, she had stayed at home to oversee the preparations for the party we were giving, and deputized Isabella in her place. Before we left the house, Mama had reminded us that the Signora was, under no circumstances, to have her way with the number of buttons on the cuffs of my dress, and then insisted, almost as an afterthought, that we wear hats. Mine was pale green and matched my dress. Isabella's was blue straw with a pin in the brim. Neither of us particularly cared for hats, but Isabella especially resented being told what to wear. She was nineteen and had just begun her second year at the University, where, she informed our mother, no one wore hats. As we left the house, she jammed the offending article down onto her forehead muttering that 'she wouldn't be surprised if it blew into the river'.

But that had not happened. Because by the time we had got our bicycles out of the shed, and made our way down the hill and through the Porta Romana and along the canyon of the Via Serragli and finally arrived at the river, we had forgotten all about hats, ugly or otherwise.

As we came out onto the Lungarno, Isabella and I both realized at the same time that something was wrong. The knowledge passed between us, swift and sure as an electric jolt. There was never much traffic any more, due to the endless shortages of petrol, but now there was none. Pausing, we looked both ways and saw that the long straight avenue was eerily quiet. Below the walls, the reed grass was dull and still, the Arno glassy and sluggish. A haze shimmered over the brown water. Yet despite the heat, no one was walking on the bridge ahead of us, or lazing against the balustrades. Instead, people were gathered in tight little knots. Groups clustered and spilled off the pavements. Voices hummed like a swarm of bees.

Isabella and I exchanged glances. The strange electricity that hung in the air was not altogether unfamiliar. The city had felt like this before, as recently as six weeks ago when Mussolini was deposed. In fact, ever since then the country had felt slightly stunned, as if it were wandering along trying to wake up from a very deep sleep. Now it appeared that something else had happened, but I couldn't imagine what it was. It was true that the Allies had made a first attempt at invading the mainland in Calabria – but that had been days ago. Old news. And was so far away that it might as well have been happening in another country.

Without speaking, Isabella got off her bike and passed it to me. I propped the handlebar against my thigh and watched while she crossed to the nearest group of people. A few moments later she came back, one hand holding the silly-looking hat, the other gesturing, as if I was supposed to guess what it was she had to say. When she reached me she became very still, her face turning inward, as if she was trying to understand what she had just heard.

'Issa?' I asked finally. 'Isabella? What is it?'

I suppose from the look on her face I thought that perhaps the king had died, or Winston Churchill, or Stalin or the Pope. But it was none of those. My sister looked at me, her blue eyes dark.

'They're saying it's over.'

'Over?'

'Yes.' She nodded.

'What's over?'

'The war.'

I stared at her.

'The war?'

'At least for Italy,' she said. Then she added, 'It's just a rumour. But they're saying Badoglio's left Rome.'

Isabella took the handlebars of her bike but did not get back on. Without thinking I slipped off mine.

'Left Rome?'

I knew I was sounding like a parrot, or an idiot, or both.

But I couldn't take the words in. Surely the Allies hadn't some-how reached Rome and chased the Prime Minister away? In less than a week? Without us hearing a word about it?

'Why would he leave Rome? What do you mean?' I asked. 'What are you talking about?'

My sister began to walk. I fell into step beside her. As we neared Piazza Goldoni I could see people coming out of build-ings and milling about.

'An armistice.' Isabella looked at me, her eyes sliding side-ways under the brim of the hat.

'An armistice?'

The parrot again. A look of exasperation crossed her face.

'They're saying that Badoglio has signed an armistice with the Allies,' she said, very clearly, as if she were speaking to some-one deaf. 'He's supposed to make an announcement on the radio, at eight o'clock tonight. To say that Italy is no longer at war. With America or England or anyone,' she added, in case I hadn't understood.

But I had. Too well. I stared at her. We were crossing the pi-azza by then, turning into the street where the tiny and fear-some Signora had her salon.

'But—' I said.

Isabella nodded. 'I know.'

She looked down, apparently concentrating on the toes of her shoes. We turned into the street and stopped. Bolts of satin, a basket of white roses made of ribbon, and several pairs of small pink shoes surrounded by wisps of tulle featured in the salon's window. Beyond them, we could see the interior of the front room, soft and pink as a womb, and the door that led to the fitting rooms at the back, ajar.

'I know,' Isabella said. She looked up, reading my face, fin-ishing the thought I had barely even begun. 'I know,' she said again. 'If we are not fighting the Allies, then what about the Germans?'

I felt my mouth go dry. My fiancé, Lodovico, was a naval

officer, a medic on a hospital ship serving off North Africa. He was due into Naples any day. In two months, he would have leave, and come to Florence, and we would be married.

'You'd better go in.' Isabella nodded towards the door of the salon and took the handlebars of my bicycle. But nothing happened. I stood rooted to the pavement. *Eight weeks*, Lodovico's last letter had said. *Eight weeks. Here is a kiss for every one of them. Then I will be home.*

Now, I tried not to shift, to stamp from foot to foot in my matching satin slippers like a horse bothered by flies. There was no point in asking the Signora. Her world was composed solely of seams and hems, of pleated lace and the exact placement of tiny satin rosebuds. Moreover, she had made it amply clear, more than once, that she did not care for 'chat'. Mothers might occasionally intervene on matters of necklines and bodices. Brides, however, were to be poked, prodded, grateful, and silent.

It was almost half an hour before the Signora stood up. For the final ten minutes she had been squatting on her haunches behind me. Oblivious to what might or might not be happening in the world beyond the salon – to anything but the quality of available silk, and whether or not the right 'foundation garments' could still be found in Milan or Paris – the little woman muttered something. Two of the pale silent creatures who shadowed her handing out marking chalk and measuring tapes stepped forward and helped me down from the stool, one on each arm again, and stood me, like a giant doll, facing a large standing mirror that was covered with a sheet. Without speaking, they arranged the train of my dress, smoothing it across the floor. A third girl appeared, carrying a swathe of tissue paper, holding it in front of her with both hands. She laid it on a bench behind me. I heard a faint rustling. Then they placed the veil on my head.

I glanced through the open door. The hat remained on the settee, but Isabella was nowhere in sight. I suspected she had gone to try to find a newspaper, or listen to a radio, and I could hardly blame her, but I wished she would come back, all the same. My heart felt strange, like something in a cage. A few more of the girls materialized. Standing behind me, they formed a semicircle in order to witness the final creation. Faces full of studied expectation, hands folded in front of them, they waited. Then, finally, the tiny Signora rose on her toes. Her hand reached up, fast as a cat's claw, and whipped the sheet away, revealing the mirror like a magician revealing a lady sawn in half.

I blinked.

A tall girl blinked back at me. Her hair was hidden, covered in what looked like a spider's web. Her eyes stared. Wrapped in white, she looked like a column of smoke. Like a woman in a shroud. Like Lot's wife, who stopped and looked back, and turned to salt.

Isabella had found a newspaper, but it said nothing. Officially, there was nothing to say, because nothing had happened. But everyone knew that wasn't true. During the almost three hours since I had entered the salon, the streets had changed. The stunned, electric feeling had gone. The storm had broken and this time no one was asleep. As we cycled home, abandoning the hats – Isabella's on the settee and mine kicked to the side of the changing cubicle with a viciousness it probably didn't deserve – we found ourselves swerving. Braking. More than once we almost collided, trying to avoid people who ran into the street throwing their arms up, shouting and grasping one another.

At home, the house was in an uproar. Emmelina, who had

been our housekeeper for as long as I could remember, stood in the kitchen marshalling delivery boys and three local women who had come in to help. In the dining room, her niece sat at the table. When I had come down that morning, I had found the girl – a small solid creature with eyes as black as river stones – polishing silver and arranging tiny spoons and flat-pronged forks in fans on the sideboard. Now she was folding white linen napkins, her square, blunt-fingered hands creasing them into triangles. On the terrace, two men in blue overalls were setting up tables and chairs. A string quartet was coming. There would be dancing. In the driveway, the grocer's old horse stood resting against the shafts of the cart that had been called back into service since petrol had become too expensive for tradesmen to use.

Our mother was not in evidence, so we escaped being berated about the hats. According to Emmelina, as soon as she had heard the news, she had gone upstairs to 'turn out Enrico's room'. My older brother had recently taken up his commission in the army and was stationed outside Rome. Emmelina said that Mama was absolutely certain, with the war now over, that his arrival was imminent. She had told Emmelina that his dinner jacket must be got out of his wardrobe and ironed.

I did not even bother to wash my face, much less change out of my rumpled, sticky dress. Instead, I went straight to Papa's study. Inside, I closed the door, and leant against it, savouring the dark, cool room that smelled of my father. Of his books, and his dusty papers. And of the Acqua di Colonna he wore and the faint, heady perfume of the cigar he allowed himself every Sunday afternoon.

I took a breath and wandered across the dark patterned carpet. There was a photograph of our mother on Papa's desk, a tall blonde girl with a wide smile. It was taken almost thirty years ago, but she did not look so very different. At fifty, she was still a handsome woman – strong boned, with fine skin and the dark-blue eyes she gave to all her children. Enrico and I had

Papa's dark hair. It was from Mama that Isabella got her lion's mane.

Lodovico had cousins in Caserta, and I was sure – being close to Naples, which after all was his home port – that they would know where his ship was. I knew that it was due in, carrying its cargo of the maimed and dying. His last letter had promised that he would write, or if he could, telephone as soon as they arrived. But I couldn't wait. On the bicycle ride home, I had become gripped again by the absolute certainty that they had been bombed. That the Germans must have attacked them at sea as soon as even a rumour of an armistice leaked out. I was sure of it. I sat down in Papa's chair and picked up the telephone. My hand was damp on the receiver. All I could hear was a dead, empty buzzing.

People tramped up and down the hall. From the dining room, I heard Emmelina fussing at her niece. I tried and tried again. But on the one occasion I did get an operator, she assured me that it was futile. All of Florence, all of Italy, was trying to get a telephone line. It was past five o'clock when the door opened and Papa came in.

He stood with the light behind him, so I could sense rather than see his expression. My father was a professor at the University, a specialist in Boccaccio. He was, like almost everyone else we knew, anti-Fascist. And like all anti-Fascists across Italy, he'd felt the air move a little more easily in and out of his lungs since the twenty-fifth of July, the day Mussolini had gone. Papa had never been an agitator, or even what one might really call an activist. His resistance had, instead, been quiet and unflamboyant and rather sly. Still, the strain of it must have been considerable. One evening about a month ago when we had been sitting on the terrace, he had turned to me, his long face soft in the last light, and told me that he had never quite believed the day would come. That he still felt surprised, as if he had found quite by accident that he had been holding his breath for over twenty years.

Now the straightness had gone out of his shoulders. His linen suit was as rumpled as my dress. Like my mother, my father had blue eyes. They were not as dark as hers, but they were wider, rounder. Behind the wire frames of his glasses, they looked like a child's eyes. Mama said once that she married him because he looked like a poet. These days, his hair was flecked with grey. It still fell over his forehead. He was in the habit of pushing it away as he spoke.

'Caterina?' The signet ring he wore on his left hand next to his wedding band caught the light that seeped through the half-open curtains.

'I've been trying to find Lodo.'

I wasn't sure the words actually came out of my mouth. If they did, they were not much more than a whisper.

Papa closed the door and came into the room. He smiled, but sadness blurred his face. He leaned down and took the telephone out of my hand. My father replaced the receiver gently in the cradle, then he placed his hand on the top of my head, stroking the snarled tangle of my hair that had long since escaped its pins and the tortoiseshell clasp I had tried to tame it with.

'Tomorrow,' he said. 'If we don't hear from him tonight, we'll get word of him tomorrow.'

I closed my eyes, my head resting against Papa's hip. The linen of his suit scratched against my cheek.

'Papa,' I said finally.

'Yes, my love?'

'Are the Germans coming?'

'They're already here.'

I knew I sounded like a child, like anything but a twenty-two-year-old woman who was about to be married, but I couldn't help myself. I looked up at him.

'No, I mean here,' I said. 'To Florence. Do you think we'll be occupied?'

For what seemed like a long time, my father didn't answer me. Then he said, 'Yes, Cati. I should think we will.'

That evening Isabella and I stood between our parents and greeted our guests as they arrived. Supper was served on the terrace by the women who had come in, all of them now in starched white aprons that Emmelina had found from somewhere. Then, just before eight o'clock, the musicians stopped playing, champagne was poured, and everyone moved into the sitting room to crowd around the big radio and listen to what we all already knew the Prime Minister was going to say. That the Italian government had asked the commander-in-chief of the Allied forces, General Eisenhower, for an armistice, and that the request had been accepted.

There was dead silence as Badoglio spoke, his voice wavering from the radio. As a result, he said, Italian forces would immediately cease all acts of hostility towards the Allies.

Then, the BBC announced that the Italian navy had been ordered to sail its ships immediately to the nearest Allied port. Issa was standing beside me. She reached out and gripped my hand.

The quartet we had hired were four old men, their tailcoats and white ties impeccable and shiny with age. Not that you would have known it, because after the radio announcement the music became quite wild. High and fast, it was like Gypsy music, flung from the strings in bright unravelling spools. Champagne corks popped. Down the hill in the city, the bells began to ring. A few minutes later, fireworks went off. Standing at the terrace wall, I watched the livid colours spiralling upwards, snagging in the branches of the garden trees and tangling in the smatter of stars.

It was well past midnight before the terrace finally emptied and nothing was left except tables covered with crumbs and empty glasses. A few of Papa's friends, colleagues from the University, had stayed on. As I went up, I paused on the stairs, listing to their voices rise and fall, lapping like waves from behind the closed door of his study. Part of me wanted to turn the handle and slip through into the safe, grave world of men's voices and cigar smoke. My father had always made me welcome, had always allowed any of us to join in his conversations. I paused. Then I realized I was too tired, and slipped my shoes off and crept upstairs.

The curtains over the window at the end of the hall had been pulled, but light still seeped under my door. I pushed it open, realizing I must have left the lamp on the dressing table on, and almost tripped over Isabella's dress. She had shed it like a skin. Dropped it on the floor, then drifted into my bed. The covers were pulled up almost over her face. A floss of hair spread across the pillow.

Standing there holding my shoes, I didn't have the energy to be angry. Issa had done this when she was a child, floated from her bed to mine as if there were no real difference between the two. At least tonight she had left me some space. I bent down and picked up the dress. It was her favourite, an iridescent blue shot with green. The silk came from Como. Mama picked it out. The bolt she chose for me was copper-bronze. With my skin, Mama said, with my hair, I couldn't wear green. Even blue, I should beware of. My colours were autumnal. Bronze, copper. Occasionally, scarlet. I hadn't said anything, but I didn't like my dresses. I didn't want to wear the colours of dying leaves. I, too, wanted to be a dragonfly.

Smoothing the skirt, I eased open the wardrobe and slipped the dress onto a hanger. Then I opened my bureau drawer, and saw that Issa had helped herself to one of my nightgowns. My trousseau was locked away, otherwise she would probably have rifled that, too. Belongings didn't really exist for my sister. She simply picked up what she liked.

Looking at her nestled in my bed wearing my nightgown, I

wondered if Isabella would ever be forced to grow up. Probably not, I thought. Probably she would be one of those people who lived forever with the special privileges allowed to youngest children – the charm and skills bred of indulgence. It was a joke in our family that Issa could get away with anything.

I was brushing my hair when I felt her watching me. I looked in the mirror.

'Are you scared?'

I put my brush down. Then I stood up and pushed open the window and closed the shutter.

'Yes,' I said. 'Move over.'

She wiggled sideways and I climbed into bed. I threw my head down on the pillow and yanked the blanket. Issa waited a moment, then she yanked it back and laughed. High and bright, the sound sparked the darkness.

By the time I woke up the next morning, she was gone. I lay in bed feeling the echo of her in the room and watching the slats of sunlight slide through the shutters. I'd been dreaming of Lodovico. I'd heard his voice. Seen him smile. As I woke up, he was walking towards me in his officer's uniform. I closed my eyes and tried to summon him back, to feel the touch of his hands. Then I remembered, and leapt out of bed. The Allied port.

Downstairs, the debris of the party was still scattered about – dirty glasses, cigarettes stubbed out in ashtrays. I glanced at the hall clock. It was past nine on a Thursday morning. Papa and Issa would have left for the University ages ago. From behind the kitchen door, I could hear a dim murmur of voices. The radio. I skirted the dining-room table, and pushed through the door.

My mother was standing in the middle of the room. Like me, she was still wearing her dressing gown.

'Mama?' I asked, my eyes straying to the counter where the radio sat. 'What's going on? What's happening?'

All of us, Issa, Rico, and I, had learned over the years that our mother was not someone to turn to for reassurance. That Papa was the one who could be relied on to chase monsters from under the bed and thwack through the bushes, proving that Count Dracula was not, in fact, at the bottom of the garden.

Mama looked from the radio to me.

'The Allies have landed at Salerno.'

'What?'

'Late last night. Early this morning. It's still going on.'

So, it had happened. I sat down suddenly, the kitchen chair rocking with the motion.

As the voices had been lapping to and fro in Papa's study, as I had been yanking the blanket with Issa and dreaming of Lodovico, the invasion – the real invasion – had begun.

After university, I had begun training as a nurse. But my skills were still not such that I was in much demand at the hospital, and it had not been much of a problem to get two days off for Mama's party. So once we had recovered from the news, and Emmelina arrived, with her niece in tow to do the 'heavy work', I spent my day half helping to tidy the house, but mostly hovering around the telephone. I still could not get a line, and no calls came in. Mama and I were like cats on hot bricks, starting every time we heard something in the street, darting to the windows in case it was Enrico or Lodo or someone with a telegram. But the only people who came were the men who folded up the tables and took away the chairs. For the most part, they were morose and silent. Whereas yesterday people had been jubilant, even giddy, now a watchful, almost sullen, mood had set in. All day long, the radio babbled.

Papa and Isabella finally came home, much later than usual. As we sat down to dinner, they recited the news of the day. But by then Mama and I had already heard it. The Germans had moved faster than anyone expected. In little more than twelve hours they had occupied Padua, Bologna, Verona. Milan would be next. Then us.

No one knew what was happening in Salerno, exactly, but Papa had spoken to colleagues who insisted they could hear the guns from Rome. Everyone expected another landing, possibly at Ostia, or even farther north – on the Argentario, or at Livorno. Badoglio and the King apparently really had vanished, signed the armistice and fled Rome. Despite his best efforts, Papa had not been able to find out anything more about the navy. There was no news about the movement of specific ships. He had not been able to get a line to Naples, nor had he been able to get any news of Enrico. Rumour said that the divisions based around Rome would attempt to defend the city, but as the country appeared to have no government, no one knew who would be in command.

On hearing this last piece of information, Mama, who had left her plate untouched, got up from the table abruptly. From the sitting room we heard the snap of the bar door, the clink of a glass and a bottle. After that, Papa stopped talking and pushed his food back and forth. I cut a potato into pieces, smaller and smaller and smaller. Only Isabella ate, methodically and without speaking, like a horse.

She was, she informed me after dinner, going out with a group of her friends, to a 'meeting'. When I asked her what it was about, she shrugged and said, 'nothing'. Which I suspected meant a visit to one of the cafes around San Marco. I had joined these outings once or twice. But most of Issa's friends were from the University mountaineering club – she shared that particular passion with both my father and my brother – and on the whole, they were rather too hale and hearty for me.

'Answer the door, will you?' Issa said. 'If Massimo comes? I just need my coat.'

'You're going with Massimo?'

We were standing in the hall. She shrugged as she started up the stairs. 'We all are,' she said. 'He has a car.'

And petrol to put in it, I thought. I had met Massimo once or twice. He was a year or so ahead of Issa at the University – in engineering, which was presumably how he had got out of being sent off to die for his country. His family came from somewhere around Siena and owned land, rather a lot of it. He was a beefy fellow, loud and opinionated, with a rather self-conscious booming laugh. The others had treated him with a certain amount of awe. I suspected he was used to getting what he wanted. Including petrol.

The doorbell rang, and I opened it obediently, wondering if Papa knew what Issa was up to.

Massimo stood on the doorstep with his hat in his hand. He looked rather more subdued than I had remembered him. At least he'd cut his mood to suit the occasion.

'Caterina.' He took my hand as I invited him in, standing half in the open doorway. Behind him I could see the shape of a car in the drive, and hear voices rustling in the warm night.

'I hear,' Massimo said, giving a little bow, 'that congratulations are in order. A doctor?'

He said this as if I had just bagged an excitingly large deer.

'Yes.'

'Your fiancé is very lucky.'

'Thank you. He's in a very dangerous position. As an officer,' I said suddenly, sounding prissy, even to myself. 'In the navy.'

I don't know why I added the last remark, probably to highlight the fact that Massimo wasn't – in the army, or the navy, or anything else, except the mountaineering club. And was therefore in no danger at all from anything, except possibly twisted ankles.

If he heard the insult, he was gentleman enough to ignore it. Instead, he smiled again and said, 'Then he matched his good taste and courage in choosing someone as beautiful as you.'

I blushed, feeling as badly as I am sure he intended me to. And probably as I deserved.

Massimo had extravagantly lashed rather pale eyes. Just then, they flicked away from me, over my shoulder, to Isabella who was coming down the stairs.

'Hello,' she said, and Massimo's charm, so evident moments before, deserted him. Looking at her, he was simply tongue-tied.

Issa shrugged into her coat, although the night was warm.

'I won't be late,' she told me, although I hadn't asked. Then she slipped past Massimo and down the steps, and they were gone.

Later, as I dried the dishes, Emmelina whispered to me that she had heard the city prisons had been opened. Cut-throats and murderers, she said, were on the streets. Prisoners of war and who knew who else. It was, she assured me, impossible to buy a lock, or even a piece of chain or stout rope. There were none left in the shops. In all likelihood we would not have to worry about the Germans because we would all be slaughtered in our beds well before they arrived. She hoped I was going to lock my door and windows. As she left for home an hour later, I saw what I recognized as the tip of one of our bread knives sticking out of the folds of her big black coat.

I didn't put much stock in the story – although it turned out to be perfectly true – if only because it was the sort of thing Emmelina loved. She had been working for us since shortly after Enrico's eighth birthday when I was five.

Every afternoon, Emmelina had collected us from school, and entertained us while walking home with some dire tale or other, usually featuring automobile accidents or train wrecks. It was Emmelina who had invariably bandaged my scraped knees when Enrico pushed me over. Who had sat with me over countless cups of hot milk at the kitchen table while I related to her all the adventures and dramas of my days.

After she had gone that night, I felt suddenly bereft. Papa was in his study. I knew I could interrupt him, but I had nothing, really, to say. And he would be getting ready for a lecture. I went upstairs instead to check on Mama. The door to my parents' room was ajar, the lamp on the bedside table on. My mother was curled on the bed asleep, the picture of Enrico she kept on her dressing table beside her on the pillow.

Mama's grandfather had made a fortune in mining. Marrying our father had been considered a romantic concession to love, but one she could afford. We had a gardener who came twice a week, and a man who helped with the car. When Rico and Issa and I were very small there had been a nanny, who had eventually been replaced by Emmelina. Until not long ago there had been a live-in maid. Now, with Enrico in the army, me at the hospital, and Papa and Issa at the University all day, the phalanx of people who had surrounded my mother had dwindled. On most mornings, she was left alone until Emmelina came just before lunchtime.

I don't know if I considered whether or not she was lonely, but I had noticed that she had developed the habit, when she thought no one was watching, of running the tips of her fingers over the surfaces of our furniture, as if she could read their history like braille. A desk that had belonged to my great-uncle. The chair that my grandfather had been sitting in when he died. It occurred to me that when we were gone she must drift through the too-big house, picking up traces of ghosts and playing the piano while she waited for the day to unravel.

My mother was not an unkind woman; she was not even what could be described as 'cold'. It was simply that she had made it clear, from the time we were very small, that she had a single reservoir of love, and that it belonged to Enrico. I don't know what my father felt about that, other than a vague sort of sadness, but Issa seemed to have decided some time ago that she did not care. I was not so lucky, not so good as my sister at being impervious. I reached for the blanket folded at the end of the bed and slid it over my mother, gently tucking it in at her shoulder.

Downstairs, I wandered into the sitting room and picked up the telephone again, imagining that somehow I would hear Lodo's voice. That he would tell me to put on my best dress because we were going dancing. Or say that he'd call for me in half an hour so we could walk down to the bridges and watch the lights on the river. This time, however, not only was there no voice – no promise of dancing or kisses in the dark – there was not even a reassuring hum or click. There was nothing on the line at all. Just silence. We had been cut off.

I replaced the receiver carefully, suddenly afraid of making a sound. Through the glass doors, I could see the empty terrace and beyond the balustrade, the city below. Crouched in its valley, it looked like a huge animal holding its breath.

I slept badly, heard Isabella creep along the hall some time after midnight, and left early for the hospital the next morning. Despite my fractured dreams – filled with the sound of cars, and Lodo's voice mingling with my father's and Massimo's – I was glad to be back in my uniform and out in the new light. I cycled fast, allowing myself the fantasy that perhaps the Germans would simply decide to go somewhere else. Or that the landing at Ostia, or even Livorno, would happen today and it would be the Allies instead who came marching down the Lungarno bestowing cigarettes and chocolate cake.

The illusion was pleasant but fleeting. When I arrived, I found the ward I had been assigned to in chaos. Explaining anything to junior nurses was not a priority at the best of times, and it took me almost half an hour to get someone to stop rushing about long enough to tell me what was going on.

Some time during the night it had been decided that we

should make a complete inventory of everything – all supplies, medication, linens – and then pack away and hide as much as we could reasonably manage in the cellars, the isolation ward, even the morgue. A rumour was going around that the Germans, on taking control of Bologna and Verona, had requisitioned all hospital supplies and sent them to their own medics at the front. There were no swastikas hanging outside the Palazzo Vecchio yet, but the Director thought we had, at most, twelve hours. After dithering through yesterday, complete panic had broken out.

I spent the remainder of the day carrying boxes downstairs where they were being bricked into a wall which had been hastily torn down for the purpose. Picking my way through dust and rubble, I refrained from thinking about hygiene, or the lack of it, or the fact that any German would surely recognize a newly bricked wall when he saw one. The decision had been made, and we slaved like worker ants. By the time I left, I was so tired I could barely cycle home. The heat had lingered. The sun was silver-pink on the river. People were loitering in the warm evening, just standing on the bridges, staring into the water or up at the hills, as if they were saying goodbye.

I wound through the Oltrarno, where I passed an abnormal number of people pushing carts and wheelbarrows laden with God knows what. Overnight, we had turned into a city of burrowers and hiders – victims of Requisition Fever. Even Papa had been infected. The night before, on one of the few occasions he had spoken after Mama left the table, he had announced that he was having the mechanic come to take the wheels off the car. It would be put up on blocks in the shed. Common wisdom said that if you wished to keep your car at all, this was the only way to do it. I wondered if Massimo was busy doing the same thing at this very moment. Personally, I thought the Germans might find an entire city of wheelless cars somewhat suspicious. It also occurred to me that if Lodo was still alive and somehow managed to appear at the appointed time and hour, I would probably have to walk to my wedding. Or sit on the handlebars of Papa's bicycle.

I turned up by Santa Felicita and saw that the side gates to the Boboli Gardens were open. I was half tempted to stop and go in, to see if there were digging parties interring knives and forks and pots and pans and whatever else they could manage under shrubs and in the grottoes the same way we had bricked our precious supplies into the cellar walls. But I was too tired and too dirty. My uniform was covered in dust. I could feel grime in my shoes. Even the pins in my hair felt dirty. I made my way out through the Romana Gate. Then my legs failed me. At the bottom of our hill, I got off and trudged, pushing my bike.

I don't know what it was that made me stop on the hill and look up at the house. But the moment I did, I knew something was different. Even here, higher up where there was often a breeze, it was stifling. The heat pressed down like a broad, heavy hand and in the thick evening light our house seemed to waver like a mirage. The ochre tiles on the roof looked soft, as if they were melting. I half expected to see streaks, long and dull red, on the greying plaster. The gate to the drive was closed, which was odd. Behind it, the huge grey-green pine tree, its boughs dripping towards the lawn, looked as if it were swaying, although the air was perfectly still.

At first, I thought it was exhaustion – that I was so tired I could not keep the world still around me any more but was instead watching it simply melt away. Then I realized my heart was running too fast. It was beating inside my chest, flailing its fists like something trying to get out.

I almost dropped my bike in the street. When I did get to the gate, I was in such a hurry to undo the latch, my hands suddenly all thumbs, that I left my bicycle propped against the stone column and heard rather than felt myself running up the drive. I must have looked wild, with my eyes wide and my mouth gaping, when I burst through the front door and then into the sitting room and saw them all standing there. Mama, Papa, Issa, and Enrico.

I don't remember what I said, if anything. All I remember is the feel of Rico's arms, and the smell of his shirt, of mothballs and soap. I remember him lifting me off my feet and swinging me around, the way he did when we were children and he used to tease me about who was stronger.

'You're not dead. You're not dead!'

I do remember, idiotically, that I said that.

And I remember that Rico laughed, and finally put me down and said, 'No, I'm not dead.' And that that was when I looked around and realized there was someone else in the room, a tall blond boy I didn't know.

My hand went to my hair. Suddenly embarrassed, I was aware of my grubby uniform, my armband that had slipped.

'Cati,' Enrico said, 'this is my friend and fellow officer, Carlo Peralta. Carlo, my other sister, Caterina.'

'How do you do?'

He was a good head taller than I, and, even in what I realized were a set of my brother's old clothes that were far too short for him at the ankles and wrists, quite simply one of the handsomest men I had ever seen. People say this all the time, but Carlo truly did look as if he had been sculpted by the hand of God. His hair was almost as blond as Isabella's. The features of his face were clear and strong without being hard. His smile was quick and generous, and in the shadowed light of the sitting room, I could see that his eyes were hazel, almost gold, like a cat's eyes. I dropped his hand abruptly, and turned towards Rico.

'But how did you get here?' I asked. 'What happened? When did you arrive?'

Papa put his arm around Rico's shoulders; together they looked like a younger and older version of the same person. Isabella, who was unusually quiet, was loitering by the terrace doors.

'Supper,' Mama said. Which was not an answer to my question. She smiled, reached out and touched the side of Enrico's face, brushing his cheek with the tips of her fingers as if she could not quite believe he was real. 'I must get the supper.'

As she said it, I looked through the archway into the dining room, and noticed that something was wrong. The table was not set; there was no noise, and no smell of cooking, coming from the kitchen beyond.

'Where is Emmelina?'

'I told her not to come.' My mother answered without taking her eyes off Enrico's face, as if she was afraid that if she stopped looking at him he would vanish.

'We thought it better.' My father looked at me, saying something with his eyes that I didn't understand. 'Now, who would like a drink?' He clapped his hands. 'There's something still, I'm sure, in the bar!'

'I'll get the food. Everything's cold,' Isabella muttered.

I followed her, waiting until the door was shut and we were out of earshot before I asked, 'Issa, what's going on? How did they get here? Where's Emmelina?'

'I went round this afternoon and told her we wouldn't need her for a bit. I said Mama had flu and she shouldn't come in case she caught it.' Issa didn't look at me as she spoke.

'What?'

I could barely remember a time when Emmelina had not been in the house. She even came in at Easter. The idea that she would not nurse my mother, or any of us, if we really were sick, was absurd.

'Why?' I asked.

Mama could barely boil an egg, and Issa was not much better. Apart from anything else, the reality of this arrangement meant that preparing meals would be left to me.

'Issa!' I protested.

'For God's sake, Cati!'

Isabella spun around, a serving plate in her hand that, for a moment, I thought she was going to throw at me.

'Don't you understand?' she said. 'They've left their regiment. They're deserters.' She waved towards the sitting room. 'If anyone sees them, if anyone says anything—'

'You can't think Emmelina—' I stared at Isabella, amazed. And angry. 'What?' I asked. 'Inform on them? On Enrico? You think Emmelina would inform on Enrico? She loves him. She loves all of us. She would never—'

I was genuinely shocked. Isabella shook her head.

'We can't take any chances,' she said grimly. 'She might mention something. She might not mean to, but—'

I shook my head in disgust. 'That is ridiculous.'

'It isn't.' Issa looked at me. 'It isn't,' she said again. 'You'll see. We aren't going to be able to trust anyone.'

So this was it, I thought. This was the real poison the occupation would bring to us.

'Well then,' I said. 'What about him?' I waved towards the sitting room. 'What about this – what's his name, Carlo? Who's he? For all you know, he might be a Nazi spy.'

'He isn't.'

Issa said it with a calm that suggested she had already considered the idea and rejected it.

'Oh, yes?' I ran my hand through my hair, shaking it loose of its dusty pins. 'Well, how do you know?'

'Because,' Issa said, turning towards the pantry, 'he's one of us.'

Dinner was not, in the end, an utter disaster. The strangeness of the menu gave the meal a slightly Dionysian air that was enhanced by the fact that Papa had gone down to the cellar and retrieved several bottles of his best wine, while Mama had laid the table with our best china and silver. I had decided, while lying in the bath, where I had retreated after my argument with

Issa, that I would fix the situation with Emmelina in the morning regardless of what my sister thought. In the meantime I intended to enjoy the fact that my brother was not only not dead, but at home. Everyone else apparently felt the same way. We ate and drank with exuberance, expecting to hear jackboots in the drive at any moment.

It was in this atmosphere that Enrico told their story.

On the morning after the armistice, their commanding officer had called his junior staff together and told them to send their men home. He had received news that the Germans were interning Italian troops – rounding them up and herding them onto trains that would ship them east, to either German labour or prison camps. With Badoglio and the King having fled south to get behind Allied lines – we now knew that that was where they had gone – the country was effectively without a government. The army was rudderless. Determined not to give in to the Axis, they were without any plan that enabled them to stand with the Allies. With tears in his eyes, the Colonel, who had fought through the previous war and through Russia and somehow survived both, had told his junior officers that it had come to this. That the best he could do for them was advise them to desert and give them the option of staying out of German hands. He hoped they would carry their honour with them, and join the fight that was to come in the best way they saw fit.

Within hours, the barracks were empty. Enrico and Carlo managed to get a train as far as Chuisi. There they heard stories of German troops, of newly resurgent and invigorated Fascisti, and of POWs – Allied officers and soldiers who had either been released or stormed their way out of prisons, many of whom spoke no Italian at all, and who were roaming the countryside trying either to move north to get into Switzerland or France, or south to join the assault at Salerno. After listening to all this, they had decided that it was wiser to stay away from both towns and train stations. They got a lift in a farm lorry to Castellina, then another to Galluzzo. From there, they had walked.

It was an hour or so later when Enrico joined me in the garden where I had gone to retrieve my bicycle and to close the gates I had left open. The others were on the terrace, talking quietly and smoking, the tips of their cigarettes glinting like fireflies as they watched the lights of the city.

'Cati.'

He caught the handle of the shed as I was wheeling my bike inside, then held it as I came back out and slid the pin through the latch.

'I wanted to tell you,' he said, 'what I heard about the navy.'

I searched his face, my eyes taking a moment to adjust to the dark, to find the familiar contours of his straight nose, his chin, his high cheekbones that were so like my own. I knew that his eyes, like mine and Issa's, were dark blue, but I couldn't make them out, couldn't read whatever message they might be holding for me.

Enrico and I had not seen much of each other since I had started as a nurse and he had gone into the army. Standing there, I realized that I hadn't known, until I dashed into the sitting room and saw him, until he had lifted me off my feet, how much I had feared that he was dead. Or how much I had wanted him to come home. He had always been the leader, even when we were babies. As adults, we had the same hands, the same arch to our brows, the same frown. Yet, despite our physical resemblance, and the fact that barely two years separated us, my brother had always been closer to Issa than to me. They were alike, and took after Papa in their love of all things outdoors.

'Have you heard?' he asked. 'From Lodo?'

I shook my head, suddenly uncertain of my voice.

'Come.' Enrico took my shoulder. 'Let's walk.'

We climbed slowly up the slope at the side of the house, beyond the loggia and away from the terrace.

'I don't know anything for certain.' His voice had dropped to a murmur, the words mingling with the soft fall of our footsteps in the grass. 'But we heard that most of the fleet have reached Malta. They turned at once, as soon as the armistice was announced. They mean to put themselves under Allied command. That's probably where he is.'

He stopped. We were under the drooping boughs of the big tree. When we were children this had been our hideout. Even after the oppressive heat that had boiled up during the day, the soil was damp and cool and smelled of moss and pine needles.

'How is Mama?'

He didn't look at me as he asked the question.

I shook my head.

'I don't know. The same.'

The unspoken flowed between us. My brother had never said anything, but I knew that at times he found our mother's love for him a burden, as if he carried a weight for the three of us.

He nodded.

'Communication's almost impossible,' he said a moment later. 'Everywhere. Rome is cut off. And everywhere south. If Lodo doesn't contact you, it isn't because he doesn't want to.' He looked at me. 'Or because he's dead,' he said. 'You mustn't think that.'

Despite the stories I told myself, it was, of course, exactly what I thought.

'This is going to be bad,' Enrico said suddenly. 'All of it. The Fascistoni will come back. The Germans will put them back, to make it look as if there is at least some support for the occupation, and they'll want vengeance. They've been locked up. Humiliated. They'll come after their enemies. Which is just about all of us.'

'But the Allies—' I blurted. 'The next landing. Surely—'

Enrico shook his head.

'It isn't going to happen, Cati. A second landing. What we've heard is that they're barely hanging on at Salerno. The Germans are fighting like demons. They have to. It's their only chance. That's why Hitler sent Kesselring. They're not going to give up easily. They can't.'

The glow of the wine evaporated like smoke. In its place, I felt a sort of hollow sickness, as if everything inside me was turning cold and leaking away.

'What are you going to do? You and Carlo?' The question didn't come out as much more than a whisper.

'You can't tell anyone. I mean anyone outside the family. Anyone at all.'

I started to snap 'you mean Emmelina', but something stopped me. I could feel as much as see Rico frowning. His voice was the same one he'd used when we were children and he was swearing me to secrecy over a catapult that broke a neighbour's window, or a penny whistle he'd stolen from the shop at the bottom of the street. I wondered if I should raise my hand, prick my thumb and mingle my blood with his.

' I'm sorry,' he said. 'Cati, I'm really sorry. That I won't be here. That you'll have to take care of everything. Of Mama. And Papa,' he added almost as an afterthought. 'And the house. I'll contact you when I can. I promise.'

I wanted to beg him to change his mind. But I couldn't. Enrico would not be much good to any of us interned in a labour camp in Germany. I tried to take a deep breath. I tried to sound brave.

'Where are you going?'

I imagined Switzerland. Rico had climbed in school. He had relished the summer holidays my father took us on as children, walking the drovers' paths through the Apennines. I imagined a series of trains, lorries, farmers' carts, hikes that would get them into the Alps, and then out – over a pass higher, colder, more dangerous than I could ever face.

He paused for a moment. Then he said, 'There's a group – you'll hear more about it – the CLN.'

'CLN?'

Enrico smiled.

'*Il Comitato di Liberazione Nazionale*,' he said. 'It's why we came. To join the fight.'

'The fight?'

I don't think I even spoke the words. I had heard them once already this evening, through a haze of wine and candlelight. Then, luxuriating in the fact that my brother was home, that we were having a family meal where even Mama seemed happy, I had not been paying much attention. This time they sounded sharp and hard, something sitting in my stomach that I had been forced to swallow.

'Carlo's from the Veneto,' Enrico was saying. 'He knows people. They're already organizing there. We're going to do the same thing here. In the mountains.'

One of the things my family professed to love about this house, supposedly the reason Mama's grandfather had bought it instead of one in the city, or on the then-fashionable Poggio Imperiale, was the fact that you could see the mountains from the terrace. Rising behind the city, the slopes were dun, grey, or green. Above them, no matter what time of year, the peaks were tinged with white.

Enrico nodded.

'We're going tonight,' he said. 'We won't be here in the morning.'

He was as good as his word. The next morning when I woke up, Enrico and Carlo were gone. By noon, the Germans had arrived. I watched them, standing in a silent crowd, as they marched down the Lungarno, their boots shined, the engines of their jeeps and staff cars and lorries humming, their uniforms immaculate, their broken black spider hovering above them.

∽

Just in case we didn't understand, the news on Radio Roma that afternoon was broadcast in German. The next morning, Kesselring himself spoke to us. Smiling Albert informed us that 'for our own protection' we were under martial law. All communications and train lines had been taken over. With immediate effect there would be no private letters. No 'uncontrolled' telephone calls. And no resistance. Anyone going on strike, or found 'aiding or giving succour' to Allied POWs would face trial by court martial. Former members of the Italian forces were to report at once to the nearest German command. Squadrons of Italian volunteers would be formed, he said, to continue the glorious fight. What would happen to those who chose not to volunteer was not mentioned.

It did not need to be. We might have been shocked by the occupation, stunned like animals who have been startled by a large noise, but we weren't stupid. It didn't have to be spelled out. At the hospital the next day, a nurse who lived near Campo di Marte told me she had seen closed trains. Trains made up of carriages like the carriages used for transporting animals, but with human hands waving through the slats.

That evening, just before I left, one of the doctors walked into our tiny staffroom. He told us that since no one knew what was going to happen, all days off, all leave had been cancelled. Then he announced that the Germans had 'liberated' Mussolini.

The first announcement did not surprise me, and I suppose after what Enrico had said, the second shouldn't have. But it did. Hearing *Il Duce*'s voice on the radio two nights later was like hearing a creature from a nightmare.

Without the possibility of a phone call or a telegram or a letter, I was reduced to hoping that Lodovico would somehow miraculously simply appear. He didn't. But Emmelina did come back. I had gone to see her on my way to work the morning Enrico left, just as I had planned, and told her that Isabella had been mistaken. Mama's flu was not contagious, after all. Really, it was just a cold. Overexertion after the excitement of her birthday party.

It was the first time I could ever remember lying to Emmelina, and I knew perfectly well that she didn't believe me any more than she had believed Isabella in the first place. As I stood in the doorway of her tiny house, shifting guiltily from foot to foot, Emmelina had given me her sideways look, but said nothing. When she asked if we had heard from Rico, I simply shook my head. Then I said I had to go or I was going to be late, and got on my bike and pedalled, my eyes filling with tears because something infinitely precious had been broken.

Emmelina sensed it too. The week that followed was almost worse than not having her in the house at all. She came exactly on time, laid the table and made dinner without comment, and was always careful to close the kitchen door while we were eating, something she had never done before. She did not ask again about Rico, or about Lodo, or anyone. In fact, she barely spoke. There were no whispered conversations in the kitchen. I noticed that the bread knife had been replaced.

Then, one night towards the end of September, she was waiting for me when I came home, standing in her huge black overcoat at the bottom of the hill. I did not have to look to know that she didn't have her uniform on, or guess that she had not gone up to the house. When she handed me her key, I thought my heart would break.

'My brother,' she said. 'He has a farm near Marzabotto, in the mountains, at Monte Sole.'

I knew about the farm at Monte Sole. I'd heard stories about it, mostly concerning dead animals and accidents. I nodded.

'Giorgio thinks it's better if we go there,' she said. 'While we can.'

Giorgio was Emmelina's husband, a thin rail of a man who had a mule and cart and worked as a coal merchant. I knew he had been born in Florence and had barely ever set foot out of the city. I also knew, because she had told me – warning of the dire internecine wars I should be prepared for when I married Lodo – that Giorgio hated her brother with a passion and hadn't spoken to him for the better part of twenty years. The idea that they would go to sit out the war under his auspices seemed unlikely in the extreme.

I hugged her, breathing in the deep earthy smell of her as if I could keep it forever, and told her that this would soon be over. That I understood, and even agreed, and that they had best go while they could, while the trains were still moving and they might get a pass to get on one. I told her that I would be fine. That we would all be fine, and that I would see her again. Soon. Even as I said it, I knew every word was a lie.

When I finally stopped speaking, Emmelina held my hand for a moment. Then she said, 'Tell Rico I wish him luck.'

Whether I cared to acknowledge it or not, Emmelina's leaving exposed a gulf between me and the rest of my family. It had probably always been there, but now somehow it seemed larger. I had been her special child, known in my heart that she had loved me best, and I was angry with them, all of them, for driving her away. But most of all, I was angry with Issa.

The night Emmelina left, I could barely look at her.

Oddly, or perhaps ominously, things became rather quiet at the hospital once the Germans arrived, and at the end of that week. I was given Sunday off. By that last Sunday in the month, 26 September, I had come to terms with the fact that there was no longer any point in hovering beside the radio for reports that might tell me if Lodovico was dead or alive. A part of me still hoped that he might, somehow, appear in time for our wedding. But I no longer thought that I, or anyone else, could do anything about making it happen. In fact, by that time, I doubted that anyone could do much of anything about making anything happen. The news seemed to get worse every day.

The Germans had cooked up a Fascist puppet government,

and there was a new Republic of Salo. On the radio we were treated to nightly chants of *I believe in the resurrection of Fascist Italy, I believe in Mussolini*, followed by that stupid song, 'Giovinezza'. You were supposed to stand up when you heard it. *Il Duce* himself ranted over the airwaves with monotonous regularity, and what news we did get from the BBC, which presumably we could now be arrested for listening to, was terrible. The Allies were bogged down in Salerno. It looked possible that Kesselring might, after all, push them back into the sea.

Yet, despite all that, we were having a run of beautiful weather. Silver mornings, followed by blue afternoons and blurred golden evenings. The days spun on, mindless in their sun and shadows, and I decided the least I could do, given the opportunity, was take advantage of at least one of them. Directly after breakfast, a piece of toast which I ate alone in the silent kitchen, I went upstairs, got my paintbox out from its hiding place at the back of my wardrobe, blew the dust off it, and took it down to the terrace.

My parents had given me the paintbox for my fifteenth birthday. I had done well at drawing in school and, although I had no real talent, I enjoyed making little watercolours. I had an album of them. That morning, I decided to paint Mama's birthday, the old men in their tailcoats and the bright threads of music tangled in the trees.

I had been at it for the better part of an hour when Issa came up behind me.

I wanted her to go away, but she didn't. Issa had a way of demanding your attention, of absolutely insisting, when she walked into a room or came anywhere near you, that you looked at her. Anger roiled inside me. Churned, like some unruly inland sea. I dabbed at a block of paint with the tip of my brush. Then I stabbed at it, and bent the bristle, and streaked the sky above my picture black.

Issa pulled out a chair and sat down at the table beside me. Without asking, she opened my album and began leafing through my collection of pictures. There were several paintings of Lodovico, none very good. In one, he stood beside a dark-haired woman in a ball gown who might have been me.

Issa studied it for a moment, then she said, 'Massimo asked me to marry him.'

I didn't want to be interested in this, or anything else she had to say, but I couldn't help myself.

'Massimo?'

The idea of Isabella being married to Massimo struck me as faintly ludicrous. But then again, Aphrodite had married Vulcan.

'Yesterday,' she said, although I hadn't asked. 'While I was sitting outside the library. He says that I ought to marry him because things are going to get worse. And that he loves me,' she added as an afterthought.

'What did you say?'

Issa fingered the edge of one of my pictures.

'That I don't love him. No matter how bad things get. That I would never love him.'

There it was, just like that. Cold as a stone.

I looked at her out of the corner of my eye. Isabella had had many beaux, none of them, as far as I knew, even remotely serious. She was beautiful, undoubtedly, like our mother, with features so perfect they were almost a statue's. But underneath that perfect flesh, there was something hard. For all her laughter, all her game-playing and dancing, I had never seen Issa melt. Not even for a moment. She had a heart, I knew. But she held it close.

'Was he angry?'

She thought about my question for a moment. Then she shook her head.

'I don't think so,' she said. 'Actually, I don't think he believed me.'

'Didn't believe you about what?'

'That I didn't love him. I think he thought I was making it up.'

35

Issa shrugged.

'It won't matter,' she added. 'He's gone now, anyway.'

'Gone?'

Back to Siena to hide on his family's farms? To Friuli, like Emmelina, if she had gone at all? To Switzerland? Where did people go?

'Gone where?' I asked.

Isabella looked at me for a moment, as if she was weighing something. Then she said, 'To join the partisans.'

Something contracted in my stomach. If I glanced up, I would see the mountains from where I was sitting. I shook my head and pushed the feeling away, concentrating on my picture.

'Do you mean,' I asked, as casually as I could manage, 'the CLN – the Liberation Committee, whatever it's called?'

'No.' She shook her head. Then she added, 'Well, yes, but not really.' Issa looked at her hands for a moment, studying the pearly half-moons of her nails. 'Here it's called the CTLN, anyway,' she said. 'Committee Tuscan. But I mean GAP.'

I put down my brush and looked at her. 'Issa,' I said, 'what are you talking about?'

'GAP,' she said. '*Gruppi di Azione Patriottica*. The CLN will direct, coordinate everything. But GAP units will do it. The work in the field.'

I didn't want to ask what, exactly, 'the work in the field' was and the look on my face must have said so.

Issa rolled her eyes. 'For goodness sake, Cati,' she said.

A patronizing false brightness rang in her words.

'You may not realize it,' she went on, rather pompously. 'But we have to organize.'

'Organize?'

'Yes.' She nodded, animation lighting her face. 'The University. All of us. That's what we're doing. Organizing. For the fight.'

'The fight?' I was rapidly coming to hate that term. Hate everything about it.

If Issa heard the derision in my voice, she ignored it. Instead, riding a wave of enthusiasm she must have assumed was infectious, she said, 'Against the Germans. The Nazis, of course,' she added, as if I might need the clarification. 'But the Fascistoni, too. We're going to have to fight them both.'

'We?'

She nodded too eagerly. 'Yes. That's what the Partisans are doing. They're forming units, brigades, in the mountains.'

'Don't you think,' I said, 'that it would be a good idea to leave "the fight" to the Allies?'

I looked at her. My sister was all of nineteen. Not much more than a child. 'Who do you think you are, Issa?' I asked. 'What role are you playing? Nemesis? This may come as a shock,' I added unpleasantly, 'but General Eisenhower just might know more about this than you do.'

Even if I hadn't already been angry with her, this refusal to grow up, this readiness to treat everything as a jolly version of yet another game or outing with the mountaineering club, infuriated me. Enrico was one thing. He and Carlo were soldiers, after all. They at least knew what they were doing. Issa and her silly friends, on the other hand, had no idea what they were talking about. I doubted Massimo had ever shot anything other than a rabbit, probably with his father's fancy shotgun.

'So,' I said, 'let me get this straight. These gaps, made up of you and your friends, you're going to do what?'

'I told you.' Issa spoke too cheerfully, as if she was encouraging a stubborn child. 'We're going to fight.'

'We'. That word again. Fear throbbed through me. I laughed as nastily as I could.

'A bunch of students?' I said. 'With pitchforks and rabbit guns? What are you going to do?' I asked. 'Line up against the Third Reich? Take on Hitler's army?'

Issa looked at me. Then she stood up. The animation had gone from her face. Been replaced by something harder, and much more frightening.

'Yes,' she said, and walked back into the house.

By noon, a high scrim of clouds had made things dull. It was still warm, but I no longer felt the heat of the day. A clammy feeling washed over me. I started another picture, this one of Papa, on the terrace, wearing his old white hat and making notes at his table, but gave up when I got to the background. I didn't want to paint the mountains. Instead, I sat staring at them. I was still staring at them when the first bombs fell.

✐

The Allies always insisted afterwards that they had been trying to hit the train station at Campo di Marte. It was, one would have thought, rather a large target to have been missed so completely, and in the days that followed a sort of sick joke went around to the effect that they must be hard up in America and Britain if their pilots couldn't even afford glasses. Because, although they did hit a couple of the factories at Refredi, the station was untouched. Most of the bombs they dropped that afternoon fell in piazzas and streets. Where they hit houses. And the children's hospital.

Of course, I did not know that at the time, while I watched it happen. All I knew was that there was a strange sound, and then, in the east of the city, a flowering of fire.

I rose to my feet, almost hypnotized as petals of smoke blossomed and turned rapidly black, washing the sky like the sky in my painting. This is it, I thought. This is our Turin, our Cagliari, our Grossetto. There, they had bombed the carousel at Easter. And killed the priest while he was giving absolution. And four little girls who were herding geese in a field.

Isabella came running out onto the terrace.

'Bombs,' I said stupidly, without looking at her.

It occurred to me that neither of us had actually seen a bomb explode before. Not that it mattered. I knew exactly what this was. I recognized it the way you recognize things in dreams. 'They're bombing us.'

Issa gripped my shoulder, her fingers digging into me. I put my hand over hers. From the terrace, we could see black specks of planes. Several explosions came, very close together. And there must have been sound, but the strange thing is, apart from the first droning, I don't remember it. Then, finally, the afternoon was split by a high, repetitive whooping sound.

Later, I would recognize it as an air raid siren, the signal that was supposed to warn us. It began almost as soon as the last bomb fell.

'Come on,' Issa was saying. 'Hurry! Hurry up!'

She had begun dragging my arm, pulling me across the terrace towards the house. I looked at her. Something was shaking. At first I thought it was the earth, that the whole city was rippling in the aftermath of the explosions. Then I realized it was me.

'Cati!' Isabella shouted. She took both my shoulders and shook me, hard. 'You have to go to the hospital!'

I stared at her. I started to say I wasn't hurt. And then, as if her shaking had rattled something loose in my brain, I understood.

In the next moment we were running – through the house, out of the front door, to the shed where we kept our bicycles. I had pulled mine out, and was about to get on it, when I stopped and shoved it at Issa, forcing her to grab the handlebars.

'Mama!'

I started to dart towards the house, but Issa lunged and stopped me.

'She's in the cellar, with Papa. They put supplies down there a week ago.'

I looked down at her hand grasping my dress and noticed that something was wrong.

'My uniform.' The words came out as a mumble, the kind

of muttering you hear crazy people making in the street. 'My armband.'

'It doesn't matter.'

Isabella thrust my bicycle towards me. She said something else over her shoulder that I couldn't hear and then, before I realized what was happening, she was gone, and there was nothing for me to do but follow her, out of the drive, down the hill and through the Porta Romana into the city.

By the time we arrived at the hospital, the first ambulances had come in. There were people running everywhere. Issa shouted something to me about a civilian defence group and pedalled away. I didn't have time to wonder where she had gone. The moment I dropped my bicycle, a sister grabbed me by the arm. There was a woman holding a little boy. It took us the better part of ten minutes to convince her to let us look at him, to prise him out of her arms and discover what his mother must have known all along, that he was already dead.

The children's hospital was not far away, and we got most of the casualties. Two nurses who had been trying to evacuate a ward that took a direct hit died in the corridor because we couldn't get them into an operating theatre. There were babies screaming in bassinets. A little boy on crutches was looking for his father. A small girl with cuts all over her face was clutching a stuffed rabbit. And then the parents began to arrive, entire families looking for their children and grandchildren. One man ran up and down, a napkin still tucked into the front of his shirt, because his family had been eating Sunday lunch in Scandicci when a neighbour came running in and told them that the hospital where his daughter had had her tonsils removed the day before had just been bombed by the Allies.

The strange thing was that during all of that, as hellish as it was, I was not afraid. Standing on our terrace, I had been terrified. Literally rooted to the spot with fear. If Isabella had not dragged me, I doubt I would have moved at all. I probably would have stood there all afternoon and all night, shaking and staring like an idiot. But once I got to the hospital, once I had something to do with my hands – the fear fell away. It shattered like glass. And was replaced by a kind of nothingness. My fingers moved by themselves. My mouth spoke. My brain clicked and whirred. It chose the right instrument, moved methodically from one task to the next. During it all, if I had a thought, it was only this: Thank you General Eisenhower, Thank you Mr Churchill, if this is how you set us free.

Sometime towards evening, Issa reappeared. She was covered in dust. The University students had formed groups of 'civilian volunteers', and were helping to get people out of the bomb sites, in some cases digging through rubble with their bare hands. Issa came in an ambulance, helping a very old woman and her husband, who was screaming like a banshee. His arm was broken in three places – painful, but he'd live. Trying to comfort his wife while they set the bones, Issa found me and kept insisting there must be somewhere where she could make the old woman a cup of tea. There was no tea, and ordinarily, I might have been angry with her for saying silly things and getting in the way – but not then. Then, all the anger I had felt towards her just hours before melted away, and for possibly the first time in my life, I felt sorry for her, for what I saw in her face. Because, for all her bravado, Isabella was not used to blood, and bone, and flesh. If I had had the time, I would have told her not to worry. I would have put my arm around her and told her that all of us are made of this.

❧

The next morning, I was told of my promotion.

I had found a spare uniform in the linen store, and managed to tidy myself up enough to start my shift on time when the Head Sister, a small stern woman to whom I had barely spoken three words since she had accepted me at my interview almost a year before, called me into her office. I had no idea what I might have done, but all at once the preternatural calm I had acquired deserted me. My hand was shaking as I lifted it to knock on the glossy dark wood of her door. Somewhere in the back of my head, I think I must have believed that perhaps she had somehow had word of Lodovico and was going to tell me that he was dead.

I stood in front of her desk feeling like a schoolchild. I had always found nuns uniquely terrifying, and I was sure she would look at me and know I no longer believed in God, and that I was too fond of creature comforts, perfume and engagement rings, and was an out and out coward to boot. It was all I could do not to look down and see if my socks had sagged.

She was writing in a large ledger. Reading upside down was something I had always been quite good at, and I realized she was making lists of those who had died. When she put the pen down and looked up at me, I jumped.

Her eyes were quite large and very dark, her skin pleated with soft lines. Wrapped in her habit, she might have been anywhere from forty to sixty. I recalled something I had heard once, about God's children being ageless.

'Signorina Cammaccio. You must be exhausted.'

It didn't sound like a question, so I said nothing. Actually, I did not feel tired. I had not even thought about feeling tired.

She considered me for a moment. Then she said, 'You will understand, it is hoped that the children's hospital will be re-opened as soon as possible. Sadly, a number of their staff were killed last night. Naturally, we will be sending some of our nurses to the new facility to make up the numbers.'

She paused. I knew nothing about children and I hoped that she was not going to ask me to go – that she was not going to condemn me to weeks, or months, or even years, of looking into the faces of parents as I had last night. Of trying to explain to them why it was that God, or the Allied command, or the

Germans, or the Fascists had seen fit to break to pieces the bodies of their little boys and girls.

'This, of course,' she continued after a moment, 'will leave us short-handed.'

She rested her elbows on the ledger, steepling her small pudgy fingers over the names of the dead.

'I have had excellent reports of your conduct,' she went on, after a moment. 'And so, I am going to ask you to take on a new job. As of this morning, I will need you to take over as a ward manager.'

I stared at her. The relief I felt at not being sent to the new children's hospital lasted for about five seconds. Then it was replaced by something close to panic. I was a junior nurse. Most of the time I did nothing more than help with meals, sort linen that came in from the laundry, read aloud to patients, write letters for them, or occasionally hold their arm while they shuffled in baby steps up and down the ward and looked out of the windows onto the garden. I held trays of equipment for the sisters, watched while injections were given, and occasionally changed a dressing. I had done some science at university and the position at the hospital had been secured for me through a friend of Mama's. That was the sum of my qualifications. For the last year, I had appeared when I had been told to, done what was asked of me, and gone home.

In short, my 'nursing' was nothing more than an acceptably genteel hobby, something to keep me out of the house and occupied until I got married. The ward managers, on the other hand, were senior sisters. They arranged work shifts and controlled supplies, made decisions about beds and food. I had only the vaguest idea of how any of this was done.

'But, Sister!' I blurted. 'I can't.'

She cocked her head and looked at me. 'Can't?' she asked.

'No!'

'But, my dear, you have two years of university education, do you not?'

'Yes,' I said. 'But—' Flustered, I shifted from foot to foot. 'I'm merely a junior nurse.' My voice sounded small and disturbingly childish. 'I have no idea what to do.'

At this, she smiled. Then she stood up, and came around the desk, and took my hand.

'My dear girl,' she said. 'In the days that are going to come, none of us are going to have any idea what to do.'

It was late evening when I finally left. By the time I got to our street, I couldn't even trudge up the hill. Instead, I had the odd sensation that I was gliding, hovering an inch or so above the cobbles, as if I myself had also died but was simply too tired to attempt leaving earth. As I put my bike away, I registered dimly that neither Issa's nor Papa's bicycle was in the shed. I knew that they had both taken to staying late at the University, but I didn't have the energy to sort through what this might mean, or why it niggled in the back of my brain. Instead, I pushed the pin through the latch and walked back along the path.

Thick light fell through the trees. Dusk was fringing the edge of the garden. In another lifetime, and if the car had not been hunched under its shroud, I might have thought Papa and Mama had gone out for a drive, up to Arcetri, or to Piazzale Michelangelo to watch the sun set over the city. I took out my key, but the front door was not locked. When I pushed it open, the house felt empty.

There were no lights on. I walked down the hall. Untouched by the last of the sun, the rooms on either side – Papa's study behind its open door, the dining room and sitting room – seemed leached of colour. And wavering, as if they were underwater, and the furniture – the tables and chairs and photographs – might slip their anchors and float free.

I blinked. Then I crossed the dining room and pushed open the kitchen door. Plates from the breakfast or lunch my parents must have eaten had been washed but not put away. The leather silver canteen was closed and locked, its brass key bright in the shadows. The wine glasses sat ghostly on their shelf. There was a coffee cup on the counter, a dark outline of lipstick kissing its rim.

'Mama?'

There was no answer. I said it again, a little louder, and this time heard in my voice the telltale high note.

'Mama?'

My shoes clacked on the tiles. I let the door swing shut, crossed the dining room and hall and went through the arch into the sitting room.

'Mama, are you here?'

The glass doors to the terrace were closed. The table and chairs beyond were empty. Suddenly, I was gripped by the idea that no one lived here. That I had not been wrong after all when I looked in the mirror at the bridal salon. Because somehow I had slid through time, and dropped into a future where all of us were ghosts.

I turned and ran up the stairs.

'Mama!'

I banged open the door to my own room, to Isabella's beyond, to my parents' room across the hall, and finally to Enrico's.

She was sitting on Rico's bed, holding one of his sweaters, stroking it as if it was a cat, her hand moving back and forth like a metronome. The ring my mother always wore – the same ring that had been my grandmother's, an aquamarine surrounded by diamonds – glinted in the light from the open window.

I was standing not ten feet from her, but she didn't look at me. Instead, her dark-blue eyes were fixed on the window sill, as if she could see something there, something beyond the branch of the tree and the roof of the house in the street below. A picture, perhaps, of the children we had once been. Of the past we had lived, the one she traced, moving from object to object, with the tips of her fingers.

I turned and had started to leave the room when she spoke.
'Cati?'

I had not bothered to turn on the lights. It was nearly dark.
I looked over my shoulder. My mother was not much more
than a ghost herself. Her dress melted into the shadows. Her
legs, her arms and hands, appeared so pale they shimmered.
Her beautiful hair was colourless.

'I miss him.'

'Yes,' I said. 'I know.'

'Are you afraid?'

The question hung between us.

I nodded, my hand lingering on the doorjamb.

'Every day?' she asked. 'All the time?'

I nodded again.

My mother looked down at the sweater in her lap. Her hand
hovered over it, floating in the half light.

'I didn't think it would be like this,' she said.

In the weeks that followed, I did not see much of my family.
My new duties increasingly kept me late at the hospital, and
demanded that I arrive early. I even began, on occasion, to stay
through the night, sleeping in a chair in the staffroom, when I
slept at all. Autumn deepened. The nights drew in, and seemed,
when I was at home, to bring ghosts with them. They clustered
in the rooms where I had grown up. Flocked under the old
cedar tree and lingered by the shed. But mostly they seemed to
stare at me through my mother's eyes, as if they had come to
dwell inside her.

She left me plates of food. Pieces of cheese. An apple with a
silver knife beside it. A slice of ham on the increasingly frequent
nights when I did not get back in time to cook dinner. When
I did, she often sat at the kitchen table, watching, and smiled
at me, her face wistful, her fine features faintly blurred, as if she

were looking out from behind a mirror. The sensation was alien and unexpected, and made me feel so guilty that I began to fancy our roles had been suddenly reversed. That I was now the one who had never paid enough attention, never given enough love, and that my neglect had somehow left her prey to phantoms – allowed them to lure her into a strange cold place beyond the glass.

The sensation was deeply uncomfortable. Yet in some strange way, it drew us closer together. We never spoke of it again, but I became quite certain that – even though she had the luxury of knowing he was still alive – she kept Enrico close beside her in the same way that I kept Lodo. More than once, when we found ourselves alone, I had the mad thought that there were not two of us seated over breakfast, but four. That Mama and I were both sharing our toast and our thoughts, not only with each other, but with Lodo and Enrico, too. The angels who hovered at our right shoulders.

The children's hospital was reopened in a borrowed villa. The arrangements were made quite quickly, largely thanks to the German command, who vacated one of the properties they had requisitioned in order to allow the children to move in. They were, by all accounts, exceptionally helpful, even volunteering to set up the makeshift wards, an act of generosity that left everyone involved feeling both grateful and confused.

By mid October the Italian 'government in exile' – in other words, the King and Badoglio who were hiding safely behind Allied lines in the south – had finally got round to stating the obvious and declaring that Italy was at war with Germany. We had resented the Germans and been afraid of them before, of their marching and their flags and their tanks. Now they became officially our enemies. What they might do terrified us. But they were also, on occasion, capable of such civility. Even outright kindness. It was hard, sometimes, to understand exactly what one felt about them.

At about this time, rumours began to seep out of Rome – stories of raids on the Jewish ghetto, of sealed trains travelling east. We believed them and didn't believe them. We told ourselves that most of the German soldiers probably loved this war and Adolf Hitler no more than we did, and were just decent men trying to serve their country.

No such conflicting feelings, on the other hand, were aroused by our compatriots. Enrico had been exactly right in his prediction. The Fascists were not only back – they had returned bloated on triumphalism and bent on revenge, and were, if anything, more loathed and more loathsome than before. Certainly they were more dangerous.

It became clear that the German command had more or less turned the policing of Florence over to the forces of the Republic of Salo – or as we called it the Republichini, the little republic – and in particular, to one Mario Carita. No one knew much about him, at first. But as summer died and autumn dropped down, his black-shirted thugs, known as the Banda Carita, had begun to appear on the streets. Rumours travelled with them the way flies travel with corpses. There was a house on the Via Ugo Foscolo where it was said screams were heard at night. And another, on the Via Bolognese, which people began to call the Villa Triste.

At the end of the month, the weather broke. There was a chill at sunset. The thick honey light of late summer, the light of harvest and evening walks, vanished and was replaced by a succession of sharp, crystalline days. So sharp, that one morning, when I had got up very early, I realized that I would be quite cold cycling with just my thin coat over my uniform. It occurred to me, as I laced up my shoes, that I might borrow a coat of Issa's, or ask Mama if she had an old one. But no one else in the house was stirring, so instead of waking them I tiptoed into Enrico's room, just down the hall from mine, thinking I would take one of his old jackets. But when I opened the wardrobe, it was empty. There was nothing in it at all. Not even on the rack where his shoes and boots had been lined up. I stood for a moment, confused, trying to push back the now-familiar feeling that time was not running in an orderly progression, that instead it had got all mixed up and tipped me into a future where we no longer lived in this house, no longer even existed.

Telling myself that these fancies were one thing when there were shadows – I had always been afraid of the dark – but altogether too stupid for the morning, I turned to the bureau, and was more relieved than I should have been to find his box of shirt studs and cufflinks in his top drawer beside the silver-backed brushes that had been my parents' twenty-first birthday present to him.

It was the night after that when I came home so late that there was not even a sliver of light showing through the chinks in the shutters. For the first time I could remember, the house was completely dark.

I left my bicycle in the shed and crept along the path as quietly as I could, turning my key in the front-door lock, and actually freezing, stopping dead when it clicked, as if I were a thief. Easing the door closed behind me, I slipped my shoes off, then turned and locked the door again. My stockings whispered on the tiles. I started towards the kitchen, thinking that, unappealing as the offerings left for me usually were, perhaps I was hungry.

I had my hand on the door when something stopped me. There was no sound I could make out, no change in the shadows. But nonetheless I stood there, absolutely convinced that someone was waiting for me in the darkness on the other side.

I could hear the faint huff of my breath, hear my heart beating. Or was it someone else's?

My hand lowered slowly. I stepped backwards, shuffling on the cold floor in my stockinged feet. When I bumped into the edge of the dining-room table, the noise hung in the air.

Without thinking, I turned and darted across the hall. I grabbed the stair banister, no longer caring how much noise I made, and once in my room, turned the key in the lock and sat on the edge of the bed, wondering if I was losing my mind.

Finally, I stood up, went into my bathroom, and splashed water on my cheeks. When I looked in the mirror, I felt a pang of relief that Lodo was not actually standing beside me to witness the fear on my face. The thought made me smile. It wasn't until I'd peeled off my uniform, and pulled a nightdress over my head and walked back into my room, that I noticed that the wardrobe door was ajar.

I stood for a moment, looking at it. Then I told myself not to be idiotic. Crossing the room, I yanked the door open and jumped backwards.

My wedding dress had been delivered and hung in my wardrobe on its padded and scented hanger, swaying gently, as if it were dancing to unheard music.

I heard about the train the next afternoon. By this time, it was impossible to tell where stories, bits of information, or rumours came from. They simply sprang up, travelled like seeds on the wind, and took root. This one had grown, and was even bearing fruit, before I became aware of it.

I was standing in an upper corridor, looking down over the hospital's courtyard. The building had once been a convent, and the square at its centre was still ringed by a fine cloister and planted with brightly coloured beds. The patients loved them, but a few days earlier it had been decided that we could no longer afford the luxury of a garden. At least not for flowers. I was watching as the last rose bushes were lifted out and the soil was turned and tilled and made ready for the planting of potatoes. And cabbages. And beans. Food was getting more and more expensive. While flowers were good for the soul, it was becoming increasingly obvious that, regardless of when the Allies arrived or didn't, we needed to survive the winter.

My thoughts were running aimlessly along these lines. I was considering carrots, and whether I could afford to buy myself a new coat, and whether it had been entirely frivolous to tell the old gardener when he had sidled up to me that of course he could keep the clump of irises in the western corner since they were the emblem of the city, when I sensed someone standing beside me.

It was the same nurse who had told me about the sealed trains at Campo di Marte. Had I heard, she asked? Her voice was hushed. She was standing close enough to touch my shoulder, but was not looking at me. No, I murmured in reply, I had heard nothing. She nodded, a slight almost imperceptible movement of her head. Then she told me. Three nights ago, the partisans had sabotaged a signal box on the railway lines just outside the station. A night train destined for Fossoli, the transit camp that was a first stop before worse to come in the East, had wheezed to a halt. As soon as it had, the carriages had been stormed. Two hundred Allied POWS had been freed.

As she spoke, the courtyard below me vanished. I no longer saw the rose bushes, their root balls tied neatly in sacking, or the old gardener with his bent back and his hand hoe. Instead, I saw Issa's face. And Massimo and his rabbit gun. And heard Enrico's voice, and remembered his empty wardrobe.

Late that afternoon the radio announced that the rules had changed. From now on, aiding and abetting the enemy, and any and all acts of sabotage that previously might have earned a court martial and imprisonment, would be immediately punishable by death.

That night, I left the hospital early. It was just after seven when I got home. I left my bike in the hedge by the gate and walked up the drive as quietly as I could, sticking to the neatly clipped grass verge so I would not make noise on the gravel. The up-stairs windows stared glassily out onto the garden. The down-stairs shutters were closed. Chinks of light slipped through the slats, winking against the dark.

Before I opened the front door, I stood for a moment on the step. Then I walked quickly back to the gate and looked up and down the street. Nothing looked different. All the other houses looked like ours – still, and glowing quietly from within. A man was making his way up the pavement. I heard his foot-steps before I saw him, and instinctively stepped back. I watched as he turned into a drive down the hill. The home of a new family, whom I did not know and who had only been on our road for a few years. The door opened. Light flooded out and was cut off. Then there was no one. I turned and walked quickly back, staying on the verge again, then slipped in through the front door, quiet as a cat.

From where I stood in the hallway, I could hear the mur-mured rise and fall of conversation. Straining, I tried to make out the words, but I was too far away. The kitchen door was closed, the voices were muffled. I considered taking my shoes off. Then, even as I had begun to bend down to unlace them, I realized that I was too frightened. And too angry. I could hear Enrico's voice in my head, *You'll have to take care of everything. Of Mama and Papa. The house.* I stood up, my heart hammer-ing, took a deep breath, and walked quickly across the dining room and shoved open the kitchen door.

I don't know what I expected, but it was not what I found.

Isabella was standing at the sink. My mother was in the act of placing a very large pot on the stove. They turned towards me at the same time, their mouths open in surprise.

To say that this domestic tableau was uncharacteristic would have been generous. With their golden hair, their fashionable dresses, and their lipstick, my mother and Issa looked like bad actresses playing housewives. Beyond that, I knew for a fact that neither of them cooked.

Mama recovered first. She smiled, wiped her hands down the front of the apron she was wearing, and then, as though she was doing a bad imitation of Emmelina herself, said, 'Cati, how nice. You're home in time for dinner.'

Issa's eyes caught mine, and I thought I saw her smile. Before I could be sure, she turned back to whatever she was doing deep in the well of the sink. The radio babbled on the table. Mama turned it down.

'Racket,' she said, too brightly. 'So loud it's hard to hear yourself think. Supper's nearly ready, if you want to go up and change.'

She picked up one of our largest bowls that had been brought out from the cupboard and was sitting on the counter.

'I'll set the table,' Issa muttered. She took a stack of plates and slipped past me into the dining room.

'If I'd known you were coming home,' Mama added, 'I'd have waited. So you could have had a bath. Papa's in his study,' she added, for no apparent reason.

The brightness in her voice was almost as alarming as the apron. Without saying anything, I crossed the room and went into the pantry.

There was cheese on a cutting board. The bags of pasta and rice I had bought the week before were in their bins. Bread. Eggs. Milk, in the cold store. Two cabbages. A basket of onions. Another of carrots. All supplied thanks to the black market and Mama's money.

I stood there, not sure what it was I was looking for. I had got very good, thanks to my new job, at doing inventories in my head, but recently I had been gone so much from the house, and certainly from the kitchen, that I was no longer sure what had been taken or replaced.

I could sense Mama watching me from the kitchen. I looked around, taking in the shelves, and the mincer, and the cold store. My eyes stopped at the cellar door. The top bolt was shot. I reached out and put my hand on the porcelain doorknob. It refused to move. Locked. I looked up. Nothing hung on the little hook beside the doorjamb.

'Where is the key?' I stepped back into the kitchen. 'To the cellar?' I asked. 'Where's the cellar key?'

My mother had relinquished the bowl and was now peering into the oven, so I couldn't see her face as I spoke. But I saw her back. It stiffened. Nothing much, just a reflex action, like someone bracing for a blow.

'Mama—'

I was about to ask – no – demand to know what was going on, when she closed the oven door, straightened up, and looked at me. At the sight of her face the anger I had built up shattered. It fell at my feet like a broken shell, leaving nothing but the naked fear underneath. The same fear I saw mirrored in my mother's eyes.

'Mama—'

As I stepped towards her, Isabella pushed through the kitchen door.

She stopped, looking from one of us to the other. No one spoke.

Then my mother smiled brightly. In the garish light of the kitchen her lipstick was too red. It seemed slightly lopsided, as if she had put it on quickly, not bothered as she usually did to sit at her dressing table or bend in front of the hall mirror. A strand of hair had come loose and she pushed it out of her face.

'Papa has the key, darling,' she said. 'To the cellar. It's in his desk.'

At supper, Papa and Issa talked too loudly – about the University, a new series of lectures on Dante that someone or other was giving, and about the fact that, although the Allies had finally broken out of Salerno and taken Naples, they were now bogged down again thanks to appalling weather in the south. Papa had heard that there were 400,000 German troops in Italy. Every bridge and road in Naples had been destroyed, and they had booby-trapped their retreat. A favourite trick, he said, was to bury a landmine in the craters left by other mines at the side of what had been roads, so that when planes came over strafing, Allied soldiers who dived for cover were blown to smithereens.

I did not ask how he had acquired this gem of knowledge. I did not ask anything at all. Instead, I sat watching my mother. She, on the other hand, avoided looking at me for the entire meal – which was suspiciously tasty – a chicken, a treat from the back room of the butcher down the road, that had been jointed and baked.

As I ate, I wondered when, exactly, either Mama or Issa had learned how to do this. But then, I thought as I looked around the room, there were a lot of things I wondered. Why, for instance, although I could see no visible change, our house was different. Why a vast pot of potatoes had been boiled when we would eat, at most, one apiece. Why Issa and Papa would not stop talking and Mama would not talk at all. Why, in short, I was suddenly a stranger in the midst of a family that looked and sounded like mine. Suddenly, I wished powerfully for Emmelina, or for Lodo. Or preferably for both of them. For allies in this alien territory I had somehow wandered into.

Mama went to bed immediately after supper, volunteering, quite suddenly, that she had a headache. When I offered to bring her a cup of camomile tea, she shook her head, saying she was merely tired and was sure she would feel better in the morning. Papa stayed in his study. Issa insisted on clearing up by herself. I left her to it and attempted to read in the sitting room, but finally gave up. Upstairs, I locked my door and sat on the bed, trying to push away the feeling that I should march downstairs and demand the cellar key. That I should slip the bolt, and open the door, and follow the stairs down into the dark.

The next morning, when I left very early, the house was silent.

The cellar door was still bolted, the key was still missing. The bowl had been put away, and the large pot had been scrubbed and hung up. There was no sign of potatoes.

Issa was waiting for me that night when I left the hospital. There was a thin mist, the beginning of rain, and it was cold. She was on foot, and had a scarf wrapped around her head and her hands dug deep in her pockets. We walked in silence for the first few minutes, my bicycle between us. As we reached the Duomo, the bells began to ring. We stopped for a moment, looking up at the striped marble and the great red hat of the dome that seemed to drift above it. A squadron of pigeons clucked at our feet, then lifted and flapped away, their wings fluttering into the grey evening light.

We had moved on, following a crocodile of schoolgirls, all with long braids and holding hands, and had reached the Baptistry – which looked derelict without its bronze doors, like the hovel of a hermit – when I asked the question.

I asked it without looking at her, concentrating instead on the spokes of my bicycle which were shiny with damp and glinting in the light of the lamp on the corner of Via Roma.

'How many are there?'

I felt rather than saw her glance at me, then felt the sharp jump of her shoulders as she shrugged.

It had been a long day. One of our patients had died. There was a rumour that Spanish influenza had broken out near Siena. I was tired and cold and had not yet had time to try to buy a new coat.

'How many what?'

The casual ring in her voice made my temper snap.

'For God's sake, Issa!' I jerked the bike to a halt. 'Are you going to tell me,' I hissed, leaning over the basket, putting my face as close to hers as I could. 'Are you honestly going to tell me that you had nothing at all to do with that train? That at this moment there is no one in our cellar? Eating our food?

Wearing Rico's clothes? Because if you are going to tell me that, I don't believe you. In fact,' I added for good measure, 'if you are going to lie to me, I don't even want to talk to you.'

'Keep your voice down!'

She grabbed the handlebars of the bike and kept walking. I stood for a moment, feeling my heart thump in my chest, feeling the colour rise in my cheeks, then scurried after her. Ahead of us, a pair of German soldiers stood on the pavement, smoking, their greatcoats spangled with damp. We skirted them, stepping into the street.

'Three,' Issa said a moment later.

I had thought as much. The pot of potatoes on the stove last night had been enough for at least six people.

'Which one of them is the cook?'

Issa glanced at me and almost smiled.

'One of the Americans. There are two Americans and one English. How did you know?'

'That they could cook?'

'That they were there.'

'No matter what you may think, Issa, I am not stupid.'

Ahead, in the Piazza Vittorio Emanuele, the carousel was going around and around, the music high and tinny in the chilly air. There was a smell of chestnuts coming from a brazier tended by an old man whose dog lay at his feet. His wife twisted cones out of newspaper, used her fingers to fill them, and dropped coins into a can. Café Paskowski was already crowded, the tables by the window bright smears of colour behind the glass.

'Does Rico know?'

Issa smiled. 'Of course.'

'And Mama and Papa?'

She did not bother to answer. She knew that I knew in any case, that I had seen it in my mother's eyes the night before – the knowledge that what was below our very feet as we stood in the kitchen, that what was behind the cellar door, that the very food that she had placed on the stove and slid into the oven, were all reason enough for us to be dead.

I stopped and looked at my sister. 'Why didn't you tell me?' I asked.

Issa looked back at me. She waited for a moment. Then she shrugged.

'Because we couldn't trust you.'

There it was again, that thing inside of her. The words were not said with any venom, not laced with any particular malice. Just stated as fact.

I felt them like a blow. Like a slap. So firm and hard, my eyes watered.

Issa was watching me – waiting, I suppose, to see what I would do – so I turned and looked up at the Orsanmichele, pretended to be studying the Della Robbia rondels, some of the few pieces of art actually left in the city, because I could not bear for her to see that I would have been the first person to agree with her. To admit that, in all likelihood, it would not have been wise to trust me. Because I was too weak, and too frightened. I always had been. Even before the war, I had not been as strong or as brave as Isabella or Enrico. I had not had noble thoughts or inclinations. All I had wanted to do was marry Lodo and have the sort of dull happy little life that millions of women like me had had for centuries.

I wiped my eyes with the back of my glove, and turned back to her.

'I don't see, then,' I said, 'why you're telling me now.'

'Because we need you.'

I stared at her. And thought of that boy – of poor Massimo with his big laugh and his cold eyes, who was probably also in this up to his neck, but who, no matter how many Nazis or Fascists he faced, would never come up against anyone harder than my sister.

Snatching the handlebars of the bike, I pulled it away from her and turned towards Via Calzaiouli.

Isabella waited for a moment, then hurried after me. She placed her hand on mine and pulled me to a stop.

'Don't!' I spun around on her. 'Don't ask me for anything.'

Issa took a step back, as if I had hit her.

'It's one thing,' I said, 'if you want to call me an untrustworthy coward to my face – I admit you may be right. But if you hold me in such contempt, you can't also ask for my help.'

She opened her mouth to speak, then closed it. Issa stepped backwards again, up onto the pavement, and I walked away, not certain where I was going, but so angry I could feel myself shaking.

In Calzaiouli, not all of the shops were closed yet. People flocked and separated, walked and stopped to look in windows. Life was doing its old imitation of normality. I could feel myself trembling, biting back tears.

I closed my eyes and wished with all my heart that I could open them and see Lodo walking towards me. He did not want me to be a partisan, or join a fight, or blow up trains, or do whatever it was Issa was going to ask me to do. He just wanted me to be his wife. Because he loved me.

I felt a hand on my shoulder and jumped. Isabella had caught up with me.

'I'm sorry. I'm sorry, Cati,' she said. 'I shouldn't have said that. That was wrong, about not trusting you. I'm sorry.'

I felt my foot falter.

'Is that what Mama and Papa think, too? That none of you can trust me?'

I stopped and looked at her. She shook her head.

'No. No.' She shook her head again. 'I said that because I was angry, because you'd made fun of us, that day on the terrace. And I wanted to hurt you.' Wisps of her hair had escaped and curled in the damp air. 'Papa said I shouldn't worry you. That you have enough to worry about, at the hospital, and with Lodo. He's right. I shouldn't have. It was wrong. I'm sorry.'

'He's known from the beginning, hasn't he?'

Isabella waited for a moment, then she nodded. 'He was – he and some of the other professors. They were helping at the beginning. To organize.' She was watching me closely as she spoke, knowing how much this would hurt, this additional exclusion. She put a hand on my sleeve. 'He didn't want any more risk than necessary. He said not knowing would keep you safer.'

'And what about Mama?'

I knew I shouldn't ask it, but I couldn't help myself. It was like pulling a scab, then pulling it some more when it started to bleed. Issa didn't answer.

'And Enrico?' I demanded, remembering how we had stood under the cedar tree. 'Doesn't he trust me, either?'

Isabella shook her head. Then she nodded. In the strange misty half-light, I saw that her eyes were blurring, welling up.

'Rico told me I should come to you, if I ever needed anything. I told him you didn't like what we were doing. He said it wouldn't matter.'

'You've seen him?'

She nodded.

I reached up and touched the bottom of her eye with the fingertip of my glove. The fawn-coloured leather darkened, matching the smear left by my own tears.

'I'm not as brave as you or Rico,' I whispered. 'You know that.'

She shook her head.

'It's true,' I said. 'We're different, Issa. I'm not like you. I'm afraid for all of us. All the time. I don't want to fight. I just want this to be over.'

A couple skirted around us. We began to walk again, reaching the corner and turning down towards the bridge. The smell of chestnuts hung in the air. I stopped at the next brazier and bought a paper twist of them. For a moment Issa and I walked and chewed in silence.

'It's not safe for Mama and Papa,' I said, lowering my voice until it was not much more than a dull murmur swallowed by the crackling of the paper cone. 'I don't care if Papa helped to organize it. We have to take care of them. We have to do everything we can for them. That's what makes me most angry with you,' I added. 'If they're found, Mama and Papa could be shot. You have to get those men out of the house.'

Issa nodded. 'I know.'

I glanced at her.

'I'll only help you if you promise – no, swear to me – that no one else will ever be in the house. Never again.'

She nodded.

'All right. Yes.'

'For Mama and Papa's sake.'

'Yes.'

'No matter what they say. Swear?'

She looked at me.

'I mean it,' I said. 'I want you to swear. On Mama's life.'

'I swear on Mama's life.'

'All right,' I said a moment later. 'Then tell me what it is you want me to do.'

We had come to the bridge. Despite the fact that it was damp and cold, there were still people hurrying home or crossing from the Oltrarno down into the city. A few were feeding the fish, dropping crumbs and the husks of chestnuts into the river. Issa took my elbow and guided me to the edge. We looked down, just able to make out the dark floating shapes, the ripples in the water, the occasional snap and gaping mouth.

'We have an ambulance,' she murmured, 'and a driver. To get them up to Fiesole. To the monastery.'

The monastery was being used as a rest and recuperation home for soldiers with shell shock and worse. The truth was, many there would never recuperate. If they were lucky, the best they might get was a little rest.

'From there the trail goes into the mountains,' she said. 'Remember?'

I did. It was the start of the Via degli Dei, the pilgrims' trail we had walked one summer with Papa that led all the way over the Appenines and down to Bologna, and the Po Delta beyond. From there, there were any number of routes north, to the Alps and Switzerland.

I looked at Issa. She glanced at me, then back down at the fish.

'There are roadblocks,' she muttered. 'We need someone, a nurse, who can explain why the patients are being moved.'

I felt a cold that had nothing to do with the mist or the evening. It blossomed in my stomach and feathered upwards towards my heart. I nodded before it could reach my mouth and seal my lips.

That night, we sat down to dinner with three frightened, cowed-looking boys who had been sleeping for the better part of a week in our cellar. Mama's English was fluent and Issa spoke a few words. I could not say a word to them, or understand what they were saying. But they were someone's brother, someone's friend, and for all I knew someone's fiancé or husband, too. Any one of them might be Lodo, or Enrico, or his friend Carlo. That I had felt angry with Issa for bringing them into the house, that I had blamed her, and them, for my own fear, filled me with guilt. For their part, they had been told of the plan. All through the meal I was aware of them watching me carefully. Summing me up. Trying to decide if I could keep them alive.

Issa had decided that it was best to move them in the late afternoon. Dusk was coming down earlier and earlier. Once in the mountains, they would walk at night. She wanted to make as much time as possible, get well away from Fiesole before they had to seek cover at daybreak.

It was not until she said this that I realized she would be

going with them, guiding them along the Via Degli Dei, over the pass and beyond the fortifications the Germans were building. Once on the other side, she would hand her 'parcels' on to a group from Modena who would get them to Novara, then hand them on again. When she told me this, she joked that she had become a postman. I did not ask her if Rico would be there too. Or how long she would be gone. Already I understood that it was better if I didn't know.

❧

By the next morning, I had realized that Issa's plan was not quite as simple as she thought it was. We had decided that it would be best for the ambulance to come to the house. To try to move three POWs through the streets, either to the hospital or to some other rendezvous spot, was simply too dangerous. Instead, we would put the story about that Mama had slipped on the stairs, fallen, and hit her head. She would stay out of sight for a few days and then 'return' from the hospital. With no staff in the house any more, that would be easy. More difficult would be pilfering the supplies to transform the three boys into invalids.

Thanks to my new job, I had access to bandages and the like. But I could not simply put them in a shopping bag and walk out with them. Or could I? I'd lain awake pondering this, and decided that was exactly what I would do. I sometimes stopped at the early market, so it was not entirely unusual to see me coming or going with a rucksack. That solved, I moved on to the two stickiest points – the papers that I should be carrying to transfer my 'patients', and how I myself would get away early without arousing suspicion.

I began working on the second problem the moment I arrived at the hospital. For once, I eschewed the small amount of powder and lipstick I normally wore. Having been awake all night, it was not too difficult to look pale and a little glassy-eyed. Around mid morning, I began to cough – not much, but regularly. By lunchtime, the senior ward sister was eyeing me suspiciously. An hour later, she told me to go home.

I protested that it was only a bit of a cold. That might be, she said. But if we were to have an outbreak of influenza, as everyone now feared, she would need all of her staff fit. She could not afford for me to become run-down. By two o'clock I was on my bicycle, pedalling back over the bridge with a bunch of carrot tops sticking out of my rucksack, rolls of gauze and a box of bandage clips beneath.

The papers were folded into a slit I had made in the hem of my old coat. Early that morning I had slipped into the records office and removed three sets of forms. It would not take me more than twenty minutes when I got home to fill them out with fabricated names and injuries and forge the Head Sister's signature approving the patients' transfer to the monastery in Fiesole.

Up until that point, to my surprise, I had found the project almost fun. Our family had always played games, especially charades, and I had allowed myself to think that this was just more of the same. Nothing but play-acting. A dare. A climb out onto the roof above the loggia. It was not until I found my-self holding Papa's pen, sitting at his desk and signing the Head Sister's name, that I felt the first cold wash of fear.

I think that if I could have put the pen down then, torn the papers up, changed my mind and run away, I might have. But, of course, it was too late. Issa was gone. She would have clothes, boots, and jackets waiting for the men in Fiesole. In the mean-time, Mama and I dressed each of them in a set of Enrico's old-est pyjamas. Then I tried not to let my fingers tremble as I wrapped bandages around their heads and hands. I tried not to look into their eyes as I fastened the clips and Mama dabbed white powder on their cheeks.

At just before four o'clock, the ambulance backed into the drive. Papa stood by the open doors appearing to fret. When we pulled out of the gates a few minutes later, I realized I had been holding my breath.

The driver was a young man with pale, long-fingered hands and the sort of face that is old before its time.

We came down the hill and crossed at the far bridge, avoiding the Lungarno with its display of spider flags, and drove slowly towards the Porta al Prato. I did not ask the driver's name, and he did not ask mine. In fact, as if by mutual agreement, we did not speak. Imprisoned in our own little pockets of fear, we sat ignoring each other.

The evening was clear. Twilight was dropping slowly over the city. At the Fortezza da Basso we saw a formation of Blackshirts. They looked like nothing more than children, baby-faced boys dressed up, playing at being murderous men. After they had passed, marching across the road in front of us, my companion spat, a sharp vicious gesture of contempt.

The roadblock came approximately a mile after we left the city, just as the hill began to climb. I suppose the driver knew it was there; he shifted downwards, slowing on the corner, but I did not see it until we were almost upon it.

The barrier was lowered. There was a sentry box on either side. I don't know how many men I thought there would be, but I was surprised when only one stepped out into the road, waving a torch. We drew slowly to a halt. I stared through the windscreen, hypnotized by the beam of light, my hands clutching the leather wallet that held the papers. Then I felt a touch on my shoulder. The driver's fingers. Even through my uniform cape they were bony and hard. His eyes met mine.

'Go,' he mouthed, and I opened the door.

Outside, the night was crisp. It had not been more than half an hour since we had left the house, but already it was considerably darker. The German soldier who walked towards me seemed huge, like a pillar of granite in his grey uniform.

'Signorina.'

I jumped at the sharp click of his boots. When I looked up, I was surprised to see that he was handsome. And young. Probably no older than I was. I forced myself to smile as I opened the wallet.

He examined the papers carefully, holding them in one gloved hand, his torch in the other. Then he looked at me.

'To the monastery, in Fiesole?' His accent was heavy and hard to understand.

I nodded. Issa had warned me that I should not say too much. But to say nothing at all would have been equally suspicious, as if a deaf mute had been sent to escort invalids.

'Allied bombing,' I said. The first thing that came into my head. 'Two are burns victims,' I added. 'Not much more than boys.'

He considered this for a moment, then nodded, and it occurred to me that perhaps he had little Italian, not much more than the few words he'd spoken. So I said it again in my schoolgirl German: 'Allied bombing. *Brandwunden. Schrecklich.*'

He smiled, and I realized that it was not because he liked the idea of burnt flesh, but because he was hundreds of miles away from home and I had used his language, even a few pathetic words of it.

'My name is Dieter.'

He still had not given me back the papers. I smiled. Issa had told me to wear my best lipstick. Not red, she had warned, but pink. Girlish. Nurse-ish. What she meant was coquettish.

'Caterina,' I replied, and the odd thing was, it never occurred to me to lie about my name.

'Caterina. Nurse Caterina.'

He smiled again. His mouth was generous. He had very white, even teeth. He looked at me for a moment, then he stepped towards the back of the ambulance.

'I must ask you to open the doors, please, Nurse Caterina,' he said in German, and my mouth went dry.

When I did not move immediately, he cocked his head slightly and motioned.

'*Verstehen Sie?*' Do you understand, he asked. 'I must see your passengers.'

'*Ich verstehe.*'

I nodded with what I hoped was cheerful efficiency. My German vocabulary was limited, but I thanked God that what there was had not entirely deserted me.

'They are feeling bad,' I said as loudly as I dared. I did not know if any of the men in the ambulance spoke a word of German, but I wanted them to be prepared when the doors opened. 'In pain. Weak. They have drugs, for sleeping. You understand?'

Dieter nodded, still smiling. Perhaps he did not notice that my legs had stiffened, that I was having difficulty moving.

'I promise you, I will not disturb them more than necessary.'

I smiled, nodded, and left with nothing more to do, reached for the door.

The handle stuck. Dieter put his gloved hand over mine, and pulled it down. He was standing so close that I could feel the warmth of him, his breath on my cheek.

The driver had kept the engine running. A white trail of exhaust wound itself around Dieter's black boots. I stepped back as he shone his torch into the ambulance. Its beam lit the stretchers, two on either side, one above the other like children's bunk beds. The bright light caught the still shapes, the grey blankets, the mounds of feet and bandaged paws of hands. It lingered over the pale moon faces, lips drawn, eyes closed.

Then one set of eyes popped open. One of the Americans. Caught in the beam of the torch they were round as marbles, staring and terrified. Dieter moved the light away.

'*Arme Jungen,*' he said, poor boys, and closed the door.

He ushered me back to the front of the ambulance, folded the papers, and clicked his heels again when he handed them to me.

'Signorina Caterina,' he said, 'it has been a pleasure. I hope we meet again.'

This time, my mouth was too dry to summon any words. All I could do was twist my lips into what I hoped was a grateful smile, and nod.

He waited as I slid into the front seat, then closed the door for me, and walked to the barrier. His hand was resting on the lever that raised it when he stopped.

I felt rather than saw the driver tense, heard the sharp intake of his breath. I knew he would be armed, that somewhere, in a pocket, or shoved down between the seats, he would have a pistol. Dieter was walking back towards us. One of his hands had disappeared into the pocket of his greatcoat.

Beside me, there was a rustle of clothes.

'Don't,' I murmured. 'Wait.'

Dieter leaned down and tapped the window with the black fingers of his gloves.

This time, his face was solemn. When I rolled the window down, there would be a straight shot to his jaw, his neck, his forehead. I didn't dare glance at the driver. The glass squeaked.

'Signorina Caterina.' Night air danced on Dieter's words.

I waited.

He raised his hand from his pocket and handed me a pack of cigarettes.

'Please,' he said in German, 'I want to give you these. Please take them for your poor boys, with my compliments.'

A moment later, when we drove under the barrier, he saluted.

I closed my eyes. I could feel myself floating, as if I had risen out of my body. When I opened my mouth, I gulped air into my lungs as if I had never breathed before.

Isabella was waiting for us. She guided us towards the dark of an old machine shed at the back of the monastery. Just before the driver doused the lights, I caught sight of two figures standing on either side of the doors. Massimo's face was lit for a moment, then he and the person who stood with him, who looked no bigger than a child, swung the wide doors shut behind us. A beam of torchlight guided us forward. I caught a glimpse of Carlo, as he banged on the hood telling us to stop. The driver killed the engine, someone lit a lantern, and a moment later we were all standing on the packed earth floor of the empty shed.

'Quick,' Massimo said, moving towards the rear door of the ambulance. 'We're all right here, but you can't be too long before going back through the checkpoint. It's best if you're gone before Mass finishes' – he glanced at Issa – 'in case anyone else uses the footpath.'

As I stood back while the driver and Massimo helped the men out of the back of the ambulance, I saw that the child who had helped to swing the door closed was not a child, but a short, slight young man. A teenager with a misshapen back, a slope to his shoulder that suggested the possibility of a deformity, a hunchback, or broken bones from a childhood accident that had never been set properly.

'Little Lamb!' Massimo saw me staring and ruffled the boy's hair with the kind of aggressive affection men use with dogs and children. 'Little Lamb is my mascot!' he said. Issa and Carlo exchanged a glance as Massimo let out one of his booming laughs.

'For Christ's sake,' Issa muttered. 'Shut up.'

If Massimo heard her, he ignored her.

Issa disappeared into the back of the shed and appeared again with three piles of clothes. Carlo produced boots, a pair of which I recognized as Rico's. As he began handing out socks I noticed that, like Issa, he was wearing mountain clothes – woollen trousers, hiking boots, a heavy jacket. He would be going with her. He murmured something to her. She glanced up at him. Then he lifted a rucksack, and she turned around so he could place the straps over her shoulders.

Concerned as I was by then with getting the bandages off the men, getting them dressed and moving as fast as possible, I was not so concerned that I did not take in the look on Issa's face, or the way Carlo rested his hand on her shoulder. A pang of loss shot through me. My hands actually faltered. My wedding day was next week.

I didn't think anyone had noticed – certainly not Issa and Carlo, or the men themselves. Then I realized that Massimo was watching me. That he had seen me look away and blink back tears.

He and the boy vanished a moment later. After slapping the driver on the back, Massimo clapped the boy on the shoulder, knocking him so hard he almost stumbled, then they slipped out of the shed doors and into the night. I could hear Massimo whistling as they walked away down the road towards the front of the monastery and the village.

Issa tightened the straps on her rucksack. She glanced at Carlo who was adjusting his own straps, then looked at the three men. They nodded, the last one pulling on a pair of Rico's old gloves.

A few moments later, as I stood outside the shed and watched them move slowly up the trail, I thought I had never felt more lonely. It was not just mistrust and anger, the pain of destruction and loss and death the war had brought, I thought then. It was loneliness. That was the true horror. The reality that, when it came to it, we were not a battalion. Or a band of comrades. On the contrary. We were each of us alone, fighting the fight we were given.

They were almost lost in the tall shadows of the trees when Issa broke away. It took me a moment to realize that she was running back down the path towards me. As she came close, I saw that her face was glowing. Her eyes were wide and sparkling in the chilly night air.

'Cati!' she said. 'I almost forgot! Here.'

She dug into the pocket of her jacket and pressed something into my hand. She wasn't wearing gloves and her fingers were cold.

'It's your wedding present, in case I'm not here.'

I looked at the familiar oval of her face, at the blue of her eyes, and the lion's mane of her hair. Then I put my arms around her, and pulled her close. I drank in the smell and the warmth of her, unable to imagine a time or a world when she would not be here.

Finally, I had to let her go. She turned and ran back up the path, growing smaller and smaller until she merged into the shadows.

I stood a moment longer. Then, when I could no longer make out any shapes, or hear even the shuffle of leaves in the chestnut forest, I looked down. There was still just enough light to make out what it was that she had pressed into my hand. A small book, with a pencil slotted neatly into its spine. The cover was red, and embossed with the lily of Florence.

I was still standing there, fingering the buttery, expensive leather, tracing the golden outline of the lily, when I felt the strange bony fingers on my shoulder.

'We should go.'

The driver's voice was soft. In the half-dark, his eyes appeared wide and colourless. I looked back and saw that the shed doors had been pulled open. I hadn't even heard the noise.

I nodded, but before I moved, I put out my hand. Issa had told me that among themselves, they used code names, things like Little Lamb, presumably. But I had no code name to offer.

'Caterina,' I said.

The driver looked at me. For a moment, I thought he was not going to repay the compliment, not going to accept even this small gesture of trust. Then he almost smiled. He placed his hand in mine.

'*Il Corvo*,' he replied. The Crow.

I nodded. Now I was one of them.

PART TWO

—◦◦◦—

FLORENCE

1 November 2006

Chapter One

The rain began right on time. It came down suddenly on the first afternoon of the month, in long hard sheets that blew through the city. Within minutes windows swam, walls wept, and the gutters churned themselves into small angry torrents. A Uffizi brochure swirled by. Botticelli's *Venus* smiled dreamily up from the foaming water, then spiralled down and was caught in the grate of a drain.

Standing in the doorway of the building where she had lived for thirty years, Marta Buonifaccio watched the street empty. People scurried, she thought, like rats, heads bent and furtive. A tall man carrying a briefcase swore and darted towards the bus stop where already two blue-jeaned teenagers stood huddled. With their cropped heads and pierced skin, they looked to Marta not like shining examples of youth, or even overgrown children bent on menace, but like penitents, cast-out creatures who shuffled with bent heads and bent shoulders, shrugging themselves into clothes too thin and too large. Far from filling her with fear, she wanted occasionally to give one of them a coat. Then she reminded herself that their parents were probably bankers, university professors, lawyers who made more in a year than she had managed in a lifetime.

An old woman stood in the opposite doorway, shrouded in black, her coat collar turned up against the wind. An umbrella,

useless in this, was clutched in one gloved hand. The other
hung onto the requisite black bag. Bought for too much money
twenty years ago, it would hold house keys, a packet of tissues,
a half-used lipstick of unassuming pink smelling of something
sweet, and a too-large wallet, its plastic envelopes filled with
fading pictures of grown and indifferent children. For a moment, their eyes met. The woman smiled and glanced to the
heavens. November rain, Marta could almost hear her saying.
Doesn't it always come as a shock? The beginning of one more
winter.

The bus swished between the buildings. The woman hob-
bled towards it, the cavernous black bag swinging from her
crooked arm like a pendulum. I wonder if that is how I look
now? Marta thought. Old and blended in, another worn feature
of this worn city that no one notices much, and no one will
miss. How, she wondered, does that happen? In what year is it,
exactly, that we begin to vanish, to fade into our surroundings
as if they are absorbing us, pulling our bones back home?

The teenagers slithered onto the bus. The man with the
briefcase reached for the old woman's arm, rain plastering his
bowed head as he helped her across the gutter. Then the doors
closed with a hiss and swallowed them all, and the street was
empty again. Marta stood for a minute more, watching nothing, before she turned back into the building.

It was lunchtime. The faint odour of mushrooms and cooking oil hung in the air, mingling uncomfortably with the
sharper tang of furniture polish. Marta could not remember
when, exactly, it was that she had taken it upon herself to start
polishing the palazzo's stairway and the sills of its huge heavy
windows. Probably at about the same time that she had begun
to fade. Twenty years ago, at sixty? Twenty-five years ago, at
fifty-five? Whenever it was that her hips had begun to thicken
and men had ceased to look at her face. She'd turned then to
the building, and it had not let her down. The windows, tall
and diamond-leaded, looked out onto the side alley. Through

them, you could see the iron rings in the walls of the next palazzo that had once held torches.

Marta had read somewhere that torches had been necessary, in the Middle Ages when the alley was still used, to light it – even in the daytime. Without the benefit of flames it was so narrow, and the palazzos on either side of it so tall, that even in broad daylight it was like walking into a tunnel. The windows back then were really for show. In those days, glass was prestige. Openings in solid walls meant you could afford firewood to heat the house.

Someone had left a pile of Chinese menus and flyers for the local taxi service on the floor beside the mailboxes. Tutting, Marta gathered them up. Moo shoo pork. Kung Pau chicken. She knew what that meant. Cats were protected by law in Florence, but no one ever did a head count.

Marta was about to drop the flyers into the waste-paper basket she had recently placed beside the long hall table when she noticed the envelope at the bottom. Distinctly creamy, it looked expensive. And unopened. She reached down and plucked it out. The envelope was thick, and rather heavy. The top corner was lifting, but the seal still held. There was a crest on the back flap, a tiny rearing dragon in a circle. She turned it over. The front was addressed in spidery writing to Signor Giovanni Trantemento. The stamp, Marta saw when she reached out and switched on the lamp she had also supplied, looked distinctly British. She sighed. Signor Trantemento was, technically, only a few years her senior, but the difference was, he was old.

At first, after Rome, after he had got that medal, he had walked with a bit of a spring in his step. Or, Marta thought, at least a bounce in his shuffle. But over the months that had seeped away, as if he were a toy whose battery was winding down. His face had narrowed perceptibly. From behind his round glasses, Signor Trantemento, who had once been considered if not handsome, at least suave, now looked bug-eyed and constantly alarmed. It had crossed her mind that he was sick, or had received bad news. But she knew that was not it. It was simply that he was getting ready to die. Feeling the chill of the shadows that stretched towards him.

Sighing, she turned off the lamp, then began to climb the stairs. It did not occur to her that Signor Trantemento and his mail were not her business. Everything that went on in this building was her business. She was as much part of it as the huge chestnut doors, and the brass knocker with the lion's head she polished every Thursday.

Giovanni Trantemento's apartment was on the fourth, and top, floor. The palazzo, as far as Marta knew, had not been built for anyone particularly important, or by any name that had been remembered. No Pazzis, or Strozzis, and certainly no bankers' balls of the Medici. She had often wondered who had ordered up these walls, who had swung open the door and climbed this staircase for the first time. Whoever it was would not appreciate being forgotten. Five centuries ago when this house was built, it would have been impressive. A monument that would last forever. Hah. Marta knew better than that. She was on the one-hundred-and-fiftieth step. She could have taken the tiny box of an elevator, but that would not keep her fit, keep what muscles she had in working order.

The windows up here let in a little more light than those on the ground floor. Rain pinged and batted against them, turning the air grey and cold. Signor Trantemento's apartment certainly had the best view in the building, and even a loggia, but it could not be described as welcoming. It was more like the eyrie of an ageing and increasingly mangy eagle. On the landing between the third and final floors, Marta switched on the light, an inadequate frosted sconce.

As she neared the summit, the top of Signor Trantemento's door with its carved pediment of grey stone fruit reared into view. Now she could see the door itself, with the knocker she did not polish. Signor Trantemento had hung a tapestry on the landing wall. A lion held a banner while a unicorn, his front feet in a woman's lap, smiled foolishly. Rabbits, foxes, and what looked like a lumpen weasel crouched amid embroidered flowers. In the rainy light, the tapestry's red background quivered. It seemed to have slipped off the bottom of the material and seeped onto the stone floor. Marta had reached step one hundred and seventy-eight before she realized that what she was looking at was blood.

❧

Alessandro Pallioti had a new office and a new title. Both were products of the Polizia di Stato's most recent spate of streamlinings and general overhaulings. Like changes in the weather, these paroxysms of modernization happened from time to time. In Pallioti's experience their effects varied. Sometimes they were simply embarrassing, like elderly ladies taking up disco dancing. Sometimes they actually achieved something, though not necessarily what had been intended. Usually they were a combination of the two – an awkward, slow inching towards Bethlehem.

His job was a case in point. Like Yeats' rough beast, it lumbered on, essentially unchanged. No matter what title you gave it, he thought, it was still a specialization in all that was worst in human nature. Greed, cruelty, violence, carelessness and their all-singing, all-dancing handmaidens – murder, theft, corruption, and any and all other general or specialized mayhem man- or womankind was able to think up.

He swivelled in his chair, as if he were stirring up the sourness inside. Shaking the cocktail of petulance and discontent that seemed to have brewed in him over the last six months. Frowning, he tapped his pen against the leather edge of his blotter, unsure if he was disgusted with himself for indulging in feeling this way, or feeling this way because he was disgusted with himself.

The bottom line was, either was unacceptable. But then again, since his fiftieth birthday he had found pretty much everything unacceptable, from the state of the world, to his job, to his own attitude. When he had complained to her about his current insufferableness, his sister had smiled and gently pointed out that he was having a mid-life crisis.

She was probably right. Despite being a full fourteen years his junior, Seraphina was almost invariably right. She had advised him, with her usual equanimity, that it would pass – and had politely suggested that he should refrain from buying a sports car or marrying his secretary in the meantime.

Pallioti had been able to reassure her on those two counts, at least. His new secretary – who had come with his new office, along with the black leather sofa and a fashionably inscrutable coffee table – was *A*, bald, and *B*, male. Neither of which was to his taste. As for the sports car, the enhanced salary and pension he had received along with the new title were generous, but did not run to the Lamborghini of his dreams. And being a perfectionist, he would settle for nothing less.

He spun his chair back again and looked out of the half-moon of his window down onto the Piazza. Rain swept across the wide empty space, blurring the buildings on the far side and the tall elegant arches of the loggia that fronted them. A throng of tourists sheltering from the downpour looked tiny and miserable. They had all read too much about the Tuscan Sun and were prone to forgetting that this was a city where winter was not only possible, but inevitable.

Glancing at his watch, he stood up and straightened his tie, which was dark blue and dotted with small gold lions who looked as if they were saluting. The Florentine Marzocco. They reappeared engraved on the oval face of his gold cufflinks. He had worn them today because he was due, in approximately half an hour, at a lunch that was being hosted by the city in honour of the members of an EU delegation who were supposedly fascinated by new and innovative methods of policing. He was dreading it. And in his present mood, rather enjoying dreading it. At least it gave him a target for his ire.

He shrugged into his suit jacket, and was pulling his cuffs down, making certain that they were exactly even, when the phone buzzed.

The secretary whom he had no intention of marrying, a blue-eyed young man called Guillermo whose head was as bare and shiny as a polished stone, said, 'Dottore, I have the Mayor.'

Pallioti rolled his eyes. He had known the Mayor for the better part of twenty-five years and, despite the upcoming lunch, considered him a friend. But he was an old-style new-style communist, a worrier and a fretter with all the instincts of an over-wrought sheepdog. Doubtless there was something he wanted Pallioti to say – or more likely, be certain not to say – that must immediately be transferred from his teeming brain, and could under no circumstances wait the thirty minutes it would take to reach the private dining room at the Helvetia and Bristol.

'*Pronto,*' Pallioti murmured.

There was a dull emptiness on the line. This was not surprising. The Mayor had been known to place calls then leave people hanging on for half an hour while he chased eight or ten other topics and phone conversations. Pallioti looked out of the window again. The three flags in front of the building, the circle of gold stars on its blue background, the green, white, and red bars – Hope, Faith and Charity – and the pennant of Florence, rose and fell in the gusty wind.

'*Pronto!*' the Mayor said suddenly out of nowhere. '*Pronto!*' He sounded like the counter boy at an especially busy pizza parlour.

'You called me, Dottore,' Pallioti reminded him.

'Oh.'

There was a momentary pause. Then the Mayor said, 'There's something I need you to do for me.'

Pallioti was tempted to point out that he was about to do something, something he loathed – standing up and spouting meaningless platitudes about policing – when he realized that that was the problem. Or at least part of it. He had worked his whole life to attain the marginally exalted position he now held, and having got it, he hated it, because he spent so much of his time talking about policing. Or writing reports about policing. Neither of which had anything to do with why he had joined the Polizia in the first place. He was, he thought, looking at the rain, like a ship that struggles through storms to reach port, then sinks out of boredom once she's moored.

The epiphany was cut short by the Mayor's voice.

'It's only just happened,' he was saying. 'Some hack called the press office for a comment. And they actually had the wit to call me. Thank God.'

Pallioti frowned; he had no idea what the Mayor was talking about.

'What's only just happened?'

'Giovanni Trantemento. Mean anything to you?'

Pallioti shook his head, relieved. It wasn't just him. The Mayor wasn't making any sense either. Again, nothing new. These conversations could be like doing a crossword puzzle. The theme only became clear at the end.

'Nothing,' he said. 'Giovanni who?'

'Trantemento. He was a hero of the resistance. A partisan. Heroic role in the liberation, all that. Decorated in Rome, by the President. You remember?'

Pallioti did, in general, if not specifically. A year and a half ago a line of old men in dark overcoats and berets, rheumy eyes watering, had finally stepped forward to receive the medals they'd earned more than half a lifetime earlier. A dinner at the Quirinale had followed. And many speeches about the Heroes of Italy, the young who gave and gave, and the memory of those who died – whether from Fascist bullets or Nazi bullets – so we can all sit here today and insult each other at liberty.

'Someone's killed him,' the Mayor was saying.

'What?'

'I know. I know. It's appalling. An old man. Eighty-seven. In his own apartment. What kind of animal does that?'

A human one, Pallioti thought acidly.

'So you will, won't you?' the Mayor went on. 'Keep an eye on this? Make sure it doesn't get ballsed up. It's the sort of thing,' he added ominously, 'that could look bad. For the city.'

'Ah.'

'I know how busy you are,' the Mayor added. 'But as a personal favour?'

'A personal favour?' Pallioti cleared his throat. He thought he had detected a hint of pleading in the Mayor's voice. 'I am, as you know,' he murmured, 'very busy with this fraud case. Very complex. Of course,' he added, 'I would like to do everything I can. But if I were to, I wouldn't have much – no, really any – disposable time to—'

'Yes,' said the Mayor, who was not stupid. 'All right. All right. Yes, yes, my friend. I understand. Completely. There are plenty of other people to trot out. Many, I'm sure, who we can find to talk about policing. None, of course, as eloquent as you might be – however.'

'However—' Pallioti echoed.

Looking out of the window, he smiled. For a moment, in the grey watery light thrown back by the rain, his face looked distinctly fox-like.

He had not lied. He was in the middle of coordinating the winding up and preparing for trial of a substantial fraud. Not that it would make any difference to Giovanni Trantemento. He would give the day-to-day running of the case to Enzo Saenz, and keep an eye on it from a distance. Nothing more would be necessary. The fraud was genuinely complex. This, on the other hand – an old man murdered in his apartment – while certainly distasteful, possibly inflammatory, and definitely the sort of thing the press loved (*Hero Survives Nazi Bullets Only to be Slaughtered in Own Home!*) was not complex. In fact, Pallioti made a mental bet with himself that it was a burglary gone wrong. Making sure the whole mess was cleaned up quickly and correctly would not only curry favour with the Mayor and prevent a dent to the city's image, it was also the right thing to do. It was the least he could do, in fact, for those old boys who, despite the rather tedious hours of TV coverage, had, sixty years ago, fought with a courage he himself found inconceivable.

'*Certo*,' he said again. 'Of course. It will be my pleasure.'

'Thank you.' The Mayor sighed. 'You know,' he added, as if he had read Pallioti's mind, 'I think about them sometimes, the partisans.'

'Yes.'

Pallioti suspected that there was not a man in Italy who did not think about them, Italy's Holy Children. Not a man who, at some point, in the dead of night, had not lain staring at the ceiling and wondered – would I have done it? Would I have had the courage?

'They were half our age, most of them. If that. Children, really.' The Mayor's voice sounded suddenly tired. 'Between you and me, my friend,' he said, 'I suspect we've made something of a pig's ear of the world they fought for. So, chasing up the thug who murders one of them, it does seem, doesn't it, the least we can do?'

Enzo Saenz was waiting when Pallioti stepped out of the lift that had whisked him silently down five floors and deposited him in the pristine new garages where his car was waiting. The subterranean depths of the recently renovated police building were every bit as impressive as those above ground. Below the explosion-proof, bulletproof, generally terrorist, mob, and reprisal-proof offices and incident rooms, there was a gas-proof, disease-proof, weapons-of-mass-destruction-proof maze that housed not only official vehicles, but labs and armouries, firing ranges and files and God knows what. Pallioti suspected that one day he would send someone down here and have to mount a missing persons operation to get them back. It would not, however, be Enzo Saenz. Enzo could find his way home from hell itself.

Today, he was wearing one of his collection of leather jackets and sporting a rough-cheeked twenty-four-hour beard. Combined with his ponytail and Roman nose, it made him look more than a little medieval. Not that that was inappropriate. Pallioti always saw in Enzo the Medici enforcer – the silent and trusted young man who slipped into the alley and did the deed.

It took them ten minutes to reach the building where Giovanni Trantemento had made his home. There was no question which one it was. Already, an ambulance, a police van, and two marked patrol cars were pulled up outside. A uniformed policewoman was placing bollards in the street. A wet young man who could only be the Mayor's reporter was mooching about on the pavement. In the bus station opposite, a crowd had gathered. They peered through the scratched Plexiglass wall, watching the police like fish looking out of a tank.

Enzo, who had shooed Pallioti's driver away and taken the wheel himself, pulled inside the bollards and stopped. Ducking from the rain, which if anything was coming down harder now than before, he and Pallioti opened the doors and made a dash for the building. The ambulance crew was coming downstairs as they entered the hallway. They carried a folded stretcher and oxygen canisters. One looked up and caught Pallioti's eye. He shook his head.

'Fourth floor. All yours,' he said without breaking stride.

A second uniformed policeman was stringing evidence tape across the front grille of a tiny elevator tucked under the stairwell. As Enzo crossed to have a word with him, Pallioti turned towards the stairs. Their stone treads and dark polished banisters vanished upwards and out of sight. Like Jacob's Ladder, he thought, without being really sure why. Taking a deep breath, he began to climb.

The front hall of the huge chilly building was so cavernous and so badly lit that it was not until Pallioti reached the first landing and looked down that he even noticed the woman. She was wearing a flowered headscarf. As she looked up at him, her face was a pale, round moon. The light was too poor to see if she blinked. Pallioti nodded. Then he kept climbing, his shoes tapping time against the endless thrum of the rain on the windows.

'Six apartments, one bottom, one top, and two on the two floors in between. I've had them tape off the whole place. A second car is coming to take statements.'

Enzo caught up with him on the second level.

'Do we know who found him?'

'Woman downstairs. Marta Buonifaccio. Sort of self-appointed concierge. She brought an envelope up for him, saw the blood under the door, opened it, saw him, went back down and called us.'

Pallioti stopped.

'Elevator?' he asked.

Enzo shook his head. 'Regards it as an instrument of the devil. Always uses the stairs.'

'And the door, Trantemento's apartment door?'

'Closed but unlocked. She said there was a line of blood. Seeping under the door. She thought he might have hit his head. Opened it to see.'

They began to climb again.

'The old guy,' Enzo went on, 'moved in a few years after she did. That's what she called him, incidentally – "the old guy". Says he was getting frail. He's a stamp and print dealer. High end. According to Marta.'

Was there a low end of stamp and print dealing, Pallioti wondered. He supposed so. There was a low end of everything. High end at least would explain the building. True, it was draughty and dark, but top floors of places like this – top floors of anywhere in the Centro Storico – did not come cheap.

They rounded the corner onto the last landing and were met with a white glare. The scene of crime team was already setting up floodlights. Pallioti stopped. He pulled the protectors Enzo handed him over his shoes and slipped on latex gloves. The landing was wide, and unfurnished except for the tapestry. The tall narrow window in the stairwell would have lit it poorly, even on a sunny day. The elevator cage was to the left. The door to the apartment, which was topped with an ornate carved stone lintel, was directly opposite the top of the stairs. It was open. The old man's body lay just inside.

The team processing the scene were stepping back and forth over the stream of blood that had snaked its way under the door and was now congealing on the cold floor. The medical examiner crouched by the body. The glare of the lights caught her white paper suit, making her look like a polar bear guarding a kill.

'Come on in. Just step over.'

She glanced up, waving them into the apartment. Beyond the body, a hallway stretched to the back of the building, where Pallioti could see glass-fronted doors giving onto what looked like a loggia. Enzo went first, hopping over the dead man and padding down the hall on the worn oriental rug. He checked the loggia, stuck his head into one room, and vanished into the next.

Pallioti followed, stopping in the hall, which was lined with bookshelves roughly to waist height on both sides. Above them, a series of prints and paintings, most in heavy gilt frames, were hung on the old-fashioned flock-wallpapered walls, making the hallway a densely patterned tunnel. The air smelled dusty, as if the glass panel doors at the end had not been opened for some time. The result was an immediate feeling of claustrophobia.

The medical examiner nodded, looking up at him.

'Single shot to the back of the head,' she said. 'I'd say three, four hours ago.'

'So.' Pallioti looked down at the body. 'Sometime late this morning, he opened the door, turned around, and whoever it was shot him?'

The medical examiner's reply was a surprise.

'I don't think so.'

She waved a hand at the thin, crumpled figure. He was wearing brown twill trousers, velvet slippers and a cardigan.

'Look at him,' she said. 'He's what? Six foot?' She leaned forward, her gloved fingers gently probing the back of the skull. 'I can't be sure until I get him on the table, but I think the angle of this shot was downward. At best straight on. It means, at the least, you have a very tall killer. Over six feet.'

'Or he bent over for some reason, to pick something up, and they took advantage.'

'Maybe,' she agreed. 'Certainly could be. Let me take some pictures and I'll roll him.'

While she reached for the camera in her bag, Pallioti stepped back over the old man's legs and outstretched arm. He examined the apartment door. It did not appear to have been forced in any way. There was not so much as a scratch.

He stepped over the body again and went into the hallway, anger rising in him. No matter how many times you warned people, especially old people, they kept on opening their doors. It was what made them such easy targets – and those who took advantage of them so despicable. How hard would this have been? To get into this building, walk up here, knock on the door saying you're the gas man, or the TV repair guy, or who knew what? Then one shot's all it takes, and the apartment's yours. Frankly, he didn't know why it didn't happen more often.

Expecting to find the main room ransacked, he stepped through the door, and stopped. It wasn't a pretty room. Up here under the heavy chestnut eaves the ceiling was too low to be gracious. But it was big, running almost the length of the apartment down one side of the hall. A line of windows gave onto a view over the roofs that was beautiful even in the rain. Santa

Croce rose up, and beyond it, the hills on the far side of the Arno. Nothing looked out of place. In the middle of a dark, heavy dining-room table a family of sculpted silver foxes sat on a silver tray. A silver letter opener lay in plain view next to what looked like an ivory-handled magnifying glass on a desk.

'There's a safe in the bedroom,' Enzo said, coming in behind him. 'Not touched, as far as I can tell.' Pallioti spun around. 'But there's no sign of a wallet, or any cash, either. Some coins on the dresser, but no notes. And there's something else. Come and take a look.'

Enzo nodded towards the bedroom. Pallioti followed him across the hall.

This room was also large. The floor was covered in another dark-patterned Turkish rug. In here, the windows – which would face the building across the alley, or more probably, its roof – were covered by heavy, and on first glance rather moth-eaten, velvet curtains. The double bed faced a wardrobe with carved doors and a mirrored front. The walls above the padded headboard were lined with rows of expensively framed prints. Pallioti stepped forward.

'Porn,' Enzo said. 'Politely known as erotica. Probably valuable. Maybe very. I'd say, eighteenth century. It looks to be some kind of set. Maybe two. I didn't study them.'

'Boys?'

Enzo nodded. 'Every one.'

Pallioti turned away from the dark etched figures, the grinning faces and flying shirt tails. He had never found pornography titillating, no matter what its date. He sighed. Sexual proclivities were people's own, what consenting adults did together the most private and inviolate of private lives. But he knew as a policeman how often and easily the word 'consent' could be twisted to suit one party and not the other. He didn't know what he had hoped to find here, but it wasn't this. A decorated partisan porn dealer. The story was not going to read well.

'All right,' he said, 'let's—' But before Pallioti could finish the sentence, or the thought, the medical examiner swore from the hall.

By the time the two men got there, she was sitting back on her heels, the body rolled over, face up, beside her.

'Dottoressa?' Enzo reached her first.

The medical examiner looked up, shaking her head.

'I've never seen anything like this.'

As Pallioti came up behind them he looked down and saw the old man's face. His cheeks, obviously lean and probably usually sunken, were puffed out, making him look like a cartoon child at a birthday party, mouth stuffed with cake. The man's eyes stared in panic through lopsided glasses. One lens was cracked. His lips were caked with something white that had spilled down his chin and onto the scrawny skin of his neck.

'It looks like someone packed his mouth with—' The medical examiner shook her head again. 'I don't know. Heroin? Cocaine?'

Enzo knelt down and touched the old man's chin. He sniffed his finger, then, before Pallioti or the doctor could stop him, dabbed at it with the tip of his tongue.

'Not coke.'

Looking up at them, he licked again, the pink tip of his tongue darting.

'Salt,' Enzo Saenz said. 'Whoever killed him packed his mouth with salt.'

Chapter Two

Marta Buonifaccio felt something like dread as she watched the man in the dark overcoat come towards her.

He was neither tall nor short, this policeman. Nor was he ugly. Or handsome – not like the young one. *Yai.* Marta did not want to think of the trouble he must cause. Or how much fun it might be to be in that kind of trouble. That would be a pleasant thrill. Which this wasn't. Because unless she was careful, this man walking towards her would cause trouble too, but of a much more serious kind. It was the quiet ones, she thought, always the quiet ones. Then she told herself that she had not done anything wrong. It was just men in well-tailored dark clothes. That was all. The ones who talked softly had always frightened her most.

'Signora Buonifaccio, thank you for taking the time to talk to me.'

As a gesture, it was gracious. Both of them knew she didn't have any choice.

'I'll try not to keep you too long at the moment,' Pallioti added. 'I realize this must have been a terrible shock for you. I will need you to give a complete statement to someone later.'

The woman nodded without lifting her eyes. The scarf she had tied over her head hid her hair, making her look curiously ageless. That, combined with a solid body that showed no signs of the frailty she had ascribed to her housemate upstairs, made it difficult for Pallioti to age her. She might be an old fifty, or a young eighty. What was apparent about her was that she was scared. Contrary to the received wisdom, Pallioti invariably found that frightened people did not fidget. They became very still. This woman was attempting to turn herself to stone.

'Could you tell me,' he asked gently, 'exactly what happened, this morning?'

The question was left deliberately vague. It was always interesting to see where people chose to begin.

'It started to rain,' Marta said. 'At about eleven o'clock.' She glanced up at him. 'You could hear it. Like drums. I came to watch. I've always liked it better,' she added. 'Winter.'

Pallioti smiled. A tiny spark of complicity lit between them. Marta looked down again, and went on.

'There isn't much to tell,' she said. 'I watched for a while. Then I came back in. Up there' – she gestured with her head towards the stairs – 'the second floor, left, they were cooking. So it was lunchtime. I don't eat lunch,' she added. 'But I was going in, my television show is on, and there were some of those things, you know, menus and things, on the floor. So I picked them up.'

'Who were they from?'

'From the Chinese place down the street,' Marta said, 'the one they closed two years ago because of the dead rat.' Found in the toilets, if Pallioti remembered the headlines correctly. It had caused quite a row. 'And a taxi company. You can look, if you want,' she added. 'I put them in the dustbin. Which is when I saw the letter, addressed to Signor Trantemento.'

'It was in the dustbin?'

She nodded. 'Over there, beside the table. It happens sometimes. People collect their mail, and throw things out they don't want. Well, they used to just drop them on the floor, which is why I got the waste-paper basket. Sometimes they get mixed up and throw out things they don't mean to.'

'Did Signor Trantemento do that often?'

'No. Not often. But he was getting old, you know? So I decided to take it up to him.'

'And the mail? How is it delivered? Does the postman have a key?'

Marta looked at him as if he were daft. How many keys would a postman have to carry if that were the case?

'It comes into the basket, through the front door,' she said, 'and I put it in the mailboxes.'

'So, you have a pass key. To the boxes?'

She nodded. 'Everyone used to collect their own. But it got all confused. So, I don't know, ten years ago, I volunteered. I don't mind.' Marta shrugged and shook her head. 'There isn't much more to tell you. I went upstairs. I saw the blood, coming from under the door. I tried the door and it was unlocked, so I opened it. And there he was, just inside.'

'Did you touch him? Feel for a pulse?'

She hesitated for a moment. 'Yes,' she said finally. 'I put my fingers on his neck. He was dead. I came back downstairs, and I called you people. Then I waited.'

'Down here?'

'Right here. Where I'm standing.'

'And did anyone come or go before the first policeman arrived?'

'No. No one. It was only about fifteen minutes. The ambulance and the police, they arrived together.'

Pallioti nodded. 'Do you have a mobile phone?'

That actually caused her to smile. A small pucker twisted her lips upward.

'So you came all the way back downstairs to call the police?' Pallioti asked. 'Or did you use Signor Trantemento's telephone?'

Again, she hesitated. Then she said, 'I came back downstairs. I – I don't know why. I'd never been in his apartment, I suppose. I didn't know where the phone was, and—' She shrugged.

And he was dead, Pallioti thought, so there was no real rush, was there?

'One last thing,' he said. 'The elevator. You didn't use that? Even when you knew he was dead and you needed to call the police?'

She shook her head emphatically.

'And can you tell me, by any chance, if you noticed where it was?'

She looked at the grille with the crime scene tape strung across it as if Pallioti had just suggested that the elevator itself might have dashed outside and into the building next door. Then she said, 'Oh. I see. No. No, I don't know what floor it was on. I don't pay any attention to it,' she added, as if the elevator were a badly behaved child.

Pallioti reached into his pocket for a card.

'Thank you,' he said again. 'I won't trouble you further now, but if you think of anything you'd like to tell me—'

She took the card gingerly and dropped it into her apron pocket. He was about to turn away when he heard Enzo call his name.

'Boss?'

Enzo dodged past the policewoman who, having placed the bollards in the road outside, was now standing guard under the portico, her neon anorak dripping onto the tiles. Enzo himself was soaked, and apparently oblivious to the fact. He had an excited clip to his stride, and was holding up an evidence bag for Pallioti to examine. In the dull light, it took Pallioti a moment to see that it was a wallet. A long black leather man's wallet.

'His ID's inside,' Enzo said. 'Initials on it.'

He flipped the bag so Pallioti could see a brightly embossed gold G.B.T. It would be Giovanni Battiste, of course. Pallioti didn't need to ask what the man's birthday would turn out to be.

'Where?' he asked.

Enzo grinned.

'Alley beside the house, about halfway down. I've had it

taped off. There's the ID, a couple of cards. Not a single banknote inside it. But there is this.'

He produced a second evidence bag from somewhere inside his jacket, flourishing it like a magician. Inside was what appeared to be a soggy piece of white paper.

'Cheque receipt,' Enzo said.

Pallioti had almost forgotten the things existed. Little plastic cards had taken over the world.

'It was in the cash pocket,' Enzo was saying. 'He cashed a cheque for five hundred euros at twelve minutes past three yesterday afternoon. I'm going upstairs to find the chequebook.' Enzo wheeled away and took the first steps of the staircase two at a time. 'The safe guy's on his way,' he called.

His words echoed in the hallway. Watching him, Pallioti wondered what it was he had been about to ask Marta just before Enzo appeared. Then he remembered. Turning back towards her, he said, 'Forgive me, Signora Buonifaccio, but the letter?'

'The letter?'

Marta was staring at the spot on the landing where Enzo had vanished, turning up the next flight of the staircase. 'Oh,' she said suddenly, 'the letter. Yes.'

She reached into her apron pocket and pulled out an envelope. She handed it to Pallioti. The paper was thick, expensive. The inky writing on the envelope had run slightly in the rain, making the address look as if it had dripped. He turned it over and saw the little dragon rearing in its circle. Then he said, 'It's open.'

Marta looked at him. Then she nodded, nothing more than a slight dip of her head.

'It was open when you found it? In the waste-paper bin?'

Marta's head dipped again. 'I thought I should check,' she said. 'Be certain he hadn't made a mistake. It didn't look like the sort of thing you'd mean to throw away.'

❧

October 25, 2006

My Dear Signor Trantemento,

It was such a pleasure to see you, as ever, last month in your beautiful city.

I have considered the proposal you made at the time in order to help me expand my collection, and after some thought on the matter, have decided that it is by far the best course of action, since – as you pointed out – I am unable to travel as frequently as would be desirable in order to view potential acquisitions. Your proposal also, as you remarked, avoids the increasingly intrusive nature of the 'wretched airport security' (may they rot in Hell!). I would therefore like to empower you to act on my behalf, as I consider your taste impeccable and in close tandem to my own. I look forward to a long and fruitful collaboration in celebration of our shared enthusiasm.

Yours truly,

The letter was typed on a single sheet of paper embossed with the heading David, Lord Eppsy, Eppsy House, 15 Pont Street, London SW1. For the life of him, Pallioti would never understand why it was that the fancier a man's title was, the less likely it was that he would be able to sign his name as anything more recognizable than a scrawl.

He pushed the letter away with a pang of disappointment. He had not seriously expected that it would hold some magical clue that would give him the name of Trantemento's killer. But he had hoped that it might be marginally more interesting than a little billet doux between pornography collectors.

Of course, he thought, looking at it again, David, Lord Eppsy might have been referring to a shared passion for stamps. But the reference to, and damnation of, the already benighted airport security workers suggested otherwise. A pair of dirty old men, he thought sourly. That was what was disappointing him. The Englishman – well, they liked that kind of thing. But somehow it made him unhappy to think of a great hero of the liberation, one of those sharp-eyed, too-thin boys with a rifle slung over his shoulder, being reduced to this – a lonely old man living out his life in a mangy overstuffed apartment surrounded by exquisitely drawn depictions of sodomy.

He glanced at his watch. The autopsy was due to start in half an hour. He had volunteered to be present, leaving Enzo free to get his team up and running. It was a strange thing, but Pallioti, who had been known to feel queasy putting a sticking plaster on his own finger, had never found autopsies bothersome. He sometimes found it difficult to deal with the wounded living, but never the dead. They had no pain left in their eyes.

∾

'It wasn't just his mouth.'

'Oh.'

The medical examiner looked up at him and nodded.

'Yes. Oh. There is salt in his stomach, oesophagus, and throat. Rather a lot of it. In fact,' she added, 'if he hadn't been shot, he probably would have choked.'

'So the killer made him—' Pallioti shook his head. There was something about it. It was brutal in a way he hadn't before encountered. He had seen stabbings, shootings, stranglings – any number of things. But there was some kind of odd, symbolic – and very personal – cruelty to this that made him cold despite the ample heating in the observation room.

'Eat it,' the medical examiner said. 'Whoever killed him, made him eat salt.'

'How much?'

She cocked her head and considered the eviscerated body that lay open on the table in front of her.

'Quite a lot,' she said. 'I'll be precise in the report, obviously. But I'd say at least half a kilogram. Perhaps more.' She glanced up at him. 'It must have been horrible. But people can do extraordinary things when they're terrified.'

'Is there anything else?'

Pallioti was no longer entirely sure he wanted to know, but the question had to be asked.

'Not really.' She shook her head. 'There are no defensive wounds. None. Which is a little strange. For whatever reason, it looks like he ate the salt more or less willingly. Didn't even try to fight back. From where the body was, I would have thought that was because he was taken by surprise. Except for the salt. I'll analyse it by the way, of course,' she added. 'But I think your Tybalt was right.'

Despite himself, Pallioti smiled at her description of Enzo. He did look suspiciously like one of the Capulets.

'My guess is ordinary table salt,' she continued, shrugging. 'He was in good condition otherwise, for a man of his age. Eyesight going, a bit. The glasses. But he didn't wear a hearing aid, or have a plastic hip or a pig valve in his heart.'

She contemplated the body thoughtfully. As of now, the investigation was following the obvious line of enquiry, looking for a burglary or some kind of rendezvous that had gone wrong. Pallioti had heard of escorts, gigolos, and rent boys who carried guns. He had never heard of one who carried bags of table salt. As far as he knew, no more than a tiny dish of sea salt crystals had been found in the apartment's kitchen. He reached behind him for his overcoat. A restless, itchy feeling had come over him and he wanted to be alone for a few minutes before he talked to the Mayor, or even to Enzo.

'Oh, and I was right,' the medical examiner added, looking up at him. 'About the bullet. I'll get it down to ballistics, pronto. But it was small calibre. No exit wound. It lodged. One shot, definitely. At contact, into the back of the skull.' She smiled. 'From above.'

Pallioti's hands stopped in the act of buttoning his coat.

'Say that again.'

'From above,' she repeated. 'I told you, I was almost certain when I was back there in the apartment, but now I've measured the angle. Whoever shot this man was standing directly above and behind him, close enough for the gun barrel to make contact. You can see clearly, the burn markings—'

'Powder burns?'

'Yes,' she agreed, 'that's right. On the back of his head. And the killer was aiming down. Definitely down.'

'So what do you think happened?'

'Well,' she said, shrugging, 'it looks to me as if his killer made him kneel, eat a large quantity of table salt, then stuffed his mouth with it and shot him in the back of the head.'

Chapter Three

'You're saying that it was an execution?'

The term was too melodramatic for Pallioti's taste. If this was a gang killing, some half-witted bunch of drug dealers picking each other off, he wouldn't have hesitated to call it what it was. An execution. A hit. An assassination. All of which implied, not a random crime, but some kind of vendetta. A planned act of revenge. Which in turn suggested that the victim had done something to deserve it.

He made a faint humming noise.

'Well,' he said, finally, 'I have to admit, I don't know how else you'd describe torturing someone, making them kneel, and shooting them once in the back of the head.'

'It doesn't fit,' Enzo said. 'The shooting, maybe. But when you throw in the salt. The kneeling.' He shook his head. Then he added, 'Or maybe it does. There's not a fingerprint anywhere. Not in the elevator, on the door, in the apartment – nothing. There's not a fibre, a hair. Anything. Maybe some grit from the street.'

Pallioti shrugged.

'That could mean whoever did it wore gloves and got lucky.'

Even as he said it, he didn't think he believed it.

Enzo glanced at him. 'On the other hand,' he said, ignoring the 'get lucky' theory, 'if whoever it was was that good, why drop the wallet in the alley? Why take it at all? Opportune cash theft and execution doesn't fit. Any more than the salt. It doesn't make any sense.'

For a moment, the image of Giovanni Trantemento's face hung in the room between them. Pallioti flicked his hand as though he was flicking away a fly. He had just had a brief conversation with the investigating magistrate who, for now, was busy enough on what he considered more important cases to be content to stand on the sidelines. Prior to that, he had filled in the Mayor. In between, he had taken a call from one of the Questura's press officers who bore the unwelcome news that a small piece had already appeared in one of the evening papers. So far, it was not much more than local colour. *Ageing Hero Slain in Safety of Own Home.* For now, the Questura had simply issued a confirmation of the tragic killing. But there was no guarantee that the story wouldn't – and in fact a fair to good chance that it would – grip, if not the public's imagination, then the imaginations of the city's editors. Should that happen, a press conference would become inevitable. Having something concrete to say at it would be advantageous.

'It makes sense to someone,' he said. 'So, what are we doing about finding them?'

Enzo sank down into one of the black leather armchairs by the window and began ticking off points on his fingers.

'We're sweeping all the gay bars and clubs. We've got good contacts, so if there's something there we ought to hear about it. Somebody with some weird salt fetishes, likes to play execution games – I don't know. We're going over CCTV footage from cameras near the building—'

Pallioti, who had been studying the edge of his blotter, looked up.

'Are there any?'

'Not really,' Enzo said. 'An indoor parking garage a couple of blocks away. But you never know, we might get lucky. Spot someone we recognize.' He ticked off another finger. 'I've got people back at the building now, going apartment to apartment while everyone's home for dinner. Did he have enemies? Get any threats? Behave strangely? Any strangers lurking around? We're checking the guy who distributes the fliers in case he noticed anybody. I'm getting hold of Trantemento's bank records. We're trying to find out everything we can about his business contacts. And with any luck, sometime tomorrow we'll get the ballistics back on the bullet. We should get something off it. If we do, we'll get it out on the databases. Between that and the salt, it should be distinctive. If our friend has done this before anywhere in Europe, it'll show up. In our dreams, we get a match to the weapon. If we don't find it first. We've impounded the rubbish containers within five blocks. The other thing,' he added, 'is the safe.'

Pallioti raised his eyebrows. The thing had looked like it came from an American gangster film from the 1930s. He'd assumed it could be opened with a bent paper clip, or at a stretch, a nail file.

'Apparently,' Enzo said, 'Signor Trantemento was security minded – at least with his papers, if not his front door. The safe is fitted with some very fancy mechanism. Our guy couldn't open it. We had to get a specialist. The closest one is in Genoa.'

Why, Pallioti thought, did that not surprise him?

Enzo glanced at his watch. 'He should be there now.'

Pallioti looked out of the window for a moment. The piazza was dark. Lights glittered on the wet pavement.

'What do we know about Giovanni Trantemento?' he asked.

'Apart from the fact that somebody, somewhere, apparently thought he was important enough to torture and kill?' Enzo shrugged. 'So far, not much. Never married. Lived in the apartment more than forty years. Forty-one to be exact. No criminal record. Doesn't own a car. Doesn't have a computer. We're going through his desk and address book, all that. And I'll send someone to Rome. But I thought I'd wait until we can get hold of a copy of his will.'

Pallioti frowned.

'He has a sister,' Enzo explained. 'Apparently his only living relative. In Rome. Polizia down there have sent someone along to break the news. But of course I'll send one of our own people as well. I just thought we might as well wait, though, see if there's a will in the safe and who inherits before we ask questions.'

'I have to be in Rome tomorrow. If you can wait that long.'

An inter-agency briefing at the Ministry had been scheduled for months. Wriggling out of it was out of the question. Paying a visit to Giovanni Trantemento's sister might not be everyone's idea of excitement, but it would at least provide a counterpoint to the rest of the day, which promised to be bureaucratic and possibly vicious.

Seeing his face, Enzo smiled.

'It would be an honour, Dottore,' he said, 'if you think you could possibly fit it in.'

∽

Marta Buonifaccio stood in her doorway and watched as the men came down the stairs. There were two of them. They were both wearing jeans, running shoes, and leather jackets. Not that it mattered. They moved like every other policeman she had ever seen.

There were others upstairs, two women knocking on doors. They had thrown her slightly at first, because they were women. And young. Barely girls. So she'd opened her door and stood there, confused. Then she'd looked in their eyes and understood. They didn't need a badge. They could go where they liked, ask whatever they wanted.

Had she seen anyone? Noticed anything strange? Or out of the ordinary? Did she know Signor Trantemento? Did he have visitors?

No, no, no, not really, and not that she noticed. As answers went, they weren't entirely untrue. But even if they had been, that's what she would have said. Because that was how you did it. That was how you made your own luck – by keeping your eyes down and your mouth shut.

The men were on the last steps. The first one, who had been talking on his mobile phone, flipped it closed and dropped it into his pocket. The second one, behind him, adjusted the box he was carrying, holding it out in front of him in both arms as if it were valuable, which it was. All of Giovanni Battiste Trantemento's secrets were in it. That's what they were taking away. They'd been at it all evening.

He hadn't been dead for a day yet, Marta thought, and already they were gutting his life – pulling his entrails out so they could read them the way the fortune-tellers had read the guts of cows and pigs centuries ago. Slit them open and thrown the innards down on the slick stones, then taken a gold coin to see the future in them, until Lorenzo got sick of the smell and banished the butchers from the bridge, handed it over to the gold-sellers who still sat there today in their rabbit hutches.

The men's shoes squeaked as they crossed the flagged floor of the hall. Marta did not move. She had been so still that they had not even noticed her, standing in the shadows beside the fireplace.

As soon as they were gone, as soon as the big front door had creaked and slammed and cut off the gust of damp air that floated in, she stepped back through the open door of her apartment. Marta closed it so quietly that it didn't make any noise at all. She was good at that.

She stood and looked around her little sitting room. The inside of her oyster shell. If they came for her, what would they find? Which pearls would they pluck?

None. Nothing. Not one thing.

She resolved it then and there. The boxes they carried away would be full of china cups, a teapot. Photographs. Frames. Worn clothes. A sweater with a darned elbow. A jacket with a muskrat collar. A hat that looked as if someone had sat on it. All the leftovers of her life.

But no secrets. She would make sure of that.

⁓

Enzo Saenz gave a low whistle.

'No wonder he wasn't happy with the original locks.'

Pallioti, who had been fingering a pile of papers, looked up. The safe had been opened. Now the heavily guarded contents of Giovanni Trantemento's little Aladdin's cave, all of which had been pirated away in a series of cardboard boxes, were being laid out for examination.

'How much is there?' he asked.

Enzo frowned, then thumbed the stack of notes he was holding. Even with the latex gloves on, he could count money as fast as any casino cashier.

'I'd say at least two hundred thousand euros, and the same again in dollars.' The bills were bound neatly with rubber bands. 'Money laundering? Drug money run through eighteenth-century smut prints?' Enzo shook his head. 'That would be a new one.'

Pallioti shrugged. 'Or purchasing cash,' he said. 'Perhaps some of his sellers didn't take Mastercard.'

'Possibly.' Enzo stood looking at the table. 'He had a couple of credit cards. But he barely used them. Like I said, no computer, no BlackBerry. Nothing like that. Not even a mobile phone. I have a feeling he wasn't a fan of the twenty-first century.' He shook his head again. 'Maybe he was saving up. Planning on taking a trip.'

'Is there any sign of that?'

Enzo glanced up. 'Do you mean did he visit a travel agent yesterday? Did we find a ticket to Rio in his desk? No. But that doesn't mean he wasn't thinking about it. Or planning it, in case he had to do it one day. In a hurry. His passport is up to date. This is a lot of money to keep in a safe in the bedroom.'

'Maybe he didn't like banks.'

'Maybe banks didn't like him.'

Enzo's mobile phone beeped. He flipped it open and turned away, muttering into it.

The investigation was headquartered in a room on the floor below Pallioti's office. It did not look out on the piazza. If it had looked out on anything at all, it would have been the wall of the building across the alley. But it didn't, because the rooms on this side of the new Questura building had no windows.

A photograph of Giovanni Trantemento stared down from a whiteboard, the presiding ghost of all that now lay before him. The photo had been enlarged until it was nearly life-sized. It had probably been taken a good ten or fifteen years earlier, but already Giovanni's high domed forehead, his hollowed cheeks, and dark eyes looking out from behind his round glasses, made him look like a death's head. Studying his face, Pallioti wondered if that came with age, and suspected not. He suspected instead that Giovanni Battiste had been born looking like that. Some people were. It was a kind of economy of bone structure. As if God occasionally took a short cut. Created beings who never needed to age because they'd always looked as if they were already dead.

The room was nearly empty. Enzo's people were out asking questions, frequenting the sorts of places where they were more likely to get answers after dark. Enzo himself finished his phone call and turned his attention to a closer reading of Giovanni Trantemento's will, which had indeed been tucked neatly between the stacks of cash. A first glance had established that it was both current – having been drawn up barely two years before – and relatively straightforward. The bulk of his estate was divided equally between his sister and her son, his nephew. There appeared to be several small bequests to city charities, a hospital, a shelter for the homeless. And one not-so-small bequest to something called the Alexandria Chess Club that apparently occupied an address somewhere on the Poggio Imperiale.

Pallioti returned his attention to the table. At the far end a collection of plastic bags lay in a heap. On closer inspection, they held what appeared to be very faded leaflets. He lifted one of the bags by the corners, holding it up to the light. It was large and sealed with a zip, the sort of thing one kept frozen food in. A number, 46, had been written on the front of it in what appeared to be black felt-tip pen. A small yellow sticker with a smudged name printed on it was stuck in the top corner. He put the bag down and picked up the next one, which was similar, although this time heat-sealed. The number on the front, again written in black felt pen of some kind, was B742. It was circled.

Pallioti squinted, then fished in his pocket for his reading glasses. With them on, he could read the tiny faded print through the plastic. The document in the bag wasn't a leaflet, but a faded and folded newspaper of some kind. He flipped it over and saw the headline in dull greying letters, *La Nostra Lotta*, Our Fight. He could just make out the date, February 1944. The other bags were the same. There were at least fifteen, possibly twenty. The quality was uniformly poor and the titles uniformly full of bravado. *Call to Freedom*, *Patria*, *The Green Flame*, and again *Our Fight*.

He recognized them at once. Any Italian schoolchild of his generation would. Slipped into Fascist papers, left on park benches, folded into menus. They were like small ghostly hands reaching out. Touching a shoulder in the jostle of a crowd. Exhorting in a whisper not to lose hope. Not to give up. These were the 'newspapers', the underground press, that had been printed and distributed by the partisans during the last years of the war when the Germans had occupied Italy and released the Fascists, allowed them back out into the light of day to have one last hurrah.

Pallioti smoothed the bag in his hand, running his fingers over the dingy plastic, and looked up at the whiteboard and

Giovanni Trantemento's face. On first glance, the old man did not look sentimental. But looks could be deceiving. The truth was, everyone was sentimental. About something. Why should it be any surprise that Giovanni Battiste Trantemento, hero of the liberation, had been proud of what he had done? That he had collected these leaflets, souvenirs, a fragile deteriorating little record of his youth with the partisans.

Pallioti put the bag down, placing it carefully on the table. He was about to turn away when a flash of colour caught his eye. Something red, also in a plastic bag. He reached into the pile and lifted it out.

The top of this bag was open. Shreds of brittle yellowing sellotape clung to its mouth. Inside was a small book, about the size of his hand. He slipped it out, turned it over, and saw, stamped on the faded red leather cover, the ghostly outline of the lily of Florence.

Chapter Four

'He was quiet. Even as a boy. He was always so quiet, so modest.'

Ensconced in a large armchair in the sitting room of her Rome apartment, Maria Valacci, Giovanni Trantemento's seventy-seven-year-old sister and only sibling, buried her face in her handkerchief and began to weep loudly. Standing behind her, her son rolled his eyes before patting her, none too gently, on the shoulder.

'Mama,' he said, 'please.'

Tall and thin, with a strangely skull-like head, Antonio Valacci bent over his mother and whispered, quite loudly, 'For God's sake, Mama, pull yourself together. This man is a policeman!'

Leaning back in the uncomfortable chair he had been shown to, Pallioti watched as Maria Valacci somewhat reluctantly followed her son's advice. He wondered if they knew exactly how dear Uncle Gio had amassed his not-inconsiderable nest egg. The size of his bank accounts – there were several – had surprised everyone. What he had amassed was not a fortune, quite. But when added to the cold cash found in the safe, it was damn close. And as his will stated, most of it, including his extremely desirable apartment in Florence, would revert to these two people. Pallioti wondered if they were aware of that fact.

'He was my older brother,' she said. 'My only living relative.'

Antonio Valacci sighed as he folded himself onto the sofa beside his mother's armchair.

'*E che sono?*' he muttered. '*Il figlio di nessuno?*'

'Don't be so silly.' His mother glared at him. 'Of course you're not no one. You know what I mean!'

'Yes, Mama.' Antonio nodded. 'I certainly do. My mother is proud,' he said, turning to Pallioti, 'exceptionally proud, of the role her brother played in the war. In fact,' he added, 'she never tires of talking about it. It's one of her favourite subjects. Which is all the more amazing since dear Uncle Gio, who we saw all of once a decade, never mentioned it at all.'

This caused Maria Valacci to wail, 'He was a modest man!' again. She produced another handkerchief from somewhere in the depths of the chair. 'A patriot,' she said. 'One of the heroes of Italy. Without men like him,' she announced, turning to her son, 'people like you wouldn't be free to walk the streets.'

'Oh, for Christ's sake.'

Antonio leaned back and closed his eyes. Pallioti thought he saw him counting to ten. A clock whirred in the corner of the room and began to chime the half-hour.

Although the day was bright the windows were half shuttered, filling the long room with light the colour of pond water. Pallioti wondered if it was always like this, or if the gloom had been specially induced out of respect for Uncle Gio.

The apartment itself was in a building in the warren of streets between Piazza Navona and the Vittorio Emmanuel. The address was distinguished, but even the police driver had had difficulty finding it. Eventually Pallioti had got out and walked, leaving the young officer and his Mercedes at Chiesa Nuova. In the end, the building hadn't been more than twenty steps away, as everything in Rome seemed to be once you actually knew where it was. He had been buzzed in and climbed the three flights of marble stairs, his footsteps ringing loud as cymbals. The fact that there had been only one other front door on the far side of the Valaccis' landing led him to suspect that their apartment took up at least half the floor. For Rome, that was large. But perhaps, Pallioti thought, not large enough to comfortably house a fifty-year-old man and his ageing mother?

From somewhere beyond the sitting room another clock, then another, joined the chorus of whirring and chiming. Antonio opened his eyes and managed a wan smile.

'An enthusiasm of my father's,' he said. 'He was a shipping agent – frozen foods, mostly. And rice. Did you know that Italy is a major exporter of rice?'

Antonio Valacci got to his feet, straightening his tie and pulling down the cuffs of his pinstriped shirt.

'I suppose you did,' he said. 'It's the sort of thing policemen know.' He glanced at Pallioti, and added, 'At least your kind of policeman. Anyway,' he shrugged, 'it was lucrative, but it bored Papa. What he really loved was clocks. He liked to collect them and disembowel them, in his spare time. He called them "his children".' Antonio smiled thinly. 'I suppose,' he said, 'that makes them my brothers and sisters. My mother's only other living relatives. May I offer you an espresso, Dottore?' he asked. 'I'm feeling in need of one.'

Without waiting for Pallioti to answer, Antonio Valacci picked up a small silver bell from a side table and rang it. The sound should have been lost in the chiming of the clocks, but apparently wasn't, because a small Asian woman in a uniform popped out of a doorway at the end of the room even before he put it down. Pallioti wondered if she had deliberately been idling in order to eavesdrop, or if she was always required to hover just out of sight. She was illegal, probably. In a perfect world he ought to check. But he wouldn't. He wasn't that kind of policeman.

'I wonder if you could tell me,' he asked, leaning towards Antonio's mother, 'how often, Signora Valacci, did you see your brother, in the last few years?'

Maria Valacci's skin was pale and finely wrinkled. A vein twitched at the corner of her eye. 'Not often enough,' she said.

As she spoke she glanced towards the fireplace. From above it, a portrait of a dark-suited man whom Pallioti assumed was Antonio's clock-loving father stared down at them.

'Not often enough. During my whole life,' Maria Valacci said again. 'I never saw Giovanni often enough.'

She paused. Pallioti braced himself for another flood of tears. But they didn't come. Instead, Maria Valacci narrowed her eyes, staring into the middle distance as if she was trying to pick something – some moment, or word, or gesture – out of the past. Failing, she shook her head. Then she said, 'Tonio is right. Giovanni did not care for us.'

'Mama—'

'No. It's true.'

Maria Valacci reached out and touched her son. For a second, her thin, almost talon-like fingers rested on the back of his hand with unexpected tenderness. Then she drew back, twisting the large sapphire ring that sat on her left hand and shaking her head.

'Perhaps we did not care for him, either,' she said. 'As much as we should have. If the truth be told.'

She glanced at Pallioti and smiled. It was nothing more than a flicker, an echo of the young woman she must once have been.

'The dead are difficult, don't you find, Ispettore?' she asked suddenly. 'They tend to be so much more present than the living. Perhaps because they can be everywhere at once.' Her pale-blue eyes dulled for a moment, then she gave herself a little shake. 'In any case,' she continued, 'my late husband did not care for Giovanni, on the few occasions that he met him. And to be very honest, I didn't know him. I didn't see my brother, after the war, for almost twenty years. I thought he was dead. So we might as well have been strangers, really. We were. I suppose,' she added, looking down at her hands, 'I thought I would correct that, one day, in the way you do. But I never did. I was ten years younger than Gio.'

She stopped speaking, her eyes searching into the past again. Pallioti waited.

'My father,' Maria Valacci continued. 'I loved him. He used to carry me on his shoulders, pretend he was a horse.' She smiled and shook her head. 'He was killed in the war, in Russia, Papa. Left to die on the retreat when our German friends decided they could not, after all, spare the resources to help evacuate their beloved brothers-in-arms. Mama, my mother – she never forgave him for that. Never got over it. It made her ill. She'd been a believer, you see.' The old woman looked at Pallioti and nodded. 'A loyal follower of *Il Duce*,' she said. 'An advocate of the Pact of Steel. So, the shame – you see, she couldn't cope with it. She believed my father was a coward, that somehow it had to have been his fault. Being left behind. Dying. Leaving her. She couldn't hate Mussolini, or the Nazis – so she hated Papa. And eventually, she did the same to Giovanni. Hated him for what he did.'

Pallioti leaned forward.

'For what he did?'

Maria Valacci nodded.

'Joining the partisans. My mother never forgave him for that. Even though he took such good care of her. He loved her, you see,' she added. 'The way children will. You kick a dog and it keeps coming back. She died in a sanatorium, Mama. In Switzerland, near Zurich. In 1947.'

Her voice stopped as abruptly as it had begun. Silence seeped into the long room, rocking on a backwash of memory. It was broken by the creak of a door and the quick tap-tap of the maid's shoes as she crossed the polished chestnut floor bearing a tray that held three tiny porcelain cups and saucers.

The coffee was bitter and strong and seemed to inject a pulse of normality into the proceedings. Which, Pallioti suspected, was why Antonio had suggested it. He wondered how much time, exactly, Maria Valacci's son spent trying to fish his mother out of the whirlpool of the past.

'Forgive me,' Pallioti said, replacing the little cup and saucer on the tray, 'but I am afraid I have to ask you. Last Wednesday, November first, can you tell me where you were?'

Antonio opened his hands in a 'who me?' gesture and smiled.

'Not in Florence,' he said, 'if that's what you're wondering. I was in my office. I work for the Ministry. Under the general umbrella of Culture. My mother,' he added, 'was having her hair done.' Antonio Valacci was watching Pallioti carefully. 'She has her hair done at 11 a.m. on Wednesdays,' he said. 'On any and all Wednesdays. I can give you the name of her hairdresser. And of my secretary.'

He jumped up and began to weave his way towards a desk in the corner.

'Don't be ridiculous, Antonio,' his mother said, her eyes following him. 'You make us sound as if we're suspects.'

'We are.'

Antonio Valacci glanced over his shoulder and smiled. He appeared to be writing something on a piece of card.

'Everyone's a suspect,' he said. 'Aren't they, Ispettore?'

Threading his way back across the room, Antonio handed Pallioti an old-fashioned address card that had a telephone number and two names – *The Bella Donna Hair Salon*, and *Anna Perocci* – written on the back. The woman's name sounded familiar, but Pallioti could not put his finger on why. He slipped the card into his jacket.

'I gave the same information to the pair who came yesterday evening,' Antonio said, sitting down on the couch again. 'But perhaps they haven't passed it along. If the police are anything like the Culture Ministry it takes about a year for one department to talk to the next.'

The police were actually not much like the Culture Ministry, but it was entirely possible that the two fairly junior Roman officers who would have been sent to inform Giovanni Trantemento's next of kin of his death had not yet got around to filing a report. Not that it mattered much. They were family liaison officers, dispatched for the purpose of bringing comfort, not casting suspicion on the recently bereaved. That was his job.

Having spoken by phone to one of the officers in question, Pallioti knew the Valaccis had not been told any more than the press – simply that Giovanni Trantemento had been shot in the course of what appeared to be a burglary. No mention had been made of single bullets. Or of kneeling. Or salt.

Now he leant forward and said, 'I know it is unpleasant, but I must ask. Do either of you have any idea, any suspicion at all, as to why someone might have wanted to kill Signor Trantemento?'

The words were so clichéd that he felt mildly ridiculous even mouthing them. But hackneyed as it was, the question was necessary, and in his experience, almost always useful. It was not so much the answer that interested him, as the reaction he got when he asked it. Sometimes outrage. Sometimes gabbled nonsense. This time, he was rewarded with a knowing look, at least from Antonio. Maria Valacci simply shook her head.

'I thought it was burglary,' she said.

'Yes. But there is always the chance that he knew his killer. So, if you have any idea—'

He looked from one to the other of them. Antonio was studying his empty coffee cup with intense interest.

'I never visited him,' Maria Valacci said. 'Not once, in Florence. Or anywhere else, I'm afraid. So I don't know anyone he knew. Except Antonio and my late husband, of course. I went to Switzerland,' she added, 'with my mother. Giovanni took us. He stayed with us for a while, then he vanished. Not surprising, I suppose. Even the most devoted dog can be kicked too hard.'

Pallioti frowned. Maria Valacci looked at him and nodded.

'It was horrible,' she said. 'Our mother, she called Gio names. Said he was a coward, like his father. We weren't even allowed to mention Papa. It was as if she wanted to wipe him off the face of the earth, pretend he'd never existed. But she couldn't because she had us. And Gio looked just like him. Perhaps that's why Mama hated him, because although we couldn't speak about Papa, or even use his name, Gio still had his face.'

She studied her hands for a moment, twisting the big ring. 'They said some heart ailment killed her,' she whispered. 'But really, it was anger. Hate. Hate turned her heart black.'

She stopped speaking. The clocks ticked like a chorus of crickets.

'After my mother died,' Maria Valacci said, 'I got married. I thought Gio was dead.' She shrugged. 'Everyone else was. So I just assumed. And I had a new husband, and—' She shook her head and looked at Pallioti. 'Everything was so confused just then. You have no idea. Nothing was the way it had been. It was as if the whole world had been taken and shaken and all the pieces broken and put back in the wrong place.'

Pallioti nodded, waiting for her to go on.

'After we were married,' she said a moment later, 'my husband and I came here, to Rome. His family is from here. And, well, I tried to find Gio. I made some calls. Wrote to the Red Cross and the CLN. The Committee of National Liberation. They were supposed to know what had happened to all the partisans. Finally, I was told he was dead. I'd thought so anyway, so why should I guess it wasn't true?' She looked at Pallioti, her face pleading, as if she were asking for his forgiveness. 'It happened,' she said. 'To a lot of people. No one knew who was dead or who was alive or who was anywhere.'

'How did you find him again?'

Maria Valacci shrugged.

'I didn't. He found us. He came here, one day. Out of the blue. Antonio was just a little boy. It was in the afternoon.' Her eyes narrowed again as she drifted backwards. 'It was a long time ago. And as I said, Gio and my husband – they didn't get on.' Her thin shoulders jumped under the sweater. 'We came from Pisa,' she added. 'Gio and I were both born there.'

Pallioti frowned. He realized that in the back of his mind he had somehow assumed that Giovanni Trantemento had been a native Florentine. It was the apartment, of course. Properties like that in buildings like the one Maria Valacci's brother had lived in were usually passed through generations as carefully as family jewels – which, in fact, they were.

Maria Valacci's hands ran across her lap, plucking at the pleats of her black trousers. For a moment Pallioti thought she wasn't going to go on. Then she said, 'I didn't have a reason to go to Florence, after that. And Giovanni – well, he was busy.' She looked up at Pallioti and nodded. 'He travelled a lot. Yes, a lot,' she repeated, as if she liked the sound of this, as if it explained   every-thing – all the years that had slipped away unattended, and left her here, surrounded by clocks and overstuffed sofas and un-comfortable chairs. 'Building his business,' she said. 'He was very successful, you know. An antiques dealer.'

Pallioti glanced at Antonio. Sunk into the couch, he had given up the coffee cup and was now studying the tips of his fingers. His nails were blunt and close clipped.

'Did he mention any friends at all? Business acquaintances? Someone he came to see when he was here in Rome?'

Even as Pallioti asked it, he realized that this was pointless. Nothing suggested the earlier answer might have changed. In fact, it all pointed to the contrary. Maria Valacci and her brother might as well have been strangers.

'No,' she replied. 'I – as I said, we weren't close.'

Pallioti nodded, and decided to change tack.

'Do you by any chance have a picture?' he asked. 'A recent photograph of Signor Trantemento that we might be able to borrow?'

Antonio looked up. He glanced at his mother as if he were wondering whether or not she was going to lie.

'Not more recent than the ceremony,' Maria Valacci said finally. 'That's the last time we saw him. On the day of the celebration, when he got his medal. The ceremony, and everything – it was on TV. Then we were invited to the dinner. At the Quirinale.'

She got up from her chair, her thin body unfolding like a spindly ladder. Her son began to get to his feet. He reached a hand towards her, but she waved him away.

'I'm not dead yet,' she muttered.

Pallioti, who had been about to rise and offer her his arm, sank back onto the lumpen brocade of his own chair.

'He was frightfully angry with me,' Maria Valacci added. 'He rang up and shouted.'

The small black velvet slippers she wore made a soft hissing sound as she shuffled towards the grand piano that sat in front of one of the windows. The top was down, and laden with picture frames.

'Because you came to the Quirinale?' Pallioti asked. For Giovanni Trantemento to deny his only relative seemed churlish, no matter how distant they might have been.

'No, no.' Maria Valacci seemed to be having some trouble seeing in the dim light. She was peering at the forest of frames. Finally she found the one she wanted, reached in and plucked it out.

'No, no,' she said again. 'When I nominated him, for the decoration.'

'Nominated him?'

'Yes. I heard about it, you see.' She turned back towards the two men, executing the turn with the care of a dancer. 'Well, actually,' she added, 'Tonio did, heard about it, and told me – that they were going to do something special for the partisans, on the sixtieth anniversary. So I, I nominated Giovanni. I put his name forward.'

She moved slowly back across the room and stopped in front of Pallioti, holding the frame, its face pressed against her black cashmere sweater as if she was afraid he might try to snatch it from her.

'I thought it was the least they could do,' she said. 'To thank them. All those people who died, throwing stones and firing silly little handguns at Nazi tanks. And he deserved it, Gio. He truly did. He fought so bravely. He saved someone's life – ran out into the street and helped a woman who had been shot. He was arrested, and beaten, and escaped, finally. But it saved her life, that woman. It was written about,' she added. 'In the paper.' She shook her head. 'My mother was so horrible about it. Even about that. She would barely talk to him when he came to see us, even when he got her to Switzerland. She never told him he was a hero. I thought someone should.'

For a moment Pallioti thought she was not going to give up the picture after all. Then she handed him the frame.

Turning it over, he saw a tall elderly man, his drawn face haunted as he struggled to smile. He wore a dark suit. Even in a photograph it was obvious that it was expensive, well cut. Probably custom made. A medal winked on his lapel. Antonio stood on one side of him, and on the other side, his sister. Giovanni Battiste's veined hand rested awkwardly on the shoulder of her pale velvet dress.

Maria Valacci turned around and shuffled back to the piano. She came back and stood in front of Pallioti, holding out a small black presentation case.

'This is his medal.'

She opened the box. Inside, a gold medallion nestled on a bed of white satin.

'He gave it to me. Afterwards. That night. He said I deserved it more than he did. I told you.' She looked at Pallioti and blinked. 'My brother was like that. Modest. He was a brave, modest man.'

Maria Valacci clicked the box closed, placed it on the table beside her chair, and nodded towards the photograph.

'You will be careful with it, won't you?' she asked. 'It's the only photo I have, of us all together.'

'Very. I will be very careful with it, I promise.'

Pallioti got to his feet and extended his hand. He was surprised when she took it in both of hers.

'I loved him, you know,' she said. 'Even if I didn't know him. He was my brother. A hero.'

'I know.'

'Will you find the person who did this thing?'

Maria Valacci's fingers were surprisingly strong. Pallioti could feel the bones, barely covered by her dry papery flesh.

'Yes,' he said, 'I will.'

❦

Antonio Valacci, who pointed out that he had already missed half a day of work and really did have to get back to his office, walked Pallioti down to the street.

'I know what he did, you know.' Antonio glanced at Pallioti as they stepped out of the building, blinking in the bright autumn light. 'To make his money, I mean,' he added. 'Giovanni. I know he dealt in – whatever you want to call it. Not stamps, anyway. More engravings. Specialized. Boys, wasn't it?'

Pallioti nodded. 'Apparently. Eighteenth-century, I gather. Very discerning. Was your mother aware?'

'Good God, no!' Antonio laughed. 'No, no. I think my father might have been,' he added. 'That might have explained the coolness. Not that dear Uncle Gio was warm himself. On the contrary, a real cold fish. I found out by mistake.' He glanced at Pallioti. 'Amazing what the ministry turns up. I kept quiet, of course.'

They walked in silence for a moment.

'It was a strange comment,' Pallioti said finally.

Antonio glanced at him. 'Which one?'

'About the medal. Your uncle telling your mother she deserved it more than he did. What do you think he meant?'

'That she was the real hero?' Antonio shook his head. 'That getting shot at by Nazis was easier than putting up with their mother? Who knows? That he wouldn't have got the wretched thing if it wasn't for her nominating him for it?' He shrugged.

'It was nice of him anyway, to give it to her. Unexpectedly gracious. It means a lot to her. Particularly after he was such a bastard. To start with, anyway. Although I suppose that was my fault.'

Pallioti stopped. 'What do you mean?'

Standing opposite him in the sunlit street, Antonio Valacci shrugged.

'Well, I was the one who told my mother about the sixtieth anniversary celebrations. That they were planning on giving medals to the partisans. The ones who were still alive.' He paused for a moment, then he said, 'You have to understand, Ispettore, she doesn't have much in her life, my mother. My grandmother, forgive me for saying it, was a rabid Fascist bitch. You know, the kind who thought Mussolini brought "honour" to Italy because he made the trains run on time and liked smart uniforms. I doubt my father's parents were much better, from what I heard of them. God knows he wasn't exactly a bargain. And of course, they never knew what Mama was, or I doubt they would have been so kind to her.'

'What she was?'

'Jewish.'

Pallioti stood for a moment in the sunlight, absorbing what this must have meant, in occupied Italy in 1944.

'Well, half,' Antonio added. 'Genetically. Strictly speaking, according to the tenets of the faith, Jewish though – since her mother was Jewish. I think that's how it works, doesn't it? I'm not really sure. Not that I'd guess the Nazis cared. Mother, father, grandparents, great-grandparents. I think Buchenwald welcomed all comers.'

'Your grandmother was Jewish?'

'Ironic, isn't it?'

Pallioti nodded. He was trying to build a picture in his head. He had heard of it before, Jewish families who were among the most ardent Fascists. And, he supposed, if they considered themselves Italian first and foremost, why not? Plenty of other people had done it. At least until 1938.

'Her family had converted to Catholicism,' Antonio Valacci said. 'Years before. They'd abbreviated their name, the whole thing. And of course, my grandmother married my grandfather. They were good party members. But, yes, my grandmother was Jewish. So my mother was, is, half Jewish. I don't think it mattered much, at first. But after the occupation, certainly by 1944, even in Pisa – well, you can see why Giovanni was desperate to get them to Switzerland.'

Yes, Pallioti thought. He could.

Antonio smiled, but the expression that flashed across his face was more of a grimace.

'I doubt my father would have married her, to be honest,' he said, 'if he'd known. But in Switzerland, my grandmother was just another refugee war widow with a daughter. To this day, my mother more or less denies it.' He shrugged. 'She can't help it, I suppose. She was brought up denying it – at first because I doubt they ever thought about it. Then because her life, literally, depended on it – on not being what she was. Of course, my grandmother probably would have died before admitting it.' He let out a bark of laughter. 'I'm sorry,' he said. 'I didn't intend that to be funny. But you see, it does explain a lot.'

Pallioti nodded. 'They were, where?' he asked. 'In Pisa?'

'Yes. Both of my grandparents' families came from there. It wasn't an issue, really, even after 1938 when the restrictions came in. No one paid close attention, and as I said, my grandparents had become Catholics, and were good party members. But the families were known. After 1943, people began to develop long memories.'

'And your grandfather was dead.'

'Yes,' Antonio nodded. 'I suspect that made my grandmother more vulnerable. She wasn't a very nice woman. She probably had enemies. Giovanni must have looked at the situation and realized she was sitting on a time bomb.'

'No wonder your mother thought he was God.'

'Oh, yes,' Antonio agreed. 'He did the impossible. He got them out. And I heard all about it. Any time my father wasn't around, my mother went on, and on, and on. How handsome her brother was. How brave he was. How he'd dragged that woman to safety. What a hero he'd been. I grew up thinking my Uncle Gio was a cross between Superman and the Pope. Meeting him was a bit of a let-down, I'll tell you. Still,' Antonio shrugged, 'when I heard about the sixtieth – that the government was issuing a new medal, and trying to dig up as many of the partisans as they could find to pin it on, I told her. Talk about good intentions paving the way to hell.'

Pallioti frowned. 'I don't understand.'

'No,' Antonio Valacci rolled his eyes. 'Well, it surprised me too,' he said. 'You see, when I told my mother, she was all excited. She wanted me to find out who to give Giovanni's name to, and make sure he got on a list for a medal. So I did. I made some calls. I told the story about the woman, and how brave he was and blah, blah, blah. My mother wrote a letter, nominating him. It never occurred to me that he wasn't proud of it – you know how old men are. Their glory days and all that. Certainly, it never occurred to me he'd be upset. But then again, I really didn't know him.'

'He was upset?'

Antonio laughed.

'To put it mildly. When Uncle Gio found out – when the Ministry contacted him with the joyous news that he had been put forward for a medal by his loving sister. Well. Let's just say it wasn't pretty. To put it bluntly, he went mental. Rang up and called her names. I happened to be home. I could hear him on the phone, even though I was across the room. He was shouting. Accusing her of ruining his life.'

'Ruining his life?'

Antonio Valacci nodded.

'That's what he said. He was hysterical, I tell you. "First

Mama and now you – you've, both of you, ruined my life!"
Those were the words. You should have seen my mother's face.
I thought she was going to have a heart attack. Honestly. She
turned grey. I took the phone out of her hand and hung up on
him.'

Antonio shook his head.

'It wasn't funny, really,' he said. He looked at Pallioti and
smiled. 'So, you see,' he added, 'the least dear Uncle Gio could
do was give her the damn medal. To this day, she thinks he just
had a change of heart.'

'Didn't he?'

Antonio shrugged. He looked up at the buildings behind
them as if he expected to see his mother at the window.

'Not exactly. I telephoned him the next day. From my office.'
He smiled, looking somewhat sheepish. 'You may not believe
this, Ispettore,' he said. 'But I do love my mother, very much.
So, I told dear Uncle Gio exactly what I thought of him.'

'And?'

Antonio sighed.

'Let's just say that by the end of the conversation – look,' he
added, 'I'm not particularly proud of this – I don't generally go
around threatening old men – but, well, I may have suggested
that some of his transactions, his sales, and his clients might be
looked into a little more carefully than they had been in the
past if he didn't, as they so quaintly say in America, Straighten
Up and Fly Right.'

Pallioti could not help smiling. He was beginning to like
Antonio Valacci.

'Straighten Up and Fly Right?'

'I had an American girlfriend, what can I say? Anyway,' Antonio added, 'Uncle Gio called my mother the next afternoon
and apologized. I came home from work that evening and she
told me she'd gone to Mass and confession for the first time in
ten years and prayed her head off for her dear, darling brother,
and lo and behold, a "miracle" had happened. Imagine.'

'Imagine.'

'And, of course, he accepted the medal.'

'And gave it to her.'

Antonio nodded.

'And gave it to her.' They began to walk again. 'But,' he added, 'I don't think it was just that, honestly – my shaming him, heavy-handing him – whatever you want to call it.'

'No?' Pallioti asked.

'No.' Antonio Valacci shook his head. Then he stopped again and looked at Pallioti. 'When I saw him at the dinner, it was almost as if—'

He stopped talking, his eyes focused back in the past. Pallioti waited. Antonio Valacci gave himself a small shake. 'I know it sounds strange,' he said, 'but before I threatened him – I doubt, incidentally, that I'd have been able to do any of that, get his sales looked into, but it sounded good – before I did that, he was angry. But more angry the way people are when they're afraid. Like an animal that's cornered. They fight and scratch because they're terrified. But at the dinner, at the Quirinale – perhaps it was just time – but it was as if he'd changed.'

'How?' Pallioti asked quietly. 'How did your uncle change?'

Antonio Valacci thought for a moment. Then he said, 'People are so strange. As I'm sure you know. And perhaps I'm wrong, but I got the feeling he'd stopped fighting. That he wasn't angry any more. He was just tired. Like someone who's given up.' Antonio shrugged. 'Perhaps he had a presentiment, you know, that it was all almost over. Now I do sound idiotic,' he added. 'Next I'll be telling you he had an aura. A blue haze around his head or something. Although it is a little spooky. Given what happened.'

Pallioti said nothing. Spooky was not the word he would have used. They began to walk again.

'I'm parked at Chiesa Nuova.'

Antonio Valacci nodded.

'I'm going that way.'

They came to the end of the narrow street. Antonio stopped, dug in his pocket, and pulled out a slim gold cigarette case.

'Is that why he was killed?' he asked. 'Do you think? Because of that stuff, the erotica?'

'I don't know,' Pallioti said. 'Possibly. At this point, anything is possible.'

'So, no leads.'

If it was a question, Pallioti didn't answer it. Instead, he watched as Antonio examined his cigarette, raised it to his lips, then said, 'The name I gave you. On the card. She isn't my secretary.'

'Ah.'

'I didn't give her name to your friends from Rome, either. Just you. She's Carlo Perocci's wife. We're having an affair. You know who he is?'

Before Pallioti could answer, Antonio said, 'Junior Culture Minister. He's an ass. It's been going on for a long time. Anna and me, I mean. Well, and him being an ass, too. If he knew, he'd kill her. We'd run off to the ends of the earth together, but I can't leave my mother. Yet.' He shrugged. 'So there we are.'

'I'm sorry.'

Antonio smiled. 'So am I. So's Anna. It's a mess. We've known each other for years. That number I gave you? It's her mobile. We were together almost all day. Certainly all morning. We have an apartment, in Trastevere. People saw us. It's not just my lover vouching for me.'

'Thank you for telling me.'

Antonio waved his hand through the stream of smoke.

'It's the least I can do, cooperate with the police. I mean, I'm just the Culture Ministry, but we're more or less on the same side. Besides,' he added, 'you'll want to clear it up, since I have a motive.'

Pallioti raised his eyebrows.

Antonio Valacci dropped his cigarette into the gutter, shook his head, and ground it out under his heel.

'I wasn't born yesterday, Ispettore,' he said. 'I'm sure people have killed for less than that apartment. I'm also sure I'm not one of them.'

He held out his hand. Pallioti shook it.

'Safe journey home.' Antonio Valacci smiled. 'Chiesa Nuova's straight ahead. Down that alley, then on the left.'

∽

The plane rose from the runway, swung out over the ancient port of Ostia, and turned north. Below, the silver sheet of the sea glittered in the setting sun. Then it turned pink, and orange, and was lost in cloud as they climbed over the coast.

A drink, vodka straight up on the rocks, and a foil envelope of 'nibbles' sat untouched on the tray table in front of Pallioti. He poked the ice cubes with his green plastic stirrer, then put it down and sipped the cold slimy liquid. Vodka was a bad habit he had picked up some years ago – he could not remember exactly when – a defence against all the times, on planes and overseas, when grappa was out of reach. As a substitute it was a poor one, but it had the comfort of familiarity. He felt the taste evaporate on the back of his tongue, considered the supposition that, in a perfect world, Alitalia would provide plump green olives instead of vacuum-packed stale almonds, and looked at the small red book he held in his hand.

Strictly speaking, he should have signed for it, or at least told Enzo he was taking it. He would remember to mention it. Not that anyone would care. It was a souvenir, evidence of nothing except the past. Eventually it would be handed over to the Valaccis, along with the rest of Giovanni Trantemento's belongings.

He had recognized it at once, from the moment he'd held up the bag. The cover was the wrong colour, but otherwise the little book had been as familiar as the face of a long-forgotten friend in a crowd. There was only one shop in the city that sold these, an ancient dark little hole of a stationer's in an alley not far from Via Purgatorio that had no name.

The little books, all with the lily stamped on the front, came in a variety of colours. They were sold in soft cloth bags, often in pairs. Appointments, accounts, liaisons, and dreams – all the crucial, forgotten minutiae of lives had been carefully recorded between covers just like these by generations of Florentine women. Pallioti's mother had kept hers in the secret drawer of her desk.

Her book was always dark blue, her favourite colour. As a child, he had often released the secret latch and pulled it out. Sometimes, instead of studying the small cramped pages, he'd simply sat there, his feet barely touching the floor, holding it against his cheek because the cover was as soft as her skin and the pages smelt of her perfume.

The memory came back so suddenly, it made him blink.

The cover of this book was battered, the red faded, the gilding on the lily almost gone altogether. The spine was intact – the hand-stitching had assured that, but the flyleaf was water-marked, the inscription on it barely visible. Pallioti turned on his reading light and held the speckled page up in the beam. There was an address – no number, but a street off Via Senese that he recognized, and a date – 1 November 1943. Then the inscription, *To Caterina Maria Cammaccio, the Most Beautiful Bride in Florence – From Her Sister, Isabella.*

The letters were ghostly. Isabella had chosen to use what must, even at the time, have been pale lilac ink. Caterina Cammaccio herself had opted for more conventional black. Turning the pages, looking at the tiny, cramped writing, he realized with a start that he could not remember what colour ink his mother had used, or – despite the fact that he was ten when she had died and had been reading for years – a single word that she had written. It was simply the fact that she had smoothed the pages with her hands, and left on the marbled paper the shape of her handwriting, marks as definitive as a zebra's stripe or a leopard's spots, that had drawn her close to him.

Glancing about to be sure no one was watching, he lifted the little red book to his nose. But there was not so much as a hint of jasmine. The scarred leather and thick ragged pages of Caterina Cammaccio's book smelt only of dust and shadows.

PART THREE

Chapter Five

Florence, 10 November 1943

I can't describe the feeling I had, getting back into the ambulance and driving away from Fiesole. An hour earlier, when we had bluffed our way through the checkpoint, watched the barrier rise and driven up the hill with – not three 'poor boys' – but two Americans and one British POW in the back, I had felt something beyond relief. A sort of deep gratitude for being alive. The air, the night, as I had breathed it in, tasted like nothing before. Then, watching Issa walk away, start into the mountains, positively glowing with joy because she was doing what she loved most in the world, and because she was in love with Carlo – that left me bereft. Utterly. Standing there watching her go, I felt as if we were an hourglass and life had turned us upside down and was spilling out of me and into her.

So, strangely, as mad as it sounds, Il Corvo telling me his name felt like salvation of a kind. A tiny affirmation. A whisper – the thud of another heartbeat in the dark.

I waited for five days for Issa to come home, and by the time she did, it seemed everything had changed again. No, not changed – tightened. As if a tourniquet has been wrapped around us and little by little is cutting off blood.

The Fascist government has announced that special tribunals will be set up to try party members who have 'betrayed the faith', and anyone else deemed 'in speech or action' to have betrayed the regime. This could, of course, be anyone. The penalty, if found guilty, for ex-party members is death. For the rest of us, five to thirty years in prison. Papa actually took some pleasure in this, claiming that it means they are truly frightened. As he spoke, Mama's eyes met mine over the table. I did not need to ask her, I knew. We were both thinking the same thing – that frightened animals are the most vicious. Especially if they believe they have nothing to lose.

This has happened frequently since that night in the kitchen. My mother, who has never been close to me before, who has seemed all my life to hoard her love for Enrico, feels suddenly as if she is part of me, a mirror I look into. In her eyes, the only physical trait we share, I see my own looking back. For the first time, there are threads between us, fine little silks of fear and sympathy. This war has turned my mother and me into spiders weaving the same web. Or, less optimistically, flies trapped in it.

She has taken to cooking. The offerings are frequently burnt, or underdone, or stodgy, or simply raw. But I do not care. Last night, I was very late getting home. The streets were dark, and it was cold. My armband gives me safe passage, but even so, I think I hear footsteps all the time now. Under the whirr of my bicycle wheels, I imagine screams. Occasionally I've heard the screech of brakes and running feet. Once, gunshots. Mama had made a crème caramel. I hate to think how much the eggs must have cost. Papa had gone to bed and the rest of the house was dark. She sat across the kitchen table, her eyes following every lift of the spoon, watching me eat as she never had when I was a child. There was barely any sugar in it and the milk was sour, curdled. I scraped the bowl. It was the most delicious thing I have ever tasted.

Food is getting more and more expensive. Thanks to Grandpapa's money, and the black market, we are all right. The necessities, and even some luxuries, can be had for those who know where to look. But that is bound to get more difficult, because the banks are refusing to cash cheques and limiting withdrawals. And with or without money, some things are getting very scarce. Fuel is hard to come by. The Germans are requisitioning everything. I heard yesterday of a lorry going down the Via Tuornabuoni, emptying out shops, clearing shelves of woollens, gloves, shoes, and boots. Our excavations in the hospital cellars no longer seem as silly as they did two short months ago. I have given up on a new coat. Mama has an old one, and I am using that. When I turn the collar up, it smells of her powder and her soap, as if she has laid her hand on my cheek.

I began to look for Issa in crowds. I knew, somehow, that she would not come home, not simply walk up to the door and into the house. In my heart, I know that this trip through the mountains, the choices she has made now, will change her forever. I think it's why I didn't want to let her go, because I knew that no matter what happened, some part of her – the little Issa I have known all my life – would never come home. It's Carlo, of course. That heart Isabella has kept locked tight has burst wide open. It's plain to see for anyone who knows her. But it's more than that as well. Mama, Papa, and I – we will struggle. Do our best. Try not to be afraid because we want to survive. But Isabella is fighting a different fight. She does not love this war any more than we do, but it has given her her place in the world.

I began to look for her as I cycled to work, to search the faces of crowds, wait for the touch of her hand on my shoulder as I stood in the street. Which was, in fact, more or less how it happened.

It was early morning on the fifth day. The light was still pearly on the river, and I was standing on the bridge with my bicycle, waiting to cross. Then, as the traffic passed, I looked up and saw her, standing on the opposite pavement. It had grown cold. The first dusting of early snow had come the night before. She was wearing a dress and an overcoat I did not recognize, and had a scarf wound around her neck. She looked at me and smiled. The mountains were in her eyes, bright and glittering. I crossed the street and she fell into step beside me, hands dug in her pockets, as if it was the most ordinary thing in the world.

'How long have you been back?'

It took me a moment or two to ask. I had expected that she would be changed, but still I couldn't quite take it in. I kept glancing at her, trying to understand how she could be so completely different and at once the same. There was a purpose in her step, and a stillness about her, and an alertness, too, that

136

was completely new. I realized that all my life I had thought of Isabella as frivolous – as prettier, younger, somehow less consequential than me. It was something of a shock to understand that I would never feel that way again.

'A day.'

'Was it all right?'

'All parcels delivered.' She smiled. 'Your cigarettes were much appreciated.'

I had slipped the packet into her rucksack. At the mention of them I thought of Dieter, and started to look back, as if I might find him looming up behind us.

Issa grabbed my arm.

'Don't,' she said. 'Don't ever look back and don't walk faster. If you want to see who's behind you, stop and look in a shop window.'

She let go of my arm and glanced at me, her blue eyes so dark they looked nearly black.

'They won't be wearing a uniform,' she muttered. 'Remember that. They're Italians. They don't look any different from us.'

I nodded, numbly. I had heard, of course, of OVRA, the Fascist secret police. We all had. But never before had it occurred to me that they might have any interest in me.

'Then how—'

'Faces,' Issa said. 'Look for faces. On the street. In cafes. At the hospital. Anywhere. People you see too often.'

'Is that why you're not coming to the house? Because—' The urge to look over my shoulder was almost more than I could bear. Issa saw it on my face. She took my arm again.

'Tell Mama and Papa I'm fine.'

I nodded, unable to contain myself any longer.

'Where are you staying?' I blurted out the question. 'How can I contact you?'

'Like this. Or I'll come to the hospital.'

We had come into the Piazza Signoria. People hurried to and fro, scurrying on their way to work. Beyond the fountain, the swastikas snapped in the wind, looking like spiders crawling into the sky.

Issa was watching me. 'I'm staying at the University,' she said. 'Or in the mountains. With Carlo.'

'Does Enrico know about you and Carlo?'

Again, the question came out before I could help it.

She stopped and laughed.

'Yes, Cati,' she said. 'Enrico knows.'

She might as well have said, 'the whole world knows'.

'Is he—' I asked, 'I mean, is he all right? Rico?'

Issa looked at me for a moment. Then she laughed again and patted my hand. 'Yes,' she said, 'he's fine, he sends you his love,' and walked on.

I stood for a moment, holding my bicycle, watching her back and the sun glinting off her golden hair. A nervousness was fizzing inside me that I could not quite place, or account for. A pair of soldiers turned as Issa went past, their eyes following her. The sight did nothing to reassure me. I pushed my bicycle forward and caught up with her as we turned into the canyon of narrow streets behind the Bargello.

Here, the shops still had things in them. The Germans apparently had no interest in jars of ground pigment, in hogshair brushes and pallet knives. I had paused at a window, and was studying a display, thinking of my own watercolours that had lain untouched since that afternoon on the terrace, when Issa said, 'Cati, we need to do it again.'

I looked up. As she promised, I saw her reflection as she stood behind me. Our eyes met in the glass.

'How many?'

My voice was not more than a whisper.

She raised a hand, holding up fingers. Four.

'When?'

Her face was impassive. Almost mask-like, familiar and completely alien at the same time. She mouthed a single word.

'Tonight.'

∞

Again, Il Corvo and I did not speak as we drove out of the city. We went later this time. Thanks to its red crosses, the ambulance can move freely after dark. The streets were almost deserted. More snow had fallen. The pavements looked dusted with sugar, and you could see chinks of light behind shutters. There were only a few cars moving and no people at all. Like some medieval village plagued by goblins and wolves, Florence has taken to hiding behind closed doors after sunset. To turning her face away while the Devil rides abroad.

We passed one Blackshirt patrol. We did not slow down, but in the darkness I felt Il Corvo tense. Neither of us said it, but I think we were both more frightened of being stopped by them than by the Germans.

This time, as we approached, we saw a car coming through the checkpoint in the opposite direction. The soldier on duty leaned into the window, then stood back and gave a smart, snapped salute.

As it passed us, large and black and gliding through the night, we made out the caps of officers in the rear seat. They have requisitioned most of the big villas up here on the hill. The houses recently filled with American heiresses and English lords now house the German command. Not so very long before that it was the French. And before that, the Austrians. We've been occupied longer than we realize. It seems everyone comes to Florence to play at being nobility. The soldier turned and waved us forward. It was not until he stepped into the beam of the headlamps that I realized it was Dieter again. Getting out and handing him the papers felt almost like meeting an old friend.

He was pleased to see me. He remembered my name, and although he made me open the doors, he gave the inside of the ambulance only the most cursory flash of his torch beam. Four men tucked onto stretchers.

'We are moving more of them to Fiesole,' I explained again in my bad German. 'Everyone we can manage. We need the beds in the city for more urgent cases.'

Dieter nodded. Then he apologized that he had no more cigarettes to give me.

In the shed, Issa and Carlo were waiting. This time they were alone. There was no sign of Massimo and his tiny acolyte, and we were faster than before and silent, getting the men out and dressed. Already we have become used to doing this. This time, the clothes were not all Enrico's, although I recognized a sweater and another pair of gloves. Issa had her hair tucked up under a cap, and was wearing men's woollen trousers and a heavy jumper and jacket.

Again, Carlo strapped her rucksack on for her, then she kissed me on the cheek, her lips cold from the night, and led them out of the side door. The men followed her, one by one, like goslings following a goose. Carlo brought up the rear. Just before he slipped through the door, he turned to me and touched my cheek.

'Don't worry, Caterina,' he whispered. He winked, and a smile lit his face. 'God shows us the way.'

Another time, I might have told Carlo that I do not believe in God. But I appreciated his kindness nonetheless.

Outside, I watched as they moved like phantoms, six figures, black against the white smattering of snow. Long after they had vanished, I could still hear the tramp of their feet on dead leaves. Then their footsteps were lost in a rustle, and there was nothing on the mountainside but the wind.

Il Corvo let me out in an alley near the Porta San Frediano. I have no idea where they are keeping the ambulance and I did not ask. I wanted to say something to him, give some sign that we were friends, or at least in this together, but in the end I couldn't think of anything, so I ended up nodding mutely. Even though it was dark, I saw him smile. The expression was strange on his face, as if it were something he wasn't used to.

I had left my bicycle at the hospital, so I walked home. Snow fluttered from the steps of the Carmine and danced in the piazza as if it were the only living thing in the city. Even the bells sounded hollow, a call to prayer rung by ghosts. Tonight there were no footsteps. No sound of gunshots, or screech of brakes. I thought of Boccaccio and the plague. I might have been the only person left alive, nothing moving but me and the wind and the snow.

I didn't see any light behind the shutters when I put my key in the lock, but Mama was waiting for me. She rose up from the sofa where she had been sitting in the dark. There was no crème caramel this time, just soup and some rather stale bread. She sat across the kitchen table again, saying nothing. Watching me eat.

Now I am writing this in my room. It is cold and I am tired, but I can't sleep. I have had a little conversation with Lodo. It's stupid, but I opened the wardrobe, and ran my hand down my wedding dress and asked him if he thought it was beautiful, and what he thinks of all of this. I closed my eyes, and saw him smile. Then I opened my window and pushed the shutters back. There is no moon tonight, and it took my eyes a moment to sort out the dark from the dark, but finally I found them on the horizon – the outline of the mountains Issa is moving through like a phantom. I stood there for as long as I could, looking – as if somehow I might see her beneath the pinpricks of the stars.

Chapter Six

'Ssandro!'

Pallioti looked up at the sound of his sister's voice. He closed the file that had lain open in front of him. His driver had handed it to him as soon as he settled himself in his car at the airport. The contents had not made cheerful reading.

The forensics report on Giovanni Trantemento's apartment had yielded essentially nothing – no unidentifiable finger- or footprints and only a small amount of debris that might have come from anyone's shoes. The report on the bullet that had been so carefully dug out of his skull was equally unhelpful. It was a .22 calibre, about three years old and common as dirt. In fact, a note in the margin from Enzo informed him, it was virtually the commonest ammunition in the world. It had been around for decades, could be used in rifles or handguns, and was favoured by hunters and shooting clubs due to the fact that it was cheap, versatile, and relatively quiet. In other words, it was a perfect choice.

Pallioti wished he thought that was a coincidence, but he didn't. However unpalatable, it was increasingly clear that someone had wanted Giovanni Trantemento dead. And had put quite a lot of careful thought into achieving it.

The only bright spot, so to speak, in this increasingly unpleasant scenario, was that the markings on the bullet were strange. Distinctive enough that Enzo had highlighted them, along with the execution-style single shot and the salt, in the profile that had gone out that evening on the Europe-wide databases. As rays of sunshine went, it was a weak one. But it did mean that if they could find the weapon, they could almost certainly match it. To be honest, Pallioti wasn't optimistic. So far, even taking the wallet into account – which he was less and less inclined to do – Giovanni Trantemento's killer had done an impressively professional job. Pallioti doubted he'd have made a mistake as silly as dropping the weapon in the river or stashing it in a rubbish bin.

For the next few hours, however, he vowed to forget about it.

He slipped the file into his briefcase, and watched his sister make her way to his habitual spot in the restaurant's back corner. What he saw was a thirty-six-year-old woman who might, from a distance, have been a teenager. Seraphina was slight and blonde, and in other words, looked nothing at all like him. Occasionally, he still found it something of a shock to remember that they were related.

Saffy – as only Pallioti and her husband were allowed to call her – was fourteen years his junior. Her mother was their father's second wife – a slight, gamine Frenchwoman called Mimi whom Pallioti senior had met in Paris and married almost three years to the day after Pallioti's mother died. Pallioti had never warmed to his stepmother, something he now regretted, because it had not been her fault. An awkward, withdrawn teenager, he had been both infuriated and embarrassed by his father's behaviour in marrying again, and had taken his wrath out on Mimi, rebuffing her repeated advances with not much more than a grunt. When Saffy was born, he had pretended not to care. He had withdrawn to school, and seen as little of her as possible for the next eleven years. By the time his father and Mimi died in a car accident, Pallioti had not seen any of them for the better part of five years. At twenty-six, he was already a rising star in the police, a young man rather too pleased with himself who had done everything he could to forget that he even had a half-sister.

He had been stationed in Genoa when he heard. It had not been his father's fault. A young idiot had overtaken at twice the speed limit on a blind corner. All concerned had been killed outright.

The drive to France had taken Pallioti all night. Morning had found him outside a convent school near Montpellier, trying to understand how he should tell a twelve-year-old girl he barely knew that her parents were dead and that a remote, rather arrogant young man who had spent most of his life studiously ignoring her was the only relative she had left in the world.

When the moment came, she had simply stared at him. But there was something in the gravity of her face, something in the way she had blinked her grey eyes, refusing to cry, merely accepting what he was telling her, that pierced him. Made him feel humble, and idiotic, and deeply ashamed of himself.

Finally, he had been able to think of nothing to say except, 'What do you want to do?'

To which Saffy had replied, 'I want to go home.'

He had stared at her.

'I want you to take me home,' she had said.

'I can't take you home,' he'd muttered. 'I can't.'

'Why not?' Saffy had asked.

And although he was sure there were thousands of them, in that moment he hadn't been able to think of a single reason.

Now, Saffy knew him better than anyone else in the world. If anyone had asked, Pallioti would have been happy to tell them that, if he had done anything to help Seraphina become the woman she was, she had more than repaid the favour by, if not eradicating, at least checking, his worst instincts. If he was a decent human being, if he was even slightly more thoughtful than the arrogant young man he had been, it was Saffy's doing.

When she had married Leonardo Benvoglio – an older and successful businessman not much younger than himself – he had taken the groom aside and told him, without any particular malice, that if he ever did anything to hurt Seraphina, Pallioti himself would kill him. Promptly and probably painfully.

Leonardo, to give him credit, had taken it in the spirit it was intended. No threat. Just a statement of fact.

'So—' They had settled in at the table, attended by Bernardo, the owner of the restaurant where Saffy sometimes joked that her brother had a 'meal plan'. 'I'm sorry I look like this.'

She looked down at the polo-neck sweater, jeans and boots that had been revealed when Bernardo had taken her coat. Her hair was pulled back in a ponytail, and her small hands were nicked and flecked with paint. Only the rather large diamond ring on her left hand and the earrings that matched it suggested that she might not be your average Florentine housewife, whoever that was.

'Is the show finished?'

Saffy nodded as Bernardo poured her a glass of wine.

Seraphina Benvoglio was a well-known photographer. Her still lifes and landscapes sold for considerable sums. Several had recently been acquired by smaller but significant European museums. She had her own gallery in Borgo San Frediano. Increasingly, her shows were covered by the national press.

'You are coming?'

She looked up from the menu. Pallioti had seen every show she had ever hung, from the first one in a grim student collective somewhere on the outskirts of Modena, to the considerably more ritzy biannual affairs she hosted now. The opening of her latest show was the next night.

'If I can.' He made a face. 'And if I can't,' he added quickly, 'I'll get there before the week is out. I promise.'

She smiled and shrugged.

'As long as you turn up at some point. It's unlucky if you don't. Tommaso will be disappointed,' she added.

Tommaso was Saffy and Leonardo's son, and not only Pallioti's nephew, but also his godson. At five, he was increasingly a connoisseur of Spiderman and Batman – both of whom he seemed to think were closely related to his uncle. Pallioti supposed he ought to be grateful the little boy hadn't become enamoured of Shrek.

'I wish I had a superhero cape,' he muttered. So much for forgetting about the contents of the file.

Glancing at him, Saffy put her menu aside. There was no point in ordering at Lupo in any case. Regardless of what they said, Bernardo simply brought what he thought they ought to be eating. He claimed to know what Pallioti would like from the look on his face. This culinary mood-reading was a little obscure at the best of times, and probably had more to do with surpluses in the kitchen than Pallioti's smiles and scowls. But it hardly mattered. The results were uniformly pleasing. Tonight they began with a plate of plump grilled wood mushrooms dusted with delicate curls of pale, hard cheese.

'It's not this old man, is it?'

Spearing a mushroom, Saffy looked up. She was the only person, other than Enzo and the Mayor, with whom he ever discussed cases. Even the medical examiner and the magistrates rarely got more than he decided they needed to know. Pallioti didn't like gossip. And speculation made him nervous.

'Yes,' he said, 'it is.' He stabbed a mushroom harder than was strictly necessary. 'How do you know about it?'

Saffy eyed him over the top of her glasses. They were round and made her look like a baby owl.

'I read the newspapers.'

He groaned. He had turned down a newspaper on the plane, both this morning and coming back.

'What are they saying?'

She shrugged. 'That this – what was his name? Trantimenni?'

'Trantemento.'

'Trantemento. That he was a partisan hero, a harmless old man, shot in his apartment in the middle of the morning in what was probably a burglary, or' – she glanced at him – 'probably not, since you were at the scene. Oh,' she added, popping the cheese curl into her mouth and licking her lips, 'and one of the papers said something about neo-Nazis.'

'Neo-Nazis?'

'Attacking ageing partisans. The Reich will never die.'

Pallioti put his knife and fork down.

'Are they?' he asked. 'Attacking ageing partisans?'

He had to admit, it was an angle he hadn't even considered. It sounded too mad. But then again, the terms 'neo-Nazi' and 'rational' hardly went hand in hand.

'I don't know!' Saffy said, laughing. 'You're the policeman. You tell me. It sounds crazy.' Pallioti sighed.

'Which paper?' he asked.

She told him. He made a mental note to get hold of the editor, or the reporter, or someone, and see if this was just hot air or something of more unfortunate substance.

'Actually,' she added a moment later, 'Maria mentioned it, too.'

'Maria?'

There were a lot of Marias in Florence, but the one Saffy was talking about, Maria Grandolo, was a particular bugbear of Pallioti's. The spoilt offspring of a wealthy banking family, she was one of the very few of Saffy's friends whom he neither liked nor approved of. Which was unfortunate, at least for Maria, because according to Saffy, Maria had once had a major crush on her older brother. She seemed to have recovered from it, but one could never be sure. His sister looked at him and laughed.

'Her cousins,' she said, 'started some sort of foundation, after the war, helping the partisans. Maria was just saying how awful it was. That this poor old fellow was killed.' Saffy winked. 'She seemed reassured knowing you were handling the case.'

Pallioti resisted the impulse to groan.

'They're responsible for those memorial plaques you see all over the place,' Saffy added. 'Her family. That's how it came up.'

Pallioti had no idea about the Grandolos and memorial plaques, but he wasn't surprised. The Grandolo family had, over the course of several centuries, done a great deal for the city of Florence. Most of it with the utmost discretion. With the unfortunate exception of Maria, they were private almost to the point of neurotic. His picture had almost never been in the papers, and his name was not plastered across the front of buildings, but Cosimo Grandolo, the head of the bank, who had recently died, had nonetheless been a philanthropist of note. Clinics, hospital wings, and education programmes had all been quietly underwritten. So Pallioti was not shocked to hear that the Grandolos had reached out to those who had sacrificed so much for their city and their country. It only confirmed his suspicion that Maria, whom he considered at best a nitwit, was some sort of genetic throwback – an equalizer, designed to ensure humanity didn't evolve too fast.

'She's not that bad,' Saffy said, laughing at him again. 'Maria's fun. And she has a good heart.'

Deciding prudence – or at least silence – was the better part of something or other, Pallioti merely smiled and reached for his wine.

Bernardo swept down on them with the next course. A platter of chicken livers sautéed and tossed in sage. Pallioti and Seraphina ate in silence, moving methodically from the chicken livers to the bowl of tiny golden roast potatoes that accompanied them, and back again. The sage reminded Pallioti of childhood winters. Tasting it, smoky and soft, he could see the pale grey-green leaves tinted with frost as they tumbled out of the pots that had lined the gravelled path to the garden of the house where his parents had lived, and where his mother had died.

He finished the plate reluctantly, knowing he did not need more and wanting it anyway.

'So, was it?' Saffy asked.

As she spoke, she took her glasses off, tucked them into her bag, and swirled the deep, almost purple, wine in the globe of her glass.

Pallioti did not need to ask what she was talking about. They had learned, over the years, to read each other's minds with remarkable efficiency.

'No,' he said, pushing his empty plate away and picking up his own glass. 'I thought it was at first, just a burglary. One more old person who assumes everyone at the door is a friend.' He shrugged. 'That's what it looked like, on first glance. By which I mean, that's what I expected. Some thug posing as the gas man barging his way into an apartment to steal the stereo. Or the BlackBerry. Or whatever it is people steal these days.'

'The silver,' Saffy said. 'They still steal the silver.'

'Well, not in this case. In fact, I don't think they stole anything.'

'No?'

'No. There are' – Pallioti glanced at her – 'circumstances.'

Saffy smiled. 'Are you going to tell me what they are?'

'No,' he said. 'Not just at the moment.'

She raised her eyebrows. 'That bad?'

'Pretty grim. And, strange,' he said slowly. Then he added, 'That's where I was today, in Rome. To see the family. Among other things.'

'Oh. I'm sorry.'

She knew how much he hated this. How much any policeman hated having to pick through the lives of victims in front of the people who, whether they had loved them or not, were desperately trying to keep some vaguely familiar picture of their husband or wife or child intact.

'His mother was Jewish,' Pallioti said. 'He got her out,' he added. 'Giovanni Trantemento. He got his mother out, and his sister, during the Occupation. To Switzerland.'

'That can't have been easy.'

'No. But the partisans were doing it. And others.'

'I can't imagine that,' Saffy said suddenly. 'Can you? What that must have been like? To be hunted like that?' She put her wine glass down. 'Or to risk your life like that – saving other people? People you didn't even know. I can't imagine the courage that takes.'

Pallioti smiled. A strand of blonde hair had escaped her ponytail and whispered against her chin. 'Yes, you can,' he said.

Bernardo was closing in on them, two tiny glasses hooked through his fingers. His other ham-sized fist gripped a bottle of grappa. He poured two thimblefuls of the bright clear liquid and whisked their plates away.

'*Salute!*' Saffy emptied hers in one mouthful, rolling the dense, syrupy liquor on the back of her tongue. 'You're busy Sunday, right?'

Pallioti nodded. If it was even remotely possible, he shared Sunday lunch with his sister and brother-in-law and whatever assorted friends Saffy had rounded up. This week, however, even that sacrosanct afternoon had been sacrificed to the fraud case.

'And I know, no matter what you say, that you won't make it tomorrow. So, come on.' Saffy put her glass down. 'I want to show you something. Then we can go for gelato.'

The Benvoglio Gallery was on the western edge of the Oltrarno, beyond the high-fashion enclave of the Borgo San Jacopo and the boutiques of the Via Santo Spirito. Unlike its trendier counterparts, the area still had a faintly raffish air. On an early winter night with the lamps throwing muzzy haloes into the damp dark, it was still possible to believe that artists worked here.

The huge honey-coloured facade of the Carmine, blank-faced and rough-hewn, loomed behind them as Saffy and Pallioti threaded their way through parked cars and chained Vespas. Its piazza was a parking lot. There was no view from its steps. It had none of the grace of Santo Spirito, or the charm of San Felice, or the serenity of San Miniato. Perhaps, Pallioti thought, that was why it was one of his favourite places in the city. The Carmine made no effort to seduce. He turned and looked back at it. Floodlights threw hard shadows across its front, making it a place of foreboding. A fitting home for the exile from Eden.

Saffy's gallery had been once been a chapel. Then a warehouse. She had spent a small fortune gutting and lighting the interior.

'Here.'

After unlocking the door, she took Pallioti by the shoulders and guided him into the centre of the dark space. He heard her step away, and for a second was left suspended in darkness with pictures he could not see floating on the walls around him. Then she switched on the lights.

Directly in front of him was a panorama of cloud – a high, thin, pale-blue scudding, broken only by the black lacings of winter treetops. Next to it was a peeling doorway, its lintel heaped with snow. Three steps led up to it. One dark set of footprints led away. An empty room with a single table and chair was overlooked by a window rimed with ice. A fallow field was striped with dark ploughed lines of earth. The exhibition title, *The Winter Line*, hung from the high ceiling, the words hovering, engraved on glass. Below them floated a print of a sculpted angel. Grey on grey, the fluted wings stood out against the rippled veins of a marble wall. Next to it was a photograph of gateposts. Snow piled at their bases. It mounded over thin fingers of grass and speckled the fields that lay on either side of the white drive that ran away, beginning and ending in a gauze of fog.

15 November 1943

Our neighbours, the Banducci – Signor, Signora,
and their two children, boy and girl – are living
with us. Temporarily. Please God, let it only be
temporarily. I am sorry. I know I should feel pity
for them, and I do. But I don't like them, nonetheless. They have lived in our street for perhaps ten
years, but we have always avoided them, as they
were known to be Fascists of the more devoted
kind. They kept a picture of themselves on the
mantel, taken years ago with Mussolini, and talk
a great deal about The Glory of Italy, and the re-
demptive quality of Mass.

Or at least the Signora does. She is obsequious
and pushy at the same time, and eyes our possessions – the furniture, and silver – and comments
on their quality. Or on what she judges to be the
lack of it. She fingers things when she thinks no
one is noticing, runs her thumb along the edge
of the gilt frames checking for dust, and stares
into the flowered Venetian glass in the hall as if
she might find something suspicious there. Her
husband is much quieter. Mostly, he hovers in the
sitting room looking bewildered – which is, I suppose, not surprising. Their house caught fire, in
the middle of the night, and burned to the
ground. It is a small miracle that they got out at
all, and they have lost everything. So as I said, I
should feel sorry for them. The Signora talks
endlessly about going to Ravenna to live with
their cousins, whose villa is much finer than
ours. There, they will each have their own room
instead of having to share our two guest rooms
as they do here. The children chorus this, as if

it's a song they have been taught. The boy wears Enrico's old trousers from his childhood trunk. The girl, one of my old dresses. Mama caught her stealing yesterday. It was only a stale roll, but bread is increasingly scarce. When Mama took it away from her, saying we all must share, the child hissed like a cat. Later, I found her in Issa's room.

I had gone upstairs and noticed the door ajar. When I went to close it, I saw her – the Banducci girl – sitting at Issa's dressing table.

She turned, her face caught in the light from the hallway, and I gave a little cry. I thought she was bleeding, that she had cut or bitten herself. Then I saw Issa's red lipstick in her hand. The girl smiled, and her crimson mouth was blurred and huge, like a clown's.

I was so startled by the sight that I jumped forward and grabbed her. As she stumbled off the bench, her arm caught a bottle of Issa's perfume and knocked it to the floor. Now the rug reeks of gardenia. It seeps under the door and drifts into the hall, hovering, as if Isabella is standing there herself.

The girl cried and I apologized to her. I took her down to the kitchen and washed her face and made her sweet tea, with extra sugar. I even gave her a biscuit. But she still eyed me as if she thought that at any moment I might eat her. Sitting across from her, looking at her, this frightened little girl, I longed for Emmelina. Yesterday, on the way to work, I cycled past her building. But the shutters were all closed. I suppose they really have gone to Monte Sole.

Poor Emmelina. And the poor Banducci. This

is a sign of how mad we are all becoming – like weasels packed in a cage. I know I'm being unfair. Everyone is tired, and cold, and frightened. This morning, the girl, who seems to have recovered, kept asking me about the hospital and what I do. I'm sure she meant nothing. She's only a child. But even so, on my way in to start my shift, I stopped three times. I looked in shop windows. I changed direction. I went into San Felice, sat, waited, and came out. I could feel my feet freezing. And my hands. But I saw no faces that looked familiar. No one I recognized at all.

I decided to stay at the hospital after that. I had a cot moved into my cupboard of an office, and told the Head Sister I was happy to sleep there in case I was needed. Which I am, because our staff are vanishing. Two nurses have disappeared in the last ten days. I don't know if they have been arrested, but it's certainly possible. We hear from Rome that the Jewish neighbourhood has been attacked and hundreds sent away on trains, and here everyone is being arrested – for nothing. Anything. Yesterday, I saw two people, a couple, dragged out of a cafe by the Banda Carita and thrown into a van. Everyone looks the other way. No one dares say anything. The arrested are taken to the house on the Via Bolognese that everyone calls the Villa Triste. Sometimes family members stand outside. They weep and cry until they are chased away. We know that people are tortured there. And we hear of worse . . .

Chapter Seven

Pallioti sighed. He had just finished relaying to Enzo, over an espresso and in some detail, the not-very-productive results of his visit to Rome the day before. They had agreed, of course, that the family would be looked into. Alibis would be given a hard knock to see if they cracked. But neither of them seriously believed that either Maria or Antonio Valacci had sneaked up to Florence and wielded the gun, or paid someone else to do it for them. It was possible, of course. Anything was possible. But without saying so, both of them had the nagging suspicion that, as a solution, it would be too easy. Out of character, so to speak. Because so far, nothing about Giovanni Trantemento's death was turning out to be easy.

Enzo glanced at him. They had eschewed the police building's shiny new cafeteria in favour of a dark hole of a bar a few blocks away – partly because it was more private, and partly because, like little boys, they enjoyed escaping because they could. Pallioti, who had been drumming his fingers on the edge of the table while he spoke, forced himself to stop.

Enzo's update had hardly been more encouraging than his own. The investigating team had more or less come to a dead end on the gay escort theory, pursuing it as far as it went and coming up with nothing even remotely promising. They were still digging into Giovanni Trantemento's business associates.

The English lord was apparently on holiday in Sri Lanka or India, or somewhere else where the British went to wear white linen. The embassy in London was tracking him down. In the meantime, along with the Valacci family, all the other beneficiaries of the will would be given a thorough going-over. But, barring any startling revelations, none of them seemed so eager for the money that they'd been reduced to either taking out a contract on the old man or buying a gun themselves. Never mind the salt. The truth was, seventy-two hours after Giovanni Trantemento had been murdered, they essentially had no leads. No clue as to who had killed him, or why.

Pallioti had had the pleasure of beginning the morning by informing the Mayor of this fact. After that, his mood had been further soured by a call from the press office, which had confirmed what Saffy had told him the night before. Goings-on in Rome were presently both slow and dull. The football clubs had not hired or fired anyone of note and the Prime Minister was out of the country. As a result, the papers had begun to run with the Trantemento story. In addition to speculation about neo-Nazis, one had carried an editorial on The State's Failure to Protect Citizens in Their Homes, and another on the dire consequences for Societies Whose Police Forces Failed to Care for the Elderly. As a result, a press conference was now inevitable. It was scheduled for this evening, in time to go live on the news. Pallioti was the designated sacrificial goat. It was one of the less welcome perks of the job. And just now, doubly odious, because he had absolutely nothing to say.

'Tell me again,' he said, 'about the Chess Club.'

Enzo shrugged.

Giovanni Trantemento had left the Alexandria Chess Club what was turning out to be an increasingly substantial sum. The club was apparently run by one Sergio Pavlakoff, the son of the Russian emigré who had started it just after the war, and admittedly it didn't sound like a likely front for money laundering, murder, or any other nefarious activities. But, let's face it, Pallioti thought, they were clutching at straws.

'It's off the Poggio Imperiale,' Enzo said. 'In the original villa. You know those places?'

Pallioti did. Most of the villas on the hill were enormous and had been built in the mid nineteenth century – not, in his opinion, a happy time for architecture. Those that remained in private hands had decayed quietly, tended by their increasingly desperate owners who increasingly resorted, with some inventiveness, to turning them into things like dentist's offices. And chess clubs.

'It's just been refurbished,' Enzo said. 'But I don't think there's likely to be anything there. Donations were given by the members, and Trantemento was generous. I saw a receipt. Signor Pavlakoff keeps immaculate books. Beyond that,' he added, 'he's either a very good liar or he genuinely had no idea that he'd come in for a windfall.'

'What about friends? Other connections there?'

Enzo smiled. 'I asked, and he looked at me as if I was mad. Or had just dropped my pants.'

Pallioti raised his eyebrows.

'I didn't understand, apparently,' Enzo said. 'The members don't go there to socialize. They go to play chess. Quite a lot of them are well known, tournament players. Trantemento went regularly, two evenings a week, Wednesdays and Fridays. He arrived at seven, usually played two games and was absolutely punctual. I gather all of them are. "Set your clocks by them," was the expression used.'

'And he'd been doing this for how long?'

'Forty-one years.'

'Good Lord.'

Enzo nodded.

'And after all that time' – Pallioti was finding this hard to believe – 'Signor – Pavlov, or whatever his name is—'

'Pavlakoff.'

'He had no opinion about Trantemento?'

'I didn't say that.' Enzo shook his head. 'He had no opinion about whether or not he'd made any friends – and yes, I have the membership lists and we're going through them. Signor Pavlakoff didn't have an opinion on his social skills one way or the other. He had quite definite opinions, however, when it came to Antenor's chess skills.'

Pallioti frowned. 'Antenor?' he asked, wondering if he had missed something crucial here. 'Who the hell's Antenor?'

'Antenor,' said Enzo, suppressing a smile, 'was Giovanni Trantemento's alias.'

'His alias?'

Enzo nodded. 'His tournament name. Apparently they all have names they play under. Or rather, should I say, they play under their 'true' names.'

Of course, Pallioti thought, attempting not to roll his eyes. What fun would a club be without secret names?

'Audacity,' Enzo said. 'Plato, Hadrian, Augustus. I think Socrates was mentioned. And Vulcan. Hammer of the Gods. Given that they're all male and the average age is about seventy-five, it's rather sweet, really.'

Philosophers, Emperors, Virtues and Gods. And why not, Pallioti thought. Perfectly ordinary old men sat down at a little table, moved pieces around a board, and for a few hours became daring, invincible, and wise.

'Unfortunately,' Enzo added, 'while Signor Pavlakoff was undoubtedly grateful for Giovanni Trantemento's cheque for lighting fixtures – and I suspect was genuinely upset to hear the old boy was dead – he was quite ruthless when it came to Antenor.'

Pallioti sat up. 'Ruthless, how?'

Enzo shook his head, as much to tell Pallioti not to get excited as anything else. 'Ruthless, in that he didn't think he played very well.'

'Even after forty-one years?'

Enzo laughed. 'I know,' he said. 'That was my reaction. But he set me straight. Chess isn't something you can learn.'

He raised his fingers in quotes. 'It is a gift.'

'And Antenor didn't have it?'

'Apparently not. He was proficient, and I believe the other word was "methodical". Possibly "conscientious". But inspiration was never mentioned.'

'Talk about damned by faint praise.'

'Yes,' Enzo said. He glanced at his watch, the look on his face suggesting that he ought to be getting back. 'That's what I thought, too. Don't worry,' he added, as they got to their feet. 'I don't think Signor Pavlakoff shares his thoughts with the regular clientele. I got the impression that if he did, he probably wouldn't have any members left.'

No, Pallioti thought, probably not. But people usually knew anyway. Or at least had the ghost of a suspicion. And often a good deal more than that. Self-delusion wasn't anywhere near as widespread as common wisdom liked to believe.

'Oh, by the way,' he asked quickly. 'Anything on the neo-Nazis?' He had called Enzo as soon as he had left Saffy's gallery, only to find that, unlike him, Enzo had read the newspapers.

'I spoke to the reporter.' Enzo shrugged into his leather jacket. 'He's thinking about it,' he said. 'He wants to talk to his source.'

'Do you think his "source" actually knows anything – or was this just the idea of the month for the editorial page?'

Pallioti tried to keep the cynicism out of his voice, and failed.

Enzo shrugged. 'I don't know,' he said. 'He's not a bad guy. He's helped me before.'

One of the legacies of Enzo's past work with the Angels, as the city's undercover division was informally known, was his extensive network of contacts across the city. Many of them *sub rosa*. Glancing at him, at today's rather ratty jacket and distinctly worn running shoes, Pallioti suspected that he might be on his way now to meet someone under a bridge, or in a corner of one of the less salubrious parks. It was one of their unspoken agreements that he never asked. And Enzo never told.

'I'm going to give him a couple more hours to think it over

before I start making his life really hellish.' The smile that flicked across Enzo's face was distinctly wolfish. 'If I get anything in time for tonight,' he added, 'I'll tell you.'

Pallioti nodded, wishing that made him feel better. 'Who was he anyway?' he asked suddenly as they started towards the door.

'Who was who? The reporter?'

'No. Antenor.'

'Oh. Him.' Enzo stood aside as a man reading a newspaper pushed through the glass-panelled door and wove through the tables to the bar without so much as looking up. 'I had to ask the same thing,' he said. 'Even Signor Pavlakoff admitted that he had to go look it up.'

'And?'

'And Antenor was an elder of Troy. An advisor to King Priam. He may also have founded Padua.'

'Padua?'

Enzo nodded. 'After the war, presumably,' he added as they stepped out onto the street. 'Which I gather wouldn't have happened, if Antenor had had his way.'

'Oh?'

The day was bright with a distinct chill under the sunshine.

Enzo pulled his ponytail out from the collar of his jacket. 'Antenor,' he said, 'apparently advised the Trojans to return Helen. He didn't think she was worth it. According to Signor Pavlakoff, he took one look at the armies outside the city, and told the Trojans to give her back post haste, or they'd be destroyed.'

⁂

27 November 1943

It was three days before I went home. The Banducci were still there, but much subdued. Even the children. Signor Banducci was, if anything, more nervous than before. They were still intent on going to Ravenna, but the trains are difficult. Driving is not possible, as very few people still have a car – at least one with wheels on it – and there is very little petrol. Beyond that, it is dangerous. Anything on the roads risks being strafed by the Allies on the off-chance that it might be German. Still, Mama knew someone who knew someone. She believed she had secured travel passes for them to go the next day, by train.

She told me all this as I was eating at the kitchen table. (I had quite deliberately managed to come home too late to share supper.) After I was finished, I went upstairs to change out of my uniform and found my bedroom door locked. When I went back down to ask Mama for the key, she dug it out of her pocket, and without saying anything, held her hand open to show me she had the keys to Issa's and Rico's rooms as well. The girl was watching this little pantomime, looking around the edge of the kitchen door. She backed away as I came through the dining room, moving into the corner by the sideboard, but not before I noticed that the clip she had in her hair was the one I left in my dressing table drawer.

I was too tired to care. I didn't look back as I heard her following me up the stairs. The hallway still smelled of gardenia. It was very cold. There is almost no fuel. I sensed the child standing behind me as I opened my door. When I went in, she moved closer, then stopped just outside and stood staring at me, my hair clip hanging in her limp curls, one of my old dresses too tight around her belly, the frill sticking out below her sweater. I stared back at her. Then I closed the door and locked it. I didn't hear her walk away. A moment later, when I took my uniform off and opened my wardrobe, I saw that all the tiny satin buttons had been pulled off the back of my wedding dress. They lay, scattered across the floor, white as teeth.

I stood there, staring at them, those little flecks, and suddenly – as one understands all at once when one is very tired – I understood. I had never thought about it much before, none of us had. But now I realize that it does not matter if the Banducci go to Mass. Or if Signor Banducci was a party member, or even if they were photographed with Mussolini. The Fascists may have cared a great deal about such things, but the Germans do not. The Banducci villa did not burn by accident. It burned because they are Jewish.

I was so ashamed at my own stupidity that at first I put Lodovico's picture into my night table drawer because I couldn't bear to have him look at me. Then I heard his voice whispering in the dark, telling me that he understood, that everyone makes mistakes – everyone is afraid and cold and stupid sometimes – and that he loves me and that I am precious. So I took it out again, and curled up, and clasped my pillow, and and closed my eyes. Tomorrow, I thought. Tomorrow I will give her all my hair clips. Tomorrow I will make this right.

But when I woke up in the morning, the Banducci were gone.

It was about a week after that, that I noticed the

holes in the side of the road along the Lungarno. They're mines. The Germans have mined the bridges. My friend, the nurse who lives near the Campo di Marte, sidled up to me later and whispered that she has heard that the gas and electricity plants and the telephone exchange have also been mined. If the Allies ever get this far, the Germans do not intend to let them have Florence. They mean to destroy the city. To retreat sowing salt in their wake.

In the meantime, a new law has been passed, declaring that all Jews are now enemy aliens. Their possessions may be confiscated and they are being deported. Trains with sealed carriages leave our stations at night, rattling north. My friend says bits of paper can be found by the tracks, with names written on them. They are pushed through the slats, so someone will know.

We have several Jewish patients. Yesterday, the Head Sister called all of the ward managers together and told us what we must do – we are to go through their belongings, take any identity papers we find, any photographs or letters, anything at all that could identify them, and bring them to her. She, personally, will take them down to the incinerator and burn them. There are reports that the Germans are searching convents. No one thinks hospitals will be spared. If they come here we are to say we know nothing and send them straight to her. She is not a large woman, but the look in her eyes as she said this was enough to make me step backwards.

To add to our woes, a few days ago Pontassieve was bombed. Another misguided effort to hit a train station, which, as usual, remains unscathed.

Not so a large number of houses in the town. We are all getting sick of making jokes about the Allies' need for glasses. Some of the survivors were brought here. One, a man who was badly wounded in the chest and stomach, took quite a long time to die. I sat with him into the evening, holding his hand, feeling it grow clammy and then warmer and then clammy again as the light dropped out of the sky. He died just before supper without saying a word. I took his clothes out of his locker – a worn jacket, a pair of shoes, woollen trousers that had been patched. It is my job now to go through pockets and to enter into my ledgers not only the details of blankets and linens, but the names of the dead. Then I must parcel the belongings up, tag them as if they were objects in a cheap sale, and be sure they are returned to the right people when the families come looking for them.

This is the part of it I hate the most, this picking over other people's lives. And yet, I know that if it was Lodovico – if he is dead somewhere – then I hope someone has wrapped his clothes, and written his name on them, and saved them for me.

I was thinking about this as I walked back to my cupboard, digging in my pocket for my key. But when I got there, I realized I didn't need it. The knob gave under my hand. The door was open. Even before I pushed it open, I felt myself stiffen in anger. Someone had broken in. Someone had stolen supplies. I heard a noise and, certain I would trap the thief, I shoved the door inward. Isabella was sitting on my cot.

We stared at each other for a moment, and then

I was so happy to see her that I actually started to laugh.

'I thought it was someone stealing supplies,' I said. 'I thought you were a thief.'

She smiled up at me.

'I am.'

There was barely room for the two of us in the tiny space. Issa had already lit my lamp. Tall shadows shot up the walls, snagging on the boxes of bandages and syringes, wiggling into the folds of the sheets.

'How did you get in?' I asked.

She shrugged, still smiling, pleased with herself. I suppose I should know that my flimsy lock would be no challenge to her. She nodded towards the bundle of clothes.

'What's that?'

'Nothing.' I shrugged. 'Clothes. Some poor man who was caught at Pontassieve.'

At that, Issa hopped off the cot and, before I could stop her, began going through them, shoving her hands into the pockets.

'What are you doing?'

I started to snatch the jacket away from her, but she stopped me. One shoulder was ripped and the front and a sleeve covered with dried blood, but his papers, somewhat miraculously, had survived. Issa slipped them out of a battered leather wallet and studied them under the lamp.

'Is he dead?'

'Yes,' I said. 'Of course. Give me those.'

'We can use them.'

'Issa, no!' I snatched the document from her. 'He has a family!' I said. 'What would you think? If they were Carlo's?'

She looked at me.

'That they were of more use to the living than the dead.'

My hands were trembling as I slipped the papers back into the wallet.

'Well, that's your decision,' I said. 'And Carlo's. But I can't help you. I have a job. And,' I added rather prissily, 'a duty.'

I thought she would argue with me, ask me if my duty was to the living or the dead, which would have put me in something of a quandary, but instead, she sat back down on the cot. Curling her legs underneath her like a cat, she watched as I dropped the wallet into my desk drawer, turned the key and then threaded it onto the ribbon that I wear around my neck. As I tucked it away, Issa patted the cot. I sank down beside her. I could smell the familiar warmth of her sweater and a faintly lavenderish scent of soap. For an hour, the war fell away as we sat there in my tiny cupboard office, talking of Rico, and our parents, and for a few moments of Carlo. And then, for some reason, of our old dog who died last year and is buried under my yellow rose bush.

Eventually our words dried up. The hospital was quiet at that time of night. Footsteps passed occasionally, a door creaked. Curled on the cot we were, I thought, like birds in a nest, huddled in our safe place. I felt my eyes begin to close. I think I was almost asleep when Issa said, 'Cati, there's something we have to do.'

Her voice wasn't very loud, not much more than a whisper, and in Issa's world there was always something we had to do. But this time something was different. Somehow, I knew that she was not talking about two more downed Allied airmen. My eyes opened reluctantly. When I turned to her, her face was serious.

'A family,' she said.

'A family?'

She nodded.

'How many?' I asked, because I did not want to ask the other question.

'Four.'

There was a pause, and then finally, I said it. 'Jews?'

Issa nodded. I felt a queasy shift in my stomach. Even since the Banducci had fled, things had changed. Convents were being searched. Hospitals were being searched. Perfectly ordinary people were hiding like rats and being hunted down like rats, simply because of the blood that ran in their veins. I knew it, of course. We all knew it. But now it was here, in our city, and Issa was going to ask me to reach out – to shove my hand, up to the elbow, into the cold filthy sewage the Germans, with their idiotic obsessions with 'purity', were determined to drown us all in.

'They've already come from Rome,' she said. 'They walked, Cati. We've been hiding them. But now, we have to get them out.' She looked at me for a moment. 'Do you know where those trains are going?' she asked.

I shook my head. I knew, and didn't know. I didn't know if I could know. But I understood that Issa wasn't going to give me any choice.

'To camps,' she said.

'Camps.' The word sounded so harmless on my

tongue. Like something healthy children did in the summer.

'Not labour camps, Cati,' Issa said. 'Not like our soldiers. The Jews go to death camps. In Germany. They're killing them. As many as they can. As fast as they can. Old men, women, children. They don't care.'

I shut my eyes and saw the red lipstick – the clown's smile on that child's face. When I opened them again, I felt as if the walls were constricting, pressing Issa and me closer and closer together.

'Are you going to take them over the mountains?'

She nodded.

'Will they survive?'

The POWs she had guided before had been soldiers, all of them young men. The mountains, in November, with the snow – I looked at her and saw the answer on her face. That they would have less chance of surviving if they stayed here.

'When?' I asked.

I could feel Issa's eyes on me like a touch.

'Tomorrow,' she said finally. 'Tomorrow night.'

Chapter Eight

'A Doctor Eleanor Sachs.' Guillermo slapped the message slips into Pallioti's outstretched hand as if they were tickets from a bet. 'Three times in the last hour and a half.'

It was past four o'clock on Sunday afternoon. The day had been warmer than usual. Outside, the city was meandering towards sunset, making its leisurely way towards a drink, an early supper. Pallioti's office had no such luxury. A lengthy and not entirely satisfactory meeting with the team prosecuting the fraud case had just wound down. He looked at the small pieces of paper his secretary had handed him and wondered what new set of problems they represented.

'Who is she?'

Guillermo shrugged and fussed with his computer.

'She refused to elaborate. She has the direct number,' he added. 'So I assumed you would know.'

Pallioti sighed. He started to point out that if he had known, he wouldn't have asked. Then he thought better of it. Working through the weekend put most people in a bad mood, and in addition, Dottoressa Sachs, whoever she was, had clearly rubbed Guillermo up the wrong way. Or, Pallioti thought, perhaps it was just the end of that kind of week.

Very few people had his direct office number. One of them, of course, was Saffy. He searched his memory to see if she had mentioned someone, some friend or business contact, she had given his number to. And came up blank. Doctor Eleanor Sachs meant nothing to him.

'Do you know where she was from, which organization?' he asked. 'Hospital?'

Even as he said it, a cold hand landed on him. He told himself it was stupid. If anything was wrong with Saffy or Tommaso, Leonardo would have called himself. On Pallioti's mobile. Besides, he'd seen Saffy less than forty-eight hours ago and she'd been in rude good health. Not that that meant anything. One phone call in Genoa had cured him of that idea forever.

'She would not say.'

Guillermo glanced up, his look suggesting this was somehow Pallioti's fault.

'Well, did she say anything at all?'

'Nothing. Not a word.' Guillermo shrugged. 'She insisted that she could only talk to you. I am minced beef.'

'She had my name?'

'Dottore.' Guillermo looked up at him. 'You are on television. And when you are not on television, the newspapers are complaining about you. Usually beside a picture, with a caption. The entire universe has your name.'

True enough. Pallioti nodded.

He looked again at the slips of paper. The number given was a mobile. The message said, *Call any time, 24 hours.* In his experience, people who asked you to call any time and refused to talk to secretaries or give any hint as to why they were calling were invariably journalists.

'Her accent was American,' Guillermo said, following his train of thought. 'Her Italian was fluent,' he added. 'But I'm sure of it. My cousin married an American.'

Pallioti grimaced. He had made the mistake, just once, shortly after he had arrived in Florence and solved a rather high-profile case, of giving an interview to the American press.

To a lady from the *New York Times*. She had had a braying voice, asked long and complicated questions, and worn very expensive shoes. The result had been horrifying. A picture of him had appeared in the Sunday magazine, under the caption, *In Europe's Most Beautiful City Is This Italy's Sexiest Cop?*

Just thinking about it made him shudder. He had not been able to go to the cafeteria for a month. The Mayor had whistled at him. He dropped the slips of paper into Guillermo's waste-paper basket and turned towards the outer door.

'Are you leaving for the day?'

Pallioti looked at his watch. It was nearly dark. He could sneak out the back service door into the alley.

'Yes,' he said, and turned up the collar of his coat. 'Go home, Guillermo. Have a drink and put your feet up.'

Guillermo raised his eyebrows and turned his computer off with a flourish that suggested he had something else entirely in mind.

30 November 1943

I should have known. I should have suspected, somehow, that something was wrong. Mainly, I suppose I should have understood that Issa had not changed. That she might be in love with Carlo, but that made her no less ruthless. She would do anything, including lie to me, in order to achieve what she had to.

But I didn't. I didn't understand any of that. In fact, the thought never occurred to me. So, when I made my by now almost habitual dawn journey to the records office the next morning, I did what I thought was necessary. I stole four sets of papers and filled them out. One for a man in his fifties, two for twelve-year-old boys – twins, apparently – and one for their mother, a woman of thirty-five. I decided that they too were burns victims, the by-product of more Allied bombing. Pontassieve. No, I would tell Dieter, we did not normally send civilians to Fiesole, but there was nothing more we could do for them at the hospital. I would say this with a sad and meaningful look, implying that the wounds of at least two of them, possibly the children, assured that they were unlikely to survive. This, I hoped, would invoke his pity, and cause him to close the ambulance doors quickly. I rehearsed the scene again and again in my head as I pushed my bike through the scrim of snow that was falling over the city. It was just after dark. Flakes dropped lazily, drifting like petals. In another lifetime, I might have tried to catch them on my tongue.

Issa had directed me to a convent in San Frediano. Il Corvo would meet me there with the ambulance. The order was closed. We would not see the sisters. Our 'parcels' would be waiting for us in an outbuilding. Since our first trip, I had used and reused the bandages I had stolen. I'd added a few more supplies, but thankfully had had to steal nothing more in the last couple of weeks. The contents of my rucksack could easily make invalids of four grown men, so I would have no problem disguising a family with two children.

It was just after five when I passed through the San Frediano Gate. The bells were ringing. The huge main gates of the convent looked as impregnable as any prison, but when I pushed them, I found they were open, as Issa had promised they would be.

I slipped through, leaned my bicycle against the wall, and pulled the gigantic wood panels closed behind me. Then I turned and saw the familiar shape of the ambulance and the tall, haunted figure of Il Corvo standing beside it. I raised my hand in greeting, but this time no smile, no matter how unfamiliar, cracked his face. Instead, as I came closer, his black eyes refused to meet mine. His hands were dug deep in his pockets. He seemed unaware of the dusting of snow that was settling on his shoulders, or the flakes that were dropping and melting, running down the high dome of his forehead.

'Il Corvo?' I spoke his name, wondering if he was ill.

Finally, he glanced at me. Then he nodded towards a door that opened onto the back courtyard we were standing in. From the bins stacked outside, I guessed it was some sort of storeroom. I looked at him, waiting for him to say something. When he didn't, I pushed the door open.

The bells had stopped, their echo hanging in the silence. Inside the room was so shadowed, lit only by one small lamp, that at first I could barely see at all. Then I picked them out. An older man, perhaps fifty or sixty, stood beside a woman who was clutching his hand. Two children, the boys, sat on the cold floor, their backs to the wall. Beside them, next to a stack of sacks they had obviously been sleeping on, was a young woman, probably younger than me. In her arms she held a little girl of no more than three or four years old.

I stared. Then I backed out, pulling the door closed. When I turned around, Il Corvo was behind me.

'There are six of them,' I hissed. 'Six! Three adults! Three children!'

He nodded.

'But there's only room for four.' I shook my head as if doing so could make two of these people vanish. 'We only have four stretchers!'

I was trying to keep my voice at a whisper – I didn't want to upset the poor family who I knew would be listening, who must have seen the look on my face.

'We can't take them,' I said. 'We can't—'

I looked at him. I could feel the air going out of me, tears welling up in my eyes.

'We must,' Il Corvo said, his eyes dark and fastened on mine. 'We must.'

We put the old man and his wife and the two boys in stretchers. The younger woman sat on the floor between them, holding the baby. She said she did not dare let her go, that it was the best way to stop her from making a noise. I bandaged her head, and the little girl's arm. I wrapped a blanket around them. I told them they would be safe. I knew that, looking into my eyes, the woman did not, for one moment, believe me. But she smiled anyway. She thanked me. The man tried to press money into my palm. I put it in the pocket of his jacket, and told him he would need it in Switzerland. Then I closed the ambulance doors.

There was no wind. The snow fell straight down, spiralling into the headlamps. Il Corvo did not look at me, but kept his eyes on the road, driving even more slowly than usual. I think he was trying to delay reaching the checkpoint, trying somehow to avoid what we both knew lay ahead of us. No matter that he had remembered my name, no matter that he had given me cigarettes and smiled at me – there had not been one trip we had made when Dieter, or the other soldier who was sometimes on duty, had not opened the ambulance doors and shone his torch inside. I could feel my heart beating. I could feel my hands growing colder and colder as they lay like dead things on the wallet and the four sets of papers in my lap.

The checkpoint was lit. The barrier was a black line in a circle of white. Beyond, the snow was a gauze curtain. As we slowed, I saw no one at all. An almost giddy sense came over me. They had forgotten about it. The checkpoint was not manned. The barrier would lift magically and we would simply drive under it without even stopping. Then I saw the tall figure step out of the dark, torch in his hand, swinging from side to side. Il Corvo looked at me. We had never spoken of it, but I knew that somewhere he still had the gun, and that if he had to, he would use it.

My hand shook as I opened the door. The cold hit me in the face like a slap. Snowflakes drifted and swirled. It was not until I began to walk towards the figure in his greatcoat and boots that I looked under the brim of the cap and saw that it was Dieter. I did not know whether to feel relieved, or even more frightened. Dieter knew me a little. Surely he would see something wrong in my face.

'Signorina Caterina.'

His face lit with genuine pleasure as he stepped

towards me. He took my bare hand in his gloved one and made a little bow over it.

'I was thinking you would not come again,' he said. 'I have not seen you in the last few weeks.'

'You weren't on duty.'

'That is true.' He smiled. 'But now I am, and we meet again. Ah! I have something for you.' He reached into the pocket of his greatcoat and pulled out a pack of cigarettes. 'Nicer ones,' he said, 'than before. I chose them for you, specially.'

I had been weaving a story in my head, grasping for something that might sound reasonable, or that he could at least pretend to believe – that this family had been bombed out and we did not have enough ambulances so were making people sit on the floor. That the little girl was not at the children's hospital because we did not want to separate her from her mother. That I had lost their papers because I was an idiot.

I looked at the wallet in my hand, and then at the cigarette packet. Dieter would not believe any of that. No one would. Il Corvo's gun flashed into my head as if I could see it. If the back doors of the ambulance were opened, he would have to use it. After that, we might survive. And we might not. All or any of us. I thought of Issa and Carlo, waiting. And of the young woman, probably no older than I was, who was sitting merely feet from me, holding her baby in her arms. Then I looked up, and smiled, and handed Dieter the wallet.

As he opened it, I dropped the cigarettes into the pocket of my uniform. I leaned towards him, shivering. He was in the process of slipping the papers out, getting ready to look at them, when

I said, 'Thank you for the cigarettes. It's so kind of you to think of me.'

Dieter smiled. He looked at me for a moment, then he said, 'It's not difficult for me to think of you, Signorina Caterina.'

His tongue lingered over my name. His eyes were blue. There was a faint flush in his cheeks. The collar of his greatcoat came up to his chin. Insignia I did not recognize shone silver on the heavy dark wool. I reached up, watching my own hand as if it was not mine, and touched them.

'I think of you, too,' I murmured. Then I moved my fingertips slowly to the warm, slightly bristled skin of his jaw.

For a moment, he froze. I could feel the thudding of my heart, and his breath on my face. Then he slipped the wallet into his pocket, and his gloved hand came up and covered mine.

'Schön,' he whispered. Beautiful. His lips were warm and hard. As his hand moved down to my waist, I glanced over my shoulder at the ambulance.

Dieter smiled. Then he stepped across the bright white circle and raised the barrier.

Il Corvo picked me up. I was walking on the side of the road like a tramp. I didn't want to get in, but it was too cold and too far to walk. Finally, I slid onto the seat and sat as far from him as I could. Neither of us spoke. Instead we watched the steady splat of the snowflakes as they fell on the windscreen, and were brushed aside, and fell again. Near San Frediano he stopped, pulling into a dark corner to let me out, so I could collect my bicycle and push it back through the snow as if nothing had happened. I had started to open the door when I felt his hand on my arm.

'Don't,' I said. 'Please.'

But he didn't take it away. The headlamps bounced off a wall ahead of us, making the shadows strange and long. Il Corvo's hand was pale and narrow. Elegant, like the hand of a pianist or a conductor. Before I could protest, he reached up and laid the cold tips of his fingers on my lips.

'Thank you,' he said.

I shook my head. I did not want him to ask me what I felt, or see me cry. I reached behind me for the door handle, but he stopped me.

'Caterina,' he said. 'My sister – my sister and my mother are Jews.'

Chapter Nine

The house was large, and lost in shadow. From where Pallioti stood across the street, it seemed swallowed by the tall drooping shapes of cedar trees. They whispered against the gabled roof, fingering the weathered tiles and the black lines of the gutters.

He had not meant to come here, at least not tonight. He had been on his way home and had stopped for a drink, had taken his glass to a side table and pulled out the little red book. Afterwards, he had sat for some time. Then he had taken out his mobile, and called the switchboard and cited his rank and made quite a fuss until he had got what he wanted.

There were no Cammaccios in the city database. But the Banduccis had been there. Only one family. Of course, they might not be the same – might be completely different, and the name a coincidence. But Pallioti doubted it. Their property was down the hill from the house he was looking at. The family had owned it since 1940. Whether or not they had got to Ravenna, they had survived, at least some of them, in their borrowed clothes, and returned. Found their way home after April 1945 to claim the ruins of what had been their home.

The villa that had been set alight and burned to the ground had not, perhaps understandably, been rebuilt. Instead, the Banducci family had taken advantage of the need for post-war housing. According to the police database, the building that now sat on their lot – a Le Corbusier-inspired remnant of its time, which to Pallioti's eye looked like nothing so much as a shoebox tipped on its side – housed three apartments. One up, one down, and a penthouse occupied by the Banducci. Probably, Pallioti thought, the son whom Caterina had not liked, and who now was likely to be a retired banker or a lawyer or small businessman with children of his own, who had children of their own, all of whom were waiting for him to die – if he had not already – so that they could move in and update the kitchen, and raise the rents on the flats below.

Up the hill from the apartment building was a small park, gated and locked. Then the darkened villa Pallioti had come to find – the home that, according to the address in Caterina's little red book, had once belonged to the Cammaccio family. It was owned now by the University of Wisconsin, and housed something called the Renaissance Foundation. He dug his hands into his pockets and stood in the empty street, thinking about ambulances. And a frightened young nurse with a red cross on her armband. And a tall thin young man called Il Corvo, whose sister and mother were Jews.

Had they been lovers? Had she given it to him as a gift? For safe keeping? Was that why he had her little red book? Why he had kept it all these years, locked away in his safe? In the last hour the weather had shifted. Rain had blown down from the mountains, not heavy, as it had been on the day Giovanni Trantemento had died, but a thin pinging drizzle. Pallioti wondered – if he was correct, and Giovanni Trantemento and Il Corvo were one and the same – would he still know this house? Had he, perhaps as an old man, come and stood here, in the very place Pallioti was now standing, and remembered?

The iron railings that ran between the road and the strip of front garden were backed by a diseased laurel hedge. Through the dead and leafless gaps, Pallioti could see the pale stuccoed facade. A front door with two steps and unlit lamps stood at the head of the short, curved drive. Shuttered windows lined up on either side of it. If he stepped downhill, he could just make out the stone balustrade of a terrace that appeared to run along the back of the house, looking out over the city. The upstairs windows were not shuttered. Their panes peered out from behind the cedar trees. The wind kicked and the boughs waved, making it look as if they were blinking.

The road was very quiet. Street lamps were lit. On a Sunday in neighbourhoods like this everyone who was coming home was home. Lights glowed from behind pulled shades in the Banducci's apartment building. Two Smart Cars, a Fiat and an Alpha were pulled neatly into designated parking spaces. Three bikes were padlocked into a rack. On the flat rooftop, the steel railing of a terrace was a silver criss-cross against the darkening sky.

The Banducci apartment building was not beautiful or romantic, but behind the plate-glass windows children squabbled, and went to school, and came back and ate dinner and watched television. Parents squabbled, and went to work, and came back and made dinner and had angry, or happy, or disinterested sex. Football was watched. Newspapers were read. Dogs were walked. Life, in short, went on. People lived there. Unlike the Cammaccio villa, where no one lived.

Pallioti stepped off the pavement, and crossed the empty street. He peered through the railings. The garden stretched steeply up the hill to the side of the house. What looked to be a garage huddled at the base of another huge drooping cedar. A street lamp shed enough light to see a new concrete apron that had been poured around it to provide parking spaces for several cars, and a patch of lawn, overgrown and tufted with winter. The cedar trees shivered. They scraped the stucco and flicked the empty glass.

The gate was closed, but there was no chain. No padlock. It was all he could do not to pull his hand out of his warm pocket and finger the cold, wet iron latch. See if it would lift, and if it did, push it aside and walk straight in as Caterina must have done herself a thousand times, exhausted after her stays at the hospital. Or cold and tired, but too frightened – or relieved – to sleep after the ambulance had driven down the hill from Fiesole and dropped her off, allowed her to slip back into the life of the city, hiding in her uniform. He wondered about her walk home that night, in the snow – the imprint of Il Corvo's cold fingers on her lips. His absolution, if that's what it was, for what she had done, what she had given, ringing in her ears.

A car went by, its headlamps bright as searchlights. For a moment, the gravel drive glittered in the rain. Pallioti looked up and wondered which window had been Caterina's. Then he remembered. Of course, it had been on the other side of the house. From her window, she had looked out across the garden and the city, and seen the mountains, and imagined her sister walking through them under the stars.

He would say he was from the police. Say he was conducting an investigation. His fingers crept out of his pocket, loosening themselves from the dense folds of cashmere. The rain was cold on the back of his hand, the iron latch colder, and flaked with rust. The gate was locked.

Pallioti turned and walked quickly away, his feet making a hollow sound on the pavement.

On Via Romano, shop windows were bright behind the criss-cross of their iron grilles. A few were even open. The supermarket. The wine co-op whose streetside blackboard announced that it was having a tasting. In the pharmacy a small Asian man sorted anxiously through a shelf of labelled boxes while a woman in a dark suit holding a dripping umbrella stood at the counter frowning. The man from the upholstery shop was locking his door. Zipping his jacket up, he dropped his keys in his pocket, turned down an alley and hurried away into the darkness. Pallioti walked on. Five minutes later, he realized he was standing in front of San Felice. The heavy door was ajar. Without thinking, he stepped inside.

The church was a cave lit by flickering candles. Pallioti closed the door and felt the cold drop over him like a cloak. Damp, and smelling faintly of incense, the air felt as if it had not been stirred for a hundred years. His eyes adjusted slowly. There were several people, nothing more than hunched shadows in the pews. Ahead, a dull light lit the altar. Beside him, next to the font, a bank of votives flickered and danced. The coin he dropped into the offering box was as loud as a gunshot. He waited a moment for the sound to settle and die, then, taking a taper, he set a tiny flame dancing in one of the red glass orbs, and looked up to see Giotto's crucifix hanging above him.

The gold leaf of the frame shone in the candles' twilight. It would have been vulgar but for the austere, sharp angles of its lines. The crucifix itself was a deep red-brown, the colour of wood, or blood. Christ's halo was bright against it, framing his bent head and copper hair, throwing its light on his narrow, naked shoulders and the stretched sinews of his arms. His mother wept at his right hand. One of the disciples, red-cloaked, covered his face in anguish at the left. In the *cimasa* above, a pelican fed her young. Pallioti had read somewhere that it was a symbol of Christ's sacrifice to the world.

He thought of Caterina, not daring to look behind her, pausing at shop windows, and finally coming here, feeling her hands and feet freeze as she sat on one of these damp pews.

Of course, the crucifix would not have been here then. Giotto's grey-skinned Christ would have been spirited away, hidden like all the city's other treasures. Pallioti could not imagine Florence without her Madonnas and saints. Without her cherubim. Her sprites and angels. She must have been as empty as a shell. Abandoned to the wanton malice of man.

In the second row, a figure moved. For a moment, he thought it was a woman. But it wasn't. An old man slid out of the pew. Gazing up, he genuflected before the great gold frame. The eyes of Giotto's Christ were closed. A lock of hair drifted on his shoulder. The old man turned, and walked slowly down the aisle. He nodded to Pallioti. As he opened the door, the noise of the city darted in. The blare of a horn, a cackle of voices. They fluttered around the crucifix, excited. Then faded, and drifted slowly to the cold stone floor.

Back outside, Pallioti felt suddenly tired. He would seek refuge at Lupo, get some dinner, and go home. The piazza in front of San Felice might once have been something greater, but now it was little more than a widening of the pavement. A spurt of traffic shot by, feeling close enough to touch. The drizzle had kept up. It would be faster to continue down Via Romano, but after the dark of the church, the lights were too garish, the noise too loud. He didn't have the energy to shoulder past people, or flatten himself against wet walls to avoid being pushed into the street. He turned down the narrow alley beside San Felice, glad to slip out of the modern world and back into the Middle Ages.

There was a wall on one side. A few lights spilled from small windows high up on the other, throwing oily shimmers onto the wet cobbles. Pallioti walked in the middle of the alley. Cars could not fit here – a horse could barely have fitted – and Vespas announced themselves well in advance. In the rain, even his own footsteps seemed muffled. He moved in silence, drifting, he thought, like a sleepwalker towards the Borgo Tegolaio. There, he was forced to stop for an electricity van. Then he crossed over, and entered the next alley.

At first, the sound was faint. Just a clack. Then it was a rattat, like a child dragging a stick along a wall. Pallioti stopped and looked back, but there was no one behind him. It must have come from above. Night in the city was deceptive. He walked on, and a moment later heard it again. This time, there was no question about it. It was the sharp click of heels – a woman's shoes on pavement.

The next street was crowded, but the one after that was empty again, lit by the windows of antiques dealers and upholsterers.

Halfway along it, Pallioti turned into the little alley that led to Lupo. He could see the tiny piazza ahead. The wash of the restaurant's lights reflected off the rain-darkened stones of the locked church that faced it. He picked up his pace. Suddenly hungry, he wondered what Bernardo would feed him tonight, and what wine he would recommend. The wind gusted, blowing across the rooftops and scuttling down the alley, slapping a fine spray of drizzle against the back of his head.

Pallioti stopped and spun around.

Behind him, darkness clung to high windowless walls. Confused, he stared into the shadows. The thin light at the mouth of the alley shimmered, and for a moment he thought he saw something, someone. He stood completely still. Unbidden, his fingers moved in his pocket. They touched the worn cover of the little red book. He was sure he saw a thickening of the dark in the alley. A shadow moving. Without meaning to, his lips whispered, began to form a name. Then, before he could make a sound, a wild beeping noise erupted.

A pair of dozing pigeons cackled and flapped skyward. As startled as they were, it took Pallioti a moment to realize that the racket was being made by his new mobile phone, and another to remember which pocket it was in and pull it out and flip the damn thing open. When he did, he heard Enzo Saenz's voice.

'Can you get back?'

'Now?' Pallioti glanced towards Lupo's lit windows. It was Sunday night, he had been working all day. He was starving. 'What is it?' he asked. 'Can you tell me?'

'Sure.' Enzo Saenz gave a bark that might have been laughter. The sound turned Pallioti away from the window. 'Some godforsaken village down south, near Brindisi,' Enzo was saying. Already Pallioti had begun to move. 'They've found a body.'

Pallioti felt his footsteps quicken.

'One Roberto Roblino,' Enzo went on. 'Eighty-four years old. He was shot once in the back of the head. His mouth was stuffed with salt.'

The Villa Triste

∽

I have packed my wedding dress away. When I slipped it off the hanger, it lay in my arms, heavy as a body.

I'd waited until Mama went out, then gone up to the attic and found an old trunk and dragged it down. So – the slippery satin, the lace from Venice, the tiny stitches, the frowns and tutting of the Signora and her girls – all of it is gone now. Lodovico's letters, too. And his photograph. I can't bear to have him look at me.

I wrapped it all in the tissue paper that came with my trousseau. Finally, I took one last piece and spread it as evenly as I could across the top. I pinched the edges, made them neat and sharp. After that, I smoothed it and smoothed it, ironing it with my palm until there was not a wrinkle, not even the hint of a crease. Then I fetched the tiny white satin buttons from my dresser drawer, and scattered them across the top like seeds.

Chapter Ten

'Tell me again what we know.'

As he spoke, Pallioti looked out of the plane's tiny window. A patchwork of dull green spread out below. Far away, the greying expanse of the Adriatic merged into a bank of cloud. It was just after dawn on Monday morning. They had left Florence in the dark. In a few minutes, they would land in Brindisi. He and Enzo were the only passengers on the flight.

'Roberto Roblino.'

Enzo didn't need to open his briefcase, or look at the sheets of notes and printouts that had been faxed the night before.

'Eighty-four years old. Has lived in the area something like fifty years. Something of a local character. He was found in his garden, on Sunday afternoon. Apparently by his housekeeper, who went by to see if he was all right when he didn't answer the phone. Autopsy is scheduled for later this morning, but the ME figured he'd been dead about twenty-four hours. Single shot to the back of the head, and his mouth was filled with salt.'

Enzo glanced at Pallioti. 'That's not the only similarity,' he said. 'Roberto Roblino was also in the partisans. Also decorated at the sixtieth. He, on the other hand, did like to talk about it. A lot. Something of the Local Partisan Hero.'

Pallioti nodded. 'What about your reporter?' he asked.

Enzo frowned. For a moment the question seemed disconnected. Then he said, 'Oh, yes. The neo-Nazis.'

The spectre of the disastrous press conference Pallioti had struggled through on Saturday night reared its head like an unwelcome third passenger.

'Did he have anything?'

'A couple of years ago,' Enzo said, 'there were some silly goings-on. Apparently someone working for an IT company that did some work for one of the Ministries turned out to be a little Hitler worshipper. Got into some databases and tried to mess up benefit payments, mainly to Jewish camp survivors, but I guess to a few of the partisans as well. They caught it and shut it down before any damage was done. But it was a good story, the highlight of our little reporter friend's career, I think. And you know how it is. If the spark lit a fire once, why not try it again?'

'But it didn't?' Pallioti, who had been concentrating on the window, turned to him.

'Didn't what?'

'Light a fire last time? I don't remember it.'

Enzo shook his head. 'No. It ended up getting pretty much buried. Apparently, before the story ran, the Ministry got hold of it. The company carried out an internal investigation and supposedly purged itself. There wasn't too much more to say.' He shrugged. 'Honestly, I think it was half rumour to start with. A sort of journalistic urban myth. Even our little newshound admitted, when I pressed him, that there wasn't too much concrete. Mind you,' he added, 'I suppose if there had been, neither the Ministry nor the company would exactly want to dwell on it. My bet is, the neo-Nazi line's the same this time. More inspiration than substance.'

Pallioti sighed. This didn't surprise him.

'So, what else do we actually know about this?' He nodded towards the window as if he was referring not just to the death of another old man, but to the whole of Puglia.

'Well, the guy in charge of the case is one Cesare D'Aletto,' Enzo said. 'I talked to him last night. He contacted us as soon as he ran it through the database and saw what we had. He figured there probably weren't two people running around doing this.'

Pallioti didn't even want to think about the ramifications of that. Instead, he asked, 'Is he cooperative?'

'D'Aletto? On a scale of one to ten?' Enzo said. 'Eleven. He only got moved down to Brindisi three months ago. My guess is, it was sort of a shake-up when he came in. He says he's got his plate full. Human trafficking. Drugs. Illegal immigrants. Illegal building. Illegal gangmasters. You name it. He's not looking for glory, he wants to clear cases.' Enzo shrugged. 'Otherwise, he would have taken his sweet ass time calling us. Or have forgotten to get around to it altogether. I think you'll find he's more than happy to take any help he can get.'

'And where did this paragon of virtue come from?'

'Turin.'

Pallioti knew his counterparts in Turin. They were highly thought of.

'And the bullet?'

Enzo nodded. 'The ME is sure it lodged. So they'll have it after the autopsy. D'Aletto thought you might want to have it compared by the same team that did ours.'

Pallioti raised his eyebrows.

'I told you,' Enzo said. 'He's cooperative.'

The plane banked. Rain splattered against the windows, smearing the outline of the coast, turning everything below them a dull, industrial grey. Wind buffeted the small jet as it began its descent. The engines shifted and purred. The landing gear made a grating sound and locked into place. Seconds later they landed with a whoosh, spray flying up from the soaking tarmac, blurring the dark car parked by the side of the runway and the figure standing beside it.

*

By the time they had taxied back, and the engines had been shut off and the door opened, Cesare D'Aletto was waiting for them at the bottom of the steps. The expression on his face – at once expectant and anxious – reminded Pallioti of the parents he encountered when he occasionally went to collect Tommaso from playschool. Young women in overcoats and fathers in suits who gathered at the gates, desperate to see their precious offspring and half afraid they would not come out of the door.

'Thank you,' he said, grasping first Pallioti's hand, then Enzo's. 'Thank you so much for coming all the way here. And so quickly.' He smiled as he ushered them towards the car.

Once they were safely ensconced in the back, Cesare D'Aletto turned and leaned over the front seat. 'It's been pouring,' he said, 'since Saturday night, when the weather broke. So it's not ideal. But I thought you'd want to see the site as soon as possible.'

He was younger than Pallioti had expected and seemed almost apologetic, as if he could somehow control the weather, or the state of the crime scene, or both. His blond hair flopped into one blue eye. He flicked it away. 'Unless,' he added, 'you'd prefer to stop? For something to eat, or coffee?'

'No,' Pallioti shook his head. 'Let's get on.'

'Good.' Cesare D'Aletto twisted back to the front and fastened his seat belt. 'In that case, it's about a forty-minute drive.'

Somewhere behind the bank of cloud that hung over the sea, the sun rose. Pallioti did not see it as they swung around the city, then joined a road so straight that it had to be Roman. The rain came down in sheets, blowing sideways, obscuring the countryside that, to Pallioti's eye, looked low and green and scrubby. Once or twice, he saw small houses standing far back from the side of the road. When they turned off the motorway, the pace slowed considerably. It slowed again as they wove through a small town, not much more than clusters of whitewashed stone clinging to the side of a hill. A church reared out of the piazza. A few sodden market stalls were set out around a fountain, their red awnings sagging and dripping.

'It's not all like this.' Cesare D'Aletto glanced back at them and smiled. 'Brindisi's actually quite nice,' he said. 'Some of it.'

Never having been there, Pallioti had no idea if that were true or if the young man was simply making the best of things. Coming here after Turin might technically have been a promotion, but it must also have been one hell of a culture shock. Not to mention a geography shock, if there was such a thing. The nearest snow-capped mountain peak was Etna. Even in the rain, he had felt the temperature a good deal warmer than the autumn dawn they had left behind in Florence. In the summer, this whole area was a frying pan. Akin to living in the desert. Pallioti knew the mezzogiorno had become fashionable with the English who had finally grown tired of Tuscany, and perhaps even with a few Italians, but he couldn't imagine actually living here. What would you do? And where would you do it?

'Was Roberto Roblino a native?' he asked.

Cesare D'Aletto twisted backwards over the seat again and shook his head.

'I don't know,' he said.

'I'm sorry?'

'According to the history we have on him, most of which is coming from his housekeeper at the moment, he came here about fifty years ago. From Spain.'

'He's Spanish?'

Pallioti had heard of plenty of Italians who had gone to fight in the Spanish Civil War, but he wasn't aware the favour had been returned.

'It says here' – Enzo was looking at the file he'd pulled out of his briefcase – 'that he's an Italian citizen.'

'Oh, yes,' D'Aletto said. 'He is. No question about that. We got his safe open yesterday, we've got his passport. But there's no birth certificate, not in the safe anyway. The housekeeper and her husband met him in Madrid, in the 1950s. He had some kind of import–export company. Roof tiles, building material, that kind of thing. When he moved back here, he brought them, the company and the couple, with him. And he fought with the partisans. So he's Italian all right. We just have no idea where he was born. It happened, apparently, during the war. A lot of records got destroyed.'

The driver braked abruptly for a pair of old ladies who stepped off the pavement and crept, tortoise-like, across the street, heads bowed in the rain.

'No family?'

D'Aletto shook his head.

'Housekeeper says not. There was a wife, or, more like, girl-friend, in Spain. She came back, stayed a few years and left. Other than that, nothing. Nothing in his will, either. It all goes to the housekeeper and her husband. Mainly the housekeeper.'

'The one who found him?'

Cesare nodded as the car began to wind downhill.

'Maria Grazia Franca. She and her family live here, in the village.' He waved at the houses that were rapidly receding behind them. 'She comes in five days a week. They naturalized as Italians aeons ago. Her husband takes care of the grounds. I've contacted the consulate in Madrid,' he added. 'But you know what that's like.'

Pallioti didn't, but he could guess. They had reached the bottom of the hill. The car accelerated, then slowed.

'We're here.'

Through the bleary glass Pallioti saw a television van and several other cars pulled up by the side of the road. Beyond them, a police car was pulled across the mouth of a track.

'Damn,' he muttered.

'We've kept them out.' D'Aletto glanced back. 'So far.'

He held his ID up to the window as they came level with the patrol car. Cesare D'Aletto spoke briefly to the driver before they turned onto what looked like a potholed gravel lane, a lesser version of the beloved Tuscan 'white roads'. There was no house in sight. The car veered and bumped.

'Luckily,' D'Aletto said, putting his ID away, 'this is long. About a quarter of a mile. So we've been able to hold them down here. But' – he shrugged – 'once they knew who it was, and that he was one of the partisans. Well – after your press conference the other night.'

Pallioti nodded. They could hardly have known that this would happen again – that in fact it had happened already as he stood at his podium in Florence long-windedly trying to say nothing at all. If they had, perhaps they would have thought twice.

'No one knows,' he asked, grabbing the door as the car lurched over a pothole, 'about the salt?'

Enzo looked up at the question. His team had essentially been told that they'd be hung, drawn and quartered if anyone so much as breathed the word. Cesare D'Aletto shook his head.

'No one,' he said. 'Well,' he added, 'the housekeeper saw. She turned the body over, it was face down. And even in the rain—But I've explained to her, and she's not a stupid woman. She won't talk to the press. My team?' he added. 'Well, there are only four of us. I don't have squads of people to put on this. And the forensic people, the ME. They won't say anything. They know it's more than their job's worth.'

Pallioti hoped so. This was bad enough – the murder of ageing heroes in broad daylight in the supposed safety of their homes, without the news getting out that it involved some macabre sort of ritual. The press would have a field day with that. Not to mention that it would probably inspire half the nut jobs running around the country. Italy was no more immune to 'serial killer mania' than anywhere else.

The car gave another lurch, did something that felt like skidding, and turned a corner. He wondered if perhaps they should have stopped for the coffee after all.

'This is it,' Cesare D'Aletto said as they turned onto a wide packed-earth parking area. 'Welcome to Masseria Santa Anna. Otherwise known as the *castello*.'

Looking through the window, Pallioti saw a large ochre-coloured cube with a crenellated crown running across the top. Two large windows stared out from either side of a broad front door that was approached by a semicircular set of white steps.

'Signor Roblino owned pretty much what you can see,' Cesare D'Aletto said, waving towards the low hills that fell away from the terraces and arrangements of shrubs. 'A couple of hundred acres. Olive groves, mainly, and scrub. He built the house himself.' He added as he got out and opened umbrellas, offering one first to Pallioti, then to Enzo, 'According to the locals, he designed it, too.'

Despite the unfortunate circumstances, Pallioti found himself thinking that it was a good thing for Italy that Roberto Roblino had been significantly more successful as a partisan fighter than he had been as an architect. The house looked like a startled red face with its hair standing on end.

He looked around. They were standing on the crown of a small hill. Apart from the village, huddled on a larger hill about half a mile behind them, and the ribbon of the road, the land was dusky green and rolling for as far as they could see. Crowns of olives ran down the slopes, criss-crossed by the white lines of stone walls. The wind that had been evident on the coast had not reached inland. The rain fell straight down in soft, oozing drops. The driver stayed in the car while Pallioti and Enzo followed Cesare D'Aletto past the inevitable loops of crime scene tape, up several sets of steps through a terraced garden, and finally into the house.

'The scene has been processed,' he said, as soon as they got inside.

Pallioti looked around. There were no members of the forensic crew, but plenty of evidence that they'd been there. Probably half through the night.

'Did they get much?' It was Enzo who asked the question, but even as he did, Pallioti had a feeling he knew what the answer would be.

'It's a little early to say definitely,' Cesare D'Aletto replied. 'But on first glance, no. Almost nothing at all.'

The inside of the *castello* was better than the outside. The walls were white-plastered stone. A tiled hallway bisected what was basically a large two-storeyed square. At the front, sitting rooms opened off either side of it, their grilled windows looking down on the bend of the drive and beyond to the town. A staircase ran up the wall of one sitting room, leading to a gallery that obviously gave on to bedrooms. Beyond the sitting rooms, a dining room opened off to the left and a large kitchen to the right. Pallioti stopped in the archway that led to the dining room. At least half of the table was covered in papers, books, and files.

'The housekeeper says he was collecting "his archive",' D'Aletto said, coming up behind him. 'Apparently, he'd been obsessed with it for the last year or so. Since he was decorated in Rome. He's already loaned the medal to a local museum. He became something of a local hero, after the sixtieth. Talked to school groups, that kind of thing. I've had a look at it,' D'Aletto added. 'But not in detail, yet. Most of it seems pretty general. You know, newspaper clippings. Excerpts from books. A teaching package he put together for schoolkids, about what life was like in the partisans. It was a nice hobby for him. She says kids liked him. I guess he told good stories.'

Cesare D'Aletto turned away. He pulled a set of keys out of his pocket.

'The back garden's out here,' he said, 'where she found him. We got it covered last night. But it's not pristine.'

Through the pebbled-glass panels of the door, Pallioti could see the top of the tent that had been erected over the old man's body and what looked to be a surrounding piece of lawn. Enzo was in the kitchen, standing at the sink.

'That's where she was when she saw him,' D'Aletto said, looking over his shoulder as he fitted the key into the lock. 'The housekeeper. Yesterday afternoon, looking out of the kitchen window. She rang on Saturday – I guess she does that regularly – to see what he wants to eat during the week. Didn't think too much of it when he didn't answer. By Sunday when she tried again after church and the same thing happened, she was a little worried. Finally, after lunch, around two o'clock, she came down here.'

'So he lived here alone?'

'Not at first. Apparently, years ago, she and her husband lived with him. There's a cottage out behind the house. They stayed there. But when they started having kids, she said he thought they were too noisy, so he bought them a house in the village. Turned the cottage into his office.'

'So why is his stuff in the dining room?'

Cesare D'Aletto, who had managed to get the door open, looked at Enzo and smiled.

'Well,' he said, 'it looks to me like part of the cottage roof fell in about twenty years ago and no one ever bothered to get it repaired. I'd say it's inhabited now mainly by pigeons and old lawn mowers. By all accounts,' he added, 'Roblino liked living alone. He was apparently healthy as a horse. And vigorous. Still rode his bicycle. Walked. Used the town swimming pool in the summer.'

'So he would have been able to put up a fight?'

'One assumes so. If he'd wanted to.'

'Were there any defensive wounds, at all?'

Cesare D'Aletto sighed. For the first time, tiredness showed on his face. In the watery light of the hallway Pallioti noticed the fine wrinkles around his eyes, the smudge on his collar. He had probably been up all night.

'On first look,' he said, 'the ME says no. Obviously, the autopsy may turn something up.' He checked his watch. 'It's scheduled about now,' he added. 'So perhaps they'll be able to tell us something when we get back to town. But nothing obvious, no.'

'Was anything stolen?' Pallioti asked, suddenly. 'Anything at all?'

'Not that we've been able to find. At least so far.'

Pallioti looked at him sharply.

'Nothing?' he asked. 'Not, for instance, his wallet?'

Cesare D'Aletto shook his head. 'His wallet was in his pocket, with seventy euros in it. There was no sign of forced entry, and the housekeeper's weekly money, which he apparently always got ready on the Saturday, for some reason, was on the kitchen table under the salt cellar.'

'And what about that, the salt?'

'I wondered, too – if it had been taken from the kitchen. But according to the housekeeper, nothing appeared to be disturbed. And she did most of the cooking at home and brought dishes in for him, so the only salt kept here was that right there, on the table. No more than a couple of spoonfuls. There's no indication that Roblino ever owned a gun, either,' he added.

'So—' The rain was patting the kitchen window, overflowing from the gutter and falling in a curtain of grey beads. 'What do you think happened here?' Enzo asked.

Cesare D'Aletto took a deep breath. 'I think someone walked in on Saturday afternoon and shot him.' He ran a hand over his eyes and shook his head. 'And I'm afraid,' he said, 'it was our fault.'

'Your fault?'

D'Aletto nodded. 'Yes,' he said. 'Yes. You see, last night, early this morning, whenever it was, I pulled up everything we had, have, on Roberto Roblino. Over a year ago, he received a threat.'

Enzo frowned.

'A letter,' D'Aletto said. 'He turned it over to the police. Made a complaint. As far as I can tell, they never did anything. I've had a copy made for you,' he added. 'Along with the rest of the file, what there is of it. It's back in my office.'

Cesare D'Aletto looked at the scrubbed kitchen table. At the four chairs pulled up around it. The blue bowl of pomegranates sitting on the counter. 'No one thought it was important,' he said softly. 'Now two old men are dead.'

The garden was walled. A rectangle of immaculately clipped grass was dotted with fruit trees. Espaliered apricots spread their arms along the red wall, meeting the broad leaves of vines. Lemons and oranges lined up in pots. A small fountain, tiled deep blue, sat in the centre of the lawn. Pallioti had never been to Granada or to the Alhambra, but he had seen pictures of it. Suddenly he understood why Roberto Roblino had come here, to the south. The relentless sun, the baked earth, even the white blocks of the villages. All of it was as much Spanish as Italian. Beside the tent was a pomegranate tree.

Cesare D'Aletto went down the steps. 'Careful,' he warned. 'They're slippery.' He stepped across the sodden and muddied grass and held back the flap of the tent. 'This is where they found him.'

In the queasy grey light, the taped outline of the body looked strangely solid. It was stretched away from them, one arm flung out towards the metal chairs that were grouped around a small table. The table's top was inlaid with red tiles that made an interlinking pattern of stars. White cushions, still sodden, were tied onto two of the chair seats. The third chair had several books piled on it. A rather rumpled panama hat lay on the grass beside it, not far from the outline of the old man's hand, as if he had been reaching for it. Pallioti bent down. The books were all to do with the war. Their pages were buckled and wet. The glassine covers suggested that they might have come from library sales, or simply been borrowed and never returned.

Pallioti stood up and turned around. A cool feeling spread through his body that had nothing to do with the rain. He looked back at the house. He could see the hall through the still-open garden doors, look straight down it to the front door. Given that someone was careful, or disciplined enough – someone who had been let in, who had been welcomed as a guest, invited, perhaps, to share the last whisper of summer under a pomegranate tree – if the door had been opened for them by their host, they could have come into the house and walked down the hall without touching a thing. They could have followed Roberto Roblino through the already-open back doors and straight out into the garden. Where they had put a gun to his head and ordered him to kneel. Invited him to eat salt. Then fired a single bullet, before turning and retracing their steps, letting themselves out of the front door with a gloved hand, leaving no trace at all. Arriving, killing, and departing as if they'd never been.

&

On this anniversary of Italy's Sorrow let it be known to All.
The flame of Truth and Justice is still alive.
It shines in all dark Corners.
All true Italians will know its Light.
Traiters may think they can hide, but they will not be
    protected from Justice by the false protecshon of their lies.
The cleansing light of purity and truth will seek them out.
The shadows will be vanqished. As long as there are brave
    men and warriers the Halls of Valhalla will never be empty.
Traiters will be clensed by the Sword of Purity and the True
    Glory of Italy will live Again.
You have been warned!

The original had been handwritten in red ballpoint pen. Even through the plastic shell of an evidence bag it had been obvious that the paper was cheap, a dirty pale blue of the sort sold by the pad in newsagents. It appeared to have been faintly lined, as if the writer would otherwise have trouble keeping the sentences straight on the page.

The plane was far short of a plush corporate jet, but it did

have a reasonably sized foldout table. With the tips of his fingers Pallioti held down the copy of the letter that Cesare
D'Aletto had provided for them and read the text again. Then
he lowered his glasses and looked out of the window. At this
height, the rain had vanished. The clouds they flew over were
tinged with late-afternoon sun. Across from him, Enzo was
leafing through the file D'Aletto had given them. It was
disturbingly thin. Apart from the usual tax, business incorpo-
ration, and car registration material, there was very little on
record concerning Roberto Roblino. In fact, if they hadn't
known better, it might have been possible to believe that he
had dropped into Italy in 1957, fully formed at age 35. Not
that it mattered much; if Cesare D'Aletto was right, the reason
he had been killed had nothing to do with anything as rational
as a thwarted lover or past business deal gone sour. Pallioti
looked again at the threat the old man had received over a year
ago.

The date, *28 April*, and a series of Roman numerals,
LXXXIII, were printed in the top right-hand corner. There was
no return address. At the bottom of the page, instead of a signature, there was some kind of stamp. It was dark and smudgy,
and looked like something Tommaso might have made for one
of his playschool craft projects. Pallioti guessed that it had been
carved out of a pencil rubber. He had several such masterpieces
carefully stuck to his refrigerator. He examined it more closely
and saw that it was a thick cross with upturned edges enclosed
in a circle.

'The Celtic cross,' Enzo said without looking up. 'It's used
by Italian and Spanish neo-Nazi groups.'

Pallioti raised his eyebrows.

'In an effort to prove their, quote, unquote, purity.' Enzo
put the tax papers he had been reading down on the table. 'It's
their answer to their Austrian and German counterparts, who
accuse them of having "tainted" Latino blood. They claim
they're actually Celts.'

Pallioti nodded, pretending he knew what Enzo was talking about while marvelling, yet again, at what a bizarre storehouse of information he was. But, he thought, undercover policemen were like that. They hoarded facts to trade among themselves, like kids with marbles.

'And the date?' he asked. 'Italy's sorrow?'

'28 April – the anniversary of Mussolini's death; 2005,' Enzo added, 'is 83 in Fascist. The purists date from 1922, the glorious dawn when Il Duce took power.'

'I see.'

'Yes.' Enzo looked at the letter for a moment then made a face. 'I was wrong,' he said. 'It appears it wasn't just smoke.'

'No.'

'I've already called ahead. We're starting with known right-wing extremist groups and working outwards. And we've got the reporter coming in again. And anyone else we can dig up who knows anything about this kind of stuff. We'll shake the tree and see what falls out.'

'Good.'

Pallioti put the letter down and cleared his throat. The plane might have a table, but it did not stretch to mini bottles of vodka, which at the moment was rather too bad. The fact that they might finally have a real lead was nothing but good news. But he had something else on his mind. Ever since this morning when he had seen Roberto Roblino's collection of partisan souvenirs carefully laid out on his dining-room table, he had been feeling particularly guilty.

'I have something to confess,' he said. He reached into his inner pocket, where he had taken to carrying Caterina's little red book, and placed it next to Enzo's file. 'I borrowed it,' Pallioti muttered. 'From Giovanni Trantemento's belongings. From the safe.'

Enzo nodded.

'Yes,' he said, pulling a paper out of the file, 'I know.'

'You know?' Pallioti looked at him, aggrieved. He had dutifully summoned the courage to confess, only to be short-changed. Enzo didn't seem to care about the humble pie he'd been preparing to eat. The apology for his presumption. The assurance that he had not been 'pulling rank', and that of course he had intended to report at once if it contained anything even remotely germane to the investigation. 'You know? How do you know?' He wondered if Enzo was just being clever.

Enzo smiled.

'I saw you take it.'

Pallioti sighed. That was the problem with working with ex-Angels. Very little got past them. They were professional watchers, all but state-sanctified peeping toms. Even with his ponytail, it was sometimes too easy to forget that Enzo had led some of the city's most delicate, and most successful, under-cover jobs. And all at Pallioti's behest. Which more or less added insult to injury.

Enzo put the paper down.

'It's a diary, isn't it?'

'Yes,' Pallioti said. 'One of Trantemento's souvenirs. From the war. Written by a woman he knew.'

'A girlfriend?'

'Possibly. I'm not sure. I haven't got there yet.'

'Is it important?'

Pallioti shrugged. 'I doubt it.'

Chapter Eleven

Christmas was so sad and strange, so empty, that I almost forgot about it. I spent most of the day at the hospital, where I am living almost all the time now, lying down to sleep when I can in my little coffin cupboard. With the door closed it does not matter if it is night or day, and sometimes I lose track. The worst thing is that when I dream, I no longer dream of Lodo. Just as I no longer hear his voice. Instead, as if I am damned to relive what I have done night after night, I dream of Dieter's lips. Of the cold of snow. The pant of breath. And his hands on my body. But in these dreams I do not see his face. Instead I see the face of that young woman, sitting on the floor of the ambulance, holding her little girl, smiling with terror in her eyes.

I have not seen Il Corvo, or had to face the checkpoint again, since that last night. It was, thank God, the last run in the ambulance. At least until the snow melts again in the spring. And who knows where we will all be then. Or if we will even be alive.

Issa is here, in the city. She does not stay at the house, but I know she goes there, to see Mama and Papa. I know not because she has told me, or because they say anything, but because after she has come and gone, our ration cards are missing. And, as often as not, some of my clothes. Even one of my spare uniforms. For whatever she is doing, I am sure it comes in handy. Carlo and Rico are somewhere in the city, too. But I have not seen them at all. I understand the need for this, but I would like to hear Rico's voice. I wouldn't even mind him ordering me about, if it made me feel that everything was not so broken. But I know it is not a good idea. There can be no 'casual visits'. Since 25 November, when the final 'amnesty' for Italian troops officially ran out, they are fugitives. From the Germans, from the Fascists, from everyone. They can be shot as deserters or partisans or 'enemy combatants'. It's quite a choice.

Issa says they move almost every night, and of course I have not asked her where. We live in closed little worlds now, each of us knowing only what we need to know. No one ever says it, but we all understand that this ignorance of each other is a perverse kind of gift – the only protection we have. That if we are arrested, we will be able to throw our hands in the air, and say, 'I don't know. I don't know. I don't know.' Deny each other three times before dawn.

It is in the interests of this that I do not even know Issa's name – the name the others call her in what I have come to think of as 'her other life'. They have come down from the mountains for the winter, all of them, to work with GAP. The

Gruppi di Azione Patriottica. Issa says that the way she says Carlo's name, as if it is another lover. GAP, she says, will 'bring the fight to the enemy'. She has not told me, and again, I have not asked her, exactly what she means by this – but I have a fair idea. The head of the Fascist party in Ferrara was assassinated last month. His body was left on a road outside the city.

I am sure that was a triumph. But if we have learned anything in the last few months, it is that everything has its price. Sugar. Tea. Bread, or a human life. Ferrara, it turns out, is a very expensive place. The next day, the Fascistoni chose eleven people at random, arrested them, marched them to the castle walls, and shot them. Their bodies lay uncovered until the Archbishop could no longer bear to look out of his window and finally demanded they be buried.

I dream of that, too – of bodies. They lie in the snow. They look up into the sun with wide dead eyes and clowns' smiles. Any one of us has already done enough to be among them.

But bullets are not all that kills. The influenza that has been expected has arrived, an unwelcome guest in time for Christmas. It does not seem to be as virulent as we had feared, but it finds plenty to attack, in the old, and the weak, and the hungry. And God knows, there are enough of those. At the hospital we have food, and at home Mama and Papa are saved by the black market. But others are not so fortunate. Ration cards do not go far, especially in this cold, and without fuel there are plenty who may die without any help from pneumonia or the flu. On Christmas Eve, they brought in a girl who reminded me so much of Issa that, for a terrible moment, I thought it was her. Then I looked into her face, and saw Issa but not Issa – Issa with the flame inside of her snuffed out.

The girl's name is Donata Leone. She does not appear to be that ill, but already death has lodged itself in her features. She comes from Genoa. Her family was bombed, all of them killed – she was only saved because she was not at home at the time. She fled to Florence because she was able to get a job here and because she thought it would be safe. And now she will die too, and she knows it. I sat with her on Christmas morning. I held her hand while we listened to the bells.

It was not long after that, that the Head Sister came and sought me out, and told me to go home. When I said I was happy to volunteer to stay, she looked at me long and hard. I have no idea what colour her hair is, whether it is light or dark or, for that matter, snow white. But her eyes are almost black, and as bright and hard as wet stones.

'Signorina Cammaccio,' she said. 'Go home to your parents. It is Christmas Day.'

And so I went.

Outside, I felt lost. I have grown used to the walls of the hospital. To my tiny cupboard and my cot. The city feels at once too much like a maze, and too large. I cannot see what is going to happen.

There has not been much snow just lately, but there is ice. I left my bicycle in the hospital shed and walked. It was near noon, and everyone was at home. I passed a few others, but the only people in the piazzas were German soldiers. Several of the cafes and restaurants were open, and they were coming and going in flocks. Pigeons and crows in their black and grey uniforms, the cackle of their laughter brittle against the cold.

And then I saw him, in a group of five or six others – Dieter.

He saw me at the same instant. He turned, as if a string between us had been jerked. His eyes widened. He was already smiling, laughing at some joke, but a different smile came over his face. His hand began to rise, his mouth opened, as if he were going to call out my name.

I ran.

I broke every one of Issa's rules. I bolted as fast as I could into an alley, my feet slipping. I looked back, and saw him staring after me. Then I scrabbled on the ice, grabbed the cold stone of a wall to right myself, and kept running, towards the river, sure I could hear him calling me, shouting my name in German through the city streets.

Issa appeared that night, after dark and out of nowhere. She had presents – a pipe she had got from somewhere for Papa, a small beaded purse for Mama, and a hair clip for me. I did not ask her where they had come from. For her, I had a brooch – a tiny enamel bumblebee that Papa gave me years ago. She had stolen it once, from my jewellery box, when we were much younger. When I gave it to her, she held it in her palm, then looked at me and asked, 'Are you sure?'

I nodded, and she closed her hand over it, smiling.

We played cards in the sitting room afterwards, pretending we were enjoying ourselves, until we turned the radio on, and heard that both

Pisa and Pistoia had been bombed. Finally, I came upstairs, leaving them below and saying I was tired.

I was sitting at my dressing table, brushing my hair, when the door opened and Issa slipped in. I hadn't heard her climbing the stairs or walking along the hall. She sat on the end of my bed. I watched her in the glass. She was wearing the bumblebee, pinned on her collar. We have never spoken about that night in Fiesole, she has never asked me why I was not in the ambulance when it pulled into the shed, and I do not know what Il Corvo told her, or what she thought.

As I sat there, watching her in my mirror, I opened my mouth. I could feel the words rising in my throat, feel them trying to push their way into the room. I was about to tell her – about Dieter, and what I had done, and how I thought I had seen him today and heard him calling me – when she got up from the bed and opened my wardrobe. She stood there for a moment, holding the door, looking at the space inside. Then she said, 'Where is your dress?'

I shrugged. 'I packed it away.'

She looked at me. Then she closed the wardrobe door.

Issa crossed the room.

'Budge up.'

She shoved me a little, and perched on the end of my dressing-table bench. For a moment, we looked at our faces together in the glass. Then Issa reached over and took the brush out of my hand, and began to brush my hair.

'It's much prettier than mine,' she said. 'Like black silk.'

This was nonsense. No one's hair is prettier than Issa's. I started to say so, but I couldn't. I watched in the mirror as tears began to slide down my face.

'Did you get them out?' I asked finally. 'The family? With the little boys and the girl with the baby?'

Issa nodded. She kept brushing, one stroke after another.

'All of them? Will they be all right?'

'Yes,' she said. Then she laid the hairbrush down and put her arms around my shoulders. 'He's alive,' she whispered. I could feel her lips moving against my ear. 'Cati, Lodovico's alive. I know he is. I can feel it.'

I reached up and covered her hand with my own. I squeezed it as hard as I could. Then I closed my eyes. Tears seeped under the lids, running down my cheeks, mingling with Issa's breath, that was as warm and steady as the slow beating of her heart.

New Year's Eve came and went without celebration. I tried my best not to notice it, and failed. A year ago, Lodovico asked me to marry him. He took me to the Excelsior. We danced. When he gave me my ring, he bent down on one knee and asked me if I would 'do him the honour' of being his wife. The people sitting at the next table and the table beyond clapped when I said 'yes'.

What would I say, if I saw him now?

I have no answer to that. So I spent the evening trying not to remember, and mending sheets – sitting in my little closet patching and darning, and listening to footsteps in the corridor outside

– and trying not to ask myself exactly how all of this could have happened. How our world could have been so completely tipped upside down. I go over and over in my head how everything was lost last summer – how we had our opportunity and didn't take it. How we did not leave and Italy did nothing to keep the Germans out. Just sat, like self-satisfied children, so pleased with ourselves that we had got rid of Fascism that we actually believed peace would follow.

I became so angry thinking about it that I repeatedly stabbed my thumb, and finally had to give up and go hunting for a thimble.

Donata Leone is a little better, and sews quite well. When I had finally found a thimble and started over, she sat with me beside the stove at the end of the ward, and we darned quietly, our needles flashing in and out like two old ladies sitting on our stoops. From time to time, she talked about her family in Genoa, all of whom are dead. Which makes my anger and self-pity seem small.

With that in mind, that we at least are still surviving – that we have a house and a family – I went home for the night of Epiphany. But, like everything else, that turned upside down too. Because Enrico was there, and instead of being overjoyed to see him, I had my first fight with him since we were children. I hadn't seen him for months – and what did I end up doing? Shrieking at him like a fishwife. I would have hit him, if Papa hadn't stopped me.

I do not really want to write it down, but I must. In the midst of my sewing fit, I opened a seam of my jacket and made a little secret pocket for this book – so no one will find it – and so I can keep it with me always, hidden and close to my skin, like a hair shirt. Writing in it has become a sort of penance. Words like the bite of a whip, falling until they bleed.

When we were children, the Night of The Three Kings was always the night when we gave presents, and received them – the night when we ran out into the garden and looked for the star, which never really was shining straight overhead. So I thought that was why Enrico had come, blessed us with a visitation, like one of the Magi. But it wasn't. I saw that as soon as I actually looked at their faces, Mama's, Papa's, and Rico's. All three of them were sitting at the kitchen table when I arrived. Issa wasn't there.

I hadn't even kissed him, said hello, or asked how he was. I still had my coat on. My hands stopped on the buttons.

'What?' I asked. 'What is it? What's happened?'

I could feel the floor shifting. I thought they were going to tell me that Issa was dead. Or that finally someone had had news and Lodovico was dead, or had been taken. But that wasn't it at all.

Finally, Papa stood up and pulled out a chair.

'Cati, sit down,' he said. Then he turned around and smiled, and clapped his hands. 'I have something still, I'm sure,' he said, 'in the cellar. Why don't we all have a drink? To celebrate?'

I started to ask, 'Celebrate what?' Then, instead, I looked at Rico.

At first, he would not look back at me. He was studying his hands – which are dirty and chapped now. Finally, when he did, when his eyes came up and met mine, I knew.

I stood up, almost knocking the chair over.

'Issa promised me.' I could hear my own voice rising, loud and shrill. 'She promised,' I said pointlessly, as if that meant anything. 'She swore! On the bridge, I made her swear that never again— Not here. Not in this house—'

I didn't know what it was. I didn't know if it was more POWs in the cellar or the attic – but I knew when Rico looked at me that that was why he had come. Nothing to do with the Magi. Nothing to do with gifts.

It was Mama who stood up and took my shoulders.

'Cati,' she said. 'Cati, please.'

The look in her eyes forced me back to my chair. I sat there, numb, while glasses were fetched and Papa opened a bottle and we all raised it and said 'Salute'. I even drank it, straight back in one gulp, although I don't remember what it was. Then they told me.

It isn't POWs or refugees. It's a radio. Not just any radio. A special American radio. The Americans are dropping them by parachute to the partisans. The transmissions from England are not reliable and they do not come fast enough to be of much help to the Allied command in the south. The armies are stuck now, still in the Liri valley at Cassino, but the spring is coming and they will break out, and then they will need information. On the Germans – anything we can find – troop numbers, mainly. And the location of ammunition dumps. Numbers of soldiers and tanks, how many there are, of what division, and in what direction they are moving. Most important, they need to know where the city is armed and mined. It is crucial for 'the liberation'.

I looked at Mama, but she would not meet my eyes. She bowed her head and played with the stem of her glass.

'Papa?' I asked.

My father's face looks so tired these days. Sometimes only his eyes seem as they used to, wide and blue behind his glasses.

'They need our help, Cati.' He reached out and covered my hand with his. 'We must be glad to give it.'

But I did not want to be glad. I thought of the trains, of hands waving through slats, of the people who have been dumped in the hospital's doorway after they have been visited by the Banda Carita.

Enrico turned to me. 'Cati,' he said, 'it's our duty.'

It was those words, it was when he said that – 'our duty', that I snapped.

I leapt out of my chair. I told him I did my duty every day – that down here in the city we ate, drank and slept 'our duty', and that he was selfish, and that while he was playing at soldiers in the mountains, we were stuck here – ducks in a shooting gallery – Mama and Papa and me. I asked him if he was stupid – if he understood? That it was us who would be arrested, us who would be dragged off to the Villa Triste. That when the Germans traced his radio, we would be the ones lying in a heap in the snow. I screamed at my brother that he was as bad as Mussolini, as Mario Carita, as the SS, or the Allied bombers – putting us in this much danger.

Papa had to grab me to stop me from hitting him.

But, of course, it made no difference.

That's what I had seen in Rico's face. And in Mama's. That's what I had felt in Papa's touch, heard in the clap of his hands.

Salute!

Before I even walked into the kitchen, the decision was made. When we raised our glasses, we were drinking to the newest member of our family. Her name is JULIET.

Chapter Twelve

By Tuesday evening, Pallioti had all but given up using the front doors of the police building. The press office had managed, in the forty-eight hours since Roberto Roblino's body had been found, to avoid confirming that his death was in any way linked to Giovanni Trantemento's. But Pallioti realized, along with everyone else – including, apparently most of the press – that they could not keep up the front indefinitely. Sooner or later, and probably sooner, someone would get hold of something concrete. Then he would have to give another press conference, and answer more questions, most of which would almost certainly contain the magic words 'serial' and 'killer'. Nothing, after all, sold newspapers better. He was just hoping he could delay the inevitable until Enzo came up with a reasonable line of enquiry – something that would make them sound as if they had some clue as to what on earth was going on. Or better yet, an arrest.

As he came out of the cafeteria service door, Pallioti spoke briefly to the guard on duty. Then he stood in the back alley, buttoning his coat. It had been a long day. He had spent most of it catching up with everything he had missed during the trip to Brindisi. The fraud case was as thorny as it had always been, but he was faintly optimistic that, as far as Roberto Roblino was concerned, they were in fact making progress.

Enzo's team was happily picking apart what little there was in the file from Brindisi. Pallioti himself had made several calls to Rome and thought that he might, finally, have found the right person to light a fire under whatever poor unfortunate it was who was responsible for the consular archives in Madrid. Enzo had met again with the reporter who had written the neo-Nazi piece. Cesare D'Aletto had dispatched the original letter to their own forensics people. It was true that a second search had revealed nothing similar in Giovanni Trantemento's papers, or tucked away inside one of his books, or anywhere else in his apartment. But that didn't mean he hadn't received a letter like Roblino's, which had, after all, been sent over a year ago. Hate mail was the sort of thing people threw out. Everyone who knew Trantemento – a relatively short list – was being questioned again to see if anything jogged their memory. In the meantime, partisan groups were being contacted to see if they knew of any other similar missives, and the letter had been circulated on the police databases. It had to be only a matter of time before they got a break. The spelling alone suggested Roblino's letter hadn't been written by a criminal mastermind. Which, oddly, was the one thing about it that bothered Pallioti. Enzo disagreed, pointing out that even morons could wear gloves and get lucky enough not to leave evidence behind. The gun had probably been kept as a souvenir.

Pallioti sniffed the air. It was warmer than it had been. A fog had rolled down from the mountains. Dusk was falling so fast he thought he could actually see it, dropping like a curtain of gauze across the roofs of the city.

He had been considering simply going to Lupo then crawling home to bed, when he remembered Saffy's show. He had indeed missed the opening, but a message on his phone had informed him that tonight she had a special late viewing. He glanced at his watch. If he was quick about it, he could still catch the florist and arrive with a conciliatory bouquet in hand.

Skirting the the piazza, staying well away from the police

building and the few lingering reporters, Pallioti stopped at the kiosk and bought a dozen irises. By now there was a proper fog. Puffs of it billowed between the buildings, making the cobbles glisten and the mouths of the alleys dark and empty. Sound came in ripples. The splishing of the fountain was counterpointed by a general tap of feet as figures drifted, or hurried, by.

As he paid the flower seller, Pallioti thought he heard someone say his name. A coin still in his hand, he looked around. But the only people close by were a pair of carabinieri walking slowly, heads bent, hands behind their backs like priests. Lost in conversation, they passed the kiosk without looking up. Pallioti shrugged, dropped the euros into the old man's hand, and started towards the alley that led to the river.

'Ispettore?'

The word seemed to come from nowhere. Pallioti was not even sure he had heard it. His step faltered. He paused by the loggia where a pair of damp backpackers hunched over guidebooks. They did not appear even to notice him.

'Ispettore Pallioti?'

This time it was louder. He whirled around, almost dropping the bouquet.

The hazy light made a silhouette of a woman's coat. Not more than a few yards in front of him, the shape seemed to be drifting, rising out of the darkness at the mouth of the alley.

Pallioti felt his breath catch. His heart thumped uncomfortably. From where he stood, he could not make out her face, but he could see that she had dark hair.

'Ispettore Pallioti?'

Her voice was strange. There was something not quite right about it, a faint flat echo thrown back from the stone walls.

'Please,' she said. 'Please. I need to speak with you.'

As she stepped towards him, Pallioti felt himself step backwards. Instinctively, his hand went to his pocket, as if the little red book could summon her up. Or make her go away.

'No!' she exclaimed, as he began to back towards the open space of the piazza. 'No, please, don't!' Her hand, small and white, almost childish, reached towards him.

'I've left messages.' She stepped closer, the words coming faster. 'At your office. I left my number with your secretary—'

Guillermo. There had been two more messages yesterday. What was it he had said? That the woman's Italian was good, but her accent was American?

The spell shattered like glass.

This was no ghost. No wandering shade who had slipped from the twentieth century into the twenty-first, her voice echoing down the decades out of a distant and war-torn past. If this voice was echoing from anywhere it was from the midwest of the United States. He knew those flat vowels. He had done an exchange year at the University of Chicago.

This had to be the insistent Doctor Eleanor Sachs.

Pallioti felt his shoulders drop. A small surge of something like relief turned quickly to irritation. He felt stupid, then angry – embarrassed at having behaved like an idiot, thinking he was seeing phantoms. Squaring his shoulders, he summoned up what remained of his dignity.

'Dottoressa,' he said, 'if you wish to speak with someone, you must follow correct procedure.' Sounding like a petty official, even to himself, he added, 'There is no point in continuing to harass my secretary. Please, contact the press office.' And turned on his heel.

'No!' she said. 'No! You don't understand.'

He spun around. 'Oh yes,' he said. 'But I do.' Pleased to have genuine cause to be annoyed, he added, 'Only too well. You are the one who does not understand. I do not give interviews. Now, if you will excuse me—'

'Wait! Wait! It's not that. Wait, I've been trying—' She grabbed his arm, her voice rising to a high, shrill note, her small white hand fastening like a claw on the black sleeve of his coat. 'Please!'

In the piazza, several people had stopped and were looking towards them. The flower seller was hurrying across the damp pavement, rising out of the fog, his bandy legs making him look like a giant wind-up toy.

'Dottore!' he called. 'Dottore, is everything all right?'

'It's about Giovanni Trantemento.' The woman's voice dropped to a low hiss.

'What?'

She was small, and dark, her glossy hair cut short, like a boy's.

'Just tell me,' she said quickly, the words not much more than a whisper. 'Please, just tell me. Was his mouth filled with salt?'

∽

'So, Dottoressa Sachs' – Pallioti's guess had been right, that was exactly who she was – 'what is it, exactly, that I can do for you?'

In the low light of the cafe he had hustled her into, and robbed of her ephemeral cloak of fog, Doctor Eleanor Sachs looked less ethereal than simply cold.

Watching her, it occurred to Pallioti that, having successfully cornered him and commanded his attention, Eleanor Sachs now found herself, as the Americans were fond of saying, 'in over her head'. Feeling no particular desire to rescue her, he leaned back in his chair, deciding to let her stew in her own discomfort. If he hadn't been so annoyed – he didn't like being stalked and ambushed any more than the next person – he might have been tempted to smile.

The table he had chosen was at the very back of the room, in a dark corner suited to trysts and arguments and people who did not want to be seen together. Having explained to the flower seller that everything was a mistake, brought on by the fog, that he was perfectly fine and had merely not recognized an old friend, he had hustled the woman who was now sitting opposite him out of the piazza as fast as he possibly could – not because he had any particular desire to have a drink with her, but because until a few minutes ago he had been under the happy illusion that the police had kept to themselves the more intimate facts of Giovanni Trantemento's death.

He cocked his head slightly, watching her. There were only a limited number of ways she could have discovered the information, and in the next half-hour he intended to find out which one she had used. If it was the most dramatic, that she'd murdered the old man herself – well, he wasn't worried about being overpowered and they were around the corner from the holding cells. If, on the other hand, it was the far more likely eventuality that someone on the inside of Enzo's or Cesare D'Aletto's investigation had told her – then he would, without delay, have their tongue cut out. He might even wield the knife himself.

He realized that the waiter was bearing down on them. Rapidly, he produced a twenty-euro note – he was in no mood to cede any high ground by letting her buy him a drink. After she'd told the boy what she would like, he muttered that he'd have a glass of red wine.

Eleanor Sachs glanced up. Something like a smile flitted across her face, as if she knew that what he really wanted was a double grappa.

'Thank you,' she said, 'that's very gracious. I thought you'd like to see these.'

She opened her wallet and slid two cards across the table. One was an American driver's licence from the state of Ohio. The other was some kind of security card issued by an Exeter University in England. Both had a picture that looked at least enough like the woman sitting opposite him. Both said she was thirty-five years old and that her name was Eleanor Angela Sachs. He nodded and slid them back to her.

'I repeat the question,' he said. 'What is it, exactly, Dottoressa Sachs, that I can do for you?'

*

The waiter returned. Eleanor Sachs poured some wine into her glass from the small carafe that had been placed in front of her. Her hand wasn't shaking, but it wasn't entirely steady, either.

'I think,' she said, 'that it's actually what I may be able to do for you.'

'And what would that be?' he asked, obligingly taking the bait.

'Well—' She paused and tucked the cards back into her wallet. Then she said, 'I can tell you about Roberto Roblino, for a start.'

Pallioti's hand paused for a fraction of a second too long as he reached for his glass. Score one for Doctor Sachs.

'I assume you know who he is?' Eleanor Sachs asked. 'Roberto Roblino?'

Pallioti sipped his wine. Eleanor Sachs was watching him. Her eyes were disconcertingly large, and ever so slightly tilted, like a cat's.

'I'm not a journalist,' she said suddenly. 'That's what's worrying you, isn't it? That's why you wouldn't return my calls.' She laughed, an odd little barking sound. 'I don't blame you,' she added. 'I read that piece in the *New York Times*. It was horrible. Honestly.' She drew her finger across her chest in an X. 'I wouldn't write that kind of crap. I'm a university professor, not a hack.'

'A university professor?'

Pallioti really didn't care what she did. All he really wanted to know, and preferably sooner rather than later, was how much she knew and who she'd got her information from. It seemed, however, that he was destined for at least an abbreviated tour of her biography, because Eleanor Sachs nodded enthusiastically, as if being a university professor somehow explained everything.

'At Exeter University,' she said. 'In England. My husband and I both teach there. He's English,' she added.

'That's very nice,' Pallioti said. 'But I'm afraid I still don't understand. Your interest in this case, in Giovanni Trante-mento, Dr Sachs, is, precisely, what?' Remembering some saying about flies and honey, he made an effort to smile. The result was not filled with warmth.

A wary look came over Eleanor Sachs's face.

'You see,' Pallioti continued, 'regardless of your profession, Signora – or do you prefer Dottoressa?'

'Signora is fine.'

'Well,' he said, 'regardless of your profession, Signora Sachs, you still have not told me what it is you think you know – I presume you think you know something – or how you came to think you know it, or why you are apparently so eager to talk to me that you have harassed my office and all but flung yourself under my car.'

She smiled. Pallioti was glad to see that it looked more like a nervous twitch.

'Well, you see, I'm writing a book.'

'A book?'

'Yes. As I said, I teach at Exeter University, in England, and I'm writing a book. I've written several others, but this is on the partisans.'

'On the partisans?'

'That's right,' she nodded. 'Social history.' Sensing safe ground, her voice gathered confidence. 'I collect oral histories, stories, really, that sort of thing. I have a PhD. About eighteen months ago, I interviewed Roberto Roblino.'

She was looking at him, he thought, as if she expected him to drop his jaw in amazement. Or leap out of his chair and applaud. Because she had a PhD. Because she had written books. Because she conducted interviews. It was all very familiar, and suddenly very irritating.

He nodded and gestured for her to continue, preferably rapidly.

She looked at him, a flash of irritation rippling across her features, took a sip of her wine and said, 'I wanted to talk to him again. To Roberto Roblino. I'm taking this semester off,' she added. 'To work on this. Finish my research. I got here about a week ago. I'd been trying to call him. Then I found out he was dead.'

She looked at Pallioti as if this somehow explained what she wanted to tell him. He gestured again.

'Go on.'

'Well, I was planning, on this trip, to talk to Giovanni Trantemento, too.' Eleanor Sachs looked at him. When he said nothing she frowned, pinching her small heart-shaped face. 'Actually, I'd been trying to talk to him for some time. But he said he didn't give interviews. So I thought I'd just go see him, arrive in person. It's harder for people to kick you off the doorstep. But when I got here, and went to his building, I found out he'd been killed. The concierge – the old lady who looks like a prison warden – she wouldn't tell me a thing. So I called Roberto Roblino. I wanted to say I was sorry. I wanted to—'

She shook her head as if the rest of what she had to say was self-evident. She picked up her wine glass, and took another sip.

'Well, you can imagine,' she said. 'What I thought – when I found out he'd been shot, in his home. Just like Signor Trantemento. Then I saw your press conference and . . . To be honest' – she had the good grace to sound slightly sheepish – 'the salt was a guess. But at least it got your attention. Not about Roblino,' Eleanor Sachs added quickly. 'I know he had salt in his mouth. His housekeeper told me. She said she ran out and turned him over and – it must have been horrible. But Giovanni Trantemento did too, didn't he?'

As she spoke, Pallioti felt a flood of relief and did not let it show. He was beginning to understand now. Not a member of Enzo's or D'Aletto's team after all. The housekeeper. Who Cesare D'Aletto had assured them wouldn't utter a squeak, but never mind. He ignored Eleanor Sachs's question about Trantemento, and asked his own.

'His housekeeper? Roberto Roblino's? She told you?'

Eleanor Sachs nodded. 'Maria Grazia,' she said. 'Signora Franca. She's the one who told me. She takes care of him, she and her husband. She's such an angel. And she was so upset, poor thing.'

'And you spoke to her, when?'

Pallioti's press conference had been on Saturday night. Roberto Roblino's death had not been reported until Sunday afternoon, and he and Enzo had not heard about it for several hours after that. Yet Eleanor Sachs had called his office for the first time late Sunday afternoon. She appeared to be claiming that she had known about it before they did.

She nodded and put her glass down. 'Sunday,' she said. 'Sunday afternoon. I called the house, Roblino's house, and Maria Grazia answered. She'd just found him. She was all upset, waiting for the ambulance. When she picked up the phone, she thought I was the police, calling for directions or something. The poor thing,' she said again. 'It was awful. I stayed on the phone with her until they came. Then,' Eleanor Sachs added, 'well, right afterwards, I remembered I'd seen you on TV the night before, so I called.'

Pallioti looked at her for a moment. Despite his relief about his own people, he could swear she was lying. He wasn't sure about what. The housekeeper story made sense, just. So, if it wasn't that, what was it?

'So,' he said finally, 'just to be certain that I have this straight. What you wanted to tell me was that, due to your work on a book about the partisans, you had interviewed Roberto Roblino. You had not, however, interviewed Giovanni Trantemento?'

'No.'

'Did you ever meet him? Speak to him?'

'No. He didn't answer my letters and when I rang him, he hung up on me.'

Pallioti nodded.

'So, you interviewed one old man, and never interviewed, met, or even spoke to the other, and now both of them are dead?'

Eleanot Sachs nodded, her eyes wide and eager.

Pallioti looked at her for a long moment, then he said, 'If you'll forgive me for saying so, Dottoressa Sachs, it doesn't seem very extraordinary.'

'Well, not when you put it that way, I suppose, but—'

'Hardly worth numerous phone calls and trailing me through the streets.'

'Trailing you through the streets? I—'

'And,' Pallioti pressed, 'I infer, although you have not actually said so, and please correct me if I'm wrong, that you are suggesting that the same person killed them, these two old men – one of whom you interviewed and one of whom you didn't – and that, inadvertently or otherwise, you know something about it?'

She nodded. 'Well, yes,' she said. 'I suppose I am. Yes.'

'And do you have any evidence for this, or is it merely an idea because you happen to have met, or actually not met, them both?'

He knew he was being offensive now, but he couldn't help it. He couldn't say he'd warmed to Eleanor Sachs, but for a moment there he had thought he detected something, like a shadow moving underwater, or a faint scent on the wind. He had thought, just briefly, that perhaps she had something to say. But she was going to turn out to be just another enthusiast. A self-important, self-dramatizing foreigner. One more of the strange and dreary breed who for some reason believed that inserting themselves into police investigations was either their duty or a rather jolly pastime – culturally enlightening, and good fodder for dinner parties. There had been any number of such idiots during the Monster investigations. Several, if he remembered correctly, had ended up in jail. As far as he was concerned, if it wasn't so expensive to keep them, they could have stayed there. Served life. For wasting police time.

'Look,' she was saying, 'I know this sounds sort of crazy. But have you ever heard of *Il Spettro*?'

'The Ghost?' Pallioti glanced at his watch and shook his head. It was hot in the back of the cafe. Saffy's flowers would be wilting. He needed to get to the gallery. 'No,' he said. 'I have never heard of the Ghost.'

'Well, there are all sorts of stories about him. From during the war. And I—'

As she spoke, Eleanor Sachs's face changed. A flush of pink crept into her cheeks. She ran a hand through her hair.

'He ran an escape line,' she was saying. 'For Allied POWs and Jews, mostly. It drove the Germans crazy – well, all the partisans drove them crazy – but they could never catch him. Some people don't even think he existed. They think the Nazis made this person up because they were so frustrated. And of course, the Italians loved it too. There are all sorts of stories. If you believed them you'd have to believe this guy was invisible and had wings. And as I said' – she finally took a breath – 'no one's ever been able to prove he actually existed.'

Pallioti glanced up. 'But you think he did?'

She nodded. 'Roberto Roblino did too.'

'Robert Roblino?'

Despite himself, Pallioti felt a twitch of interest.

Eleanor Sachs nodded. 'That's why he sent me to speak to Giovanni Trantemento.'

Pallioti frowned. That was it. She had said something about calling Roblino to 'say she was sorry'. He had heard 'an apology'. She had meant 'condolences'.

He picked up his glass. 'Go on.'

'There's nowhere to go.' She shrugged. 'Actually, Roberto Roblino wasn't very helpful. I mean, in general. He wouldn't even tell me what his name had been. You know, in GAP – sorry, the *Gruppi*—'

'*Di Azione Patriottica*. Yes, I know.'

'Oh.' She raised her eyebrows. 'Well, they all had names. The Wolf. The Lion. That kind of stuff. It was supposed to hide their real identities. I don't know how much it did. Anyway, Roblino didn't really have too much to say, nothing specific anyway that was very interesting about that. I almost would have doubted he'd ever done anything, except for the medal.' She shrugged. 'Anyway, I finally asked him about Il Spettro. If he'd heard of him? If he thought he was real? And he told me to go talk to his old friend, Giovanni.'

'His old friend, Giovanni?'

'That's right,' Eleanor Sachs nodded. 'Roberto Roblino said, if I wanted to know about ghosts, I should ask Giovanni. Then he gave me Signor Trantemento's name and address.'

She looked at Pallioti and shook her head.

'But I never had the chance,' she said. 'I had to go back to England. I wrote, he didn't reply. I telephoned, he hung up. When I got back here, he was dead. Then Roblino was dead. The same way.'

'And on the telephone, he said what?'

'Signor Trantemento? About Il Spettro?' She shook her head. 'Not much. Nothing. The first time I called, I managed to get it out – what I wanted to ask about, and that Signor Roblino had told me to call. I thought he'd, you know, talk to me, because they were friends.'

'Are you sure they were friends?'

It wasn't, Pallioti supposed, that unlikely. Old partisans staying in touch with one another. But it was the first he had heard of it. As far as he knew neither Cesare D'Aletto nor Enzo had found any suggestion in Giovanni Trantemento's papers, or Roberto Roblino's, that the two men knew each other.

Eleanor Sachs shrugged. 'Well, acquaintances,' she said. 'Whatever. Like I said, Roblino gave me Giovanni Trantemento's address.'

Pallioti thought about this for a moment. Then he asked, 'But Giovanni Trantemento didn't talk to you?'

'No. I said my bit, and there was silence. Just a long silence. A minute maybe. Then he put the phone down. Quietly. As if he'd just pressed the button on the receiver. I called back, right away. Because I thought there had been, well, a fault on the line, or something.'

'And what happened?' Pallioti asked.

'He told me to leave him alone. Then he hung up.'

Pallioti nodded. It was not that surprising. By all accounts Giovanni Trantemento was a very private man who didn't like talking about the war. Between the letters and the phone calls, she'd probably been driving him crazy.

He drank the last of his wine. Over-oaked and faintly sweet-smelling, it left a furry feeling on the back of his tongue. Eleanor Sachs was watching him. He wondered how long it would take her to say whatever it was, to present the final trump card he could sense her holding back. He put the glass down.

'There is something else,' she said, finally. 'But I don't understand it. I mean, how it fits. What it means.'

Pallioti resisted the urge to smile. Policemen like being right just as much as anyone else.

'And what might that be?' he asked.

Eleanor Sachs regarded her hands for a moment. The blunt rounded nails were painted exactly the same colour as her lips, a paleish sort of pink. She folded and unfolded her fingers, flexing them as if they were stiff from cold.

'The salt,' she said finally. She looked up at him.

'The salt?'

'Yes.' Eleanor Sachs nodded.

'I thought you just told me the housekeeper told you, in Roblino's case, and Trantemento was a guess.'

Was that what she had been lying about?

'Yes,' Eleanor Sachs said. 'That's right. But that's not it.'

'No?' Pallioti wondered what on earth she was talking about now.

229

'No,' she said, sliding her glass aside and leaning forward. 'Look,' she went on, 'I don't know if this means anything, or if you already know. If you do, I'm sorry. But by the winter of '43 to '44, the Germans were getting really frustrated. It was the start of what some people call the Terror. The partisans were causing serious problems – and threats, civilian reprisals, none of it, was doing much to slow them down. So the Nazis did what they'd done with the Jews. They put a price on their heads.'

'On the partisans' heads?' Pallioti felt his hand move towards his pocket, towards the soft shape of the little book he had taken to carrying there.

Eleanor Sachs nodded. 'That's right,' she said. 'Food was really scarce by then. Sugar and salt were almost impossible to get. So, that was it.'

'What was what?'

'The price.' She picked up her glass and drained the rest of her wine. 'That's what you got,' she said. 'For betraying a partisan.' She put the glass down and stared at him. 'You ratted one out, and the Germans gave you five pounds of salt.'

Chapter Thirteen

30 January 1944

Donata Leone died. Three weeks ago. She went downhill quite suddenly. Sometimes it happens that way. I've seen it before. And yet, I admit, I had allowed myself to think that she was getting better, that somehow she would survive. She had become my friend, and I miss her.

On her last night, I sat with her, holding her hand for a very long time. I was looking out of the window, telling myself it was almost dawn and watching for the grey haze that seeps through the sky. The truth is, I wasn't thinking about her at the time, even though her fingers were clasped in mine. I was thinking about last year, when we were still officially 'in the war' and everything was still halfway normal. And then I was thinking about our childhood, and the skiing holidays, and how I had never really enjoyed skiing itself, but how I did enjoy the chalets, and the hotel, and sitting in front of the fire all together at night with the snow falling outside. All the times when winter was something to look forward to. That's what I was thinking of, when something made me look down, and I realized she was dead.

She looked so much like Issa – like a thinner, paler version of her – that for a moment I thought, 'This is what it will be like when Issa dies, when they finally catch her and shoot her, or when she slips in the mountains and falls. She will look like this.' I reached down and smoothed Donata's hair off her forehead. Then I did something I have never done before. I opened her bedside locker, and took out her handbag, and found the little comb I'd seen her use, and combed her hair. She was proud of her hair. At the end of her life she had nothing left. I wanted, once more, for her to look beautiful.

After that, I stood up. The ward was quiet – sounds of breathing, sleeping, the occasional juddered moan of a dream, a footstep in the hall outside. No one was watching me. No one saw. I looked down at Donata, then I lifted the sheet gently over her face, and turned away, and walked through the doors and down the hall and into my cupboard, still carrying her handbag.

The honest truth is, I don't know if I meant to steal it. I don't know what I meant to do. Perhaps I was going to list her belongings in my ledger. But then it occurred to me that it was pointless, because she had no family. All of them had been killed in the bombings in Genoa. I knew their ages, their names, what they did. And I knew that all of them were dead. So I kept it. I told myself she would have given it to me, as a gift. I put her handbag under the pillow on my cot.

That night, when I went home, Issa was there. She and Papa were full of the news – eighteen of the nineteen members of the Great Council who voted last summer to get rid of Mussolini had been shot after some kind of so-called trial in Verona. More men hailed for their bravery, all now dead. Our new dawn did not last long.

Mama said nothing, and I did not want to talk about it, either, so it was not until after we had eaten that Issa pulled me aside and told me the radio had arrived. She took me up to her room and showed it to me.

Looking at it, I didn't know what to say. Finally, I murmured, 'I don't know how you can sleep with that under your bed. It's like sleeping on a bomb.'

And to my surprise, Issa nodded.

'I don't like having it here.' She laughed, but I could see she didn't think it was funny. Then she said, 'You were right. I don't care what they say about wanting to help, it's too dangerous for Mama and Papa. But I don't know where else to go.' She sighed. 'At least I know I can trust them.'

I looked at her closely. There were circles under her eyes, and her cheeks were hollower than they had been the last time I saw her. Perhaps it was because of Donata, but I felt a pang of fear. A white bright flash of it, like lightning. I didn't realize until that moment how I have always depended on Issa to be stronger than me. Stronger than all of us.

'You look tired.' I sat down beside her.

'There's been arguing.' She smiled, but again I could tell she didn't think it was funny. 'The men argue. They're like rats, cooped up in the city. I want to go back to the mountains. But there's no point until the snow clears, and this—' She leaned down and patted the box. 'This is more important. Something's going to happen.' She looked at me. 'I don't know what. But the Americans, they've made us understand. It's coming soon.'

She was right. It was in the air. Everyone could sense it. The bombing had become more intense. Livorno had been all but destroyed, and train lines were being hit everywhere. This time the Allies seemed to be aiming a little better, because supply lines were seriously damaged. It was one of the reasons food was so expensive.

But I was not thinking about that. I was worried about what she had said, who it was she couldn't trust. I wanted to ask her about the arguing, but before I had a chance she said, 'You have to start remembering, Cati.' She squeezed my hand. 'You have to start remembering everything you see. And counting. Count everything and remember it.'

Like the drops, I thought. The sticky drops of time I'd counted on that last day when I'd had my wedding dress fitted. Then I'd resisted, and failed, because at the hospital it was something the hysterics did – walked up and down and wrung their hands and counted – steps, nurses, beds, windows. That way madness lies. Now I was being ordered to make a wilful effort to be like them – to unhinge my mind for the sake of the Allies. Enrico, doubtless, would say it was my duty.

I almost laughed, and would have shared the joke with Issa, but she stood up, stretched, and ran her hands through her hair.

'Papa's going to help me,' she said. 'We'll find

somewhere to take JULIET. Somewhere—' She smiled and shook her head. I knew she was going to say the word 'safe', and that the other joke was that there is nowhere safe. So instead she just said, 'Somewhere away from here.'

And that was when I opened my mouth and the words came out.

'I can help.'

Issa stopped and looked at me.

'I can help,' I said again.

And so it began.

For once, Issa did as I told her and came to the hospital the next afternoon. I found her sitting on my cot when I finished my rounds after teatime.

'Budge up,' I said quickly, and before I could think about what I was doing, I pushed her aside and reached under the pillow and pulled out Donata Leone's handbag.

I knew Donata's address, and that her apartment was in an attic, because while we had sat sewing, she had told me all about it. Told me about her room, and the books that were in it, and the few things she had been able to salvage from the ruins of the house in Genoa. She'd recreated it in words, I think, the sanctuary she had made for herself, because she was afraid she was never going to see it again.

Now I was giving it to Issa. I handed her the keys.

'No one knows she's dead,' I said. 'There's no one to tell. I didn't enter her in the ledger. She had no family. The room will be empty.' Then, as an afterthought, I pulled out Donata's papers and her ration card, too. I looked at her printed name. Donata Maria Leone. There was no one in this world who would miss her.

'Here.' I put them quickly into Issa's outstretched hand. 'Perhaps,' I said, 'you can find a use for these.'

That is how I became a thief.

Eight days ago, we found out what we had been waiting for. The Allies made a second landing some thirty miles south of Rome. The fighting is intense. German troops are moving south, and JULIET needs to know all about them. So we hoard scraps of information, anything we can find, so she can send them off to ROMEO in what I call her 'love letters'.

Donata's room was a great success. It worked just as I had hoped. Issa and Papa simply walked into the building, climbed the stairs and used the keys. JULIET was quite happy there – she needs to be somewhere high up in order for her antenna to work properly. But the problem is that it is too dangerous to transmit more than once or twice from the same place. GAP has kept its promise to 'bring the war home', never let the enemy sleep safely in his bed – in particular by throwing hand grenades at German officers in the station last week, and again a week ago, outside the Excelsior. As a result, Fascist patrols are greatly increased. Everyone is suspicious of everyone. And the Germans can trace radio signals. They are good at this.

So, if JULIET is to continue, she must move frequently.

Unfortunately, there are few buildings we can

get to now where we won't attract attention. Mama had the idea that she would prowl through the city herself, looking for places JULIET could transmit from – she says no one ever sees ladies 'of a certain age', especially if they carry a shopping bag. But I couldn't let her do that. So I have sunk to the lowest of the low.

Quite a lot of people are dying just now, one way and another. And when they do, before I make the entries in my ledger, I rifle their belongings. I get their addresses from their papers or wheedle it out of them in conversation, and if they lived alone or I find that their family has fled or died, I steal their keys and give them to Issa. If I think they will be useful, I also steal their papers. And their clothes. Their worn boots. Their gloves and woollen socks and overcoats that smell of cigar smoke or perfume. I have not been caught out yet, but if I am, I will lie. I will say I have no idea where the papers or the keys went. I will say that things get lost in hospitals. I will say that it is sad, but in difficult times, people steal.

Issa hugs me and tells me that all of this has made me a heroine for Italy – a true partisan. But I don't feel like that. I feel like a liar and a graverobber. I feel like a crow, picking the bones of the dead.

Chapter Fourteen

The night before, as he had walked away from the cafe after meeting Eleanor Sachs, Pallioti had been of two minds. He very much doubted that she was a murderer. But his instincts still told him, with some certainty, that she had been lying.

He could call Enzo, who would run a background check on her, and pull her in and question her, and generally make her life miserable. He could do nothing, and see what she did next. Or he could carve a route between the two – run a background check and then wait.

He found himself inclined towards the last of these, partly, he realized, because he liked the game. Liars interested him, especially when they had gone to the lengths Eleanor Sachs had. He had no idea what it was she was really after, but he would find out eventually – if only because she would tell him. Liars always told, in the end. If you had enough patience. Because at heart, they were show-offs.

He had pondered the paradox of that – that half the thrill of any con was showing how you did it, thereby destroying what you'd built – as he'd made his way to Saffy's gallery, moving through the night streets of the city like Jonah through the belly of the whale.

He was still considering, even as he arrived and had a glass of champagne stuck into his hand, how they might verify the connection between Roberto Roblino and Giovanni Trantemento. Eleanor Sachs's game, whatever it was, was probably irrelevant. But the connection between the two old men, if it existed, was not. He'd sipped the wine, and had been on the verge of accepting the dreary reality that either he, or more likely Guillermo, would have to spend some considerable time on the phone and/or in a library and online in order to see if they could back up a single thing the good Dr Sachs had said, when a potential solution had presented itself in the unlikely guise of Maria Grandolo.

'Alessandro!'

Despite the fact that it was November, Maria was wearing a wisp of a dress. She might have the brains of a peahen, but they were definitely housed in the body of something, well, just short of a goddess. Her legs, which were perfect, went on for approximately half a mile. Her stomach was flat. Her hair shimmered and her face was a perfect oval. But what really interested Pallioti about her – in fact, the only thing that interested him about her – was that, while he was as bewitched as any man for about three minutes, that was it. By minute four, the idea of actually having sex with her was invariably replaced by an almost panicky desire to flee.

Maria had clasped him by the shoulders – she was stronger than she looked – and kissed him rather too enthusiastically on either cheek.

'Alessandro!' she'd exclaimed again, demonstrating that she did, in fact, know his name.

'Hello, Maria, you're looking well.'

'We have been on holiday! One last one before the horrible winter. Beautiful! We took over the hotel. You should have come! Such fun. The spa. I tried to get Seraphina, but you know what she's like. Work! Work! Work! Just like you, Alessandro.' She paused and took a breath. 'But at least you're here tonight,' she added. 'Seraphina didn't tell me. If I'd known I'd have invited you. We're going for dinner afterwards.' Maria had named one of the glitzier restaurants in the city. 'Let me see if they can add another place!'

She had whipped out her mobile as Pallioti began to protest. Then, quite suddenly, he had remembered the organization Saffy had mentioned – something run by Maria's family that dealt with the partisans – and stopped in mid sentence. He could, of course, have used his not-inconsiderable clout to contact whatever the group was and ask for help. But that would have made it official. Which would have meant potentially public. Which was not only un-Florentine, but an anathema to the notoriously private Grandolos.

Maria had looked slightly startled when, instead of protesting, he'd smiled, put his hand on her elbow, and said, 'How delightful. I'd love to join you.'

Later, he'd told himself it was a small price to pay, and if nothing else, would give him a chance to make up for Sunday by spending an evening with Saffy and Leo, both of whom had spent the next hour glancing at him as if he had gone off his head.

As he expected, the dinner had been loud, the restaurant pretentious, and the food ordinary. But the experience hadn't killed him, and he had got what he wanted. Maria, flattered that he deigned to speak to her at all, had been more than helpful. The eagerness with which she'd made a call even before the first round of champagne had been poured, had made him feel a heel. But it had borne fruit. As soon as he arrived at the office the next morning, Guillermo handed him a slip with an address on it and informed him that he had an appointment with a researcher at Remember The Fallen.

Now he was standing outside a suite of offices in an expensive and anonymous building not far from Piazza D'Azeglio. If he had been expecting genteel eccentricity, elderly ladies in cardigans or little old men in fusty tweed suits juggling manila files, it looked as if he was going to be disappointed. The young woman who greeted him was crisp and professional. She smiled brightly and extended a well-manicured hand.

'Ispettore,' she said. 'We have been expecting you.'

The room he was ushered into had several sofas, low tables with magazines, and what was obviously her desk. On it sat neat stacks of papers, a potted orchid, and a large computer. There wasn't a manila file in sight. It could have been the outer office of an upmarket psychiatrist, a lawyer, or an estate planner.

'I am Graziella Lombardi,' she added, as she crossed the thick blue carpet towards a closed door. 'The administrator. I would be happy to help you, of course. But our Director has insisted that she would like to meet you herself.'

She rapped on the door – which, like the rest of the room, was painted a pale golden colour, its mouldings picked out in pale blue – pushed it open, and said, 'He is here, Signora.'

Pallioti heard a murmured voice. There was the sound of someone getting up from a chair, then the door swung open and the Director of Remember The Fallen stepped into the room.

She was wearing a sweater of pale pink, lipstick that matched it, and a single strand of pearls. Her white hair framed her face in loose abundant curls. Pallioti had no idea how old she was, and understood at once that it didn't matter. The woman who was extending her hand to him put paid to any idea that youth and beauty were connected.

'Ispettore Pallioti,' she said, her face lighting into a smile, 'what a pleasure it is to meet you. Your sister is a dear friend of my great-niece, Maria.'

Pallioti extended his own hand nervously. He had not intended for Maria to summon up her great-aunt in person. A researcher would have done, would have been more than enough. Now he found himself pressing an utterly trivial issue on Cosimo Grandolo's widow herself.

'Please, please.' Signora Grandolo was gesturing towards the open door of what was apparently her office. 'Do come in,' she said. 'And tell me how I can help you?'

∽

'My husband started this organization, quite soon after the war. Did you ever meet him?'

Signora Grandolo had settled herself behind her desk, which was wide and highly polished. The fog of the night before had cleared and a bright, sharp sun fell through the tall windows of the office, burnishing the glass-fronted bookcases that lined the walls and the great ship of a desk to a deep chestnut brown.

'No.' Cosimo Grandolo had died only a few months earlier. 'I'm very sorry,' Pallioti said, 'that I never had the pleasure. It was a terrible loss, for the city. And, I am sure, for you.'

Signora Grandolo smiled, acknowledging the compliment.

'There was a great need, you see,' she said. 'After the war. So many of them, the partisans, were so young when they were killed, and quite a few had families. Parents, grandparents, who would have been depending on them, had they lived. And in many cases, of course, small children.'

She spread her hands, her wedding band catching the sun.

'Cosimo realized that they needed help. The country, the new government, was in its infancy. Germany bled us dry.' She glanced at him. 'Not many people understand that – how much they looted. I'm not talking about paintings and fur coats. I mean our machinery – they stripped it out of the factories and took it, you know. Also our gold reserves. Literally, our coin. After that, and after more than twenty years of Fascism, when we finally had our freedom my husband felt the least we could do was try to help the families of the people who made it possible.'

Pallioti nodded. He knew, everyone knew, he supposed, about the devastation at the end of the war. But the truth was, he had never considered what had happened to the families who had been robbed of the generation that would have been expected to care for them – those in their twenties and thirties who would have taken on the role of provider.

He shook his head. 'I'm sorry. Do you know, I had never really thought about it.'

Signora Grandolo regarded him for a moment. Then she smiled.

'Very few people have,' she said. 'The practicalities, I mean. After the parades were over. And those that did are mostly dead.' She shrugged. 'At your age, why should you have thought of it? You have other things to worry about. And the state has always taken care of you. But back then, there were so many other things to deal with. And in the meantime, where would children's clothes come from? Who would buy their books? Who was going to make sure the Nannas and the Nonnos who had been bombed out, who all those young people had died fighting for, that they had a place to live? It's not just countries and factories and bridges that wars destroy.' She looked towards the window. 'It's families.'

A shaft of sunlight caught her hair and turned it white-silver. Beneath her fragile skin, the bones of her cheeks and the straight line of her nose were hard and clean.

'The scale of the problem was larger than anyone anticipated,' she continued. 'Do you have any idea,' she asked, looking back at him, 'how many members of partisan brigades, organizations, groups – whatever you want to call them – there were by the summer of 1945?'

Pallioti shook his head. 'None. I am embarrassed to say.'

'Don't be. I'm sorry to lecture. I shouldn't.' She smiled. 'It's a privilege of age. The best estimate is two hundred thousand. Of those, some fifty-five thousand were women. Approximately thirty-five thousand of them fought in armed engagements.'

'I had no idea.'

'No,' she said. 'Well, Italy was quite different, in that respect. Our women didn't just run messages and clip telephone lines. They fought shoulder to shoulder. And died. Just like their men. My husband spent the war interned. He was in the army, arrested and shipped to Germany within hours of the armistice. He never quite recovered from the guilt of not having taken part. Not fighting for his country. He tried his whole life to make up for it.'

The story was not unfamiliar.

'I think,' Pallioti said, 'that a lot of people felt that way. Especially men.'

Signora Grandolo smiled. 'Yes,' she agreed. 'I think that is probably a male cross. Not uniquely. But I have always believed that women are better at giving up regret. In any case,' she added, 'Cosimo just wanted to do what he could to help. Hence' – she spread her hands and gestured to the office – 'Remember The Fallen. And now, of course, it would run perfectly well without me. It's just a hobby for an old woman with too much time on her hands, to come in here and meddle. More interesting than needlepoint, or playing bridge.' She laughed. 'And safer than meddling in my daughters' lives. Do you have children, Ispettore?'

Pallioti shook his head.

'Just the police.' Signora Grandolo smiled.

And Seraphina, he started to say. Then he realized she was teasing him.

'Now,' she said quickly, before he could become embarrassed, 'I think you did not come here to discuss any of this – the ruthlessness of women and the superior sensibilities of men.'

'No.' As agreeable as that might be, she was right.

Signora Grandolo appraised him for a moment. Then she said, 'So, tell me. What can I do? Maria said you needed a favour?'

'Yes.' Pallioti leaned back in the armchair she had shown him to. 'Giovanni Trantemento,' he said. 'In a word. Or rather, two.'

Signora Grandolo nodded. 'I suspected as much.'

She pulled open a drawer, extracted a file, and placed it on her desk.

'I took the liberty of asking Graziella to pull together anything we might have on him. I'm afraid it isn't much. We really only concern ourselves with partisans' family members who need our help – the children especially. Who have now turned into parents and grandparents themselves. As children have a habit of doing.' She produced a pair of glasses, slipped them on, and opened the file. 'It doesn't appear that he had any.'

From where he was sitting, Pallioti could see that the folder contained only one typed page. 'No. A sister and nephew in Rome are his only remaining family. The father was killed, in Russia. The mother died at the end of the war. In Switzerland.'

She looked up. 'Switzerland?'

'Yes. He got them out. The mother died there, in a sanatorium. The daughter married, and moved to Rome.' Too late, he realized that, having now heard what Remember The Fallen did, there was little chance that they would have come across the Trantementos. 'I'm sorry,' he said. 'Now that I understand what you do, I doubt that Signor Trantemento was the kind of case that would have come to your attention.'

She nodded, flipped the file closed and slid it across the desk towards him.

'Then,' she said, 'I'm not sure I understand how I can help you?'

'Actually,' Pallioti said, 'there is someone else.'

Her blue eyes fastened on him.

'Someone else?'

Pallioti leaned forward.

'A Roberto Roblino. Possibly from the south. He also fought with the partisans, and was also decorated, like Trantemento, at the sixtieth anniversary celebrations. We're having some trouble,' he added, choosing his words carefully, 'with his background.'

As he spoke, he thought of Eleanor Sachs's small, intent face, so completely unlike that of the woman sitting opposite him. And of her suggestion that Giovanni Trantemento and Roberto Roblino had been friends. Possibly old friends. Yet, when he had spoken with Enzo this morning, he had been told again that they had found no connection between the two. Nor had they been able to locate Roberto Roblino's birth certificate.

'I understand,' he added, 'that records were – confused – after the war.'

She smiled at his choice of words.

'Your diplomacy serves you well, Ispettore. Confused is a very polite way of putting it. Chaotic comes closer. In a lot of cases, destroyed.'

'So a missing birth certificate, for instance, wouldn't be unusual?'

'Quite the opposite. Birth, death, marriage, baptism. In a lot of cases there was no evidence that anyone was anyone.'

'But you were able to verify genuine families of partisan members?'

'Well,' she said. 'Yes, at least in many cases. We used what records were available. And, yes, word of mouth, too. Letters sent home, reports of comrades and commanding officers – that sort of thing. That having been said,' she added, 'I wouldn't die of shock if we paid for a few books, bought a few pairs of socks for children whose parents weren't exactly what you and I would call heroic. But as far as this man is concerned, if he was from the south – well, of course that was behind Allied lines. If he was with the partisans, he was away from home. As I said, we deal almost exclusively with the families of combatants who came from this area. There are other similar organizations. One in Turin does excellent work – the Piedmont, of course, was very active. And there is another in Padua.'

She picked up a fountain pen, unscrewed the cap, then put

it down and clenched and unclenched her fist.

'Arthritis,' she said, shaking her head. 'Such a bore. I don't suppose it's anything you have to worry about yet.'

Before Pallioti could reply, she picked up the pen again, and reached for a pad of paper. As she began to write she said, 'I know the directors of the organizations in Turin and Padua personally. I'm sure they would be most helpful.'

'I'm not certain,' Pallioti said, 'where Roblino was active.'

Signora Grandolo stopped writing and looked up. 'You mean you think he may have been in Florence?'

Pallioti nodded. 'He may have stayed in touch with at least one partisan member who was here. So, yes, I think it's possible.'

'Well, in that case,' she said, 'let us check.' She swivelled towards her computer. 'I take it,' she added, 'by the fact that you are asking me and not the man himself, that Signor Roblino is no longer with us?'

Not surprisingly, she apparently did not keep up with the tabloid papers, who had run yet another story this morning. Pallioti shook his head.

'Sadly, no.'

Signora Grandolo's computer, unlike the mother ship on Graziella Lombardi's desk, was slight and silver, and looked as if it could not possibly weigh more than a pound. She tapped quickly on her keyboard, then stared at the screen. From where he was sitting, Pallioti could not see what came up. Whatever it was made her frown.

'Nooo,' she said slowly, running her finger down what had to be a list of names. 'Roberto. Robbicci. Robeno. But no Roblino. No, I'm sorry. We don't seem to have any record of anyone with that name at all. Of course,' she added, glancing at him over the top of her glasses, 'I could look further for you, if you like. Contact you, if anything came up. If he's not here, though' — she gestured towards the computer – 'I tend to doubt it. Graziella is quite good at keeping our data in order.'

Pallioti decided he wasn't surprised. Trantemento and Roblino could have met in dozens of other ways. They could have met through some old partisans' network – after all, the souvenirs Giovanni Trantemento had kept suggested he wasn't entirely dedicated to forgetting his past – or they could have met for the first time in Rome, during the sixtieth celebrations. Or this could be one of the things Eleanor Sachs was lying through her teeth about. In fact, rather than being disappointed, Pallioti decided he felt rather smug.

'Tell me,' he asked, wondering if he was on a roll, 'I don't want to waste your time, Signora. But have you ever heard stories, anything, concerning a character called Il Spettro?'

As he spoke, her face broke into a smile.

'Ah, Ispettore,' she said. 'Someone has been pulling your leg. Telling you tall tales all about the Scarlet Pimpernel of Florence.'

'I'm afraid it's possible,' he agreed. 'I take it you think there's nothing in it?'

She smiled. 'No,' she said. 'I'm sorry. Stories are lovely. Especially exciting ones, aren't they? But no.' She shook her head. 'Perhaps it's the cynicism of age. Or perhaps,' she added, 'I prefer to believe in real heroes. There were a lot of them, you know. And most of them, what they did was extraordinary. But to my mind, the most extraordinary thing of all was that they were shockingly ordinary men and women.'

'I'm sorry,' he said. 'I should have known. The source was hardly reliable.'

'Well, many of them aren't. Especially when it comes to the war. That's human nature. Everyone wants to remember themselves as a hero. I know they had quite a lot of trouble, for instance, verifying the stories behind the medals, at the sixtieth.'

'Were you involved in that, at all?'

She shook her head.

'No. As I said, we deal largely with surviving families. And with the memorials, here in the city. We were invited, of course,

We have all heard of people, women usually, who have put on their best clothes and gone to the Café Paskowski or the Excelsior bar and thrown themselves at officers and the black-suited Gestapo men. Sidled up to them and slipped pathetic rolled-up wads of money, jewellery, little pieces of paper with a name written on it, into their pockets. Some people go to the Questura. Others stand in the street outside the Villa Triste until they are chased away. The German consul, Herr Wolf, is said to be sympathetic. In the right circumstances.

In the meantime, we hear whispers of informers and occasional gunshots and ignore the air raid sirens, when they go off at all, and curse the Allies for the rubble that blossoms across the city, while at the same time we long for them to come, and fear what will happen before they do, and fear even more what will happen if they do not.

GAP goes on throwing grenades and hiding news-sheets in menus and bibles, but no one speaks any more of triumph, or freedom, or ideals. Instead, we simply bow our heads – narrow time down to a day, an hour – and fight on. Not because we are lit with inspiration and hope, but because we have no choice. Because the alternative is death.

And each of us would like to meet it thinking the best of ourselves. But these days that is unlikely. Still, we do our best. So, as I have said, this book, these words, are a type of penance. And given that, I think I'll write about Valentine's Day. Because that was the day Issa was shot.

Dawn that morning was as fragile as the inside

of a shell. It had been bitter. The river was white
with cold. A skin of ice, powdered with snow, covered the water. In places it cracked, allowing a
swirl of black to show through. I had been working most of the night, and had gone out to
breathe, just to feel air on my face that did not
bear the cloying smell of illness. I had gone also
to think of Lodovico. I find I can no longer do that
at home or at the hospital. Instead, when I am
desperate and can no longer bear not to summon
him up, when I must reach for memories of him
like an addict for a drug, I walk fast and alone
through the city. Then, sometimes, I can outpace
the person I have become and find him in my
mind as what I used to be. The moments are fleeting, I admit. But on the whole, better than
dreams. Even if I never see him again, or never
know, I am determined to believe that he is still
alive, as if my thinking of him eating, breathing,
laughing could make it so. Although I know, of
course, that this is nonsense. What I think does
not matter. Any more than what I wish for matters. This great machine of a war grinds on, and
does not care what we think or wish.

It was very cold on the bridge. I peered over the
edge and thought of the fish, still there beneath
the ice, their world untouched. And then I wondered, when they blow the bridges, when the Allies finally come and destruction is truly loosed
upon us, when the Trinita and the Carraia and
the Ponte Alle Grazie all come falling down, will
the fish even notice? I hoped not. Walking back
to the hospital, I hoped the fish, at least, would
be untouched.

I thought about them all day. And I was still

thinking of them in the evening – about their
darkness and their open mouths – as I finally
made my way back to my cupboard at the end of
my shift. I was carrying a bundle of clothes, that
day's bounty. No sets of keys or useful papers, but
several pairs of socks. The decent boots of a sev-
enteen-year-old boy beaten by the Banda Carita
who then dumped him here so his death could be
on our books, not theirs. A scarf.

Things were unusually quiet, and after the
night before when I had not slept at all, I thought
I would get an hour or two. I was pulling my
keys out, tugging at the ribbon around my neck,
when I sensed that something was wrong. My
door was closed, but I thought I heard something, or someone, inside, and I was certain, absolutely positive that this was it – that I had
finally been found out, that I would come face to
face with the Head Sister, tipping up boxes of
supplies where just the day before I had hidden
two ration cards and a set of papers. My hand
was shaking, but I felt something almost like relief as I finally pushed the door open.

I suppose I must have been expecting what I
saw for some time, but still it took my breath
away. It's not that I haven't dealt with the
wounded, God knows. It's just that they have always been anonymous. They haven't had faces I
love.

Issa was huddled on my cot, wrapped in her
coat – her best coat, the black one with the fur collar. Which made it look worse, because her skin
was so pale against it.

'Issa! For God's sake!'

I dropped what I was carrying and darted forward, but she put her finger to her lips and pointed at the door. I shut it behind me, and stared at her.

'What happened?' I demanded. 'What happened to you?'

As I came close, I could see that the sleeve and shoulder of the coat were ruined, ripped and dark, and that blood had seeped through the thick wool and matted the fur.

'I was knocked down by a car.'

The minute she said it, I knew she was lying. And I knew again the moment I touched her. There was the sticky warmth, the spongy softness. Finally, she let me peel the coat back. I have been doing this for six months now. I know a bullet wound when I see one.

'What happened?'

It took me a moment to realize that she was wearing some of her best clothes. Her black suede shoes, soaked and ruined. Her black skirt, a silk blouse, the coat.

'What happened to you?' I asked again.

But even as I did, I knew it was pointless. 'I know nothing, I know nothing, I know nothing.' We hold it to us like a prayer, but in that moment I realized that I no longer know what it is for – who it protects or doesn't. All I know is that we live in our own little shells of silence and fear.

'Come on,' I said, finally. 'You have to let me get this off.'

I was worried that she was badly hurt, that the arm was broken or the bullet lodged. But she was very lucky. The flesh wound was ugly, and she had lost some blood. But that is all it was, a wound. A few inches towards her back, and things might have been quite different.

'This is GAP,' I muttered. 'Isn't it?' But I might as well have been talking to myself. Even when I prised the torn flesh open and cleaned it, she didn't make a sound.

I gave her some morphine. I tucked a blanket around her, and sitting in the chair at my desk, I watched as she fell asleep on my cot, her fingers fluttering in dreams. I waited until midnight. Then I gathered up all her clothes and took them downstairs to the incinerator.

When Issa woke up the next day, I knew that she was in pain, but again she refused to say anything about what had happened. She had visited me before, and while I did not tell anyone what was the matter with her, I thought it was safer not to deny her presence, either. I went about my business, and planned that, if asked, I would say the flat where she was staying had been hit. But no one did ask. No one asks anything any more. We all avert our eyes and scurry about, hands busy, seeing nothing.

By the afternoon of the third day, there was a little more colour in her cheeks. She did not have a fever and she was hungry. I found her some clothes. She asked for men's trousers and a jacket. I don't know if the boy's boots fit, but she put them on. When I came back that evening after my rounds, I found her sitting up, in my chair, at my desk.

'Cati,' she said. 'You have to cut my hair.'

I don't know why, but of all the things she had asked or done since last September, I found this – this stupid, trivial thing – the most shocking. She

must have seen it in my face, because she
laughed. It made her wince, made her eyes water
with pain, but she laughed anyway.

'It won't change anything,' she said. 'It won't
change me.'

I nodded, and muttered that, of course, she was
right. I told myself that we were so changed already that it could hardly matter.

She left the next afternoon. Carlo came for her.
He was waiting in the bicycle shed. I don't know
how dangerous it must have been for him to be
there, probably very. My heart went out to him. I
do not trust Issa to take care of herself, and
plainly, neither does he. He reached out and put
his arms around her. If the sight of her startled
him, with her cropped hair and in her men's
clothes, he didn't let it show. He has changed, too,
since I last saw him, what feels like so very long
ago now, in the autumn. He is still as beautiful
as an archangel, his hair is still gold, and his
eyes are still the same tawny cat's colour. He still
smiles. But he is no longer a boy. Something has
changed in his face. There is a hardness about
him.

'Thank God you're all right.' He clasped Issa to
him and buried his lips in her hair. Then he
reached out and put his arm around me. He drew
me to them until the three of us were standing
there as one.

'Bless you,' he said. 'Bless you, for what you
have done. And for taking care of her.'

I told him I had not done much, but I was
moved again by his kindness, and ashamed that
I had ever been jealous. Now I am just glad that

Issa has an archangel to watch over her. Before they went, I warned her, and him, that if she did anything stupid the wound to her arm could easily become infected and kill her. Both of them promised she would come back and let me look at it.

But I did not know when that would be. So I didn't dare leave the hospital in case she came and I was not there. Our telephone occasionally still worked, which was a mercy – not only so that Mama and Papa would not worry, but because, although it's true that I have become a better liar, when it came to this, I was not sure I could look into their faces and not tell them what had happened. So it was better I stayed away.

I made a point of going out every evening, and sometimes just after dawn as well, to the shed where the bicycles were kept and where the old gardener stored his things. I carried my rucksack, fiddled with my tyres or the basket, giving Issa a chance to see me. For almost a week she didn't appear. Then, one night, she was there.

She was alone, and at first, I barely recognized her. She had hennaed her hair and was wearing men's clothes again. But it was not just that – the hair and the clothes. She had changed the way she moved, the way she walked, held her head. She had made herself into someone else. When I think about it now, I realize that I shouldn't have been so surprised. For once, it was a talent we shared. All of us were good at charades, but especially Issa and I. Papa usually won at cards, and Rico could run faster than either of us, but we excelled at turning ourselves into things we were not.

She laid her hand over mine, and the moment I heard her voice – the one thing she had not changed – I knew something was wrong. At first, I thought it was her arm. I reached out to touch her cheek, to see if she had a fever, but her skin was cool under my fingers. Then I had a horrible lurch in my stomach. Mama? Papa? JULIET had been discovered? She saw my expression and shook her head.

'Let's go to your cupboard,' she said, smiling at the name for my so-called office.

When we got there, I insisted on changing her dressing. Then she made me sit down beside her, and what she said made me feel ill.

Issa insisted that we had to discuss what would happen if either of us 'went missing'.

I stared at her. I opened my mouth, trying to suck in enough air to make the ballooning inside me go away.

'I will come for you,' she said. 'No matters what happens. I will come for you.'

'Don't be stupid.' Fear made my voice sharp. 'You can't. No one "comes for" anyone in the Villa Triste.'

She nodded. 'I know that. I know. But they don't keep you there. They'll question you, then they'll send you to the women's prison at San Verdiana. The Mother Superior is sympathetic.'

She told me that they had bought German uniforms from Austrian deserters, that already 'German officers' had gone to San Verdiana and other prisons to 'remove prisoners'. If that failed, if there was not time, they knew where the trains went. They knew where they stopped on the route to the detention centres and the holding camp at Fossoli.

'No matter what happens,' she said. 'I won't forget you. I won't abandon you. Remember that.'

GAP, she said, takes care of its own.

Then she told me that the rules are not equal. That if it is her – if she vanishes – I must do nothing.

I stared at her, but before I could object, she went on.

I must understand. If I go to the Questura, if I throw myself at black uniforms in the Excelsior, or cry, or scream, I could make it worse for her. GAP, she said, would care for her, one way or another. I didn't like to think about what that meant. If she were dead, Issa said, someone would come and tell me.

'I haven't told Mama or Papa.' She looked at me. 'This is between us.'

I nodded as she spoke. Not because I agreed, but because a numb feeling had washed over me. The tiny space of the cupboard smelled of cabbage and the warmth of our bodies. I stood up, half expecting that I would be shaky on my feet, and pulled out the desk chair.

'What are you doing?' Issa asked.

'Wait,' I said. 'Wait. I have something.'

She watched me, half amused, as I climbed up onto the chair and reached into one of the high cupboards. I couldn't see above my head, and I was afraid for a moment that I would drop it. Then my fingers found the cool smooth neck of the bottle and lifted down the brandy that I had been secreting away in my rathole.

I stole it out of a suitcase about a month ago, from a fat black-marketeer with appendicitis. He wasn't even dead – in fact, the operation was a great success, and he was fine – but I didn't care. He had his good little Fascisti badge displayed prominently on his lapel. I told myself he'd find another bottle where this one came from.

For all that, the brandy was cheap and quite nasty. I climbed down and we sat side by side on the bed, handing the bottle back and forth, drinking it as if it was cough medicine.

'Issa,' I said finally, 'why are you talking like this?'

She was so close I could feel her shoulder against mine. Smell the liquor on her breath when she spoke.

'You can't tell anyone.'

I shook my head. Then I remembered when we were children, and held my hand up.

'I swear.'

Issa smiled. She held her hand up, and pressed her thumb against mine.

'Remember?' I asked. 'We'd pilfer Emmelina's sewing box, steal her needles, prick our skin? Blood bond?'

Issa nodded. 'Blood bond,' she said. Then she told me.

Thanks to us, or rather to JULIET, there was an air drop on the night of Valentine's Day. The first to Tuscany. They had not trusted us before, or hadn't thought us important enough. But with the spring coming, and with the advent of JULIET, all of that has changed.

The drop was in the early hours of the morning, probably about the same time as Issa's hands were dancing to morphine dreams. It was somewhere near Greve, and it very nearly went wrong. There were nineteen parachutes in all. They saw them come down, but the snow was so deep that the canisters fell and sank. In the dark it was impossible to see them. They thought they had lost everything. But GAP had gathered a lot of people, several groups, and they fanned out. Dug them out of the snow. Every single one. Thirty-six canisters in all. Fifty-one Sten guns, ammunition, grenades, incendiary bombs and explosives. All of it for the liberation, which, despite the stalemate at Cassino and Anzio, everyone believes will come in the spring. The Germans cannot hold out forever. When the Allies finally break through and Rome falls, Kesselring will fall back. They believe he will retreat as far as the mountains, to the fortifications they call the Gothic Line that Issa has been watching them build. They also believe that as the Germans go, they will try to destroy the city. That's the lesson of Naples. But, Issa insisted, it will not happen here, because we will be ready. We will drive them out before they can cause utter destruction. This is what the weapons in the air drop were for.

'By some miracle,' Issa said, 'they got it back into the city. All of it. Over three days, they brought it to an apartment in a safe house, somewhere near the Pitti. From there it was to be divided up and moved again.'

'Was?'

I looked at her. The lamp in my tiny room does not give much light, and with the high walls and strange shadows and her newly short hair, she looked both familiar and strange, like a relative I had forgotten. Only her voice and her eyes were the same.

'It was all going to be moved last night,' she said. 'But yesterday, in the afternoon, Carita came.'

I felt my mouth go dry. I understood now why she had told me what she told me.

'But—' I murmured. I could barely say it.

She shook her head.

'We didn't have anything to do with this, our group,' she said. 'But Carita must have known. It wasn't luck.' She looked at me. 'If they had come today, they would have found nothing.'

'And they got it all?'

She nodded.

'Everything. And more. There were other things. A printing press. Supplies.' She stood up, wincing at her arm. 'Too many people,' she said. 'Too many people knew.'

'Do they have any idea who it was? Who—?'

She shook her head.

'How would we know? We all knew this could happen. But we didn't believe it. Someone slipped. Someone made a mistake. Or – ' she ran her hand through her hair, not saying what we were both thinking – 'or someone betrayed us. Someone did this, not by mistake. But because they chose to slip through the shadows to Carita.'

'There are all sorts of rumours,' Issa said. 'Of arrests. But no one knows. If GAP finds out who it was – well.' She shrugged. 'They'll make sure it doesn't happen again. But it doesn't change it. About the weapons. We've lost it all.' She looked at me. 'The Americans are furious. They won't trust us again. They might as well drop guns straight to the Germans.'

'How bad is it?'

I had no idea about grenades or ammunition or explosives. I'd never even held a gun. Until that moment, I had never thought much about where things like the pistol Il Corvo carried had come from.

'They won't drop more,' Issa said. 'We can raid and steal,' she shrugged. 'But we can't make up for this. So, when it comes, the glorious day, we'll be left to fight with one hand tied behind our back.'

She looked at me as she said this, and for the first time I saw something I had never seen before in her face. It was just a moment, as fast as a dab of wind on the water. But it was so naked – so hard and bright in her eyes, that I felt as if the floor had shifted. She was afraid.

Chapter Sixteen

'Did you believe her?'

'Signora Grandolo? Of course.'

Enzo Saenz said nothing, but his expression suggested he found this mildly surprising. As if, having heard his account of being ambushed by Eleanor Sachs, he thought Pallioti might never again believe a single word uttered by a female.

Pallioti glanced up. They were standing on either side of the table on which Roberto Roblino's life, or what they understood of it so far, had been laid out. He picked up one of the photographs of the old man and put it down again. The idea of Signora Grandolo lying was ridiculous.

'Of course,' he added rather waspishly, 'if you care to waste the time, you can have one of your people confirm it. I shouldn't think it would be too difficult.'

Enzo shrugged, suggesting he'd do just that.

'Well,' he said, picking up a copy of Roberto Roblino's autopsy report and thumbing through it, 'if the salt fits—'

Pallioti assumed that was supposed to be funny, but had no idea why.

Glancing at him, Enzo elaborated.

'Most of these neo-Nazi, neo-Fascist – whatever you want to call them – groups don't think the liberation should be celebrated. They see it as a betrayal. Of the true Italy.'

'So anyone who fought for it, for the liberation, is a traitor?'

Enzo smiled. 'Yes,' he said, dropping the report back on the table. 'At least, that's how I'd read it. Traitors get executed and have their mouths stuffed with salt because, if Signora Grandolo was right – and I'm sure she is,' he added diplomatically, 'salt was the price of betrayal. It makes sense, in a warped kind of way. Which,' he added, 'is how most of their thought processes make sense. At least in my book. We are, after all, talking about people whose idea of a great holiday is a sightseeing trip to Dachau.'

Pallioti sighed. There were days when the sheer evil in the world still amazed him.

'And what about the others?' he asked.

Enzo's unusually buoyant mood was due to the fact that, since Tuesday morning, his team had unearthed seven other members of the partisans who had received both medals at the sixtieth ceremonies, and letters virtually identical to the one sent to Roberto Roblino.

'Well, they're all alive and kicking.'

'That's a plus.'

'Especially for them.' Enzo glanced up. 'I've contacted the local boys, and suggested in the strongest possible terms that they keep as close an eye as they can on any ex-partisans in their area and take any threats seriously, and then some. We've put that advice out across the country. And, for that matter, circulated it through Europe.'

'Any disagreements?'

Enzo shook his head. 'None. For once it's something we can all agree on. No one's happy about thugs threatening old heroes. As for the others, the letter recipients – at least the ones we know about – one had his house broken into, about six months ago. But none of the others have experienced any kind of attack. At least,' he added, 'that they'll admit to.'

'That doesn't mean they didn't happen.'

'True,' Enzo agreed. He was sifting through a pile of folders.

'Point of pride. Refusal to be intimidated. Not giving in to thugs. Not making a fuss. Old people are like that to start with, and I wouldn't be surprised if it's all doubled for ex-freedom fighters. We're checking it out. Asking them to think again, and going through reports from the local police. After all, they're not your average octogenarians.'

Perhaps not, Pallioti thought. Although he suspected Signora Grandolo might disagree. What had she called them? Astonishingly ordinary people who did extraordinary things.

He turned towards the copies of the letters that had been put up on a third whiteboard flanked by those dedicated to the two old men. The wording was similar, some of the phrases – most notably the assertions concerning the Halls of Valhalla – were repeated. All had been written in red ink. So far, all of them also featured the same smudged cross. And all of them were dated 28 April, LXXXIII, the Fascist year 83, otherwise known as 2005. In other words, not only the anniversary of Mussolini's death, but also three days after the liberation celebration, which, as Signora Grandolo had pointed out, had been watched live on TV by most of Italy.

The general consensus was that the targets could have been picked out that way – simply names the letter writer had been quick enough to note down while he watched TV and was able to follow up on. Or, more likely, the broadcast had provided the inspiration and local press had provided the details.

Three of the newly uncovered letter recipients, like Roberto Roblino, currently lived in the south. Another was from Rome. Two were from Milan, and the last from near Ravenna. Three of the seven had thrown their letters out immediately. The lady in Ravenna had turned hers in to her local police after correcting the spelling – having spent the end of the war blowing up bridges, she had become an infant school teacher. Three others had kept them.

The corrected version had been lost by the police station in question, but the remaining letters had already been collected and sent for analysis. No one really doubted that they would be a match. In addition to possible fingerprints, Enzo was counting on getting DNA off the stamps. Even murderous bigoted halfwits often wore gloves. Very few, on the other hand, thought not to lick. The forensics on the bullet that killed Roberto Roblino had also come back. Much to no one's surprise, it had been fired from the same gun that killed Giovanni Trantemento.

Pallioti accepted that these developments probably rendered his efforts of the morning superfluous, if not completely irrelevant. The fact was, he'd wasted his time chasing his tail. He suspected he'd also embarrassed himself in the process. Signora Grandolo had been charming, but she'd made him feel like a bit of an idiot.

Still, setting his ruffled feathers aside, it was good news. Finally they were making some real progress. The investigation had shifted almost exclusively towards the now-promising, and disturbingly large, array of neo-Nazi and neo-Fascist groups that seemed to mutate across the country, and indeed across Europe. In fact, Europol was being most helpful. Already the French had confirmed cases of harassment involving some of their surviving Resistance members. Now, all Enzo needed was the identity of the letter writer and to find something to link him to Giovanni Trantemento. A letter would be useful. Or at least a threat.

In the meantime, the Mayor was delighted. Even the investigating magistrate was happy. Going after neo-Nazis was a little like shooting fish in a barrel – rewarding for everyone, with the notable exception of the fish.

'By the way,' Enzo said suddenly, 'about your Doctor Sachs?'

Pallioti, who had been studying the letters on the whiteboard, looked over his shoulder.

'I hate to tell you this,' Enzo said, 'but I think you may be being a bit hard on her.'

Pallioti raised his eyebrows.

'Not just about the salt.' Enzo picked up another sheet of paper, glanced at it and put it down again. 'About Roblino and Giovanni Trantemento knowing each other, too.'

'Oh?'

Enzo nodded. 'A couple of hours ago,' he said, 'D'Aletto tracked down the stuff Roberto Roblino'd already given to the local museum. A suitcase full of it. Odds and ends, newspaper clippings, mostly. Apparently, they'd never even bothered to open it. I guess they get piles of crap like this all the time. It all goes down into a store room somewhere until, someday, maybe, if nothing else is going on, they get a summer intern or a student volunteer to go through it.'

Pallioti nodded. Provincial museums were like the nation's storm drains. Full of Pandora's boxes no one ever got around to opening.

'They did have the decency to be sheepish,' Enzo added. 'Admitted they took the medal for display, but they never even looked at the rest. Anyway, the citation is here. Or rather a fax of it.'

'The citation?'

Enzo nodded. 'That's right,' he said, rifling through a pile of papers. 'For the medal. And the nominating letter. Which was written by – *voilà*!' He pulled out two stapled pages.

'Giovanni Trantemento.' Pallioti did not even have to look.

'Correct. I'm afraid your Doctor Sachs was right on the money.'

Accepting the flimsy sheets of fax paper, Pallioti felt a jolt of sadness. This letter had almost certainly represented the high point of the old man's life. He had spent the last year refining his 'archive', and sent his most precious papers to a local museum that had never even bothered to look at them.

The letter itself was two pages on Giovanni Trantemento's letterhead. It appeared to have been written with a fountain pen. The copy was not bad, but the old man's hand had not been steady.

*

I, Giovanni Battiste Trantemento, do vouchsafe that I witnessed the following and that this account is true:

In February of 1944, I took part in an assassination attempt carried out by my GAP unit in Firenze. The proposed target was the German consul, Gerhard Wolf, and two high-ranking officers of the SD, the Sicherheitsdienst, Nazi intelligence police, who were visiting the city and would be attending a concert at the Teatro del Pergola. I was not told their names. I worked with three fellow GAP members from my own unit – a man known to me as Massimo, a second man known to me as Beppe, and a woman known to me as Lilia. I was known to them as Il Corvo.

In order to minimize civilian casualties, it was decided that the attempt would be made by means of a firearm rather than a grenade. Beppe and I would pose as coal merchants coming along Via Pergola while the man I knew as Massimo and the woman I knew as Lilia would pose as concertgoers attending the performance. They would arrive late, in order to get close to the consul and officers, who traditionally arrived after the general public was seated. The woman, Lilia, would carry an evening bag in which a firearm suitable for close-range targets would be concealed. Beppe and I would overturn our coal wagon in front of the car in order to make an escape by the consul and officers more difficult, and in order to create confusion, thus allowing Lilia and Massimo to escape after the shooting.

It had been very cold. On 14 February, the day in question, there was ice on the road and pavement, making it very slippery. Beppe and I entered Via Pergola from Via degli Alfani as planned just before four o'clock in the afternoon. A few minutes later, the consul's car approached from the opposite direction and stopped in front of the theatre. We saw the woman, Lilia, and the man, Massimo, approaching from the direction of Via M Bufalini. As we pulled the cart close, the consul and two German officers emerged from the car.

The cart was heavy and not easy to handle on the ice. As we began to pull it across the road, I heard three shots and shouting.

As planned, Beppe and I tipped the cart, abandoning it in front of the car and spilling the coal into the road. At that time I saw the woman, Lilia, running towards me. A shot was fired. She was hit, and fell. I helped her up and told her to run. Lilia ran towards Via Alfani, as planned. The German consul and one officer were unharmed. The second officer appeared to have been shot. Soldiers ran out of the theatre. I saw Massimo struggling with them.

It had previously been decided that after the shooting all of us should run in different directions. Since Lilia would have been seen firing the weapon, it was paramount that we do everything we could to facilitate her escape. We had previously agreed that, if arrested, Massimo would claim that he did not know Lilia, and had only met her walking to the theatre. Beppe and I would claim that we were merely delivering coal when our cart overturned on the ice.

In the event, although Lilia did escape, all three of us were arrested.

Massimo, Beppe, and myself were taken immediately to the Intelligence Headquarters, known as Villa Triste, at 67 Via Bolognese.

That night, we were interrogated separately. I saw Beppe and Massimo the next morning as I was taken out of my cell. I saw that they had been badly beaten, but they were able to communicate to me that they had stuck to their story. We were all interrogated again the next day. Then we were put in a cell together. The next day, we were told that we would be spared execution, and instead sent to a labour camp. We took this to mean that our stories had been believed.

By this time, I could not see because of the very bright lights that had been shone into my eyes during my interrogation and because of the beating.

Sometime after dark the next night, we were taken out of the Villa Triste and put into a truck. We guessed that we were being driven to the train depot. There was one guard in the back with us and one guard in the front with the driver. We had been driving for perhaps twenty minutes when the truck accelerated suddenly, then skidded on the ice and slammed into a wall.

At that moment, although he was severely injured from the beating he had received the night before, Beppe helped me to escape. The driver was stunned and the guard in the front was injured. Beppe got the tailgate open and helped me out of the truck. Normally we would have split up, all running in different directions. But I could not see. At considerable risk to himself, Beppe helped me to run down the street and into a park where we hid for several hours. Later that night, Beppe helped me through the city to a safe house. Without him, I would not have survived.

For verification, an account of this incident can be found in the records of the Villa Triste, and also in the later record that appeared in the Firenze CLN newspaper, Patria.

I hereby certify that the man whom I knew then only as the member of my GAP unit Beppe, is Signor Roberto Roblino and is currently known to me under that name.

Pallioti took his glasses off. For a moment he stood staring at nothing. He felt as if the past and the present had suddenly collided, mixed like the currents of two great rivers that sucked flotsam and jetsam under and bore it along – polishing it, hiding it, until it was ready to let it go, swirling it back to the surface six decades later.

Chapter Seventeen

10 June 1944

Spring came suddenly. But not before we endured a darkness that, in my worst moments, I thought would never end. I survived, I think, oddly enough, because of JULIET.

Her transmissions became an obsession. Or less the transmissions themselves, than the collecting for them. The counting. It became – as it is – an illness, a fever of the brain, akin to only turning left, or having to say good morning to magpies. Thirteen jeeps heading south. Fifteen tanks moving west. Twenty cans of fuel under the tarpaulin behind the church. Once the mania began, I could not stop.

Wheeling my bicycle along the Lungarno, I saw between the silver spin of spokes the rough patches in the road which meant that there were mines. I studied sandbags. I climbed to high places as the weather warmed, and, pretending to admire the view, picked out the snouts of guns. With my new eyes, I saw a city primed for death. Machine guns nested in the towers. Munitions were stacked in the thickets of the Boboli Gardens. I saw and counted them all. At night when I lay down, I mapped them in my head. I repeated the quantities – twenty-five of these, seven of those – until I was letter perfect. Until I could feed them to JULIET piece by piece.

As the nights shortened, the air raid sirens howled more frequently. Rifredi was hit again and again. Campo di Marte, Porta al Prato, and the theatre – our beautiful theatre. And then, one morning, the Allies changed. Instead of factories and stations and railway lines, they decided to have a day of bombing villas. I assume they intended to hit only those that had been sequestered by the Germans. Unfortunately, however, they lost their glasses again and made a mistake.

The villa that had been taken over as an evacuation centre for the children's hospital they bombed last autumn suffered a direct hit. I saw the Head Sister in the ward that night. The Red Cross had been informed, she said. The German consul swears that the Allies had been informed, as they are informed of the sites of all hospitals. To think of it now still makes me so angry I can barely write. I have to stop and twist my hands to keep my fists from clenching.

There were tiny bodies. Rubble, and fire. In the middle of it all, an old man grabbed my arm. He told me he was looking for his granddaughter. Then he burst into tears and told me his cat had run away and that all he wanted was to die.

Then, at the end of March, GAP attacked a column of German soldiers in Rome. Thirty-two were killed, and more wounded. The next night an announcement was made by the German high command. From now on, for every German killed, ten civilians will be executed.

My life, Issa's life, Mama's and Papa's lives, any man or woman you see in the street – it is official now. We are each worth one-tenth of a German.

It was about a month after this that we resumed the ambulance runs and I saw Issa again for the first time since February. Our 'parcels' were once more Allied POWs. I understood that we had to do what we were doing, that a choice is not possible, but looking into their faces as I bandaged them, turned them into victims of their own bombs, I felt laughter rising in my chest. Not happy laughter, but the laughter of insanity. Of madness – that we should rescue these men, so they may return and bomb us, in the name of freedom.

Il Corvo must have seen my face. He must have read something in my eyes. I had not seen him since the horrible night in December, since he watched me step into Dieter's arms. He was as quiet as ever, even more withdrawn, as if the winter had driven him back inside himself. When I looked into his face, behind his glasses I could not see his eyes at all. But when he placed his hand on my shoulder, it was oddly comforting, and caused the laughter to die in my throat.

He touched me again as we came to the checkpoint for the first time; a slight, steadying pressure on my elbow. I was prepared. I thought Dieter would be there. I thought I would have to look into his face. I thought I would have to smile and say his name. But in the end, I didn't. The soldier manning the checkpoint was a stranger, and he didn't seem to care much. He barely listened to my explanation about the monastery at Fiesole, about casualties and beds, glanced at the papers, and waved us through. Just before we drove under the raised barrier, he leaned down to the window. For a moment, my heart skipped. But all he wanted to do was warn us to douse our lights because of Allied bombs.

The shed was the same. Everything was the same, except it was spring and instead of bare branches and fallen leaves, the woods above the monastery were furred with green. It was twilight, and there was no need for a lamp, even inside. Issa and Carlo were waiting for us, as usual, and the moment I got out, took her shoulders, kissed her and came face to face with her, I knew. She saw it in my eyes, and nodded. Then she pulled me close and whispered, 'Don't tell anyone.'

'Does Carlo know?'

She smiled. 'Of course. But that's enough for now.'

I knew why she wanted it that way – she thought that if they knew she was pregnant they might try to stop her going over the mountains, try to prevent her from doing the thing she loved best.

We ran several more trips in May, and I saw Issa frequently. But with the men's clothes she had taken to wearing all the time by then it was impossible to guess, if you did not know, that Carlo's baby was growing inside her. They were rarely without one another. I almost never saw her alone. Every time we met, she seemed to me more radiant, more glossy and whole, and I felt again that we were like an hourglass. As my life diminished, as I felt myself wither and grow mean with fear and emptiness, Issa blossomed. She turned, like a beautiful flower, towards the sun.

Oddly, it was Il Corvo who seemed to sense what I felt. I don't know what he knew, or what he didn't, but there was something similar in us – a natural fugitive. As if we both had at our core a secret and undrainable little pond of fear that all the time we struggled not to slip into.

It was this sense that we could see inside one another, and recognize familiar territory, that made me ask him, one May night, about his sister. He had never mentioned them again, his sister and his mother, but I wondered if perhaps she also was younger, more beautiful, more blessed – if that was something else we had in common. And so I asked him. I asked first if they were safe, and he nodded. Then, emboldened, I asked if she was precious. I meant, like a treasure, or a jewel, that must be safeguarded. It was a stupid question, probably, and for a moment he didn't speak, and I didn't think he was going to. Then he said something very strange and probably true.

He said, 'It doesn't matter, because they are my family.'

He turned and looked at me, sitting in the front seat of the ambulance, and his face, his long strange face with his little round glasses, was different. What I saw in it was not fear, or love, but sadness. Which I suppose may be the same thing.

'They are my family,' he said again, as if that answered everything.

Later, I thought I would have liked to have asked him if that was what he meant – that in times like this the bond of blood reaches beyond love, beyond notions of sacrifice, or choice. But I never got the chance, because those were the last words Il Corvo and I ever spoke.

In late May, Issa came back into the city with the news that heavy fighting had broken out on the northern slopes of the mountains. The partisan group she and Carlo handed their 'parcels' on to, who call themselves the Stella Rossa, had heard that there was going to be a rastrellamento – that German and Fascist troops were preparing to sweep down on them and wipe them out. This time, however, instead of fading away, they chose to turn and attack. The Nazi-Fascists lost 240 men before they retreated. The Stella Rossa lost one.

The news was electrifying – and more so the next day when we heard that after four months, almost overnight the Allies had broken out of Anzio and were pushing the Germans north towards Rome. Even I was excited. Suddenly it seemed everything was splintering around us, like a great ice block breaking up. For the first time it seemed a real possibility that the Allies might be in Florence in a matter of weeks. No one thought any more about ambulance runs or smuggling POWs in coffins – which I knew Issa had been doing – or even using German uniforms to demand the 'transfer' of prisoners. Now, all anyone thought about was JULIET. Any piece of information, any titbit about a gun emplacement or the movement of a column, could be crucial.

In the days that followed, the German troops began to buzz like hornets. The Banda Carita seemed to be everywhere, and the bombing got worse. Finding places to transmit from, which was already difficult, became close to impossible. Then, on 5 June, Rome was liberated. The first European capital to fall to the Allies. The next morning, on Swiss radio, we heard of the invasion of France. That night, ROMEO asked us for anything and everything we could send.

Mama, Papa, Issa, Carlo, Enrico and I met at home. The men and Issa came one by one, after dark, slipping onto the terrace like shadows. The night was warm, but we did not dare to open the windows or the shutters. We sat in the kitchen, with the pantry and the cellar doors open, in case anyone came and they needed to hide, burrow themselves away like animals in their own home.

No one wanted to stay together for longer than necessary, and there was not much time for niceties. I did not even have a chance to whisper to Issa, to ask her how she is – although I saw Mama's eyes roving over her, deft as fingers, and I am sure she guessed. When Mama looked at me, I saw the question in her eyes, and had to look away. I was spared being Issa's Judas by Papa's hushed voice.

He pointed out that, despite my best efforts, it is getting harder and harder to find anywhere safe for JULIET. Using the same place twice is not possible, but every time we move, we take a risk. Papa paused and looked around the table.

Then he suggested that we gather everything we can – on the city, on the fortifications, on the railways and the mines and the power stations, and send it all at once. Make one final transmission before the Allies arrive. One final love letter from JULIET to ROMEO.

When he had finished speaking, there was a silence. Mama and Papa were at either end of the table. I was sitting next to Enrico. Carlo and Issa were across from us. We had not lit a lamp, and none of us were much more than familiar shapes, outlines in the half-dark of the summer night that crept through the slats in the shutters. I was looking at my own hands, folded on the familiar wooden slab where I had sat every day after school with Emmelina, and more recently, on nights when I came home, with Mama. Where I had given the poor Banducci child sweet tea and a biscuit. Where we had sat with those first POWs barely six months earlier and described to them a plan to save their lives with some gauze and an ambulance.

'We should vote,' Papa said.

I knew Issa was watching me. I could feel her eyes in the dark. Papa raised his hand. Then Enrico raised his. Then Carlo, and Mama, and finally me.

We sat there in the dark like good children in a school class. No one spoke. We waited, and waited. But Issa did not raise her hand.

Finally, Papa stood up and said, 'Well then, we have a majority. That's decided.'

And so it is. The date is set. Two days from now, on Monday, 12 June, ROMEO will be waiting. It was left to me to find the place, and I have.

The old lady who owned the house died a week ago. I have been watching it for the last four days. There is no question, it is empty. I've even been there myself – it's just off the Via dei Renai – in the morning, the evening, the afternoon. I let myself in. I walked through the rooms, looked in her closets and climbed her stairs.

It is an old house, with the servants' quarters downstairs and the family living rooms above: dining room, sitting room, and parlours. On the next floor there are bedrooms, and above that, an attic. I was prepared, if anyone challenged me, to tell all sorts of lies. 'She told me to find letters she had left for her family.' 'She gave me the china cat on the mantelpiece.' But the place is deserted. I have seen almost no one in the street. People are packing and fleeing. Going north, trying to get out of the line of the Allied advance.

I have not told anyone, even Mama and Papa, where we are meeting. I will give the address to Issa the night before. She will, in turn, tell those who need to know. It is because of the baby, I think, that she is wary as a fox. To me she mutters that meetings are dangerous. That all of us being together in one place is too risky. I know she is re-membering last February. But I have pointed out to her that even she said there were too many groups, too many people who did not owe each other enough, involved in that. This is different. I have tried to reassure her. There will be nine peo-ple, yes – but five of them are us, Carlo is the sixth, and the others are GAP members she has worked with through all of this. They have a bond of trust. And they are risking as much as we are.

I tell Issa this, and still she is not happy, but finally she has agreed that we have no choice. It is too dangerous to attempt several transmissions. Impossible, even. This will be our last. Afterwards, Enrico wants Mama and Papa to leave the city. I am trying to convince Issa that she must go with them. I will stay at the hospital, but she has more to think of now than herself.

I have been going home. Suddenly I want to sleep in my own bed. I walk through the rooms of our house at night. I memorize the shadows and the shapes of the trees in the garden. Yesterday, I arrived just at sunset and found Mama and Papa in the garden, digging beneath the cherry trees. When I asked what they were doing, they replied that they are getting the house ready, in case the Allied soldiers move into it. The glass and silver have been packed away in the attic. Papa has taken his favourite books and hidden them in the cellar. But Mama did not want to risk her jewellery that way, in case the house is bombed, so they decided to wrap it in oilskin and bury it. When I looked down, I saw that their hands were naked. No wedding rings. No aquamarine. Mama said it took a precious tablespoon of oil and almost an hour to prise it off her finger. A white band ran around Papa's wrist. The watch his father gave him when he turned twenty-one was gone. Mama looked up at me.

'What about you?' she asked.

I looked down at my own hand. Despite everything, I have continued to wear the engagement ring Lodo gave me.

'It will be safer here,' Mama said.

I nodded. Standing there in the warm honey

light, I slipped it off and handed it to her. She wrapped it in an oilskin envelope, stuck her trowel into the dark earth and began to dig.

Chapter Eighteen

Two days of meetings in Genoa caused the week to slip by almost before Pallioti noticed. Sunday dawned hard and bright. The rain that had dogged the early days of the month had retreated, leaving the air crystalline and cold. Deciding to book a table instead of cooking herself, Saffy had chosen a restaurant on the hill above the Boboli Gardens for lunch. Tucked behind one of the old villas, it looked out over the olive groves towards the *fortezza* and the pale sugar cube of the Medici villa. By 1 p.m. it was crowded; their group alone was made up of more than a dozen people.

Pallioti looked around him. There were several couples with children. A university professor, and a curator from a museum out of town. His sister sat across from him, Tommaso beside her in a high chair. Several other children, buoyed by cushions and phone books, peered across the table making faces and trading secrets. His brother-in-law was deep in conversation with a business partner, his greying curly hair bobbing as he nodded at whatever the other man was saying. Pallioti did not know any of these people well, and some of them not at all, but on Sunday, for a few hours, they were his family. Out of his suit and his habitual dark overcoat, he slipped in among whatever group Saffy had convened all but unnoticed, no one but her brother.

The antipasto had been devoured. In the lull between courses the conversation had shifted from the funding crisis in the arts to a general discussion on the merits of Sardinia as a vacation spot. Pallioti accepted another glass of wine and drifted, bobbing along on the waves of voices and laughter. He was half listening to a comment concerning something to do with a block of new flats when he looked up and saw Eleanor Sachs.

She was alone at a table in the far corner of the big room, her head bowed intently over a menu. The lack of a bottle on the table and the way the waiter was hovering suggested she had only just arrived. Today, she had forsaken her black polo neck for one of a russet colour. Her trench coat was hung on a coat hook at her shoulder. Her short dark hair had been ruffled by the wind.

As Eleanor Sachs put the menu down and spoke to the waiter, Pallioti felt a pang of guilt. In the big busy room filled with conversation and families, she looked very small and very alone. 'Excuse me,' he murmured to the woman beside him, and got to his feet. He could feel Saffy's eyes following him as he wound his way through the tables and crossed the room.

'Signora?'

She looked up, so startled that Pallioti almost felt the need to apologize as he extended his hand. Eleanor Sachs shook it gingerly, then smiled.

'*Posso?* May I?' he asked, indicating the chair across the table from her. 'Just for a moment?'

'*Certo.* Of course. I'd be delighted.'

She glanced across the room, her eyes darting to the big table by the window.

'Is that your family?'

He nodded. 'More or less.'

'How lucky.' She looked back at him. 'I mean, it must be nice. All of you being here together.'

Pallioti looked at the table, and saw for himself what it must look like. A large, affluent, happy group of people, talking and eating together on a Sunday afternoon in early winter. He'd never really thought of it that way before, but she was right. He was lucky.

Before he could think of how to phrase that, or whether he ought to at all, the waiter appeared with a bottle. He looked in confusion at the table. He had already removed the second place setting.

'I'm visiting. Just for a moment.'

'But you'll have a glass?' Eleanor Sachs smiled. 'I think you'll like this rather better than the grape cordial the other night.'

The waiter brought a second glass and pulled the cork. She was right about that, too. Pallioti put his glass down.

'Dottoressa Sachs,' he said. 'I owe you an apology.'

Eleanor Sachs had the good grace to appear surprised.

'You were right,' Pallioti said. 'About the salt—'

She smiled. 'So you didn't believe that?'

'And about Roberto Roblino and Giovanni Trantemento.'

The smile vanished.

'They did know each other,' Pallioti said. 'In fact, Giovanni Trantemento wrote the nominating letter for the awarding of Roberto Roblino's medal.'

'What?'

Pallioti nodded.

'They were in the same GAP unit. They worked together here, in Florence, in 1944.'

She shook her head, as if it was she who now didn't believe him.

'It's so strange,' she said.

Eleanor Sachs picked up her glass. Pallioti had not been sure, in the cafe the other night, what colour her eyes were. He had only noticed their shape. Now, in the daylight, they almost glittered, bright and vivid, caught between lashes as dark as her hair.

'It's just that – well, I told you.' She took a sip of the wine.

'He was kind of a windbag, poor old guy. You know, a boaster. I don't know why he wouldn't have just told me.'

'But he didn't?'

'Nope.' She shook her head. 'Absolutely not. He talked about all sorts of other stuff. You know, general derring-do, killing Nazis. But not that. Nothing specific about GAP. He certainly didn't tell me that's how he knew Trantemento.' She shrugged. 'I mean, I sort of suspected. But, go figure.'

'Well, his code name, for what it's worth, was Beppe. Giovanni Trantemento was known as Il Corvo. I don't know if that helps you at all.'

Eleanor Sachs put her glass down.

'Why are you telling me all this?' she asked. 'Not that I'm not grateful.'

Pallioti, who had begun to get up, sat down again.

'Because,' he said, 'I thought you'd like to know that you were right.' He smiled and began to get to his feet again. 'Perhaps,' he added, 'it will help you in your hunt for Il Spettro.'

'So, you still don't believe me about that?' A smile played across her face. 'It's all right,' she said. 'No one else does, either. Much less thinks he's alive and kicking and going around knocking off old men. I guess that would be too easy a solution? Death by ghost?'

Pallioti thought of the smudged crosses and the inky red lettering. The misspelt messages of hate.

'Perhaps,' he agreed. 'Now,' he said, glancing towards the front of the room where the children were being summoned back to their chairs for the next course, 'I really must return to my table.'

Eleanor Sachs held out her hand as he stood up.

'Thank you,' she said. 'You didn't have to do this. I appreciate it.'

When she smiled, she looked like a different person. The waif vanished, replaced by a pretty woman. He took her hand. The bones felt as fragile as a bird's.

'I hope it helps,' he said. 'And you'll let me know? If you prove me wrong and find Il Spettro?' Pallioti's smile transformed his face almost as much as Eleanor Sachs's transformed hers.

'Oh,' she laughed. 'You bet. You'll be the first to know. It's a deal.'

Pallioti had got halfway across the room, in sight of the plate of osso bucco that had been delivered to his empty place, when he turned back. Eleanor Sachs looked up. She didn't seem particularly surprised to find him standing beside her again.

'There is one thing.' He hesitated, feeling slightly foolish. She waited. 'I don't suppose,' he asked finally, 'in the research you've done on the partisans, that you've ever come across two sisters?'

'Two sisters?'

'Their name was Cammaccio. Caterina and Isabella. I think Isabella's code name was Lilia. They were here, in Florence.'

'Cammaccio?'

Eleanor Sachs thought for a moment, then shook her head.

'It doesn't ring a bell,' she said. 'No. Sorry. But I can check it out, I'm in the archives all the time. If you want?'

Pallioti gave a wave of his hand.

'Don't bother,' he said and smiled again. 'Really, it's not important.'

'Who was she?' Saffy leaned across the table and dropped her voice, the words coming out as a conspiratorial whisper.

'Who was who?' Pallioti smiled.

His sister grinned, plucked a breadstick off the table and broke it in two.

'No one,' he said. 'An American.'

'A very pretty American.' She handed the breadstick to Tommaso. 'Very gamine. Very Audrey Hepburn.'

'Very married,' Pallioti replied, and wondered why he'd

bothered. Laughter erupted from Leo's end of the table and rippled towards them. Pallioti smiled at his sister and shook his head. 'She contacted me,' he said, 'because she thought she knew something about Giovanni Trantemento. It was purely business.'

'Ah.' Saffy smoothed Tommaso's hair. 'And did she? Know anything ?'

Pallioti shook his head. Women, even his sister, were as tenacious as pit bulls once they got an idea in their head. Still smiling, he reached for his glass. 'No,' he said. Then he added, 'Well, that's not quite true. No and yes. I didn't believe her. I wasn't very pleasant. In fact, rather unpleasant. So I went to apologize. You see,' he shrugged. 'I told you. Nothing important.'

Saffy nodded. She was making an effort not to laugh at him. 'Then,' she asked, 'why did she leave after you spoke to her?'

'Did she?'

Pallioti looked up. A family was rising from their chairs. Several waiters flew by. Conversation and laughter reached a crescendo and fell again as the departing couple and their children moved towards the coat rack. Across the litter of plates and discarded napkins, he saw the little table in the corner. It was empty. The half-full bottle of wine and two glasses stood abandoned beside an untouched plate.

The crime scene tape that had festooned the landing outside Giovanni Trantemento's apartment had been taken down. The blood that had seeped under the door, meandering like a lost little river bearing the old man's life along with it, was gone. Scrubbed away. Lozenges of pale afternoon sun fell from the high windows and danced on the wide polished boards. Standing on the top step of the stairs, Pallioti could smell lemon oil and beeswax hanging in the still, chilly air.

Marta Buonifaccio stood outside her apartment door. She'd

heard him come in – in fact, had buzzed open the door when he rang her bell – and had sensed as much as seen him climb the stairs. She'd opened the door a crack, but hadn't come out until he was well out of sight, on the second or even third landing. She hadn't needed to check on him. She knew where he was going, and why. He'd come on a pilgrimage, like an explorer on a solitary voyage of discovery. And he'd come on Sunday, in the late afternoon, when the other occupants of the building were likely to be lingering over family lunches, or watching television, or asleep, because he wanted to be alone. Because he wanted to stand outside Giovanni Trantemento's door. To whisper the old man's name. Because he wanted to stretch his hand into the still, cold air, and try to feel what had happened.

'Dottore.'

He was wearing a suede jacket over a sweater and corduroy trousers. No tie with marzoccos. No gold cufflinks. Not that it mattered. Leopards didn't change their spots.

'*Buona sera*, Signora Buonifaccio.'

She had spoken as his foot hit the last step of the stairs. Now he gave a little bow. 'I'm so sorry to disturb you.'

That was another thing about men like this. They were unfailingly polite.

Pallioti stopped in the middle of the cavernous hallway. If it hadn't been for the lamp on the table below the mailboxes, and the fact that she had coughed, he doubted he would have seen her.

Marta Buonifaccio stood exactly where she had stood before, on the far side of the empty hearth. For a moment Pallioti felt as if he were playing the childhood game of statues. As if she might not have moved since the day Giovanni Trantemento died. She still reminded him of a Russian doll, so solid and compact that several people might be squeezed into her body.

She had dispensed with the headscarf. Wiry strands of grey hair framed her round face.

'I'm sorry to disturb you on a Sunday evening,' Pallioti said again as he stepped closer. 'But since you are here, might I take just a moment of your time? There was something I wanted to ask you.'

Marta's shoulders dipped and rose, a gesture that was almost half a curtsey. It reminded him of the maid in his parents' house when he had been a child. She had been a silent, almost ghostly girl. Someone, to his shame now, that he had barely even been aware of. She had polished silver and made beds and swept the stairs and always been there, until she had left. Her name might have been Anna or Angela, or – the truth was, he had no idea. Marta gestured towards the door of her apartment.

'Tea?' she asked.

Marta reached for the teapot. Like the cups and saucers, it was covered in a pattern of pink rosebuds. Pallioti wondered when they had last been used. He reached for his cup and tipped a dead bug out of it. He had come more or less on a whim, feeling the need for a walk after lunch, and had planned to stop for a grappa at his favourite bar on his way home. The truth was, he wasn't very keen on tea.

Marta's small round eyes glittered.

'Shouldn't throw away protein, Dottore,' she said, glancing at the bug. 'You look like you could use it.'

She cackled at her own little joke. If she had ever been shocked by Giovanni Trantemento's death, she'd obviously got over it. This evening, she seemed determinedly cheerful, as if she was trying very hard.

Pallioti wondered why. He had the impression it was an act. But perhaps he was wrong. Perhaps she was like this because it was Sunday. Or because the rain had finally stopped and the sun had been shining. Not that you would have been able to tell. The single window in Marta's sitting room looked out onto the alley. The opposite wall was so close you could probably reach between the iron bars of the grille and touch it. Even at high noon in the summer, light would barely penetrate. Originally these rooms had probably been used as storage, or possibly stables. And yet, although this was the least desirable apartment in the building by a long shot, tucked as it was behind the fireplace with a charming view of a wall, it would still be hard to come by at a reasonable price. In today's market it was difficult to buy closet space in a palazzo like this.

'This is delightful,' he lied. 'Have you been here for a long time?'

Marta paused, her teacup halfway to her lips. 'Forty-five years,' she said finally. 'Next week.'

'Ah.'

She regarded him over the rim of her cup, then answered the question he hadn't asked.

'It belonged to my husband's aunt. She was the building's caretaker.'

Pallioti nodded, feeling strangely chastened. He sipped his own tea. It tasted roughly the way he imagined rusty water might taste. He suspected it would make his teeth feel strange.

'I was hoping,' he said, 'that you might be able to help me with something.'

The smile again.

Pallioti replaced his cup carefully on its saucer, reached into the pocket of his jacket and produced a recent photograph of Roberto Roblino that Enzo had had copied. He laid it on the table.

'I was wondering if you'd ever seen this man?'

Marta replaced her cup on its saucer, and leaned forward. She stared for a moment, then shook her head.

'Are you quite certain?'

No smile. The glance she threw him suggested instead that it had been a stupid question.

'I am certain, Dottore.' She picked up her cup again. 'I have a very good memory for faces.'

Pallioti believed her. Suddenly, he wished he had a picture of Eleanor Sachs.

'Who is he?' she asked.

'Was. He's dead.'

Marta did not look as if she found this particularly surprising.

'He was a friend of Signor Trantemento's,' Pallioti added. 'His name was Roberto Roblino. Does that sound familiar to you?' he asked. 'Did Signor Trantemento ever, perhaps, mention him? An old friend, from near Brindisi?'

Marta shook her head.

'Signor Trantemento didn't mention much. His shopping. Occasionally, the rain.'

'Old friends?'

'No.'

'Roberto Roblino? Please try to remember. Did you ever see it on a letter? A return address? A postcard. From the south?'

Marta put her cup down.

'Signor Trantemento did not get postcards.' She studied him for a moment. Then she asked, 'Does this have to do with the girl? The American?'

'Doctor Eleanor Sachs?'

Marta shrugged. 'Dark hair. Coat like a spy. In the movies. *Casablanca*.'

'Yes, that would be right. Did you speak with her?'

She nodded. 'The once. I told her he was dead. Questions, questions.' She looked at him for a moment. 'I told her to ask you.'

'To ask me?'

'I gave her your card.'

'My card?' So, that was how Eleanor Sachs had got his direct number.

'*Certo*,' Marta said. 'That's what it's for, isn't it? She was lost,' she added.

'Lost?' Pallioti put his own cup down.

'Not like that, Dottore.' Marta smiled. 'I didn't tell her anything and I never saw her again,' she said a moment later. 'As for him—' She pushed the photograph of Roberto Roblino back towards him, sliding it with the tip of her thumbnail as if the glossy paper might be toxic. 'I've never seen this man. He never came here. If he put an address on an envelope?' Marta shrugged. 'I don't know. I didn't see it. Signor Trantemento didn't have friends, and I've never heard this name before.'

Pallioti took the picture and slid it back into his pocket. For the second time in a week he was being dismissed by an old lady. Grateful to abandon the tea, he got to his feet. She edged past him to open her apartment door, pulling the locks back.

Marta Buonifaccio's hand was not as elegant as Signora Grandolo's, but her grip was, if anything, stronger. As he dropped it Pallioti realized with a jolt that the two women, on first glance polar opposites, were in fact rather similar. It was something about their eyes, the directness of their gaze. The way they held themselves.

'The war,' he said, stopping suddenly. 'Were you here? In the city?'

Standing in her doorway, Marta looked down at her feet. Today she was wearing lace-up sneakers. They were pink and had small green dots on them. She considered them for a moment. Then she shrugged.

'Where else was there to go?'

'But you didn't—' The question suddenly seemed ridiculous. 'You didn't know Signor Trantemento, back then?'

There was a pause. Somewhere on a landing above a door closed. The smell of onions drifted down the stairs. Marta glanced up. Then she said, 'No, Dottore. I did not know Signor Trantemento then. I never laid eyes on him until he moved into this building.'

'But did he talk about it?' Pallioti asked. 'Did he ever say anything at all, to you? Or to anyone else you know of, about his experience in the war?'

Marta Buonifaccio looked at him for a long moment. She appeared to be studying his face. Finally she said, 'No. No, Dottore. Even when he got his medal, Signor Trantemento never said a word.'

Chapter Nineteen

June 1944

The morning began with a silver sky. I left the house early, coasting on my bicycle down the hill, feeling my hair blow back and listening to the morning sounds of the city that seemed almost normal around me. The high cheeping of swallows, the clack of shutters being thrown back. The roll of wheels in the street. It is strange to say now, but I was happy. More than that, I felt almost a sort of elation, the kind of excitement that makes you feel as if fireworks are going off inside you – makes the world vivid and beautiful, every detail standing out clearer than you have ever seen it before.

Rome had been liberated. The Allies were coming. For the first time since September, I actually believed that the war was nearly over.

As I neared the old woman's house, I slowed down. I turned and rode along the empty street, checking that the shutters were as I had left them the day before, that the overturned geranium pot was still on the doorstep, soil spilled as if by accident, so anyone coming to the front door, anyone standing on the step to open it, would have to leave footprints.

Nothing moved as I rode by, and nothing appeared to have changed. I went on nonetheless, careful not to pause – not to look as if I was looking – and left my bike two streets away as I had planned, then walked back, cut down the alley, and let myself in by the scullery door. For the next hour, I walked through the rooms. I had already cleared the dining-room table so we could lay maps out. I found a broom and swept the front step. I went up into the attic and checked the window again. When Papa arrived in mid morning, strolling, a newspaper tucked under his arm, I opened the front door to him with a little curtsey, as if the house were truly mine. The maps were rolled in his paper. We laid them out, smoothed them on the polished mahogany, so we would not get anything confused. When we were all assembled, there would be nine of us. Nine reports of roads, munition dumps, power lines, railway switching boxes. The city had been divided into sectors, as had the areas beyond, especially the roads running south and west that the Allies would use. We were each responsible for a different area, so it was important not to get muddled, not to get confused. The maps would be marked before the transmission so that when we finally made it, it could be kept as short as possible. Mama arrived next, carrying JULIET, bearing her along in a suitcase as if she were just another once-fashionable lady who had been bombed out and was dragging her belongings from place to place across the city.

The others came one by one over the next few hours, mostly through the scullery, which I had told Issa would be open. As each person arrived, Papa took their information, and marked it onto the maps. Issa appeared after lunch. I saw her out of the window, walking down the street in a skirt and blouse, her short chestnut hair glinting in the sun. She made a point of smiling, idling slowly, as if she were just another pretty girl on a summer day. Carlo was with her. She held his arm. They came to the front door, a young couple paying a call. As they reached the step, Carlo leaned down and said something to her and she laughed.

Enrico was last. Then we were ready. We all stood in the dining room, clustered around the table as if we were having an odd sort of party, checking that everything we had was marked – that nothing that might help ROMEO had been forgotten, that no mistakes had been made. JULIET had already been taken up into the attic. Finally, Rico and Papa went up to turn her on. It sometimes took a moment to tune her, for her to find a signal. I was listening to them, to the creak of the floorboards and the sound of their footsteps on the attic stairs, when I heard the growl of engines and the screech of brakes.

We were still in the dining room. I was looking at Issa. She knew at once what it was. I saw it in her face before I understood it myself.

There was the sound of running feet on the pavement outside, and shouting. A shot was fired. Issa ran to the table. She grabbed the maps, darted to the window, and threw them out, while the men scrambled for the attic, or for the back stairs to the scullery.

LUCRETIA GRINDLE

Then they burst in, screaming.

Mama was magnificent. She demanded to know what they were doing breaking into our house. But it didn't work. They pushed her aside without even looking at her. By this time, Issa was shouting, and I was shouting too. I don't remember what I said – something stupid, something about private houses and thugs. None of which made any difference. It took them only moments to find the attic stairs.

I had unlatched all the windows, made sure the shutters would open, and although the attic window was very small, I think a couple of the boys almost got out and onto the roofs. But 'almost' doesn't count.

They marched them down and past us. Papa's glasses were crooked, falling off. He looked at me, and at Mama, who was holding Issa by the shoulders. Enrico was behind him, and then some of the others. Carlo was last. Until that moment, there had been hope in Issa's eyes. As they marched Carlo through the dining room, he shouted her name, and they hit him.

The others, the ones who had run for the scullery door, they trapped like rats in the alley. Then they took us, me and Mama and Issa. Finally it was our turn to live the story we had heard repeated so often in the last months.

There were two guards with us. As I climbed into the truck one of them took my hand to help me up. I looked at his fingers, and the scrape on his knuckles, and then up into his face with the mad idea that it would be Dieter. That somehow I would be able to talk to him, tell him this was all a mistake, offer him something that would make

298

him let us go. But of course it wasn't Dieter. The
boy was tall and skinny and a stranger. And despite his gun, despite his uniform, when I looked
into his eyes they were as terrified as mine.

We drove through the city. The men were not
with us, it was just Issa, Mama, and me. We said
nothing. Just clung to the rough wooden planks,
pressed our faces to them and saw people who
looked up, or looked away, or hung their heads
and hurried on, their bodies bowed with fear.
Once, Issa looked at me.

'Where will they take us?' I whispered. I knew
the answer, but I wanted her to say something,
anything, else. To the train depot. To the women's
prison at San Verdiana. But she didn't. Instead,
she mouthed the two words, 'Villa Triste.'

That first night, Issa and Mama and Papa and I
were kept together in a room upstairs. We could
hear noises, footsteps, all night long. From time
to time, someone looked in on us, but no one
would tell us what was happening. They didn't
seem to care about us, and for a few hours I
thought they might just forget us, might open
the door and let us go. I knew Mama was thinking the same thing, and Papa, too. The only person who was not thinking it was Issa, and so I
tried not to look at her, not to read what I saw in
her face. It was not cold, but we huddled very
close together, as if we could make ourselves disappear, or somehow become one and never be separated. Then, in the morning, they took Papa
away.

He was taller than both of the guards who
came for him. In his rumpled summer jacket, still

wearing his tie, he stopped and looked back. I saw his long face, the lock of greying hair he was not free to push away. Behind the lenses of his glasses, the blue of his eyes. He smiled at us. Then the door closed, and he was gone.

Issa and Mama and I were put in a cell in the basement. As soon as we got there, Issa changed. She was sure the others were close to us. She took off a shoe, and kept tapping on the wall with the heel. And for the whole day, and most of that night, and some of the next day, taps came back. Then they stopped. And that – that terrible silence – was more frightening than anything.

I thought Issa was going crazy. When the tapping stopped, she became like an animal, pacing and prowling. She screamed and banged on the door, demanding to know what was happening. But despite the fact that they had brought us down and locked us up, no one seemed very interested. They came in once or twice, and asked us some questions – stupid things we pretended not to know – then left. But they wouldn't tell us anything, and I don't think they cared what we said. They had already decided that we were just stupid women who did not matter.

Then, on the third day, they took Issa away.

I clung to her. I screamed at them. I thought they were going to kill her.

'I love you, Isabella!' I shouted. And as they led her away, even after they had slammed the door, as she went down the hall, I could hear her shouting back.

After that, Mama and I sat without speaking. Mama put her arms around me. From time to time, she smoothed the hair away from my forehead. She looked into my eyes, and I felt it again, the thing that binds us, the new thing that, in this horror, we have found – a love that flows between us without words.

Issa came back perhaps two or three hours later. The door opened, and she just walked in – wasn't shoved, didn't stumble.

Mama jumped up, and so did I. We threw our arms around her. We pulled her close to us. We asked her if she was hurt, if she was all right – but the moment I felt her body next to mine, I knew she wasn't. She held herself stiff, straight and hard, and she would not look me in the eye. I put my mouth close to her ear. I whispered to her that I was a nurse, that if they had done something – something like that, to her – I would understand. I could help her. Mama asked her, too. But Issa wouldn't say anything. She just shook her head and despite our pleading, said nothing at all.

All that night, she sat beside Mama, holding her hand. From time to time, she smoothed Mama's hair. She ran her fingers across the back of her wrist. Down her cheek. I watched, and the sight scared me. Because I had held Donata Leone's hand in much the same way. I had smoothed her hair. And it had done no good at all.

The next day they took Mama away.

The silence after the door closed felt as if it would go on forever. Then, finally, Issa looked at me. She did not cry or even frown. Her face was blank. It was filled with an emptiness I had never seen before. She was alive. She was breathing, she was sitting beside me. But her eyes were dead.

'What?' The word came out of my mouth in a breath, in a thought.

Issa nodded.

'I had to wait until Mama left.' She was whispering. She looked at the door, then back at me. And then she told me.

They didn't rape her. Or beat her. Or even question her. In fact, they didn't talk to her. She said she was demanding, shouting, asking over and over again what was happening. What had happened? Where was Carlo? And Papa? And Rico? What had they done with them? But they didn't answer. Or even acknowledge that they had heard her. Instead they marched her upstairs, and she thought she was going to be questioned, or see Papa, or Carlo. That they might show her their broken bodies or the broken bodies of the others to try to make her talk. But instead, they took her out and put her in a car, with an officer from the SD – the Sicherheitsdienst, the SS intelligence corps – not one of Carita's thugs, sitting in the back beside her. The driver was SD, too. Although they said almost nothing, ignored all her questions, both of them were very polite. Very correct. They drove her up into the hills.

They didn't seem to care that Issa saw where she was – there were no curtains on the windows of the car – and she was sure that meant they were going to kill her. When they stopped and told her to get out, the driver coming around and opening the door as if he were a chauffeur, she thought they would order her to run, then shoot her. She was ready, she said.

But they didn't do that, either. Instead, they walked her into the woods, down a path.

It was beautiful. Speckled shade. Sun falling through the beech trees. Birds singing and that smell, warm earth and the furred scent of leaves, that means it's summer. They went for perhaps a mile. Again, very polite, very considerate, not forcing her to hurry. Finally they came to a clearing. The view stretched back to the city. At first she didn't know why they had stopped. Then she saw the trench.

The SD officer took her arm, almost gently, and led her to the edge.

Papa and Enrico appeared unmarked. She said they looked almost peaceful because they had been shot in the back of the head, given a neat single bullet. But not Carlo. He had a hole in his forehead. She kneeled down, she tried to reach out and touch it, to cover the hole in his face with her fingers. But the SD officer wouldn't let her. He held her by the shoulders. Then he told her that the others had all done as they were told, but that Carlo had refused to turn around. He had refused to look away when they shot him.

The others were underneath. Issa saw legs, arms, shoes, hands, all in a jumble. They'd been made to dig the trench themselves. The spades were still there, stuck in the earth.

Issa stood up and turned to the officer. She asked him to kill her. She begged him. He smiled at her, almost as if he had expected it. Then he gave a little bow, like a perfect gentleman, and told her that the German Reich did not kill pregnant women. After that, he took her by the arm and marched her back to the car.

After she told me, Issa stopped talking again. She just sat with her back to the wall and said nothing at all. When they came to give us something to eat, I asked where they took Mama. They wouldn't tell me, but it is San Verdiana, I hope. Mother Ermelinda, who runs the women's prison, is very kind. She is sympathetic, and a good nurse. Mama left us believing Papa and Enrico were alive. That was what Issa wanted.

The next night Issa and I were put on a train. Now we are in some kind of warehouse in Verona with probably a hundred other women. Some are dying. Some may be dead. Some have been tortured and I have tried to help them, but I have nothing to help them with. We barely have food, and nothing of our own, just the same clothes we have been wearing – which is why I still have this book. They took my watch, but they never checked the hem of my jacket.

In the days that have passed, I have thought and thought of that house near the Via dei Renai. I was the one who chose it, so the mistake must have been mine. I was so careful, or I thought I was. I've gone over and over it in my head to see what I did or didn't do. I know it's there, the mistake I made, but I can't find it. When I think back, I see everything. The shutters. The unlocked scullery door. The upturned pot, the spilled earth. I play them over and over again in my head, every step of the visits I made. I was so sure. I thought I was so careful. I was even proud of myself. But I was not careful enough, that's the only answer. It is my carelessness that killed Papa and Rico and the others. My carelessness that has taken Mama, and cost Carlo his life, and broken

Issa's heart, and brought us here. To this godforsaken human warehouse.

∽

Digging his hands in his pockets, Pallioti thought he had
walked down this street a hundred times. Perhaps two hundred.
Three. There was a restaurant here where he sometimes ate. A
bar where he had been known to have a grappa.

The lower half of Via dei Renai faced the Piazza Demidoff,
a small rectangle of greenery where sad-faced old men sat on
benches and talked to their dogs. A row of stone palazzos
looked out through the winter trees onto the river. Four centuries ago, they had been built by the great and the good. Sixty
years ago, they had been lived in by families. Now their lower
floors were almost entirely taken up by discreetly fashionable
restaurants and trendy cocktail bars. One, facing the park, was
a hotel.

It was barely 9 a.m. The morning, which had not been warm
to start with, seemed colder. The top of the street closed in on
itself, narrowed until the buildings faced each other like dancers
in some renaissance ritual, identical and po-faced. There had
been a frost overnight. Thin patches rimed the paving stones,
turning the shadows white. Pallioti walked slowly. He was
nearly at the end of the pavement when he turned abruptly,
and found what he was looking for.

Set into the wall, the plaque was not large. He must have
walked past it countless times without noticing. There were
plaques on walls all over the city. Everyone knew they were
there, but no one ever actually stopped to read them. He
thought of the machine-gun nests Caterina had counted so
carefully, the metallic snouts she had seen everywhere, once she
knew how to look. In the towers. In the thickets of the Boboli
Gardens. She had learned to see death wound round with vines
and flowers. As he would learn to see plaques set into walls.

Reaching up, he ran his gloved fingers over the engraving.

12 June 1944
In Memory of the Members of Radio JULIET
Who From This Place
Carried on the Brave Fight for Freedom and Justice
In the Face of Nazi-Fascist Oppression
Their Memory and Courage Shall Live Forever

A small iron bracket, similar to the ones often found in grave-
yards, was mounted next to the stone tablet. It was newly
painted, a discreet grey. The glass tube that rested in it held five
white roses. A condolence card hung from their raffia cord. Pallioti turned it over and saw the words, Remember The Fallen.

PART FOUR

Chapter Twenty

'Yes. Yes, Ispettore. You are correct, of course. We are guilty as charged.'

A ripple of laughter came down the phone.

'It's one of the little chores we take upon ourselves – to keep the flowers fresh. On the memorials. It's an irrelevance, I suppose. But then again, one finds that most of the important things in life are, don't you think? And of course it's nicer, for the city. There's nothing worse than dead things, all dried up. Or, God forbid, plastic.'

'*Certo*,' Pallioti murmured.

He held Signora Grandolo's card in his hand, turning it over and over. She was as polite as ever, but was probably wondering why the city paid his salary. He looked out of the window. He had taken her at her word, called on a whim. Perhaps, he thought, simply to hear the sound of her voice – the sound of a voice of someone who cared. Or simply knew what had happened.

The bright weather of the day before had held, although it was distinctly colder. Sun lit the piazza below. Pallioti blinked.

'Of course,' Signora Grandolo added, 'it's a particularly horrible story. Radio Juliet. Then again, I suppose the stories behind all of the plaques are horrible. Or else they wouldn't be there.'

'No,' Pallioti murmured.

He was watching the fountain. The arch of water sparkled and glistened. Beyond it, outside the restaurant, a few people sat determinedly huddled in overcoats at the outside tables, sipping coffee and trying to read the newspaper in gloves.

'I don't suppose you know—' he heard himself asking, 'or rather, if you have any information on any of them? Or their families—'

'From Radio Juliet?'

Pallioti sensed as much as heard the shift of tone in her voice. The laughter was gone now, replaced by a sober quietness.

'No, I'm sorry,' Signora Grandolo said. 'None of them survived. That was one of the things about it that made it so awful. Of course,' she added, 'it was a hazard with the radios. That the signals would be traced.'

'Yes,' Pallioti said. 'Yes, of course.'

He realized that he could have blurted out that this was not, in fact, what had happened. That the transmission had not even begun, that they had only just gone up into the attic – Enrico and his father and Carlo – that they probably did not even have the set turned on before there was the screech of brakes in the street, running footsteps on the stairs.

'I understand,' he added, 'that there is another monument?'

He did not bother to explain that it had taken him the better part of a frustrating half-hour online to find the very obscure municipal website that mapped Florence's monuments and plaques to its dead.

'That's right,' Signora Grandolo said after a moment. 'There is. Another monument to Radio Juliet. Up in the hills.' She paused. 'You see,' she added, 'after they were taken to the Villa Triste, they were shot. Executed.'

In the piazza, the three flags snapped and danced. The tablecloths at the restaurant fluttered and jumped, trying to escape the clips that held them down. As Pallioti watched, a waiter came out. One of the people lowered a newspaper and spoke to him. It was a woman. Her short dark hair ruffled in the wind.

'Ispettore?' Signora Grandolo said. 'I'm sorry, I didn't mean to pry—'

With a start, Pallioti realized that she had asked him something, and he had no idea what.

'No, no,' he murmured. 'Not at all.'

Holding her paper down with one hand as she spoke to the waiter, the woman sitting outside the restaurant turned up the collar of her coat. Pallioti squinted. He was sure it was Dr Eleanor Sachs.

'You hadn't mentioned it,' Signora Grandolo said. 'When we met before. So, I didn't realize you were interested in Radio Juliet?'

'Some research.' Pallioti turned away from the window. 'Just something I came across. The story is, so, well—'

Signora Grandolo sighed, rescuing him.

'Horrible,' she said. 'Yes, it is horrible. I suppose that's why the flowers matter – at least to me.'

'This other monument—' Pallioti was looking at his desk, but instead he saw Issa and Caterina's father – a university professor, a man of dignity – his face naked without his glasses, his son beside him. Below them, a tangle of arms and legs. Beside them, Carlo, Issa's archangel, the father of her unborn child with a bullet hole in his forehead because he would not turn around. 'I don't suppose you could tell me where it is, exactly?'

'*Certo*,' Signora Grandolo said. 'Of course. It's—' she paused, then she said, 'Well, since you're interested – I do go up there, to change the flowers. I could— But, well. You would probably rather go alone. Enthusiasts are a bore, I know. And—'

'No,' Pallioti replied quickly. 'No, not at all. I'd be very interested. To come with you. If that's what you were suggesting, if you would show me.'

'Oh.' Signora Grandolo sounded genuinely surprised. So much so, that it occurred to Pallioti that she had not meant to invite him at all.

'Forgive me,' he said, 'if you didn't mean—'

'No, no,' she said quickly. 'Of course I did. I'd be delighted. To have the company.'

'When,' he asked, 'were you thinking of going?'

He heard her flip a page, of a diary or a calendar.

'I'm free,' she said, 'this afternoon. Or, if that—'

'That would be fine.'

'Very well,' she said. 'Shall we say one o'clock? I find,' she added, 'that it's sometimes easier to get away when everyone is at lunch.'

⁓

Signora Grandolo's car, a large black Mercedes, was significantly more impressive than the police pool vehicles assigned to Pallioti. It was more impressive than anything that transported the Mayor. If Enzo Saenz ever got behind the wheel he'd probably have to be prised out with a lever.

'I used to have an Alfa.' She glanced at him out of the corner of her eye. 'But the truth is,' Signora Grandolo said, 'it was uncomfortable. Old bones,' she added. 'The Germans make very comfortable seats.'

Looking at her, it occurred to Pallioti that he had no idea how old she was. He had heard that you could tell a woman's age by the backs of her hands, but he had no idea what that meant, and Signora Grandolo was wearing gloves. In dark woollen trousers, a matching roll-neck sweater, and what he thought Saffy might call a 'car coat', she looked even more elegant than she had before. There was no doubt about it. Maria was not a fluke. The Grandolos were beautiful women.

She glanced in the rearview mirror. Two long white boxes rested on the back seat of the car.

'I hope you don't mind,' she said, as they slid out into the traffic. 'But I have one other stop to make, on the way. We go right past a school that was used as a collection point, before loading people on to the trains. It will only take me a minute.'

Pallioti shook his head. 'Not at all.'

Leaning back in the seat, which was indeed very comfortable, he experienced the unfamiliar, and in no way unpleasant, sensation of letting someone else make the decisions. He realized that he had no real idea where they were going – 'up into the hills' could cover a multitude of sins – or how long they would be gone. Nor did he care. He had slid out of his office past Guillermo's empty desk – Signora Grandolo had been right about lunch – taken the side elevator and escaped again through the service door. Then he'd backtracked into the piazza and caught a cab at the rank, amusing himself, childishly, with the idea that if the loitering reporters had just looked the right way they would have seen him.

But of course they hadn't. Because people only looked where they expected to see something. The juvenile glee at 'pulling a fast one' had lingered as the taxi pulled away. He'd even considered turning off his mobile. He'd settled for vibrate. If Enzo called, it would jump in his pocket like a bed bug.

The school was an ugly brick building ringed by a wrought-iron fence. It was not more than a couple of blocks from the station. As they parked, Signora Grandolo followed his gaze and nodded.

'They were efficient,' she said. 'You have to hand them that. Just a few minutes' walk. Not much chance to get away between here and the trains.'

She killed the ignition and looked towards the school building.

'This was bombed, actually,' she added. 'Most of this area was. It wasn't completely full at the time. But over a hundred people were killed.'

She opened her door. Pallioti got out as well. He took the box she indicated from the back seat and followed her as she passed through the iron gate and into the paved school yard.

The ugly metal-framed windows were bolted closed against the cold. Even so, they could hear children inside, the rustling and twittering of voices.

A simple marble column no more than a few feet high, the monument was set on a grey stone plinth a few feet from the front door. As they got closer, Pallioti saw that it was engraved.

In Memory of Those Who Were Taken From This Place
Never to Return
Martyrs in the Struggle for Freedom Against Nazi-Fascist
Tyranny
They Will Not Be Forgotten

The old arrangement of lilies was wilted and dead.

Pallioti bent and picked up the faded bouquet. Bright-yellow pollen dusted the grey marble and speckled the sleeve of his coat. He watched as Signora Grandolo opened the white box and lifted out a new arrangement of pale-pink lilies. She brushed away a dead leaf and placed the flowers carefully at the foot of the monument. Then she stepped back.

'Half the blooms will probably be gone by tomorrow.'

She took the old arrangement out of Pallioti's hands, placed it in the box and put the cover back on.

'But,' she added, 'at least they don't graffiti it. Or they haven't. Yet. I've always thought,' she added, 'that really, they should have carved every name of the people who passed through here, on the column. I thought it would be good for the children to see that – names just like theirs, even if they only walked past them twice a day. But, of course, we couldn't. There were too many.' She looked at Pallioti. 'It's one of the more perverse things,' she said. 'At least I think so – that they kept such complete records. Listed every single person who walked in or out of the prisons, or the Villa Triste. That was the SS headquarters. Of course,' she added, 'no one ever walked out of the Villa Triste. They were marched or carried.'

Behind them, a harassed-looking man angled a bicycle through the gate. He nodded to them as he manacled it to the rack beside the wide glass doors, carefully removing the front wheel and so many other pieces that by the time he was finished it looked like a skeleton.

'Really, I suppose I should thank them,' Signora Grandolo went on. She pressed the top down on the box and shrugged. 'The Nazis. For keeping such excellent records of who they killed. Without them we would have been quite lost.' She turned back towards the car. Pallioti held the gate for her.

'Did they lose many?' he asked. Then he realized it was a stupid question. How would you know who was lost? Roberto Roblino, for instance.

She glanced at him, opening the Mercedes' boot and placing the box inside.

'Surprisingly few,' she said. 'They didn't really make mistakes. The SS. Or the Fascists, for that matter. They didn't misplace people.' Then she smiled and added, 'At least that we know of. Of course if they did—'

'And if you knew about it, they wouldn't be lost.'

'Ah,' Signora Grandolo smiled across the roof of the car as she opened the driver's door. 'The Mayor warned me, Dottore,' she said. 'You really are more than just a pretty face.'

The small road they took out of the city wound rapidly uphill. Apartment blocks gave way to modest villas, and then to straggling woods. Unlike the hills that led to Fiesole or Settignano or Arcetri, where Saffy lived, this area was not fashionable. It had frequently been used in the past as a graveyard for the stripped carcasses of stolen cars, and worse. If he looked back Pallioti knew he would see, not a panorama of dreaming spires, but the squat boxes of factory warehouses and the columns of apartment buildings. The big car purred. A truck hurtled down past them. Pallioti glanced over his shoulder as its horn squawked and saw it narrowly miss a taxi climbing behind them.

Unfazed by the increasing steepness, the curves, or the occasional hurtling truck, Signora Grandolo drove steadily, with both hands on the wheel. Through the passenger window, Pallioti watched the hill fall away, taking the shoulder of the road with it. Trash, plastic bags and bottles, scattered among skinny trees. Through their bare winter limbs, he saw a glint of metal, an upside-down shopping trolley half submerged in the dark water of a stream. When Isabella was brought up this road, there was almost certainly no rubbish – no plastic or valuable shreds of scrap metal. The trees would have been in leaf and the water would have been nothing but a bright thread, a flash of silver playing hide-and-seek in the sunlight. She had thought she was going to die, be told to get out and run. She'd told Caterina she had been ready. He wondered if she had decided to go down, towards the water, or up, to her mountains?

As if in answer, the road twisted, then straightened. The big car accelerated, and for a second the horizon was filled with jagged peaks, their teeth sharp and white against the pale winter sky.

The Borgo, where they eventually stopped, was nothing more than a cluster of dark stone houses, a bus stop, and a tiny church set back from a widening in the road. Signora Grandolo parked beside what might once have been a fountain, or perhaps more likely a watering trough. Across the street there was an old shuttered building that looked as if it had been a coaching inn, a last chance to change horses or get a bed for the night before starting the long trip over the mountains and down to Bologna.

Pallioti lifted the second white box off the back seat of the Mercedes. Signora Grandolo locked the car, and started to lead him across the road. They stopped as the taxi that had been behind them chugged into view, its engine straining with the climb. It slowed as if it were going to stop, then disappeared around the next corner. The sound of its engine died. There was no noise from any of the houses, no ringing of telephones or chatter of lunchtime voices. The wind blew a plastic cup that danced in front of them, escorting them towards a narrow opening in a high stone wall that had a small yellow arrow of the kind hikers use stencilled on it.

As they got closer, Pallioti saw the ghostly letters of the old inn's name bleeding through a thin coat of dirty whitewash. *Il Buon Riposo*. The Good Rest. He wondered if the SS had a sense of humour.

The old drovers' path was narrow and cobbled. Beyond the wall it led steeply downhill for a few yards before twisting across the slope and evening out. Here the trees were older, their branches more generous, as if they were remnants of the primeval forest that had once crept down to the city. Beech and chestnut leaves rustled under foot. They walked in silence, Signora Grandolo apparently as absorbed in her own thoughts as Pallioti was in his. She obviously knew the path well. The sound of her boots didn't falter on the worn stones. Pallioti wondered what shoes Isabella had been wearing. Had she stumbled and been righted? Helped by the strong hand of the officer who was holding her arm, polite to the last, proud of his treatment of pregnant women?

The monument stood at the side of the clearing. It had been kept open, the narrow stumps of saplings recently cut back. In the spring, the slope below it would be an undulating wave of green, new growth transforming even the scraggy litter-ridden forest they had driven up through.

The old bouquet had been rained on. The ribbon was bedraggled. Brown threads of rot ran through the unopened ivory buds of the roses and wilted the white trumpet faces of the lilies. Putting the box down, Pallioti picked up the dead flowers carefully and moved them aside while Signora Grandolo removed the lid and lifted out the new arrangement.

This one, too, was white. Its bow was crisp, the buds tight

and creamy. She laid it at the base of the simple gravestone and stepped back. There was no sign now of the trench, or of rusted spades. No echo of shots. Just the words:

Caduti per Italia
Radio JULIET
15 *Guigno,* 1944

They walked back slowly. Pallioti carried the box with the old bouquet in it. As they climbed the final slope back towards the high crumbling wall, Signora Grandolo turned to him.

'Thank you,' she said. 'For coming with me.'

'It's been a pleasure.'

That shouldn't have been the right word to use, on a grey chilly day, visiting a memorial, but it was. Signora Grandolo was good company, not least because she had little difficulty in keeping quiet. Companionable silence, Pallioti often feared, was something of a lost art.

He looked at the box in his hands. A piece of bedraggled white ribbon had escaped. There was a card dangling from it. The name of the florist, printed in discreet gold letters, was one of the most expensive in the city. Signora Grandolo reached over, plucked it off, and tucked it into his coat pocket.

'For your lady love,' she said, smiling. 'I recommend roses. Every time. Tell them I sent you.'

Seeing the expression on his face, she laughed. 'Oh, it's an extravagance, I know, for the living. And for the dead, an irrelevance. At least that's what my daughters say. But they indulge me. It's one of the perks of being very old. And of being a banker's wife.'

'I'm glad you do it.'

Pallioti thought of the five pale, perfect buds, like dots of snow, against the hard stone wall of the building in Via dei Renai. Of the lilies, their tiger faces opening to children who ran back and forth through the shiny glass doors of the school.

'I'm glad someone does,' he added.

'Yes.' She looked at him for a moment. Then she said, 'Yes. So am I.' And led the way through the gap in the wall.

As they stepped onto the edge of the road, an engine growled on the hill above. Out of sight beyond the corner, it surged and coughed as the driver shifted gears. Signora Grandolo stopped by the old inn, waiting. Pallioti joined her. As he did, he looked instinctively towards the Mercedes, parked in front of the church across from them, and saw something pale move in the porch.

He looked again. The church door, which had been closed when they arrived, was open. A figure was standing just inside. A woman in a belted coat.

Pallioti felt a flash of anger. He was about to step forward, stride across the road, when a truck, a big eighteen-wheeler, snaked through the corner. The gears ground again as it straightened out, tarpaulin flapping, and gathered speed, juddering past the front of the Albergo Buon Riposo. Looking down, Pallioti realized that Signora Grandolo was holding his arm.

'What is it?' she asked.

'It's—' He shook his head as the truck passed, the sound of it withering down the hill. When he looked again, the church door was closed. The porch was empty except for shadows. 'It's nothing,' he said. 'Really, nothing at all.'

Chapter Twenty-One

2 July 1944

I became obsessed with finding out what day it was. I counted on my fingers, trying to understand how much time we had lost in the Villa Triste. I wanted to know what day Papa died. I wanted to know when I last saw Mama, but every time I thought I had worked it out, that it was a Friday, or a Sunday, or a Wednesday, it slipped away from me, ran like water through my fingers. So, finally, I asked a guard. They come when they feed us. I chose an older boy – they're all boys, but some are barely more than children, and they make me nervous, because they are afraid and clutch their guns. I simply stepped up to him, and smiled as if I was still pretty, and said in my best German, 'Excuse me, please. But could you tell me what day it is?'

It was absurd, really. We might have been on a crowded street. Or in a cafe. I might have turned, held out a cigarette, and asked him for a light.

For a moment, he looked so startled that I thought he was going to hit me – or issue an order for me to be dragged away, shot there and then for daring to speak to him. Then he made a little bow, and said, 'Donnerstag, Juni, zwanzig-zweitens.' Thursday, twenty-second of June.

I wanted to run away. I wanted to snatch this morsel and scurry back to my cot, hoarding it so no one could steal it from me. But I didn't. I was very careful. This time, I didn't make a mistake. I said, 'Vielen Dank.' Thank you very much, as polite as could be. Then I turned, and walked away slowly, and did not look back.

When I sat down I was shaking, coddling this tiny piece of civility, holding it like a moth in the cup of my hands, feeling the flutter of its wings and trying not to crush it. Finally, I turned to Issa. She was sitting with her back to me, holding a piece of bread that had been handed out in the line.

'I know what day it is,' I whispered.

She did not turn around. I leaned close to her, smelling the hot, sharp smell of her skin – there is little water here, not enough for washing.

'It's Thursday, the twenty-second of June.'

I gave it to her like a gift, but she didn't even look at me. I was so angry I didn't speak to her for the rest of the day.

It was a few days after that that the new women arrived. They were not more than a handful, twelve or fifteen. They came late at night. Doors opened. There was the sound of feet and some shouting. I had been dreaming – the same dream I always have now, of my own footsteps, slapping on the pavement, walking too fast towards the house on the Via dei Renai. Sometimes Mama is

with me. Sometimes Carlo. Sometimes they all
follow me in a line, blindly, as I lead them down
the street, and turn a corner, and see – not the
house, nor even the open scullery door – but a
clearing in the woods. And spades. And a trench.

My heart juddered as I sat up in the dark.
There was light near the open door. Then it went
away and in the silence that followed, I could feel
other eyes, many of them, like mine, staring into
the dark towards the figures that stood there.
They huddled together, and suddenly reminded
me of the trip Papa and Mama had taken us on
when we were children, to Venice. There, in the
corner of Saint Mark's, Papa had shown us the
sculpture of the Turkish soldiers, all huddling together, terrified because they found themselves
in an enemy city.

The women moved, finally. They crept to a corner and lay down on the floor. Even though there
were empty cots, they did not claim them, because they did not know where they were supposed to be and which would be safe to take.

In the morning, we crowded around them.
They looked stunned and very dirty, even more
dirty than we are. But they had news. They had
been moved from a prison outside Livorno, where
there had been very heavy bombing. On the way
to the trains all they saw was rubble. It looked,
one said, as if a monster had come, gnashing
through stone and brick, destroying anything
that lay in its way. We formed a cordon around
them, keeping out the women we do not trust,
those who hand out the food for the Germans,
while they whispered, telling us they had heard
that the Allies were somewhere south of Siena,

that the line was inching forward, that the Germans were being pushed back but only with massive effort. There was heavy fighting. And terrible stories. Of all the divisions, none are feared more than the Hermann Göring Division, and any of the Waffen SS, and the Fallschirmjäger – the Hunters who Fall from the Sky. Women and children have been herded together like sheep, and shot. Bodies have been hung from lamp posts. Half a village that had sought sanctuary was burned alive in a church.

Even when they finally stopped talking, we refused to leave them alone. We made them repeat everything. We peck, peck, pecked at them, like hens starving for kernels of news.

Issa did not join in. She lay on her cot and merely blinked when I told her what I had heard.

This went on for two more days before I understood – and when I did, I was so ashamed of myself. I did not see what was before my very eyes. And I should have. Because I have seen it before.

Last winter, in the hospital, we had more and more people, usually women, who would stop eating. Who would just sit and stare. Or hug themselves and rock. At first, we would try to make them move, stand them up and make them walk, up and down the halls, or around and around the cloister. Some got better. Some began to look about, to ask a question, respond, reach for a spoon or a cup of water. But others didn't. And finally, the Head Sister made us move them. She ordered beds to be set up in a cramped little room of their own, behind a closed door, where no one could see them. When, with another nurse, I protested, she listened to us. Then she fastened us with her small dark eyes and asked us which we thought was more dangerous. The Germans, the influenza, or despair?

She looked at us. 'You are too young to understand this,' she said, her voice still hard. 'But despair, that is what will kill you faster. More efficiently than the flu. More completely than a bullet. And it is contagious. Very contagious.' She shook her head. 'You think me cruel,' she said, 'I know. You think me far from God. But I cannot risk hopelessness spreading through my patients.'

So they were locked away, out of sight. Amongst ourselves we called their room the corsia degli perduti. The ward of the lost.

Now I looked at Issa and saw what I should have seen before.

That night, there was soup. There was cabbage in it, and some potato, and it was even warm. I had to stand in line for a long time, and I could only fill one cup. The woman with the ladle didn't look at me, her eyes didn't look at anything as she slopped it over my hand and over the rim. I turned away, then I stopped and bent to lick the back of my hand. I looked at the soup in the cup. In three swallows I could have drunk it all. Issa wouldn't care. She didn't want it anyway. I took a breath, then I held the cup carefully in both hands and walked back to her.

She was sitting up, on the side of her cot, staring at nothing. I sat down next to her.

'Here,' I said. 'It's good. It's even warm.'

She didn't move.

'Take it, Issa. Please.' I could hear the wobbling of tears in my voice. 'If you don't eat, you'll die,' I whispered.

She turned and looked at me.

'Good,' she said. And I slapped her.

The soup spilled onto the mattress. The cup clattered to the floor. My palm hit her cheek so hard and fast her neck snapped.

'You!' I jumped to my feet. 'You are the most selfish person who has ever lived! I didn't want to be a hero, Issa,' I said. 'I did it for you. Because you asked me to. I'm here because of you, and you can't even be be bothered to try to live. You have everything!' I shoved my face down, so close to hers that our noses were almost touching. 'You have a baby,' I hissed. 'Don't you think that I would give my left arm, my life, to be carrying Lodovico's baby?'

She stared at me, her eyes wide, but I couldn't stop.

'Carlo died.' I spat the words at her. 'Yes. But at least you had a chance to be with him. And he did everything he could to keep you alive. Who do you think told them you were pregnant? This is how you repay him? By letting his child die? He saved your life, Issa. You don't know what love is!'

I whirled away from her but she caught me by the hair. Even without eating, even in despair, Issa was stronger and quicker than I was. She yanked my head backwards. She was reaching, trying to claw at me, when two other women pulled us apart.

'For God's sake, for God's sake. You'll get us all in trouble, stop it!'

I was shaking. Tears poured down my face. One of the women put her arm around me, she pulled me away. When I looked back, I saw some-one else pushing the cup aside and snatching the piece of potato.

Huddled, turned in on herself, curled like a snail in its shell, Issa cried all that night. But the next morning, when I brought her a piece of bread, handing it to her without speaking, she ate it.

That night, a woman died. No one knew until the morning, when it was light and she did not move. Did not get to her feet to jostle for water. They took her body away. I didn't know her name. No one did. And to be honest, no one really cared. Be-cause something was happening.

In the afternoon, they lined us all up and called out our names. I was terrified that they would begin to split us up, march us away – suddenly that awful place seemed preferable to any number of other awful places. We could at least cower here until the Allies came. Surely, I thought, they must be in Florence by now. Must be about to burst and spill over the mountains. I grasped Issa's hand. She was standing beside me. Then I felt a flood of relief, because they weren't splitting us up. Instead they called our names, then pinned little triangles of cloth to our clothes – on our shoulders, like medals. Yellow, red, black. Anyone who took hers off – anyone without one – would be shot.

When they had gone away again, we compared them all, trying to understand what they meant. Someone said yellow was for the Jews, and that seemed to be right. Red was rumoured to be for political prisoners. No one knew what black stood for. Issa and I were both red.

They came for us the next day, at around noon. We knew when it was because we could hear the bells. They lined us up, four abreast in our tatty, filthy clothes, like some kind of beggars' brigade, and told us we were marching to the train station.

The guards were pleased with themselves, you could tell. They had shined their boots for the occasion and they shouldered their rifles as if they were having a parade – marching about in their idiotic step, barking orders and pointing their guns at a miserable group of half-starved women. I told one, who looked about seventeen, barely old enough to have fur on his chin, that his mother, wherever she was, was ashamed of him. I think he would have hit me if we hadn't started just then.

I had Issa by the arm, because although she had begun eating again, she was still not strong on her feet. I was afraid that if she stumbled or fell, she'd be trampled. Or shot.

'Stand up,' I whispered. 'Stand up and stay close to me.'

When we came outside, it was raining a little, not enough to make us clean, but enough to make it cooler than before. They marched us over the Ponte Nuovo, and down the Via Stella towards the forum. Despite the drizzle, on both pavements, either side of the street, there were crowds. They were silent, just staring, so quiet all you could hear was the tramp of feet. I don't know if they were ordered to be there, or if we were entertainment, like a circus, or animals in the zoo. Perhaps they felt a sense of relief, seeing us. Or perhaps even gratitude, because any one of us could have been one of them, but wasn't. We marched on past those blank faces, a brigade of Judas goats.

Then, as we got close to the forum, something happened. There was some kind of disturbance. The street is narrower there, and Issa and I were towards the back, so I couldn't see, but there was shouting and our little parade slowed, then stopped completely. This upset the guards. Anything that isn't planned upsets them. An officer started to bark orders, and one of the soldiers near us ran forward. And that was when I heard the sound – the mewing hiss men make in the street – and looked sideways, and saw them.

They were two men standing in the crowd, at the edge of the pavement. One was rather grubby, in workman's overalls, and the other was wearing a suit. They beckoned. It wasn't much, just the tiniest motion of a hand, but I saw it.

I don't remember the message getting to my brain. I don't remember a voice in my head that said, 'run!'

But that's what I did.

I had Issa by the elbow and the wrist, and with both hands, I dragged her.

I didn't think. It was four, five, six steps. And I was waiting for the moment – for the crack and the blackness. But it didn't come. Instead, I saw shoes, legs, arms. As we reached the pavement, they parted, and surrounded us, and pushed us down and backwards – parcels passed hand over hand, into the crowd.

When we were upright again, coats had been shoved onto us. The triangles had been ripped off – I saw a tiny scrap of red under my shoe that someone bent down and grabbed.

It all happened very fast, and in silence. Lire notes were stuffed into my pocket. A hat was jammed on my head. I was still clutching Issa's hand when someone shoved me hard from behind and hissed, 'Go.'

Chapter Twenty-Two

Pallioti sat at his desk, the result of enquiries he had set in motion the day before in front of him. In proper secretarial fashion, Guillermo had collated the material and placed it in a neatly labelled file. Pallioti opened it and looked at it again. He drummed his fingers. Then he stood up and walked to the window. It was just past noon. The flower seller's buckets were bright smears of colour in the grey of the piazza. He could see people eating in the restaurant across from the fountain.

He thought about the two old men who were dead. Two weeks ago, Giovanni Trantemento had opened the door of his apartment to someone who had apparently walked unchallenged into the building. Several days later, Roberto Roblino had done the same thing – opened the door and let someone into his house. 'Someone' who had probably been known to him – had possibly even been expected. 'Someone' who appeared so completely unthreatening that he had allowed, possibly even invited, them to walk straight in.

Pallioti returned to his desk, snapped the file closed and snatched it up.

Guillermo took one look at his boss's face and kept his head down as he passed through the outer office. The guard at the cafeteria service entrance started to say something – good afternoon, or a comment on the weather – then thought better of it. The wind kicked as Pallioti stepped out into the alley. It might have been chilly without his overcoat, if he had slowed down long enough to think about it, but he didn't.

Pallioti crossed the restaurant's deck in three strides. He wove through the outer tables, and pushed open the door, feeling the rush of food-scented warmth. Inside, he paused just long enough to take in the fact that she was seated at the far end of the long room, at the last table by the window. Which had a perfect view not only of the police building, but also of the taxi rank. Anger rose in him. Waving away the owner, who had scurried towards him, he strode between the tables.

Just before he reached her, Eleanor Sachs looked up, her mouth a startled 'o'.

He slapped the file down, rattling glass and silver.

'Tell me—' Pallioti leaned over, bearing down, his voice barely louder than a murmur, 'Tell me,' he said, 'exactly why it is that I shouldn't arrest you this moment, and take you across the street and charge you with the murders of Giovanni Trantemento and Roberto Roblino?'

She stared up at him, her cheeks paling.

'I suggest you make it good, Doctor Sachs,' he added. 'Because I am in a very, very bad mood. You have approximately one minute.'

She opened her mouth. Then shook her head.

'I didn't kill them,' Eleanor Sachs said. 'I've never killed anyone. I told you, I—' She swallowed, nodding towards the file. 'What is that?'

'That,' – Pallioti put his finger on top of the file and pushed it towards her – 'that, Doctor Sachs,' he said, 'is a complete – no, probably not complete – list of the lies you told me.'

They stared at each other. Then Pallioti sighed.

'Honestly,' he said, straightening up. 'Did you honestly think I wouldn't find out?'

She shook her head.

'I don't – I don't know. I suppose I didn't think. I just – I needed to—'

She ran her hand through her hair, causing it to stand up from her forehead, making her look like an unruly teenage boy. 'I didn't kill anyone,' she said again. 'I didn't. I couldn't. I wouldn't even know how.' She let out one of her strange little barks of laughter. 'Please,' she said, looking up at him, 'you have to believe that.'

Pallioti sat down in the chair opposite her.

'Why,' he asked, 'should I believe anything you say?' He reached for the file and opened it. 'Nothing – not one thing you have told me so far has been true.' He glanced up at her. 'Your name,' he added. 'That appears to be correct. And you do appear to teach at Exeter University, along with your husband, one Robin Sachs. But that's about where it ends, isn't it?' He pulled out the first page and perused it. 'Let's see,' he went on, 'let's start with what you teach. Not history. Not social history. Not Italian or even European History. How about the history of literature? Petrarch is your speciality. With a little Dante thrown in. The only book you've ever written concerns rhythm patterns in medieval and Renaissance poetry. No one's ever heard of any work of yours concerning the partisans.' He looked up. 'No folk history, Doctor Sachs. No collecting stories. Apparently the only ones you specialize in are the ones you make up.'

She shook her head.

'That's not true. I—'

Before she could continue, Pallioti cut her off.

'No?' he snapped. 'Well, how about this, for being true? You didn't arrive in Italy a week ago, as you told me. You arrived over three weeks ago. You flew from Bristol via Charles De Gaulle to Naples, on Air France. You landed at approximately three o'clock in the afternoon on Wednesday, 18 October. After which, you collected a rental car.' He closed the file and put it down. 'I don't know where you went immediately after that, but I presume you drove south. Because I do know, Dottoressa Sachs, that on the night of 21 October, the following Tuesday, you checked into the Locanda Azzura in the town of Ostuni where you stayed for approximately three nights. Ostuni,' he added, 'is what? A twenty-minute, thirty-minute drive from Roberto Roblino's house?'

Eleanor Sachs reached for her water glass, but didn't pick it up.

'Are you,' Pallioti said, 'honestly asking me to believe that you didn't go and see him again?'

She shook her head.

'Yes. No.'

'Which is it, Doctor Sachs? I suggest,' he added, 'that you think very carefully before you answer.'

'Both.' Eleanor Sachs looked at him. 'It's both,' she said. 'You're right. I tried to go see him. I did. But I couldn't reach him on the phone. So, finally, I drove to the house. He wasn't there. I saw Maria Grazia, the housekeeper, instead. She told me he'd gone away, to Taormina, that he wouldn't be back until the following week. I couldn't wait that long. I – I'd arranged to meet my husband in Positano for a long weekend, that Friday. Then I was going to Rome, and then coming here. I thought—' – she ran her hand through her hair again – 'I thought,' she said, 'that I'd just go back and see him. Later, before I finally left.'

'Why?'

'What?' She looked up at him.

'Why?' Pallioti asked again. 'Why did you want to see Roberto Roblino again?'

'Oh.' Eleanor Sachs nodded, as if she was having trouble following what he was asking. 'Right,' she said. 'The birth certificate.'

Pallioti looked at her. What was it Saffy had said? That Eleanor looked like Audrey Hepburn? Who was also Holly Golightly. Who'd been a liar, too.

'His birth certificate,' she said. 'I wanted to ask him about it. About where I could find a copy of it. About where he'd grown up.'

'Why?'

Eleanor Sachs didn't reply.

'Why?' Pallioti asked again. 'Why do you care, about Roberto Roblino's birth certificate?'

'Because,' she said finally, 'I don't think he is who he says he is.'

Pallioti leaned back in his chair.

'Maria Grazia—' She looked at him. 'The housekeeper, she says – I got to be friends with her – she says he never, ever talks about his past. Signor Roblino. Nothing specific, anyway. Just vague stories about the partisans. She says he has never once mentioned his parents, or where he grew up or if he had brothers and sisters. And there's no evidence of him,' she added, 'nothing that I can find, before he returned to Italy in 1957. Roberto Roblino just doesn't exist. It's like he fell to earth, aged twenty-something, in Madrid. That's why I was so surprised—' – she looked at Pallioti and shook her head – 'by what you told me in the restaurant, on Sunday. It was the first evidence I'd heard that he was really here.'

'Did you follow me there? To the restaurant?'

It was not the question he meant to ask, but it came out anyway. She looked down at her plate, ran her finger over the tines of her fork. A waiter approached and hovered. Pallioti waved him away.

'Did you follow me?' he asked again. 'To the restaurant, and yesterday?'

'Sort of.' She looked up. 'I'm renting a cottage. I told you. It's near the restaurant. I walk around there, a lot. Up near San Miniato and down the hill. I saw you. I saw your group go in. I wasn't going to. I walked on. Then I turned around and came back and, yes. I guess I followed you.'

Pallioti leaned back in his chair, watching her.

'And yesterday?'

'Yesterday, yes.' She looked up. 'Yes. I saw you get in a taxi, out there, in the piazza. And I got in a taxi, and I followed you, and that woman. Up to the monument for Radio Juliet.'

'Why?' Pallioti asked. He leaned forward. 'I don't understand, Dottoressa Sachs. Why would you follow me?'

She sighed and looked down again. The dark top of her head was tousled. For a moment, she reminded him powerfully of his sister. When Saffy was thirteen, on the anniversary of their parents' death, she had run off from school and been picked up by the police in a bar in Genoa. It was the only naughty thing she had ever done. The conversation he was having with Eleanor Sachs reminded him painfully of the conversation he had had that night with Seraphina.

'Because,' Eleanor Sachs said.

Even the answers were the same.

'Because? Because what? I don't understand, Dottoressa. Why would you want to follow me?'

Today she was wearing no make-up, no lipstick or mascara. Under the tousled hair, her pale heart-shaped face looked both very young and very old at once.

'For the same reason that I made contact with you in the first place,' she said. 'Because I thought that maybe, if I could get close to you – if I could follow you, maybe you would lead me to—'

She looked at him, her eyes pleading.

'Il Spettro,' Pallioti said. 'You thought that I would lead you to Il Spettro. Is that it?'

She nodded.

'Because you think Il Spettro killed these two old men? In what? Some sort of partisan revenge vendetta? And that if you told me about him, I would go off like a hound on the scent, and lead you to him?'

Eleanor Sachs didn't answer.

'Dottoressa,' Pallioti wanted to reach out and take her hand, but didn't. 'Il Spettro does not exist.'

She shook her head.

'I'm sorry,' he said again. 'He doesn't exist. He never did.'

'He does,' she said. 'I know he does. He has to.'

'Why?'

She swallowed.

'Because,' she said, 'because I think he's my grandfather.'

Eleanor Sachs had taken a tissue out of the large black bag looped across the back of her chair and was wiping her eyes and blowing her nose. Pallioti gestured to the hovering waiter. He ordered two grappas. He waited until the small glasses had been placed in front of them, then he said,

'All right. Now. Why don't you start at the beginning and tell me?'

Eleanor Sachs picked up her glass. Today, her fingernails were painted a pearl colour. They reminded Pallioti of the milky shells of baby whelks. Or of kitten claws – translucent, and unexpectedly sharp.

'I grew up in Cleveland. In case you don't know, that's nowhere.'

'It has a very good symphony orchestra.'

She smiled.

'I guess. We didn't go. Anyway, my parents – well no, my Dad was Italian. My Mom left us when I was little. She remarried, and I stayed with Dad. And he used to tell me – he used to talk about Italy. And about the war, and what happened. And the partisans. He used to talk a lot about the partisans. All these stories. About the stuff they did. About the Garibaldi Brigades, and how they fought the Germans, and the Fascists, and ran escape routes. All that stuff. But mostly about the escape routes. He talked about that a lot. About what happened here, in Florence – and how there was this one famous guy, the Ghost – Il Spettro – who got lots and lots of people out and who the Germans could never catch.'

She shrugged and sipped the grappa.

'I didn't think about it when I was a kid. You know, you don't. My Mom left us when I was little. I grew up with my Dad. He still spoke some Italian at home, and when I got to college, that's what I majored in – Italian literature and language. Then I remembered all this stuff, so I asked him again, and he told me his mother told him. I never knew my grandparents, they died when I was really small. But he told me his mother told him all these stories, about the partisans, and Florence, and Il Spettro.'

'His mother?'

She nodded.

'That's right. You see, his Dad wasn't his Dad. I mean, he was, but not really. My father always knew that. My grandmother married my grandfather here, in Italy. My grandfather – well, the man she married, her husband – was working with the Allies in the south, and she married him and he brought them out to America. A lot of people who worked with the Allies were given the right to repatriate. But the man she married wasn't the father of her baby. Do you understand?' Eleanor Sachs looked up. 'She had the baby, my Dad, before they were married. He was someone else's. My Dad found out sort of by mistake. An old army friend of his father's let it slip, after his father died. His parents never told him. I asked him once why he thought that was.' She smiled. 'He said, he guessed they didn't think it mattered. He always thought of his Dad as his real Dad. He adored him.'

She shrugged, fiddling with the stem of her glass.

'Anyway, I came here to do graduate work.' Eleanor Sachs glanced up, a smile flitting across her face. 'On Petrarch. With, as you said, a little Dante, a little Boccaccio on the side. But I kept thinking about the partisans and those stories and I thought, why would my Grandma talk like that? Why would she tell my Dad all those stories, how would she even know about them, and in such detail? Unless she knew who Il Spettro was, and had a reason for telling him.'

Pallioti could see the jump coming.

'So you thought she was telling him about his real father?'

Eleanor Sachs nodded.

'I think she wanted him to know. But she didn't want to hurt her husband, or her son – damage their relationship. That's why she never told him his father wasn't his father. But all the same, she wanted him to know, wanted him to be proud. Of who he was. Where he came from. What his people had done.'

Her eyes searched Pallioti's face.

'Do you see?' she asked. 'Does that make any sense to you? And now that he's gone, that my Dad's gone, I want to know. More than that. If my Grandpa's still alive, I want to find him.'

'Even if he'd killed Giovanni Trantemento and Roberto Roblino?'

Eleanor nodded.

'Even if he's killed them.' He noticed she used the present tense, refused to hear what he had told her. 'It doesn't make any difference to me,' she said. 'If he's alive, I want to know.'

'And tell me again, why did you think Il Spettro killed them?'

She shrugged.

'I don't know. Because I was asking about him, I guess. I just had this feeling. Like I was getting close. That sounds crazy to you, doesn't it?'

Pallioti sipped his grappa and said nothing. Feelings often sounded crazy to him. He had them all the time. He was saved from commenting on the fact by the sound of Eleanor Sachs laughing.

'You know,' she said, 'it wasn't really until the sixtieth, until all the celebrations and the medals, until I saw all those old men, that it really occurred to me that he might still be alive, and that if he was, I'd better find him before he died. Before that it was just a research project. You know, kind of fun, in my spare time, when I got sick of the Middle Ages – like, hey, isn't this interesting? There are archived interviews,' she added, 'that you can find on the web. It was kind of a game. Like I was looking for clues, in a half-assed way.'

Pallioti glanced up at her. 'And did you find any?'

'No,' she said. 'But I kept nosing around, in my spare time. I started to pick up threads, about Il Spettro. All sorts of stories. Mythologies, really. Obviously some of them are pretty wild. Derring-do with the Nazis. And then,' she shrugged, 'honestly? My husband's right. It became kind of an obsession. My Dad got sick. I'd taped the medal ceremony, from TV. I started watching it over and over to see if any of them, those old guys, looked like me. Or my Dad.' She toyed with her glass. 'I guess I wanted to give him that,' she said. 'I guess I thought it would be so great, you know, if I could find his father for him, before he died.' She shook her head. 'I didn't. But afterwards, I couldn't just stop.'

She finished her grappa and dropped her hands on the table

'It's about ruined my marriage. My husband says it's ridiculous. For a grown woman.'

For the first time, Pallioti noticed the white band on her left hand, a marking on the skin where a ring would have been.

'I guess you Europeans don't do that,' she said. 'It's kind of an American obsession, isn't it? Genealogy.' She shrugged. 'I guess it's a legacy of the melting pot. Wanting to know who you are. As if it makes any difference. Anyway,' she smiled. 'Now I've made an ass out of myself. I am writing a book,' she added. 'Really. And it is about the partisans.'

Pallioti nodded. Eleanor Sachs laughed again.

'Do you believe me?' she asked.

'Yes,' he said. It was true. Despite a strong hand of, admittedly circumstantial, evidence to the contrary, despite the giant shoulder bag she lugged around that was more than big enough to keep several pounds of salt and a sub-machine gun in, despite the fact that she had all but stalked him and lied through her teeth to him, he did believe her. Now. He drained his glass and signalled for the bill. The lunchtime crowd was coming in.

'You should know,' Pallioti added, as they waited, 'that the investigation is running in a very different direction. It doesn't appear to have anything to do with the partisans.'

'No ghosts, huh?' Eleanor Sachs sounded sanguine, but Pallioti doubted she believed him. Obsessions, in his experience, did not roll over and die quite so easily.

'I have a proposition,' he said.

She glanced up and raised her eyebrows.

'Of the most innocent kind, Signora. I will do a deal with you.'

'A deal?'

'Yes. If you agree to stop following me – which I promise you will lead you nowhere in any case – I, in turn, will promise that if I find out anything that might lead to Il Spettro, or the idea that he even existed, I will let you know.' He looked at her, and held out his hand. 'Do we have a deal?'

Eleanor Sachs seemed to consider it for a moment. Then she reached across the table.

'Deal,' she said.

Chapter Twenty-Three

10 October 1944

I began to walk. Slowly. My legs were shaking. I could feel Issa's hand, her fingers entwined in mine as we jostled in the crowd. There was shouting in the street. Even if I could have seen over the shoulders and heads, I don't know if I would have dared to look. I didn't dare do anything except stare straight ahead. I could hear the tramp of footsteps. The miserable parade we had, until a moment ago, been part of, had been restored to order and had begun to march again.

'This way.'

I had not quite been aware of it, but we were being led, guided by a tall blonde girl in a fashionable suit. She smiled as she shouldered past a group of men, then turned and caught my eye.

'In here.'

I saw that she was pushing open the door of a restaurant. The gold-painted letters shimmered on the glass. We stepped through and the world closed behind us. Ahead was dark wooden panelling and white tablecloths. My foot faltered.

This time it was Issa who pushed me, gently, her palm in the small of my back. The smell of food very nearly made me ill. My head was swimming. Surely, I thought, the other diners would look at us and see. Our filthy hair was hidden under the hats and our dirty clothes under the coats, but surely they would see in our faces, in our eyes, where we had come from. I don't know if they did or not, because none of them looked up. They looked at each other, or intently at their plates. Cigarette smoke hung in the room. There was the clink of glasses, and of silver on china. Suddenly I was afraid that I was going to cry.

The girl led us to a round table in the back corner. She chose the chair facing the door, indicating that we should take the seats with our backs to the room, but no sooner had she sat down, than her face changed. The bland smile that she had been wearing vanished.

'Don't.' Issa grabbed my hand under the table as I started to look over my shoulder. She squeezed hard. 'Pretend you're talking to us,' she said. And then I heard, the flat, hard sound of German-accented Italian. The mispronunciations, the slight guffaw at the end of words, as if not only we, but our language too, were a joke.

Three soldiers had come in. I saw them out of the corner of my eye. They swam into sight, brushing rain off the sleeves of their jackets, laughing, taking out cigarettes and passing them around.

The girl leaned towards us, her smile full of false animation, as if we were nothing more than old friends sharing gossip.

'There's a powder room,' she said. 'By the side of the bar and to the left. Talk for a minute, then get up, slowly, and go there. Lock the door. I'll come for you.'

I glanced at Issa. I could see the tiredness in her face, a sort of fragile exhaustion, as if suddenly all of this had become too much for her and at any moment she might shatter. I reached out slowly, took two of the bread rolls from the silver basket on the table and slipped them into my pocket. Then I stood up.

'Come,' I said, forcing myself to smile and holding my hand out to her. 'Come and keep me company.'

I could feel one of the soldiers watching us, feel his eyes as surely as a hand on the back of my neck. I knew that if I turned around his eyes would meet mine. I took her arm, bending my head low to hers as if we were whispering girlish secrets. We skirted the bar and pushed through the door into the back hallway.

After we had locked the door, we washed our faces and ran our fingers through our hair. There was soap. And a towel. We scrubbed our hands. Then we put the hats back on, and sat on the side of the sink and ate the bread rolls, waiting for the sound of footsteps in the corridor. When they came, they were not the girl's, but a cook's, an older woman from the kitchen. She beckoned to us without speaking and mouthed for us to hurry. I wondered whether we should follow her, whether it was a trap, but Issa pushed me, so I went. The cook led us down the corridor and through the kitchen. No one looked up as we passed. At the back door, a priest was waiting.

He led us through the back streets, and into a

church. There was a blanket for us to share. Despite the fact that it was summer, the vestry was chilly. He left us, locking the door. There was one window, high up. We sat against the damp wall, and watched the light vanish, and listened to the bells as they marked the offices of the night – Vespers, Compline, Matins – then finally, at the first glimpse of dawn, Lauds. It was just after Prime when they came for us.

The local GAP in Verona wanted to talk to Issa. It was then, watching her, and seeing the look on the faces of the men as she was speaking, that I realized. She is famous. People in GAP units may not know her real name, but they know who she is. They know what she has done. Some of them probably owe her their lives.

Watching her as she told them the story of what had happened in the house off the Via dei Renai, and later at the Villa Triste, and then in the wooded clearing; listening as they offered their condolences for Carlo, for all of Radio JULIET, I realized I was watching someone I knew and did not know. In those moments, I saw Issa for the first time through their eyes. She was not my younger sister, but a woman these men sought out and listened to. Whose skill and daring were both known and respected. Who had become a small legend of her own.

When she was finished, they fed us. Then they told us that we were going to Milan. Before they put us on the train, they gave us papers. We are sisters still, but now our name is Bevanelli. I am Chiara and Issa is Laura. We are from Livorno, evacuees fleeing Allied bombs.

This apartment is cramped. It is only two rooms and a bathroom. But we were handed the keys, and told that it is ours. I didn't want to think as we walked in, as we saw the worn furniture and even the clothes in the wardrobe, what had happened to the people who were here before. Papa would be horrified, but one of the lessons this war has taught me is that it is sometimes better not to have an 'enquiring mind'. There has been bombing. Perhaps that answers the question. Or perhaps there are nurses like me in all our cities, in all our hospitals – crows plucking bright things from the dead.

There is no question of us trying to go back to Florence. That was what Issa wanted – but they won't hear of it. After what happened with JULIET, it is far too dangerous. We are known there, and are needed here. The local network means for us to earn our keep. I am to be put to work in a doctor's office. Issa has already been told she will be asked to serve as a staffetta – a courier. Pregnant women are especially valuable – such is the reverence for motherhood among both the Nazis and the Fascists that they can move about almost unquestioned. Issa pleaded, but they were very firm with us. 'Considerable resources were expended' on our behalf. When I heard that, it came as a shock to me. Then I realized again that it isn't 'us' – it's Issa. GAP has kept its word and stood by its own. I am alive, I am free – more or less, I may yet not die in some godforsaken German camp, because I was with her.

I did not write in this book again until October –

10 October, Lodovico's name day. The truth was that I was going to put it away, as I had tried to put away thoughts of Lodo himself – and of the woman I might have been if I had married him. But in the end, I couldn't. The past kept creeping back.

It happened first when we got the news that Florence was liberated. The fighting was very bad, apparently, and there was much damage along the lungarnos. But most of all, Issa was right. GAP and the Garibaldi Brigades and the CLN – all the partisans – they went into the fight, the real one, before the Allies came, with one hand tied behind their back. They did not have enough ammunition or weapons to do everything. In the end, they could not stop the Germans from blowing up the bridges. The Ponte alle Grazie, the Carraia, and my favourite, the beautiful Trinità – all of them are gone. Only the Ponte Vecchio survived. For four days and nights while the fighting raged in the Oltrarno, the partisans used the Medici's secret corridor to scurry back and forth, supplying what ammunition and explosives they had, and finally liaising with the Allied command, who, when they arrived, were apparently distressed to find the CLN government already in place. If they thought we had fought through all this to replace one occupier with another, no matter who they were, they were much mistaken.

The Germans withdrew, in the end, up into the mountains, as we had known they would, to their Gothic Line. The Fascists were not so orderly. Some, like good lapdogs, went with their German masters. But others stayed in the city – tried to blend in or pretend they were no longer what they had been. Yet others were more honest. They took up as snipers, and had to be rooted out, tracked street by street and shot. Most disturbing, perhaps, was the news that Mario Carità escaped. He decamped, apparently, last July, and has taken up his 'work' in Padua. News of Mama, which both Issa and I had been hoping for, was thin at best. Issa discovered that she was taken to San Verdiana, but we were unable to find out anything else about her. The person I did find out about, however, was Lodovico. He sent me, of all extraordinary things, a letter.

Of course it was not sent to Chiara Bevanelli. It was sent to the girl I used to be. When Issa put it in my hand, I simply stood and stared at it. I think if she had not been there, I might have lit the gas and burnt it.

The envelope, thumbed and grubby by that time, lay on the table. It was a warm, lingering autumn day. The nights had become brisk, but the sun was still syrupy on the windowsill and on the scuffed boards of the floor. Outside, a tram rattled by. Issa was leaning against the kitchen door, watching me. Quite pregnant by then, she seemed to feel little effect from it. No complaining of swollen ankles or a sore back for Nemesis. She was working as a courier, and more besides, I think, although I do not know – and she would not have told me if I asked her. Sometimes she was gone for days at a time. That morning, she had returned from Bologna, bearing not only my letter, but the news of what had happened at Monte Sole.

The Fallschirmjäger and Waffen SS had conducted

another of their infamous rastrellamentos, this time against the Stella Rossa who had fought so bravely and with such success in the spring – a victory they would not be forgiven. The offensive had been launched in the last days of September. The partisans, surrounded, had held out in the hope that the Allies, who were not more than a day to the south, would relieve them. But no help came. They were wiped out. The local villages were destroyed. Two hundred civilians who had sought shelter in a church were herded into a cemetery and machine-gunned. I guessed that last year Issa must have passed through the area often, delivering her 'parcels', and that morning, for the first time, she told me that she had visited and sometimes stayed with Emmelina, at her brother's farm outside a village called Caprara. When she heard what had happened, she had left Bologna, made her way to Marzabotto, and gone to see for herself. Bodies were still being buried when she arrived. Dead animals lay in farm-yards. Houses and barns were destroyed, their gutted rafters open to the sky. Emmelina and her husband, her brother and his family were among the dead. Their bodies had been found at the farm, piled in a half-burnt barn. There was no sign of Emmelina's niece, the stolid quiet girl whom Mama used to accuse of being 'light-fingered', stealing cigarettes, and once, suppos-edly, a teaspoon. Some people thought she might have tried to get back to Florence.

As far as anyone could tell, almost eight hun-dred people had been killed. Most were civilians. Two hundred were members of the Stella Rossa, many of whom Issa had known. A few, including their leader, Lupo, had escaped and were hiding in Bologna. It was one of these survivors who had passed her Lodovico's letter. It had come up a chain, through the Allied lines which were now high in the mountains which I had watched so often from the terrace or from my bedroom window – from what I thought of now as another life.

Issa was watching me. The shadow of what she had seen in Monte Sole was in her face, a reflection of death in her eyes at the same time that life beat in her belly. I realized that I had not heard her laugh since that morning in Via dei Renai, when I had looked out of the window and seen her walking arm in arm with Carlo.

I picked up the envelope. My name, Caterina Cammaccio, was written across the front in Lodovico's handwriting. Seeing it was almost as startling as hearing his voice.

'I can't.'

I dropped it on the table. Issa said nothing.

'I can't,' I said again. 'It's not for me. Not any more.'

She stepped forward. She was still wearing her coat. Her hair had grown out. It was blonde again, the colour of dusty gold.

'Yes, you can.' She picked the envelope up and held it out to me.

'No, I can't.' I shook my head. 'It's not for me. It's for someone else.' I could hear panic rising in my voice. 'It's for the person Lodo thought— She doesn't exist any more, Issa,' I said. 'She's gone. She's dead. It's better if it stays that way.'

'No, it isn't.'

She kept holding out the envelope, stubborn, as if she could force me to take it, to open it like

Pandora's box, and face all the past, all the dreams that I had wanted, and had believed were mine.

'You don't understand.'

I closed my eyes and heard the crunch of snow under boots. The scrape of the trunk as I pulled it across the attic floor. I saw the back of the ambulance, the red cross on the rear doors growing smaller and smaller, drifting away from me into the snow. I felt the skin on the back of Dieter's hands, the tips of his fingers, his calloused palm. And the sleek, cool satin of my wedding dress. I heard the rustle of tissue paper, and the patter of satin buttons falling on it like rain.

'You don't understand, Issa,' I said again. 'You don't understand at all.'

'Yes, I do.'

She reached out and grabbed my chin. Twisted my head, so my eyes looked into hers.

'I do understand,' she said. 'I know what you did. I understand.'

We stared at each other.

'Six people lived, Cati. And you, and me, and Carlo, and Il Corvo.' She looked down, then took my hand and placed it on her belly where recently the baby had begun to kick. 'We wouldn't be here,' she said. 'None of us, if that door had been opened.'

Issa dropped my hand.

'None of us are the people we used to be,' she said. 'Even Lodovico.'

She looked at me. Then she held out the envelope again. That time, I took it.

'My Love.' Those were his first words. 'They tell me you are alive—'

Lodovico did not get to Florence until weeks after the liberation. He had been with the Allies, in field hospitals south of the line, since Salerno. All through May and June, he was just behind the advance. On the day we were arrested, he must have been somewhere just south of Grossetto. As soon as he got to Florence, he went straight to the house – which had miraculously survived – and then, when he found it empty, to the hospital. There he heard the news that we had been arrested. At first, he thought we had been shot with the others. Then he discovered that Issa and I had been transported. Apparently, in their haste to depart, the SS had neglected, or been unable, to take with them the records from the Villa Triste. So it was all there, in black and white. Every scream. Every drop of blood.

Not that that helped Lodo much. He knew that we had been put on a train to Verona, to a transit camp where we would be held until we were sent east. The Red Cross couldn't help him any further. But the CLN, who had taken over the city, eventually agreed to put him in contact with someone in GAP. Finally, he was given the good news – that we were alive, and still in Italy. And the bad news, that we were behind the German lines. He was not told where, or what names we were using. But he was told that if he wrote a letter, they would do their best to get it through.

He gave me contact information. Letters sometimes get through via the Red Cross. GAP and the CLN here in Milan were also in contact with the south. With the other Italy. The country behind the mountains, where the war is over.

'By the time you read this,' he wrote, 'I will

most likely be back in Naples, at the Allied field hospital. I pray nightly that I will hear from you. I imagine you reading these words, and hold you in my arms.'

I sat down at the table. Issa had gone into the other room. I could hear her moving about, the soft shuffle as she took off her coat and shoes, the creak of springs as she lay down on the bed. I don't know how long I sat there, holding that piece of paper and watching the sunlight play on the windowsill.

Over the next days and weeks, I read it again and again. And each time I did, I felt a strange feeling inside my chest, no longer the flowering of that blossom of fear I had become so used to, but something else. A different kind of flower, as fragile as glass. And so alien, that at first I did not realize it was happiness.

Chapter Twenty-Four

There was no question about it. Bruno Torricci was an unattractive specimen of humanity.

His flat pancake face was probably made paler by the video that had been taped in Cesare D'Aletto's interview room. But frankly, Pallioti doubted even a fake tan or tropical sun could have made him palatable. His eyes were a watery blue, his skin close to albino. The quarter-inch cut of his hair did not help. Nor did his nose, which looked as if it had been broken more than once. Probably in one of the numerous fights, brawls, and public nuisances for which he had been arrested. Nor was he the brightest light in the firmament. His fingerprints had been found all over all four of what Enzo's team had come to refer to as 'the April 28 letters'. A fact that was no great surprise, given that Bruno prided himself on his membership of the Aryan Sons. Their motto was 'the Halls of Valhalla Will Never Be Empty'.

Pallioti sighed, keeping one eye on the video and the other on the file Enzo had handed him. Cesare D'Aletto had located Bruno earlier that morning, within hours of the time a match for his fingerprints appeared on the database. Not that it was a great feat of detection. Signor Torricci had been sitting in a jail in Pescara where he had been in yet another punch-up at yet another motorway service station.

In the brief interview on the tape Cesare D'Aletto began with Torricci's name, address – somewhere on the outskirts of Rome, age – twenty-seven, and occupation – builder. Then he'd moved on to the letters, which Bruno cheerfully admitted to having written.

The idea, he insisted, had been all his. It had come to him in a flash of brilliance after he saw a piece on the local news about a group of 'traitors' who were going to receive medals on the sixtieth anniversary of the liberation, which was not a liberation at all but the occasion when Italy had finally been sold down the tubes by the Jews, the gypsies, and black Americans. He and some friends had watched the national disgrace on television, and decided that 'something had to be done about it'. The medal recipients' names had not been hard to find. His girlfriend had been a big help getting their addresses. She was very good with computers. Very clever in general. She'd also made the stamps, and thought up the idea of using red ink because it looked like blood.

Cesare D'Aletto had already established that neither Bruno nor his genius girlfriend had an alibi for Wednesday, 1 November. It was not immediately obvious that they had been in Florence at eleven o'clock that morning, but Enzo's people were working on it. The following weekend, however, they had been staying with her parents who lived, conveniently, just outside Bari. Bruno claimed they had been 'sightseeing' all day on his motorcycle, but so far couldn't remember exactly where they had gone. Cesare D'Aletto was busily rounding up other members of the Aryan Sons and looking for the girlfriend to see if her memory was any more precise. He planned to continue interviewing Bruno Torricci the next day, by which time Enzo would have joined him in Brindisi. He was flying down late that evening.

The Mayor was delighted. The press office was already drafting statements. Even the investigating magistrate was happy. Pallioti closed the file, wondering why he alone seemed to feel

no joy at the prospect of closing this case. Something was niggling at him, stuck like a stone in his shoe. He turned away
from the screen where the tape was being watched yet again,
and wandered into the side room where Giovanni Trantemento
and Roberto Roblino's papers and address books and bank
statements and letters – everything that might be remotely rel-
evant, including their shopping lists – were laid out on two
long tables.

The stacks of cash had been removed to a secure evidence
locker, but everything else was much as he had seen it last. At
the very end of the table were the plastic bags that held the
creased and fragile pages of the partisan news-sheets. Pallioti
wandered towards them and then, as he picked one up, realized
what it was that had been bothering him. He had been waiting,
in Caterina's account, for the moment of intimacy between her
and Il Corvo, for something that would explain how and why
Giovanni Trantemento had come to have her diary in his safe.
But now she was in Milan and he was – who knew where? He
had dropped out of her story with the last ambulance run. She
had wanted to ask him something, about his family, or his sister.

Pallioti pulled the red book out of its habitual resting place
in his pocket and thumbed back through the densely written
pages. Yes, there is was, a little smudged, but in black and white
– *because those were the last words Il Corvo and I ever spoke.* The
entry was dated June 1944.

He returned the book to his pocket, and plucked one of the
plastic-covered news-sheets off the table and looked at it again.
The date on it was also smudged, but visible, even through the
plastic bag. February 1944. When Pallioti had glanced at them
previously, that had meant nothing to him. Now he thought
of it as the month when Issa had been shot.

Well, he thought, it was hardly unusual, that the old man
would want a souvenir. The shooting at the Pergola, Issa's – or
rather Lilia's – escape, and his own subsequent escape thanks

to the wreck on the way to the train station was the reason that Giovanni Trantemento, otherwise known as Il Corvo, had received his medal. His sister had said so – 'he ran out into the street and helped a woman who had been shot. He was arrested and beaten and escaped. But it saved her life.' The same incident had caused him, in turn, to nominate Roberto Roblino, alias Beppe, for his medal. Even if he had never talked about it, it was still one of the major events in his life.

Pallioti picked up another of the bags. Like all the others, it had a number, or a series of numbers and letters, on it. He smoothed the plastic and read the badly printed headline. It was a different news-sheet, but was also dated February 1944. He put it down and selected a third. This one was dated June 1944. Again, that had previously meant nothing to him. Now it was the month when Radio JULIET was blown. When the Cammaccio family was arrested, and shot, and transported. He gave a little mental shrug. Il Corvo had known the women; presumably he had known many, if not all, of the people arrested at the Via dei Renai that day. Why wouldn't he be interested in accounts of what had happened? He picked up a fourth news-sheet. It was different again, but covered the same month, June 1944. As did the fifth. The sixth and seventh were February 1944 again.

Pallioti stood back from the table. Now he saw something else he had not paid any real attention to before, either. Some of the bags were heat-sealed. Some were taped. Very few had been opened. Only one or two, and the bag that had contained the little red book.

Meaning that Giovanni Trantemento had not spent his evenings reading about his own exploits, or those of his fellow GAP members. He had not read the contents of these sheets at all. At best he had, like Pallioti himself, peered through the plastic. Then he had taken them and locked them up in his safe.

Pallioti spent the next five minutes sorting Giovanni Trantemento's collection of partisan newspapers into two piles.

There were twenty-seven in total. When he had finished, one pile contained those dated February 1944. The other, June 1944. Twelve in one, fifteen in the other, none left over. He looked at the two piles for a moment. Then he got out his glasses. On closer examination he saw that not all of the flimsy little partisan news bulletins were from Florence. There were a couple from Bologna. One from Genoa. One from as far away as Turin. But all of them were dated one of the two months. Not one covered May, or January, or July. There were none at all from 1943 or 1945.

Pallioti picked up the empty bag that had contained Caterina's diary. He looked again at the shredded tape, at the letters PJ and numbers 653 that had been written on the bag with what looked like a laundry pen. Suspicion nudged at him. He sorted quickly through the news-sheets until he found what he was looking for. He had been right. In addition to the handwritten numbers, one of the bags had a small, smudged, red sticky label in the upper corner. He peered at it.

Luckily, his eyesight was not as bad as he sometimes thought it was.

It took Pallioti the better part of an hour of sorting through Giovanni Trantemento's bank records before he found what he was looking for. He doubted that the old man would have used a credit card for this kind of transaction. According to Enzo he had had one but almost never used it. Cash, on the other hand, of which he had plenty, might have been favoured. And perhaps it had been. Auction houses, especially those that handled the kind of material Giovanni was interested in, often insisted on it. But not always. Which was fortunate, because otherwise Pallioti would have been out of luck. His instincts told him that this collection had been built some time ago. So he'd started in 1960, before Giovanni Trantemento had even moved to Florence, when he had still been a relatively young man, building his business in Naples. It was not until 1965 that he found the first cheque made out to Patria Memorabilia. After that there were several. They seemed to stop in 1975.

Pallioti took out his telephone and called Guillermo. Then he stood by the table, drumming his fingers and waiting for his secretary to find what he needed.

Patria Memorabilia had probably never been a particularly lucrative business. Pallioti imagined that the trade in bits and pieces relating to the war was probably a crowded field. The selling of news-sheets, train timetables, and old letters, was hardly likely to make anyone a fortune. With the advent of the Internet, he was surprised any actual shops survived at all. But this one did, just. The display in the small and very dusty front window suggested it was as much a bookshop as anything else. The man who had answered Guillermo's telephone call had described his business as a 'search agency and auction house' specializing in 'material related to the partisan struggle'.

The shopfront itself, such as it was, was buried deep in a warren behind Santa Croce. It wouldn't have taken Giovanni Trantemento more than twenty minutes to walk there from his apartment. Pallioti himself had covered the distance from the police headquarters in just under half an hour. He was about to reach out and press the tarnished brass bell when the door opened for him as if by magic. A tortoiseshell cat slipped out, looked up at him with wide golden eyes, then slunk into the alley.

'She's a hussy,' a voice said. 'We feed her and feed her, but still she hunts.'

The comment was followed by laughter. The interior of the shop was so dark that Pallioti could not immediately see where it came from. Then a face presented itself, peering out from behind the door. The owner was probably older than he appeared. His skin had the pallid tightness of someone who looked as if he hadn't been outside, much less in the sunlight, for at least twenty years.

'Come in, come in,' he said.

As his eyes adjusted, Pallioti saw that the front of the shop was more crowded that it had appeared from the outside, and possibly better organized. The back was covered in shelves that held catalogued piles of papers, all in the now-familiar plastic bags. One wall was filled by bookshelves. Posters lined another. Some of them were old-west style 'wanted' posters printed by the Germans and featuring blurred photographs that might or might not have been of partisan leaders. Others were announcements made by the CLN, or posted by the partisan governments of the few short-lived 'liberated republics' that had flourished briefly in the winters of 1943 and 1944, before sinking without trace into the chaos of the Allied advance and German retreat.

Alongside them were framed photographs, some of individuals, some of the Garibaldi Brigades – their members young and thin-faced and intent, ammunition belts slung over their shoulders. Some of the photos were of women. A group on bicycles carried a placard that read *Gruppi Difesa Della Donna*. Another trio in dark skirts walked in formation, carrying sniper rifles. A woman in a flat cap lay behind a ridge, one hand resting on a Bren gun, her eyes intent on the horizon. Some of the photographs were simply of bodies. Three men hung from a public gibbet, swaying in an unseen breeze as a girl with a bicycle stood looking on. A line of men, hands tied behind their backs, slumped, dead in front of the wooden fence they had been lined up and shot against. Another photograph showed a trench, arms and legs sprawling from it, more bodies filling it than Pallioti could possibly count.

'Sant' Anna Stazzema, August 1944, the 35th Panzer Grenadier Regiment. Five hundred and sixty civilians killed.'

The man, who introduced himself as Severino Cavicalli, was standing behind him.

'Excuse the light,' he said. 'Or rather, the lack of it. We like to keep it low because so much of what we have is fragile. But if there is anything that interests you particularly?' He cocked his head, his strange green eyes blinking.

'No, no.' Pallioti turned around. In truth there was much here that interested him, but it would have to wait for another time. 'I'm afraid,' he said, 'that I'm here in an official capacity.'

Signor Cavicalli glanced at the credentials he held out and nodded.

'Ah, yes. I believe your assistant said you wished to speak to us about a client? A Signor Trantemento?'

'Yes,' Pallioti said. 'Yes, that's correct. We are making enquiries, as you have probably gathered, into his death.'

Severino Cavicalli gave a little bow that either did or did not indicate that Giovanni Trantemento's passing was a cause for regret.

'Then perhaps,' he said, gesturing towards a door that he moved to open, 'I think you will be more comfortable in our back room.'

The back room was large and windowless, its centre almost filled by a very large table. Unlike the front of the shop, it was very well lit.

'We hold private sales and auctions,' Signor Cavicalli explained as he ushered Pallioti in. 'Now and again. Please. I won't be a moment while I fetch my father. He always dealt with Signor Trantemento, you see. Exclusively.'

He left the door open. Pallioti heard the creak of stairs as he climbed to the apartment above.

The old man who stepped into the room a few moments later was barely more than a wisp. Beyond frail, he appeared so light that he almost hovered above the floor. He wore a bow tie, a tweed jacket, dark trousers and green velvet bedroom slippers. His face was almost identical to his son's except for the fact that the fuzz rising above his unlined forehead was snow white.

His hand, when Pallioti shook it, was feather-like. But his eyes were sharp and his voice louder than his appearance might have suggested.

'A visit from the police. I'm honoured.'

'I'm sorry to take up your time.' Pallioti moved towards the chair he was offered. 'But I was hoping you might tell me about Giovanni Trantemento?'

The old man nodded. His son had seated him at the head of the table, in what Pallioti suspected was his habitual place.

'And what was it, exactly,' he asked, 'that you were hoping I might tell you?'

'Well, I am trying to find out anything, anything at all, about his activities in the partisans. Were you a member of GAP or—'

Before the old man could answer, his son said, 'My father was not in the partisans, Dottore. My family is Jewish. They didn't return to Florence until the 1950s.'

'We owed them our lives.'

Severino Cavicalli's father allowed his eyes to rest on Pallioti's face.

'I would say,' he added, 'that we were among the blessed. But the truth is, God had little to do with it – it was the partisans who got us out. This shop,' he said, 'was my enthusiasm. My way of saying thank you. Keeping the flame alive, if you like. But no, I was not one of them. I know only what I read about Signor Trantemento in the newspapers, after he had received his medal.'

'So, he never spoke of the war to you? Of what he'd done? He didn't talk about that when he was a client?'

The old man made a gesture, his hand wobbling, as if in the wind.

'Professionally,' he said. 'Of course Signor Trantemento spoke of the war. That's why he came to me. But personally, no. He was a client, Dottore.'

Pallioti heard the rest of the sentence, *Not a friend*. He

waited for a moment for the old man to voice it, but the words
didn't come. Finally he asked, 'Why? Why did Giovanni Trantemento come to you, Signor Cavicalli?'

The green eyes glittered in the bright overhead light.

'Because I am a specialist.'

'And what he was looking for required specialization?'

Signor Cavicalli nodded. 'That is correct.'

'And what was that?'

The hands gestured again, then rested on the table, fingers
splayed. For a moment Pallioti thought he was going to push
himself out of the chair, state politely but firmly that there were
questions he could not, or would not, answer. But it didn't happen. Instead, the old man looked him squarely in the face.

'Signor Trantemento,' he said, 'was interested in only two
things. As I said, highly specialized.'

Pallioti felt the stillness in the room, deep and abiding, as if
somehow it reached back through time.

'And what would those be? Those two things?'

'February 1944 and June 1944.'

'When did this begin?'

The old man nodded.

'1965. I believe he had only recently arrived, or perhaps I
should say returned, to the city. Signor Trantemento sought me
out. I had something of a reputation then, as a researcher. A
collector. I bought up private collections, the contents of people's attics. It was around that time that a great deal of unclaimed property that had sat about in municipal cellars
gathering dust since 1945 was finally auctioned off. The odds
and ends of the dead. Mail. Unclaimed personal property. From
the hospitals. From bomb sites. Photographs. Things that had
been turned in to the Red Cross. Eventually, they needed the
space. They were tearing buildings down, building new li-
braries. New museums. They kept what they thought might be
interesting, and virtually gave away the rest. Dealers, collectors,
auctioneers, acquired quite a lot of it.'

Pallioti nodded. 'And Signor Trantemento?'

'He asked me to watch for anything that might be of interest to him. As I said, his field was narrow, but he was willing to pay for what he wanted.'

'Did he come here?'

'Sometimes. Sometimes I delivered it for him. He came to trust me. I don't think he ever turned down anything I found for him.'

'So he wasn't discerning?'

'Oh yes,' Signor Cavicalli nodded. 'Yes, don't mistake me. He was discerning. That was all he was interested in. February 1944. June 1944. Florence only. And in particular, the shooting at the Pergola Theatre. And anything, anything at all, that pertained to Radio Juliet.'

There was a beat, as soft and steady as a pulse. Pallioti could feel Severino's eyes on him, but he did not look away from the smooth pale skin of his father's face.

'Anything concerning the Pergola shooting and Radio Juliet?'

'Correct. That, if I found it, he bought without question. Often unseen. He took my word for it and never questioned the price. But not secondary material, mind you.' Signor Cavicalli shook his head. 'He didn't care for the speculation of others. He was only interested in original source material.'

'And why do you think that was?'

The hands rose and fell again. 'We all have our little enthusiasms.'

Signor Cavicalli watched Pallioti, the bright eyes moving over his features like the fingers of a blind man.

'If I may, Ispettore,' he said after a moment. 'If you would not mind, if I was so bold as to offer my opinion? As a collector?'

'*Certo*, Signore.' Pallioti leaned back, watching him. 'I would be honoured.'

'Well,' the old man nodded. 'I have found,' he said, 'that, on the whole, people collect for two reasons. Because there is something they want to show off, something they want people to know. Or because there is something they don't.'

'And Signor Trantemento?'

The green eyes blinked. Pallioti could hear himself breathing. It was the only noise in the room.

'How much did you sell him?' he asked finally.

'Over the years?' The thin shoulders shrugged, jumping like bony wings under the checked tweed. 'Not much. There wasn't much. Eventually, it dried up more or less completely. As I said, he was only interested in primary accounts, original material. Perhaps two dozen of the partisan news-sheets? That was the main thing. I kept an eye on letters, of course.'

'But you never found any?'

'No.'

'What about this?' Pallioti took the small red book out of his pocket and placed it on the polished surface of the table. He had a feeling it had been there before. 'Did you sell him this?'

The old man did not reach for it. He simply looked at the cover and nodded.

'Of course,' he said. 'I was very excited when I found it. I telephoned him. He sent me a cheque without even seeing it. He paid handsomely.'

'Why?'

For the first time, Signor Cavicalli smiled. 'I imagine,' he said, 'that it contained something that interested him.'

'And did you ever ask him what that might have been?'

'No.'

'And where did you get it?' Pallioti retrieved the little book, oddly comforted to feel its worn cover in his hand again, as if he had exposed it to some danger by laying it out as he had.

'Shall I look it up, Papa?'

Severino was getting to his feet. The old man waved him down.

'The Red Cross,' he said. 'They were clearing belongings,

things that had been handed in and were unclaimed. It was in a job lot. A box I bought. One of the last, in the early seventies.'

'Here in the city?'

'Yes.'

Pallioti nodded and got to his feet.

'Thank you, Signor Cavicalli,' he said. 'For your time.' He paused. 'May I ask you something else, while I'm here?'

The strange pale face turned up towards his.

'*Certo*, Dottore. We are at your disposal.'

'Il Spettro.'

'Yes.' The old man nodded.

'The stories are apparently extraordinary.'

Signor Cavicalli said nothing. Pallioti thought of Eleanor Sachs, saw her small heart-shaped face, its features young and old at once.

'Do you believe he existed?' he asked.

The old man smiled. 'People believe many things,' he said. 'But surely I don't have to tell you that.'

Signor Cavicalli held out his hand. Pallioti took it. The fingers quivered.

'There is one thing' – he looked up at Pallioti and smiled again – 'that I do find extraordinary. In fact, Dottore,' he said, 'it never ceases to amaze me.'

Pallioti could feel Severino watching them. Under the lights, his father's hair was hazy, as white and floating as a halo.

'And what is that?' Pallioti asked.

The old man shook his head again.

'That even in this day and age,' he said, 'in any day and age, that people always insist on believing their heroes are men.'

Chapter Twenty-Five

In late November, I had another letter.

Every summer, when we went to Viareggio as children, I would worry that I had forgotten how to swim. I would stand on the beach, watching Issa and Rico running and leaping into the waves, and be afraid that if I followed them, I would sink. That the cold slap of a wave would rise up, and that in the face of it, my body would desert me. My legs and arms would flail, my mouth would open, and I would be pulled under. Washed away. Rolled along the ocean floor like a shell.

That is how I felt when I held the flimsy sheet of paper in my hand and thought of Lodovico, alive and in Naples – as if my past was a great ocean I had turned my back on. I did not know, if I faced it again, whether I would remember how to swim or be pulled under by it.

By that time, I wanted to write back. And I thought it would be easy to lie to Lodovico. I felt I had lied so much, and committed so many sins

– stolen and whored myself – that lying to him should be something I would not even think about. But instead, when I finally sat down and picked up a pen, I found that the truth between us seemed one last tiny thing I had hoarded to myself, and could not give away. So, I found I did not know what to say. Or how to say it. In the end, I told him we are safe. I described our apartment – the piazza at the top of the street. The rattle of the tram. The cat that sits in the open window of the apartment opposite. The bells from the church next door and the sound of footsteps on the stairs.

That was what I wrote. But there was a part of me that wanted to say instead, 'Go and be happy and find someone else. Because I am not who you think I am. Go. Because you can no longer know me. I no longer know myself.'

I did not sign it – because if it falls into the wrong hands it must not give us away. I just made an X. Then, after I folded the paper and sealed the envelope, I lay on the bed, and thought of my ring, wrapped in oilskin and buried deep in the frozen ground.

I gave the letter to Issa, who promised that it would reach him. It took me three days to do that, because I barely saw her. Sometimes we could pass a week, coming and going and not seeing one another. Finding only clues – a washed plate, a cup left in the sink or the indent of a head on the pillow, as if each of us were living with a ghost.

For Issa that time was particularly difficult. A few weeks earlier, the British general, Alexander, had issued a directive to the partisans, instructing them on how to behave and when to act. They had no intention of obeying these particular orders, but it did nothing for their morale to realize that they were not trusted. I think though that the thing that hurt her most was not being able to guide through the mountains. There, she felt most alive. And there, too, she was closer to Carlo. If she was going to find his ghost, it would be in the high passes, on the worn steps and ancient stones of the Via degli Dei, the Way of the Gods. And, she railed at me, they needed her. In a reversal, downed airmen were now being taken south through the Gothic Line and delivered back to the Allies. Reports were filtering back of accidents, of guides who did not know what they were doing, while Issa, who knew those mountains so well she claimed she could walk them blindfold, was left out.

Pregnant as she was, however, she could not go climbing through ice and snow. And in any case, she was more valuable as a courier. The more her stomach swelled, the less likely she was to be stopped or questioned, so the information she carried became more important. That, at least, was some consolation to her. Bologna, Ferrara, Ravenna, Modena, Piacenza, even Genoa and Turin – she went back and forth to all of them. Everyone knew the final fight was coming in the spring; plans were being laid, and Issa carried them from one CLN command to the next. She and the baby. Each time I saw her, her belly had grown larger. Sometimes the kicking was so fierce it made her gasp, her blue eyes widening in surprise.

In the meantime, as the Allies bombed us from the air, another war was being fought on the streets. Mario Carita was in Padua, not Milan, but he had soulmates here, and I daresay in other cities, too. At the clinic, we saw the results of their handiwork. In daylight we treated good society ladies, the upright Fascisti matrons of Milan. But after dark it was different. They came three, sometimes four, a night. Shot, bleeding, limbs and jaws broken. Sometimes I was so tired I felt I could barely walk home. I didn't even realize that it was Christmas Eve until someone in the street, with half a smile, wished me Buon Natale.

That night, on Christmas Eve when I got home, Issa wasn't here. I saw no trace of her at all, and for a moment, as I came in and turned on the lamp, I felt a terrible pang of fear – convinced myself that what I had dreaded, what I had almost known would one day happen, had finally come to pass. That she had been caught, turned in, spotted by the Abwehr spies who we know exist – Italians who work for the Germans, who speak and look like us, and move among us, undetected and deadly as a virus. Or that she had been killed, trapped finally by an Allied bomb. Or hit by one of the machine guns that strafe everything that moves on the road, firing blindly from the air in the hope that what they kill may be an enemy.

I sat down at the kitchen table, fear and tiredness washing over me in that wave I had dreaded since I was a child. And knew, sitting there in my hat and coat, that if it was true – if she was gone – I wouldn't have the energy to go on. I wouldn't even try.

I don't know how long it was before I got up and walked into the other room. I suppose I must have got cold, and decided that I would get into bed, that I would lie through the night and wait to see what came. I didn't turn on the light. I just sat down and took off my shoes. So it was not until I turned to pull back the blanket that I saw the little package on the pillow. It was wrapped in tissue paper and tied with a piece of string, and more than anything, it made me happy because it meant at least that she had been there. Picking it up, I felt the touch of her hand.

Issa's gift to me that Christmas was another little book. On the first page, she had written – 'For 1945, a New Year and a New Life'.

It was some three weeks after that, that I came home and found her in the kitchen, pacing like a caged cat.

'They've told me,' she said, furious, 'told me to stop work. They say it's no longer safe!'

She glared at me as if this was my fault, that she been sent home to wait for the baby. The order made her livid. She had apparently argued and fought – not just, I think, because of her desire to 'keep up the fight', but because, like me, she was trying to outrun the past. Even more than bullets or bombs, I think both of us were afraid of being still – afraid of giving ourselves a chance to look back.

I remembered that day in September, looking in the mirror and seeing Lot's wife. I had not been so wrong after all.

That night, we sat up and played cards. Issa won, accumulating a large pile of the bits of paper we used as tokens, which cheered her up a little. Then, three days later, in the early hours of the morning, and without much warning, my nephew was born. She screamed only once, for Carlo.

Issa's baby was perfect. I had to go to work the next day, and left her staring down into his tiny face, watching his hands as they closed around her fingers. Four days later, on Sunday, we baptized him ourselves. We waited until sunset, then bathed and dressed him in one of my white blouses for a christening gown. I assumed that Issa would want to call him after Carlo, but she shook her head.

'No?' I asked. 'Are you sure?'

She nodded.

'I know who his father is.' She looked from her son to me and smiled – not her old smile, but a different one, laced in sadness. 'He's going to grow up in a different world,' she said. 'That's what I want for him. And Carlo would, too. He should go into his own life with his own name.'

The new book she had given me had an appendix of name days in the back. We found the right one, squinting at the tiny script, and named him for the day he was born.

It was after that, that she began to change. I didn't notice it much, at first. I was too busy, often working through the night. And Issa, who was still at home with her son, still smiled. She even laughed. But there was a shadow on her. While she was working, while she was waiting for the baby to be born, she had been able to concentrate on those things. On getting to a rendezvous, on remembering the right information, the right names and faces. On keeping herself alive long enough to give birth to Carlo's child.

One afternoon, I came in and found her sitting, staring at something in her hand. When I looked, I saw it was a photograph: tiny, the edges dog-eared. Apparently I was not the only one who knew how to hide things in my clothes. She held it up without my asking. From her hair, I guessed that it had been taken the previous spring, somewhere in the mountains, probably at around the time she found she was pregnant. She was standing with Carlo in a meadow. Their arms were wound around one another, and they looked very happy. And very young. She ran her finger across it.

'I didn't understand,' she said. 'I never understood, when I was with him, how much I loved him.'

I was holding the shopping, what scraps I could gather with our ration books, but standing watching Issa I forgot them. All I could think of was what I had done to her. What I had done to Carlo, and Mama, and Papa, and Rico. To all of us. To everyone who came that day, and to the baby, who had woken up and was beginning to fuss, reaching out to his mother – the only parent he would ever know, thanks to my carelessness.

Issa slid the photograph into her pocket and got up to go to him, and I turned away, muttering about supper so she would not see my face.

That night, I dreamed again of the Via dei Renai. I saw the shutters opening and closing, as if of their own free will. The pot tipped itself over and spilled soil across the step. I saw Mama's face in the window, looking down at me, her hand raised to the glass. She tried to speak. She mouthed words, but I couldn't hear her. I was deafened by the sound of my own footsteps on the pavement.

I woke with a start and sat up, feeling sweat run down my chest and pool between my breasts, even though it was cold in the room. Then I noticed Issa was not in bed. When I looked up, I saw her, standing in the doorway, barefoot, holding the baby.

'What is it? What is it?' I asked. 'What's wrong?'

I thought the baby was sick, that he had a temperature, or there had been a warning for a bomb.

But she shook her head. 'Nothing.'

Moonlight, cold and silver, stretched in from the window.

Issa came and sat down beside me. Her son stared up into her face and she stared back at him as I had often seen her do before, studying him intently, as if she was looking for Carlo – as if in their child's eyes, in the tiny mouth, the round of his cheek, she could find the piece of him she had carried inside her.

I watched her, both of them. And when, finally, she stood up and placed him gently back in the bassinet, I thought that in that chilly light she looked like a phantom, looked as if she was wavering, slipping away in front of me.

'He's sleeping,' she said finally. Then she sat on the edge of the bed again. 'I have to talk to you.'

I pulled the blanket back, and she climbed in. I could feel the warmth of her, her heart beating

next to mine as it had when we were children.
But there was nothing childish about this. It was
as if my dream had travelled through the dark to
her.

'Do you think of it?' she asked. 'That day? What
happened?'

'Yes,' I said. 'Yes, of course I do.'

'So do I. I can't stop.'

'You must, Issa.' I turned towards her. 'You
must try.'

'Someone knew.' She was staring at the ceiling.
Moonlight picked out the lines of her cheek and
nose, the curve of her mouth and chin. 'I go over
and over it in my head,' she said. 'Everyone who
was there – who it could have been. I think about
when we arrived. Where we came from. Where we
had been the day before. What order we arrived
in, and where we were when the noise started
outside. And why. Why would any one of us have
done that? And how?' She turned towards me.
'That's what I don't understand, how? How? We
knew each other so well. We were bound.'

The GAP code, I thought, the unbreakable honour and trust among comrades that she put so
much stock in.

I could have spoken up then. I could have told
her that I had walked too fast, that I had been so
confident I had not stopped to look for reflections
or faces I saw too often. I could have told her
about the scullery door, or that I must have made
a mistake, with the keys. With the shutters. I
could have told her how careless I had been.

But I didn't. Because the truth was, I was
afraid. Of Nemesis. Of what she would say, and
what she would do. I was afraid that in my care-

lessness, I had broken the pact, and that Issa would take the baby and go away. Leave me all alone. Even worse, I was afraid of what she would no longer feel for me.

And so I lay there and let her go on.

'We were so careful,' she said. 'We didn't tell anyone. No one knew, except us, the people who were there. And it was only us. And we were – after what we'd been through, we would have died for each other. I keep thinking and thinking of them, in that trench. Each one—'

She ticked her fingers then, like she had when she was tiny and learning to count. Lying beside me, she held her hands up in the dark and repeated, as if it was a litany, 'There was you, and me, and Rico, and Carlo, and Mama, and Papa, and—'

She stopped counting, but her hands still hung above the blanket, fingers outstretched into the moonlight. As if she was reaching for something.

'All of them killed,' she said. 'The silence, Cati. I can't get it out of my head. When the tapping stopped, on the wall. And I keep seeing them, Papa and Rico and Carlo and the legs and arms . . . They wanted me to know.'

She turned to me in the dark.

'That's why they took me up there, Cati, to that place. They wanted me to know. To see for myself, and understand – that one of us betrayed us.'

Chapter Twenty-Six

Signora Grandolo was waiting for him, just as she had promised. On the telephone half an hour earlier, she had not seemed surprised to hear Pallioti's voice. Instead, after remarking that she was delighted to hear from him, she had listened, and then simply said that she would be happy to stay on at her offices and share with him any records Remember The Fallen had from the Villa Triste. She would, she had added, wait in the building's lobby, now that the receptionist was gone, in order to spare him ringing the after-hours bell and waiting, and getting soaked. Rain had not been forecast, but as he left the Cavicallis', it had begun to pour.

Now, he opened the door of the official car he had requisitioned, ducked, and ran for the entrance. Little cascades dribbled down the steps and formed pools on the pavement. He stepped in one, soaking his socks. Signora Grandolo held open the heavy glass door and gestured him in.

'Not cats and dogs,' she said. 'Elephants and giraffes. I have always hated the Florentine winters!'

The glass panels swung closed. Their footsteps sounded like Morse code on the marble floor as he followed her towards the elevator. There did not appear to be another soul in the place. Whatever went on in these offices clearly ended promptly at 5 p.m.

'Thank you again,' Pallioti said as the doors pinged open.

He couldn't believe that she didn't have something better, or at least more interesting, to do on a rainy evening than guide a befuddled policeman through computerized records. He could, of course, have asked someone on Enzo's investigation, insisted that they drop what they were doing and chase his particular wild goose. But it would have taken days. And annoyed everyone to boot. And besides, he didn't even know what he was looking for. Possibly nothing at all.

But he doubted it. The thing that had been niggling at him had not gone away. He should be as satisfied as the Mayor. As optimistic as Enzo, who was currently winging his way through this storm to Bari, confident that in a day, or two or three at most, they would place Bruno Torricci in Florence and wring a confession out of him and tie this case up neatly with a bow. But he wasn't. And he couldn't think of any of those things. Instead, all he could think of was Signor Cavicalli's face. And those plastic bags. Paid handsomely for. Never opened. Locked in a safe.

'Graziella's gone home,' Signora Grandolo said as she bent to unlock the doors. 'It's tedious, to have to do this, but we had a break-in here a few years ago. Well, not really a break-in, a burglary of opportunity, while Graziella had gone around the corner for lunch. Now I don't go downstairs without locking up. Our records aren't valuable,' she added as she led him across the front room and into her office, 'but they are personal.' She glanced at him. 'May I take your coat?'

The curtains on the big windows had been pulled, shutting out the rain and the city night. A vase of roses sat on a side table. With the rug and the upholstered chairs, the bookshelf and sofa, Signora Grandolo's office looked more like a personal sitting room. A pair of glasses had been left on the coffee table, a scarf was folded on the edge of her desk beside a teacup. A pile of mail was held down with a silver letter opener. It occurred to Pallioti to wonder how much time exactly Signora Grandolo spent here, since her husband died.

She closed the closet door and returned to her desk.

'Please,' she said, gesturing towards one of the chairs, 'bring it close enough so you can see.'

The computer was already on. A click of a key brought the screen to life. She reached for a pair of glasses and slipped them on.

'Thank you so much again,' Pallioti said. 'For doing this. I could have gone through official channels to access these, but—'

'It would have taken forever.' Signora Grandolo smiled at him over the top of her glasses. 'Yes, I know. I'm afraid I took shameless advantage of Cosimo's connections to get us as many complete 'in-house copies' as I could. The archives are impossibly slow. And often rather confused.'

She turned to the computer.

'It was Villa Triste you said you were interested in?'

'Yes,' Pallioti said. 'Yes. If you have—'

'Well, we have some bits and pieces. What I could get hold of. Not all of it, believe it or not, is computerized yet. And quite a lot is missing. They're nowhere near as complete as the Red Cross or the CLN papers.'

'You've seen them? The originals?'

'Of the Villa Triste? Oh yes.' She glanced at him. 'Unfortunately. In the early days, when Cosimo first started this, right after the war – well, of course we were a few light years from the digital age. Someone had to go and do the sifting and digging. They didn't even have microfilm then.' She shrugged. 'Frankly, I much preferred the original paper.'

'You?'

Pallioti tried to keep the surprise out of his voice. He didn't succeed. Signora Grandolo smiled.

'I worked for him,' she said. 'I was a secretary at the bank. That's how we met. As for the archives, well, it wasn't glamorous.

Quite the opposite – dark and dusty. I volunteered because Cosimo felt so strongly about all this, and, well, women will do anything when they're in love.' She smiled, and added, 'The secret of your power. As if you didn't all know that.'

She tapped a command on the keyboard.

'To be honest,' she said as the page loaded, 'the Villa Triste records always gave me the creeps. I suppose I expected blood-stains on the pages or something. But I also suppose we should be grateful for them. So many of the people we were interested in passed through there. Having them to hand certainly made searches faster. Not,' she added, 'that I've looked at them in ages. We don't need these much any more – we're admin now, mainly. For the monuments. And for care homes. The occasional pension arrangement. That kind of thing. The searching has been over for a long time.'

She swivelled the computer towards him so he could see the screen.

'You see,' she said, 'we scanned full pages in. Even in that hellhole, their good Nazi-Fascisti handwriting was immaculate.'

It was. Upright black-ink letters marched across ledger pages, as neat and precise as an old-fashioned accountant's. Which, Pallioti supposed, had been exactly what this was. A massive accounting of the beaten, the tortured, and the dead. She was watching him.

'What is it exactly,' she asked quietly, 'that I can help you with, Dottore?'

Pallioti sat back in his chair.

'I'm looking for the records from a specific date. Well, two. The first is 14 February 1944.'

'Valentine's Day.'

'Yes. Yes,' he said again. 'Something happened. An attack. Assassination attempt, by a GAP unit, on the German consul and a pair of SD officers. At the Teatro del Pergola. Three men were arrested.'

Signora Grandolo looked at him for a moment. Then she nodded. 'Well,' she said, turning to her computer, 'let's see what we can find.'

She tapped for a few moments, her fingers moving swiftly over the keys, then stopped, waiting for the screen to load. A few seconds later, she said, 'It seems to have been an unusually quiet day.'

Pallioti leaned forward.

'There's no trace of them?'

'Yes,' she said. 'Oh yes. They're here. Three of them. It looks as if they were Saint Valentine's only customers. I always have thought he was a very strange choice, for the Day of Love.'

'And their code names – are they recorded?'

'Their code names?' She glanced at him. 'You mean from GAP? No, never. They never gave them away. That was the point. If they were arrested they gave their own names, or the ones on their papers. The defence was usually that they were just ordinary citizens, in the wrong place at the wrong time.'

Of course, that was exactly what Giovanni Trantemento had said – that Il Corvo and Beppe, he and Roblino, would claim they were just in the wrong place, and Massimo that he had never seen the woman Lilia – Issa – before. What was it Caterina had called it? A perverse kind of gift, the ability to deny even those closest to you – to say, I don't know, I don't know, I don't know.

'Here,' Signora Grandolo said, 'you can see for yourself. They were arrested in the late afternoon, all three at the same time. Does that sound right?'

He nodded. She swivelled the screen again. Leaning forward, Pallioti saw the three names entered clearly, as if in a school attendance book. They were recorded as having been arrested in Via Pergola at 4.10 p.m. and arriving at Villa Triste exactly thirteen minutes later.

Signora Grandolo read out loud: 'Giancarlo Menucci, Piero Balestro, Giovanni Rossi.'

Pallioti heard the names fall like rain. Like stones dropping into a deep, dark pool. He did not recognize them.

'They arrived at the Villa Triste on the afternoon of Valentine's Day,' Signora Grandolo continued. She clicked at the keyboard. 'And were removed three days later. On the 17th, at 8.40 in the evening, and put on a transport to the labour camps.'

Pallioti sat still for a moment. The timing matched too well. Two of them had to be Giovanni Trantemento and Roberto Roblino. Il Corvo and Beppe. In which case, the third man was Massimo. He leaned forward.

'What would have happened,' he asked, 'if they had escaped? Would that have been recorded?'

Signora Grandolo laughed. The look she gave him, the rise of her finely plucked eyebrows might as well have said, 'Are you kidding?'

'No,' she said. 'No, that wouldn't have been recorded. No one "escaped" from the Villa Triste. At least officially.'

'And unofficially?'

She shrugged. 'It would simply have been entered like this – that they were put on a transport.'

'Pass the buck down the line if they didn't appear at the other end?'

She nodded. 'Something like that. In the meantime, they would have hunted them down. And killed them. They were diligent about it. Often beyond reason. Escapers weren't just bad for morale, they were a personal insult. Not to mention an affront to order.' She gestured towards the neat-lined page on the screen. 'The Nazis and the Fascists, among the other things they had in common, shared a disdain for loose ends.'

Pallioti thought about this for a moment. Then he asked, 'Could you check? Can you cross-reference to see if you have any further record of them, of those names? If, say, anyone came looking for them after the war, or if they appear anywhere again in your database?'

She nodded. 'Of course.'

Signora Grandolo flexed her fingers for a moment, then began to tap out commands. The screen changed, and changed again. She watched it, frowned, and typed in another command. The screen changed yet again. Finally, she shook her head.

'No,' she said. 'I don't seem to be finding any record of them in our databases. None at all. Just this.'

She tried a few more commands, then shook her head. Her hands stilled. The screen had returned to the pages showing the records of Villa Triste for the second week of February 1944. The names stood out on the neatly lined page. Giancarlo Menucci. Piero Balestro. Giovanni Rossi.

Signora Grandolo turned towards Pallioti.

'Are you sure these are the men you are looking for, Dottore?' she asked.

Pallioti stared at the computer. In his mind's eye he saw the icy street, the coal cart, two men, their faces grimy with dust. He saw the sleek German car swing around the corner and glide to a halt. He heard the click of boot heels, the snap of salutes, doors opening, the rapid fire of shots. The sound of a woman running, and another crack as she fell. He heard Signor Cavicalli's voice, felt the featherweight of his hand. *The shooting at the Pergola Theatre, and anything at all that pertained to Radio Juliet.*

Signora Grandolo sat very still. She laced her hands on her desk and looked down at them.

'You know,' she said, finally, 'in my line of work, I find sometimes that the greatest danger is seeing what I want to see.'

Her eyes, in the lamplit room, were so dark they appeared almost black.

'It doesn't happen so often any more,' she said softly. 'Frankly, there isn't much opportunity. But when I first started this kind of work, I wanted so badly to help. To find at least some trace of the father or the mother or the daughter or husband. To say, "Yes, they were here." Even if it meant they were dead. Because it gave people something. Something to hold onto when everything else had shattered. It allowed them the rest of their lives, freed them – knowing what had happened. It's a peculiar kind of prison,' she added, 'not knowing.'

She smiled.

'Of course,' she said, 'I'm not telling you anything you don't know. But you see, I think we are a bit the same, you and me, Dottore. We want to be the ones to provide the key. Lift the bars. Have the power to make that prison vanish. I'm sure the church would insist that it's a monstrous act of ego – the refusal to settle for "I don't know."'

She unlaced her hands and looked down at her plain gold wedding ring and the small engagement ring that sat above it, the only jewellery she wore.

'My husband,' she said after a moment, 'Cosimo. He was a wise man. Small. Very ugly. Quiet. But no one's fool.' Signora Grandolo looked up again. Her eyes met his. 'He warned me,' she said, 'early on, when I started this work. He said I could do more harm than good, seeing connections where they didn't exist.'

Pallioti could hear a clock ticking in the room, and behind the heavy curtains, the spat of rain against the windows.

'Of course,' Signora Grandolo added, 'I didn't always listen to him.'

'And did you regret it?'

She thought for a moment, then shrugged.

'Usually,' she said. Then she smiled and added, 'But not always. Let's say, nine times out of ten.'

Pallioti ran his hand over his eyes. The tiredness that had plagued him more and more often recently had crept back, tiptoed up like a beggar child and pulled his sleeve. It whispered that he had not eaten, that Enzo was on his way now to solve this case, that he had better things to do. Pallioti gave the waif a morsel of reward by admitting it was probably right – then ruined that act of generosity by adding that he didn't care.

'Tell me something,' he said. 'How much do you know about GAP?'

'*Gruppi di Azione Patriottica*.' She smiled. 'What would be called now, I suppose, a terrorist organization. The Red Brigades modelled themselves on them, you know.'

Pallioti didn't. But when he thought about it, it didn't surprise him.

'You must have picked up quite a lot about them, GAP I mean,' he asked, 'over the years?'

'*Certo*,' she said. 'Of course. A lot of the people we deal with were members. Those who were working in the cities, in any case. The Garibaldi Brigades were in the countryside, up in the mountains, mainly. GAP dealt with sabotage, assassination. Weapon movements. Printing. And of course, getting people in and out. Jews. POWs. Allied escapees. But all the partisans did that.'

'Can you tell me—' Pallioti asked, 'I mean, how much do you know about their code names?'

She looked at him for a moment, then shook her head.

'Nothing extraordinary. They were given to them when they joined. You can understand.'

'Given to them?'

'Oh, yes.' Signora Grandolo nodded. 'At least, that's what I've always heard. They didn't choose them themselves, if that's what you're asking. Oh,' she added, 'I suppose the famous leaders might have, the legendary men like Il Lupo. But the rank and file, as far as I know, those were assigned. Just pulled out of thin air or made up.' She smiled. 'A lot of the survivors I've talked to, they weren't very happy with what they got. Hedgehog. Goat.'

'Why did they do that? Assign the names?'

'I assume,' Signora Grandolo said, 'for security. Wouldn't you think so?'

'The fear being that if you made up your own name you might, however unwittingly, give yourself away?' he said. 'Yes, probably.' After all, most people used part of their address as their PIN code.

'Yes,' she smiled. 'Most people aren't really very imaginative. Besides,' she added, laughing, 'they had to be assigned. Otherwise you'd have had sixteen Wolves, twenty Stallions, and thirty-five Thunderbolts in a sector. Which would have got rather confusing.'

Pallioti laughed. She was right.

'There's one more thing,' he said finally. 'The other date. Would you mind looking for me? Since we're here. It's two, actually. Or rather, anything between 12 June 1944 and, say, June 20th.'

Signora Grandolo, who had raised her hands over the keyboard ready to type again, dropped them.

'Ah,' she said. 'Radio Juliet?'

He nodded.

'I'm afraid not.'

Pallioti looked at her. An outright refusal was the last thing he had expected. Before he could ask why, she shook her head.

'I'm afraid,' she said, 'I did warn you. The records are not complete for Villa Triste. They don't go beyond April. April 23rd, to be exact.'

She leaned back, flexing her hands again.

'It's very frustrating. I've run into this again and again,' she explained. 'What they decided to destroy and what they didn't.' Signora Grandolo took her glasses off and looked at him. 'Chance plays more of a role in our affairs than we care to think. I suppose the most recent papers were probably the closest to hand during the final days, when they were leaving, so they went on the fire first. We should just be thankful that they didn't have time to make a barbecue of all of it.'

As she spoke, tiredness skittered across her face. Hiding his disappointment, Pallioti stood up. What didn't exist didn't exist. He had kept her long enough.

'I've taken up enough of your time,' he said. 'Again. Thank you.'

'Not at all. I'm just sorry I couldn't be of more help.'

'Not at all, Signora. You have helped immensely.'

'Well, I'm glad of that.'

She stood up, rubbing her stiff arm again, and moved around her desk to retrieve his coat from the closet. 'Is it very important?' she asked. 'Whatever it is you're hunting?'

For a moment he was tempted to tell her – to fish the little red book out of his pocket, tell her about Signor Cavicalli and Eleanor Sachs and the papers in the safe, and ask – for what? The balm of her agreement? Her understanding? For her at least not to think he was crazy?

'To be honest?' Pallioti said. 'I don't know. Probably not. At least not to anyone but me.'

'Well,' she smiled. 'That is no small consideration.' Opening the closet door, she looked over her shoulder. 'Will you do me a favour?' she asked as she retrieved his coat.

'*Certo*. If it is in my power, of course.'

'When you decide,' she said, 'if it is or if it isn't terribly important, to you or anyone else – or when it's over, whichever comes first. Will you tell me about it?'

He took the heavy coat out of her hands.

'Of course,' he said. 'Of course, Signora Grandolo. I will be delighted.'

'It's a date, then.'

She smiled and held out her hand, and for a moment Pallioti thought he had never seen a face more beautiful.

As he came out of the elevator, Pallioti looked around the empty lobby of the building. The thick glass muffled the storm outside. He took his phone out of his pocket, flipped it open, punched a number, and watched as the rain flung itself against the front of the building, hammering frantically before it scuttled off in the next gust of wind. The ringing echoed in his head.

Six, seven, eight. He was about to hang up when Giovanni Trantemento's sister finally picked up the telephone.

'*Pronto.*'

After he had introduced himself, she paused.

'Have you—' she asked. 'I mean, how nice to hear from you. Is there—'

The words wavered, sounding as if they were coming from farther away than Rome. In an instant, he saw the large gloomy room, overstuffed with furniture, with brocade and needlepoint, the piano groaning under the weight of photographs of the dead.

'No, no,' he said quickly. 'I am sorry, Signora, but I cannot tell you anything definite yet.'

'Oh.'

He didn't know whether it was relief or disappointment he heard in her voice. Probably both. The naming of killers to the families of murder victims was always a strange business. Unlike Signora Grandolo, he was not so certain that knowing set anyone free. It was rather more, he thought, a case of exchanging one prison for another. Bartering the blank screen of ignorance for the dreadful pictures of reality.

'We are making progress.' Pallioti forged on. 'And I am sorry to bother you in the evening. But I was hoping that you might be able to help me with something. About your brother.'

'Yes,' she said quickly. 'Oh, yes. Of course.'

'You told me,' Pallioti said, 'I believe, when we met, that when you were a child, after your father died, you weren't allowed to use his name?'

'Yes,' she said. 'Yes, that's right. My mother, she was so angry.'

He could almost see Maria Valacci twisting the sapphire ring, rolling it back and forth on her claw of a hand as if it somehow conjured the past.

'It was fear, really,' she said. 'She was afraid, and she had to hate someone for that, so she hated my father. For being dead.

389

For leaving us all alone. Abandoning us, she called it. She was so angry, she stopped using his name. Went to the town hall and changed my name. It was one of the things that made her so angry with Gio, that he wouldn't.'

'Wouldn't change his name?'

'No. Well,' she added, 'not until we went to Switzerland. Then he did. Not that it made her happy,' Maria Valacci added. 'She was still horrible to him.'

Given what Antonio Valacci had told him about his grandmother, Pallioti suspected nothing would have made the woman happy. Hate was the Fascist tipple of choice. Clearly, she'd drunk deep.

He did not voice the thought. Instead, he asked, 'And Trantemento? Am I correct in thinking, then, that that was your mother's name?'

'Yes. Yes,' Maria Valacci replied. 'Francesca Trantemento. That's right.'

'And Signora—' Pallioti took a breath, feeling as if he were a gambler throwing a dice. 'Your father's name?' he asked. 'Could you tell me what that was?'

'*Certo*,' she replied. 'Of course. It was Angelo. God rest his soul. My father's name was Angelo Mario Rossi.'

She could not see him, but Pallioti nodded.

'So,' he asked quietly, 'if I understand correctly, before you went to Switzerland, your brother Giovanni was known as—'

'Rossi,' she said. 'Giovanni Battiste Rossi, the name he was born with. He changed it, finally, to make my mother happy, when we went to Switzerland. So we could be a proper family. All of us the same.'

Pallioti said nothing.

On the other end of the phone, he heard the slight rasping intake of breath. 'Actually,' she said abruptly, 'it must have been just before.'

'Just before?'

'Yes. Now that I think about it. Yes.'

'Just before what, Signora?'

'Well, just before we went to Switzerland, that he changed his name. Because, you see—'

He could hear her thinking it out, piecing the past together as she spoke the words.

'When he came home,' she said, 'that day, out of the blue. We had no idea that he was coming. But he had all the papers. The travel passes and train tickets, all ready. And all the names were the same. Trantemento. So he must have done it before, mustn't he? I never really thought about it,' she added. 'I was so excited. But looking back on it, he must have planned it. Quite a long way in advance, I mean. Because, apart from anything else – travel permits. Train tickets. They had to be for a specific day, even a specific train. And they weren't easy to get. All the trains were being used for – well. Other things. It was such a panic.'

'A panic?' Pallioti murmured.

'Oh, yes,' she said. 'Yes. Anyone who could was desperate to get out, of course. Because of the advance. But it just wasn't possible. There weren't any trains. So you can imagine, when Gio just turned up, out of the blue, with everything – all with our names and photos, all correct – and told us we were going to Switzerland. That night. Well, you can imagine.'

'Yes. And this was,' Pallioti asked, 'exactly when, Signora? In March? April?'

'Oh, no,' she said quickly. 'It was the day after my birthday. As if he'd planned it.' Maria Valacci laughed. 'I think I thought he had. Or I allowed myself to. As if the whole thing was a present for me. So of course I remember. Gio came in the morning. It was a Friday. He told us we were taking the train that night. Mama was angry, of course. That we didn't have much time to pack, but I was—'

'And the date was?' Pallioti cut her off.

'Oh, I'm sorry, Ispettore. June. Friday, the 16th of June, 1944.'

Pallioti looked across the empty lobby to the glass doors. The blowing rain had turned to sleet. In the mountains, it would probably be coming down as snow, would be feathering the brown upland fields, coating the ancient stones and paths of the Via degli Dei.

'Are you certain, Signora Valacci?'

His voice was low, as soft as the flakes that would be fluttering into the chinks of the refuge cabins, and blurring the windows of the huts where the partisans had sheltered all through the autumn and Christmas of 1943 and into the bitter first months of the new year.

'You were only a girl,' he added. 'It was a long time ago. A confusing time. You could have—'

'No, Ispettore,' Maria Valacci said, 'I couldn't.' Her voice hardened. 'I wasn't that much of a girl, I assure you.'

The steel in her words, Pallioti suspected, had less to do with the perceived insult that she might have mistaken the date of one of the most important events of her life, than with the fact that it was precisely that. A memory of such significance that every detail was etched on her heart. Recited through the watch hours like a prayer. Engraved, as hard and pure as words on stone.

'I am absolutely certain,' she said. 'Giovanni came to Pisa and took us to Switzerland on Friday the 16th of June, 1944.'

Chapter Twenty-Seven

It was Friday morning. On the radio, the weather forecaster was making dire predictions. There would be snow. Sleet. Hail. The end of the world! Pallioti stood without moving. He was staring out of his office window onto the piazza, but he wasn't seeing it. Instead, he was seeing the neat lettering on the ledger pages of the Villa Triste, and, for some reason, the Cavicallis' cat.

She had been blotched and multicoloured as a jigsaw, her wide golden eyes as round as marbles. Slipping back into the shop, she had moved so fast that she had not been much more than a shadow. If he hadn't felt the brush against his leg, he might not have noticed she was there at all.

He was missing something, and he couldn't understand what it was.

He drummed his fingers on the sill, reluctant to admit that it probably didn't matter. When he had called Enzo on Wednesday night, catching him moments after the plane had landed in the warmer and drier South to give him the names he had dug up, Enzo had been grateful for his efforts, but not particularly interested. Enzo Saenz had made it clear, politely but firmly, that he didn't actually care what Giovanni Trantemento or Roberto Roblino had called themselves over sixty years ago. What he was interested in was the present.

Cesare D'Aletto had obtained permission to hold the charming Bruno Torricci and his equally charming girlfriend for another forty-eight hours. They had a witness who could place both of them in a bar within ten miles of Roberto Roblino's house on the Saturday afternoon when he was killed. In addition they had found a receipt from a jeweller in Bari dated November 3rd, for a silver charm bracelet priced at three hundred and twenty euros, and paid for in cash, from Bruno Torricci's wallet. Even more important, however, they had a lead on the weapon.

A week earlier, when Cesare D'Aletto had received the forensics reports on Roblino's house, he had noticed something strange. A fragment of a composite plastic that 'resembled Bakelite' had been one of the very few things found in the garden. It had struck him as unusual because Bakelite, while common in the thirties and forties, wasn't used much after 1950. A check had confirmed that nothing in the Masseria Santa Anna was made of Bakelite. Roberto Roblino was not, for instance, an antique wireless enthusiast. Still, something about the fragment had rung a bell with D'Aletto and he had called a colleague in Turin who had reminded him of a case where a vintage pistol had been used. It had had a Bakelite grip. They crumbled with age. That had been enough to prompt D'Aletto to send his bullet to an analyst in Naples who specialized in antique weapons. He had explained that the markings on the casing suggested that it could have been fired by a small sidearm called a Sauer 38H. The gun in question was, apparently, a particularly prized specimen among Nazi enthusiasts. It had been the weapon of choice during the war for the SS, the SD, and the *Fallschirmjäger*, and a certain number of them had been manufactured to fire .22-calibre ammunition.

Cesare had not even got round to telling Enzo about all this when Bruno Torricci had responded to the standard question of whether he had ever owned a firearm by launching into a soliloquy on the beauty of authentic Nazi weapons. The wording he had used had suggested strongly that he had one weapon in mind.

By now, both Cesare and Enzo were convinced that he was teasing them – that Bruno Torricci knew perfectly well that a Sauer 38H had been used to kill Roberto Roblino. They were responding by widening the search for witnesses, seeing not only if they could place him in Florence, but also obtaining warrants to search his flat in Rome and his girlfriend's parents' house outside Bari. Enzo was staying on in Brindisi. He hoped to be back, possibly as early as today or tomorrow, with a confession.

The door opened.

'I'm sorry.' Guillermo's head appeared, his bald pate shining in the overhead lights. 'I did buzz you,' he said, 'but you didn't hear. Doctor Eleanor Sachs is on the phone.'

Pallioti nodded. As he went to his desk, Guillermo handed him a message slip.

'This came for you.'

Pallioti glanced at it. It was from the London Embassy, a mobile contact number for Lord David Eppsy, the aristocratic and vacationing collector of 'erotica' whom Pallioti had, to be honest, forgotten all about. He shoved it into his pocket.

'I'm sorry,' Eleanor Sachs said. 'I hope I'm not disturbing you.'

On the phone, her voice sounded exactly the same as it did in person. In Pallioti's experience this was rarer than one thought. For some reason, it made him smile.

'Not at all,' he said. 'Actually, I was going to call you.'

'You were?'

He heard the hesitation, and the excitement underneath it, and felt a pang of guilt.

'I haven't found Il Spettro,' he said. 'I'm sorry. But I do have three names. I was wondering if you might have come across any of them. In your research.'

'Oh. Sure,' she said. 'Of course. Like I said, my memory's not perfect. But – shoot.'

'Giancarlo Menucci. Piero Balestro. Giovanni Rossi.'

He could hear her writing them down, the faint scratch of a pen on paper.

'No,' she said after a moment. 'Not right off the bat, anyway. Who are, were, they?'

'Well, Giovanni Rossi was Giovanni Trantemento.'

'What?'

'Rossi was his father's name. He stopped using it sometime in the spring of 1944 and started using Trantemento. One of the other two was, I believe, Roberto Roblino.'

Eleanor Sachs made a humming noise. 'Well,' she said. 'That would explain the birth certificate. Or lack of it.'

'Yes.' Pallioti went on, 'I'm not sure who the third man is. But I do know that they were in the same GAP unit. I believe his code name was Massimo.'

'Massimo.' Pallioti could hear the pen again as she wrote the name down. 'So. Let me get this straight. Massimo joins Beppe, Roblino. And Trantemento, Il Corvo, who was formerly Giovanni Rossi?'

'That's right.' Pallioti nodded. 'So I believe Massimo and Beppe-Roblino are Giancarlo Menucci and Piero Balestro, or vice versa. I don't know which is which, but I do know they were using those names in the spring of 1944.'

'Interesting. There are lots of reasons people change their names. I wonder what theirs were?'

'No idea,' Pallioti said. 'But all three of them were arrested and taken to the Villa Triste. On Valentine's Day, 1944. They escaped together, three days later, from a truck on its way to the train station. It skidded and crashed into a wall. On the night of the 17th.'

'*In bocca al lupo*,' she muttered, the phrase for 'good luck'.

In the wolf's mouth indeed, Pallioti thought. 'Yes,' he agreed. 'Given that they were on their way to a labour camp.'

'Well.' Eleanor Sachs paused. 'Thank you for this. I'll – I'll look into it. See what I can see.'

'But the names mean nothing to you?'

'Off the top of my head?' She gave a little laugh. 'Do you mean are any of them my family names? My father's middle name, perhaps? No. But you never know,' she added, 'what you find if you keep turning over rocks.'

'There is something else—' Pallioti hesitated, not sure if what he was about to do was exactly right, then deciding he could see no harm in it. 'You might,' he added, 'want to talk to a Signor Cavicalli. There are two of them, senior and junior. The father started a business called Patria Memorabilia. I don't know how active it is any more, but it dealt almost exclusively in partisan memorabilia. Giovanni Trantemento did some business with them,' he added. 'It's in Santa Croce.'

'Yes,' she said. 'I've heard of it. The only time I went, the shop was closed. I'll try again.' She hesitated. 'Thank you,' she said again, finally. 'For all of this.'

' Eleanor—' He tried to keep the urgency out of his voice. 'If you find anything,' he said, 'on the three men—'

'Of course,' she said. 'Of course. Don't worry. I'll let you know right away, I promise.' Pallioti wondered if she was making an X over her heart. 'In fact,' she added, 'that's why I was calling you. About those two women, the sisters—'

'Ah,' he said. 'I'm afraid I gave you the wrong name.'

'Oh. Because I was going to tell you, there was one who died. In San Verdiana, in the winter of 1944.'

Pallioti thought about that for a moment. 'Yes,' he said. 'That would have been their mother. I'm sorry. I didn't mean to send you on a wild goose chase.'

Eleanor Sachs laughed again.

'No harm done,' she said. 'I barely came up with a pin-feather. What was the right name, just out of interest?'

'Bevanelli. Chiara and Laura. They were active in Milan. In 1944 and 1945.'

'Oh. OK.' He could hear the scratch of the pen. 'Well,' she said when it stopped. 'If I find anything. I mean, if I stumble across it – if you're interested. I don't suppose,' she asked, 'you know what happened to them?'

'No.' Pallioti shook his head. He put his own pen down. 'No,' he said. 'I have no idea at all.'

∽

March 1945

The bombing got worse.

We all understood that this was in preparation for the 'final assault', but that in no way lessened the terror of it. Or the destruction. The main targets were, of course, the railway lines and stations and marshalling yards, but the church near our building was hit early one morning. The sound was deafening, like a volcano. Issa grabbed the baby and we ran downstairs and out into the street, not certain at all that our old building was going to remain standing. It did, but the doctor's office I worked in was not so fortunate. Two days later it was destroyed completely. I was spared because I had a cold and had gone home early.

The sadness of it when I went to look the next day was like a blow in the stomach. The lovely Liberty building was a pile of rubble and a crater. There were no survivors. There was nothing.

We had been in Milan only a short time, but those months were the first time I had worked, day in and day out, with a group of fellow resistants, all of us in that office knowing what we were doing – where our extra supplies went, what the nights would bring. I could not say that they were my friends – they never knew my real name or where I came from, and perhaps I did not know theirs – but for the first time I had experienced the comradeship, the bond of trust that Issa must have shared, not only with Carlo and Rico, but with the others in her GAP unit and in the mountains. It brought home to me, as I walked back that evening, the depth of the betrayal over JULIET, the loneliness of it, that she must have felt, that she must still feel every time she thinks of it.

The thought made me ill, and again, that night, I almost told her. Almost confessed that I was sure we had not all been betrayed by someone inside – that the fault was not theirs, it was mine. But once again, I was too much of a coward. I couldn't bring myself to do it. Instead I vowed, as I have before, that I would do anything, forever, to make it up to her.

The chance came earlier than I thought.

I could not go back to work. I had nowhere to go. I was going to volunteer at a hospital or a clinic, but instead Issa asked me to take care of the baby. In the spring, probably some time in the next month, the Allies will make a final effort to break through the Gothic Line. Everyone believes that this time, they will succeed. But we also understand that, with their backs to the wall, the Germans will fight savagely. They have little left to lose.

Intelligence is crucial, and of course the Allies do not have enough of it. Once more, they needed to know the location of every gun emplacement, every anti-tank trap and mined stretch of track. This is especially difficult in the mountains. Issa told me that in the past month there have been

attempts by the troops dug in around Monte Sole
to capture German soldiers in order to get information from them. These efforts have met with
some success, but spies are more effective – spies
who know the mountains and can get in close to
the German positions.

As she told me this, my first reaction was to
protest. To say 'no'. To plead with her that it was
too dangerous. Beg her not to do it. Then I saw
her face. For the first time since the baby was
born, there was that other light in her eyes.

And so we fell into a routine. Issa was not gone
all the time, but sometimes for several days. I
stayed in the apartment, in our two rooms, to
care for my nephew.

He is a fine boy. Already I can see Carlo and
Issa in his tiny face. He gurgles when I sing to
him, though I dare say from the way he waves
his hands, he does not always think much of my
singing. When his mother comes back, he twists
his body towards her. He cannot yet control his
little arms and legs, but his eyes look to her voice,
widen at the sight of her face.

During all of this, the bombing went on. It
seemed crazed, as if the Allies had adopted the
same scorched earth policy the Germans favour
on their retreats. Perhaps they are competing, to
see who can destroy the most first. Issa reported
that the corridor to the Brenner was a corridor
of death. Anti-aircraft guns firing into the skies
and explosions dropping from the heavens. There
is heavy bombing on either side of the Po, and
anything on the road is in danger of being
strafed. There is almost no petrol, and no coal at
all. So the Germans have taken to towing two

supply trucks behind one that is still running, or to using oxen and carts. People say that a great number of the poor animals lie dead in the ditches.

Issa moved mostly at night. I could never tell when she was going to arrive or go. A few nights ago, it was very late when I heard footsteps on the stairs, then the rasp of the key in the door. I did not realize until the next morning that she had brought another letter from Lodovico. By the time I opened it, she was gone. Which was a good thing, given what it said.

Lodo said the assault was coming and everyone knew it. The Germans had their backs to the wall, the Fascisti, too. They would fight like cornered dogs. As for the Allies, they would throw everything they have at this effort in order to stop the enemy getting to the Alps. We would be in the middle of both a devastating attack and an equally devastating retreat.

But Lodo had a plan. He could get me out. There was a fishing boat called the Santa Maria leaving Genoa. The captain would be looking for me and would take me aboard. Lodovico had already paid him one half of the fee. The Captain would receive the other half when I landed safe in Naples.

I stared at the words. They swam in front of me, refused to stay still, as if they were slipping off the page. The date Lodo named was three days away.

I folded the letter and hid it.

What I did not count on, of course, was Issa.

The next day when I came in, she was sitting

at the kitchen table, the single sheet of paper smoothed in front of her. She held it down with both hands, as if it might fly away.

'What is this?'

I stopped dead. Then I closed the door behind me.

'You know what it is,' I said, trying to keep my voice as even as possible. 'You've read it.'

I was kicking myself. I should have kept the wretched thing on me. I should have destroyed it when I had the chance. I should never have fooled myself that I could hide anything from Issa.

'It doesn't matter.'

I set my few pathetic parcels down, then turned and looked at her.

'I won't leave you,' I said. 'I'm not going. I won't leave you,' I said again, trying to reassure her that I would never betray her.

'What do you mean?'

I shrugged and laughed.

'Exactly what I said. I'm not going,' I repeated. 'I don't want to. And I couldn't get there if I did want to. And, in any case, I don't. I won't leave you.'

'But you must. You must!'

It took me a moment to realize she was angry.

'You can't stay for me.' She shook her head. 'I won't let you. I don't need you,' Issa said. 'I'm fine on my own.'

Not believing what I was hearing, I stared at her, and saw again that cold, hard thing in her eyes. That thing I had seen that afternoon on the terrace – in another lifetime. Nemesis.

'I wouldn't do it for you,' she said.

The words hit me like a slap. They took my

breath away. I stared at her, as if she had suddenly become someone I didn't know.

'If Carlo was alive,' she said quite calmly, 'and I could be with him, I would. I'd run. I'd crawl, if I had to. I'd leave you in a minute.'

I could feel myself shaking. My eyes were blurring.

'Well, I,' I said, gasping for breath, 'I, thank God, am not you!'

I pushed past her and stormed into the other room. I slammed the door. The baby began to cry. I heard Issa go to him, heard her singing to him. I stood for a moment, feeling the walls slip and slide around me. Then I sat on the bed and rocked – back and forth, back and forth, in time to her voice coming through the thin wood of the door. Then I cried. I cried until my throat was sore and my eyes were swollen, until I finally fell asleep.

There was an old armchair in the kitchen, next to the bassinet. Issa must have slept there, because she did not come near me. The next morning, I heard her moving around very early. I fell asleep again, hoping, I think, that she would simply go. Disappear into the mountains and leave the baby and me in peace; return in a few days, another person. But when I finally opened the door, I saw that both of them had gone. I stood there in the kitchen, alone. She had stuck to her word, I thought, but the other way round. She had abandoned me so I would have no choice but to leave.

I sat down at the table. I had no idea what to do. Without her, I was adrift. Even if I had wanted to go to Genoa, I had no idea how I would begin to get there. I could hardly go to the station and get on a train. The day was brighter than it had been. Sun was spilling through the single window in the kitchen. I sat watching it play on the sill, and thinking of what my life would be like without her, of how the years would echo into emptiness. I was still thinking that when I heard her footsteps on the stairs.

She walked in, carrying the baby, and set him down in the bassinet without speaking to me. When she turned around, she had that look – the one I remembered from when she was going into the mountains or came to the hospital in Florence and wanted something. She was not angry any more, but very calm. She had made up her mind.

'You have to go,' she said. She looked at me. 'You have to go, Cati. And you have to take him with you.' Before I could even open my mouth, she added, 'It's all arranged. They'll come for you this afternoon, and take you both to Genoa.'

I stared at her. Then I shook my head.

'No,' I said. 'I can't. I can't, Issa. I—'

Before I could stop her, she got down on her knees in front of me and took my hands.

'Cati,' she said, studying my face. 'I'm begging you. I'm begging you, for my son. You can take him out of all this. Out of what's coming. He'll be safe in Naples.'

I opened my mouth. I started to speak, and then couldn't. Because she was right.

'You take him,' Issa said. 'If you love me, Cati. You take him.' I had always known that she was utterly ruthless. That when she thought something was right, she would stop at nothing. She squeezed my hands. 'I'll join you. I'll come as soon as I can.'

'No,' I said quickly. 'No.' I saw my opening and took it. 'We must all go together, the three of us.'

Issa shook her head.

'There won't be space on the boat. And, even if there was, rail passes are all but impossible. I could barely get one for you and him. I can't possibly get another.'

'You could try. You could—'

She shook her head again.

'The captain won't wait. He'll sail tomorrow night. He has to. He has to get to sea when there is no moon.'

'Then you go,' I said. 'You go in my place, with your son. And I'll follow. I'll get there. Lodovico will look after you.'

At that, Issa actually smiled. She rocked back on her heels, still holding my hands.

'The best way will be to come through the mountains,' she said. 'Who do you think is more likely to survive that?'

I looked at her. We both knew that the answer was not me.

'I can't bring you and a baby, Cati, through the mountains. And there isn't room on that boat, not for all of us, and it won't wait. Besides,' she added, 'I have a job to do here. When it's finished, I'll come. I promise you.'

I looked at her then, and saw the loss of Carlo in her face, and remembered what I had promised myself. What I had vowed – that I would do anything for her.

Isabella told me to listen to her. She told me she had thought about it all night, and that she had already planned to go to Bologna. She said she would see out the fight there – that they needed her, and that it was close to the mountains. When she was ready, she would disappear, follow the Via degli Dei home, find Mama, then get them both to Naples. She could walk the mountains blindfold. She knew where and who to turn to for help. She studied my face.

'Could you do that?' she asked.

I shook my head.

'Don't you believe that I can?'

Even as a child, Isabella always understood how to ask the right questions, how to stop me in my tracks. And of course, she was right. She was a legend. If anyone was going to survive, it would be her.

'You must take the baby and go now,' she said. 'As it is, it will be hard enough. Please,' she added. 'Please, Cati. I'm asking you to do this for me. To save him. Get him out of here. If you love me.'

I looked down into her face. I felt her hands, gripping mine. 'If you love me.' What could I say to that?

So we are going. In an hour. Or two. A man is coming with a set of papers that says I am his wife and we are travelling with our infant son to live with relatives in Genoa. All signed, sealed, and stamped. That is what Isabella was doing this morning. I forget sometimes who and what she is. That there are people who owe her things. Favours. Their lives.

A few minutes ago, she pulled me into the bedroom, as if the baby might overhear us, and said there was something I had to swear to: that if anything happened to her, I would never tell her child that he was not my son.

'You have to swear,' she said. This time she did hold her hand up. 'You have to swear, if I don't get there, if something happens to me, that you will take him, and keep him, and make him yours and never let him know, never let him guess, that his mother gave him up. That she let him go. Even for a moment. I don't want him to live with that. Promise me.'

I looked into her eyes. I wanted to tell her it was stupid – that if anything happened to her, he would understand, I would make him understand how much she loved him.

'Please,' she said. 'For me, Cati. Swear.'

And so I raised my hand. I held it against hers.

'Blood bond, Cati,' Isabella whispered.

I nodded.

'Blood bond, Issa.'

Even now, I don't know if I can bring myself to leave her. I feel as if my stomach is being ripped out. Only looking at the baby makes the pain bearable – I am doing this for him. And for her. Because she has asked me.

But I can't bear her feeling abandoned, betrayed and alone as she did when she stood by the side of that trench. So this is what I am going to do.

I am going to fight you one last time, Isabella. With guile. And this time, I am going to win. Do you hear me? You have no one to blame but yourself if you do not like it. You taught me to walk slowly, to look in the glass – you taught me courage. And you taught me defiance. So if you are angry with me, you have no one to blame but yourself. You showed me the way.

I am almost at the end of this book now. It will not see out the war, as I planned. I do not have a photo of myself to leave for you, for you to keep next to your heart where you keep Carlo's. Instead, you will have to make do with these 'word pictures'. In a moment, I am going to get up and hide this book in the bedroom, somewhere easy. Somewhere, where – tomorrow or the next day – you, being you, will find it. And then you will keep it for me until we meet again, and know that my words are with you, and that you are not alone just because we are gone.

I wish I had something else, something better, but this is all I have to leave you – this piece of me. And this last picture.

We are sitting here, the three of us now, at this little table in a tiny apartment that belongs to strangers that we have made our home. There is sunlight coming through the window and Isabella is singing to the baby. She looks into his eyes and rocks him. Then she gets up and dances with him. She holds her son in her arms while we wait for the knock on the door.

PART FIVE

Chapter Twenty-Eight

The city was silver. The much-anticipated storm had blown through some time around midnight, taking all the colour with it. It had sucked the red out of the roofs, leached the gold and the soft creamy warmth from the stuccoed palazzos. Runnels of sleet froze in the cracks of the cobbles as Saturday hovered between dawn and sunrise.

Despite lunches at Saffy's, Pallioti had come to hate the weekends. This was a recent development, and he saw no particular trigger or cause for it other than turning fifty. Previously, he had been as jealous of his time off as anyone else, and quite happy spending time with, and by, himself. Now, if he was not in the office, he was restless. These days, he found it a relief if there was an urgent case, a 'flap' on, a drama that required one hundred per cent of his attention. The last two weekends had been ideal. But the fraud case was winding up. And so, apparently, were the murders of the two old men. Enzo did not have his confession yet, but he was still in Brindisi. And if anything, more optimistic. In short, everything was running smoothly. Which left Pallioti at a fidgeting, bored dead end.

He was not even sure how long he had been walking. Eventually, he found himself off the Via dei Renai. Perhaps he had been coming here all along. He really didn't know. With no more writing in the little red book, with the final few pages dog-eared and slightly grubby, but resolutely empty, he felt bereft. Betrayed, and a little annoyed. As if he had been sucked into an affair and then abandoned. Believed in a story only to find that it had no ending.

The five roses were still in the little glass tube. Now their petals were battered by sleet, tiny crystals of ice hidden in their soft white folds. Taking his glove off, he reached up, and ran his fingers over the words on the plaque. His hand lingered, and began to freeze, dwelling on the icy letters. Putting his gloves back on did not help. Neither did clapping vigorously. Finally, the cold propelled him into a tiny bar where the street sweepers and traffic patrolmen stopped for the earliest coffee of the day.

He did not ask, or pay, for a cognac with his coffee, but the girl behind the counter took one look at him and poured one anyway.

Taking Caterina's book out of his pocket, he set it on the table he had chosen by the window. He did not care to admit it, but Signor Cavicalli's revelation that he had bought it in a job lot of unclaimed bits and pieces from the Florentine Red Cross – that it had ended up as one more piece of flotsam and jetsam, one more fragment consigned to the rag-and-bone box of the country's past, had upset him. He had slept badly the night before, his dreams full of ragged women marching four abreast past silent crowds. Of trains lurching and gathering speed, leaving in their wake a confetti of names and addresses, final messages, falling onto the tracks like snow. A girl had danced with a baby in her arms. Men stood in a clearing, holding shovels.

Irritated, he told himself it was a long time ago, and that none of it mattered, and swallowed the coffee. It met the brandy, and gurgled and burned in his chest. A raucous guffaw came from two workmen. A traffic cop teased the girl behind the counter. Having spent the night in the company of ghosts, it was a pleasure to be again in the world of the living. He got up and returned to the bar and was waiting for his second espresso, actively resisting the compulsion both to order another brandy and to drum his fingers, when his phone vibrated in his pocket. It was a text, from Eleanor Sachs. *Didn't want to wake you. Call me when you're up. Found something.*

༄

'Eleanor?'

'Oh,' she said. 'I hope I didn't wake you up.'

The table teetered as Pallioti reached for the lemon peel balanced on the saucer and bit it in half.

'I've been up for hours,' he replied, wondering if this was strictly true. 'Well, anyway, a couple of hours.'

'Join the club. I used to go running. Every morning at five. Before I screwed up my knee. No more marathons, but I still wake up.' He thought for a moment that she was going to ask him what his excuse was, but she didn't. Instead, she said. 'Anyway. I wanted to tell you, I found something – about those women.'

He swallowed the lemon peel and began the tricky manoeuvre of opening his sugar packet single-handed.

'Go on.'

'Well—'

Pallioti could hear her doing something in a kitchen, the clink of china. He imagined her with the phone clamped between her head and shoulder. Any moment, it would probably clatter to the floor and go dead.

'Both of them,' she continued. The clinking had stopped and her voice sounded less muffled. 'Cammaccio and Bevanelli.'

Before Pallioti could tell her that that couldn't be, that there was a mistake because they were one and the same, she went on.

'A Caterina Cammaccio is listed in a field hospital in Bologna. In April 1945. Then she's listed as dead in the '45 Red Cross records for Florence.'

Pallioti paused. Caterina must have decided to stay, after all. Or something must have gone wrong. With the trains. Perhaps she couldn't get to Genoa, in the end. Or perhaps something happened to the baby, and she came back. Perhaps she just couldn't bring herself to be without Isabella.

Outside the bar's grubby plate glass window a flowering of paper gelato cups lay in the gutter, their blue and pink polka dots bright in the cold morning.

'Then there's an L. Bevanelli,' Eleanor Sachs said. 'That's the right name, right? Bevanelli?'

She spelled it.

'Right.'

She could not see Pallioti, but he nodded, abandoning the sugar packet.

'Well, according to the CLN, L. Bevanelli was last seen on 17 April, near a place called Anzola. I looked it up. It's just west of Bologna. The main rail line runs through there. There was heavy bombing around then. A softening up, before the last Allied advance, trying to finish off the German retreat – force a surrender.'

Pallioti wanted to ask her to stop. But he didn't.

'This Bevanelli,' Eleanor Sachs said. 'Definitely a woman. She was apparently working on a sabotage unit. They'd moved into a farmhouse to get some rest. It was hit by an Allied bomb. One guy was outside at the time. He reported all the rest of them as dead.'

'Are you still there?' Eleanor Sachs asked a moment later. When he didn't answer, she said, 'I'm sorry. I'm really sorry. I thought it was just something to do with this case thing. I didn't realize you knew them. I mean, that you were connected to them.'

'No.' Pallioti glanced at the little red book. 'No. I'm not.' It wasn't, strictly speaking, a lie. But it felt like it. 'Did you say CLN?' he asked quickly.

'Yeah,' Eleanor replied. 'Their records are great. I made a copy of the guy's report – there wasn't any point with the Red Cross. At least I didn't think so. It was just a couple of sentences. The Bologna field hospital and then the Florence lists. I can tell you right where to find them, though. If you want them.'

'And the CLN, the Red Cross, they had nothing on the other three, the men?'

'Not that I saw. But to be honest,' she added, 'I didn't have all that long. They were closing early yesterday, at the archive. Some kind of maintenance, or something. I'm going to take a longer look, first thing Monday morning. I'll let you know,' she said. 'I can drop off the copy of this report too, if you want. I'll—'

'Eleanor, do you have it now, with you?'

She hesitated.

'Yes. Sure. I can read it to you. It's—'

'Would you mind,' Pallioti asked, already standing up, 'if I came and looked at it?'

ೲ

'Well, so much for the idea that nothing happens in Italy before noon.'

The address Eleanor Sachs had given Pallioti was a cottage on an estate up behind San Miniato. Yet again, she had been telling the truth. It really wasn't far, not more than a ten-minute walk, from the restaurant Saffy had chosen the Sunday before. Backed by a high hedge that shielded it from the main house, the cottage sat just off the drive looking down towards the city. A small Renault of some sort with Roman rental plates was pulled up on the apron outside. There were no curtains. He had seen her moving about inside before he knocked on the door.

'Come on in,' she said. 'Take a pew.'

Eleanor Sachs nodded towards the high stools pulled up at the breakfast bar.

'Here.' She ducked around the counter and retrieved a piece of paper from the table, handing it to him as he unzipped his jacket and sat down.

The CLN report didn't add much to what she had already told him. A Bevanelli, L. had been working with a GAP unit from Bologna that was engaged in sabotaging the main railway line to Modena. They had been a few miles east of the town of Anzola on the afternoon of 17 April 1945, and were waiting for the safe cover of dark in an abandoned farm not far from the tracks when the line was hit by Allied bombs.

I had gone outside to relieve myself and was standing in a shelter of trees when I heard and saw the incoming planes. They were flying very low. There was danger of machine-gun strafing. I threw myself into a thicket of bushes and heard several loud explosions. When I eventually got up, I saw that the house had taken what appeared to be a direct hit. To the best of my knowledge, all five of the comrades listed below, who had been sleeping inside at the time, are dead.

It was signed by someone called Bernardo Fabbro. Pallioti ran his eye down the list of names below the signature. It was not alphabetical. Bevanelli, L., was the second to last. There was a capital *F* beside the name, presumably denoting female, since all the others were marked with an *M*.

He stared at the piece of paper for a moment as if it would tell him something, as if, in looking at it, he could reach out and touch her. Speak to her. Reassure Issa that, although she had missed the liberation by days, it had not been for nothing. There was some consolation, he thought, in the knowledge that four others were with her. That she had not died alone.

As for Caterina, he hoped that she had not lived long enough to know that Isabella had been killed. Hoped that whatever had taken her life – whether it was a piece of shrapnel, a German mine, or an Allied bomb – had done it before she understood that she was the last one. That none of her family had survived. They would never know, he supposed, what had become of the baby. He would almost certainly have been with Caterina which meant he too had probably been killed.

He was aware of Eleanor watching him.

'I'm sorry,' she said again.

'No.' He shook his head. 'No, I just thought – it doesn't matter. May I?'

He held up the paper. She nodded. Pallioti folded it and put it in his pocket.

'Your grandparents,' he asked, wanting to change the subject, 'what were their names, by the way?'

'Oh.' Eleanor smiled. 'Victor and Maria. Fabbionocci. They changed it to Faber. You know, a lot of people did. It was just easier. On forms and stuff. My father was Antonio. Tony Faber. Doesn't even sound very Italian, does it?'

The kitchen was tucked into the corner of the large front room which made up most of the cottage. Through an open doorway, Pallioti could see a second room, an unmade bed, books piled beside it on the floor. A laptop computer was set up on what was supposed to be the dining-room table. Papers were scattered across the sofa. Eleanor, who had just poured him a mug of coffee from the requisite American-style machine, saw him taking in the mess and laughed.

'The ruins of my great book.' She shook her head. 'I had this fantasy that I would come here and find out who my family really was and write this great, moving memoir. I guess I should have stuck to Petrarch, huh?' She perched on a stool across from him. 'I'm obviously not too good at this partisan detective work.'

Pallioti regarded her for a minute, her small heart-shaped face, the dark eyes and the features that pretended to be sharper and harder than he suspected they were. Saffy was right, she did look like Audrey Hepburn. A little more dishevelled. But just as pretty.

'I don't know that I'm so good at it, either,' he said. Then he added, feeling that he wanted to give her something, to thank her, 'The woman, Laura Bevanelli, as she was known then. Her name was also Isabella Cammaccio. She was in a GAP group in Florence. I think she used the code name Lilia.'

'Lilia?'

He nodded. 'That's right. Or at least I think it is. If I'm right, she was part of the same GAP unit that worked with your friend Beppe—'

'Aka Roberto Roblino and previously somebody else.'

'And Il Corvo, and the unknown Massimo.'

'Rossi, Balestro, Menucci.' Eleanor looked at him. 'So that's why you wanted to know about her. Not because she was a relative, but because she was connected to them?'

'Yes. I found some – references, to her and her sister. In Giovanni Trantemento's papers. Since they all knew each other.' He shrugged. 'It doesn't matter.'

She smiled at him. 'A wild goose chase?'

He smiled back. 'Something like that. You were right about the salt, by the way,' he added. 'Giovanni Trantemento's mouth was stuffed with it. So was his throat.'

Eleanor Sachs made a face. 'I won't tell anyone.'

'Please don't. Or about Roblino and Giovanni Trantemento knowing each other. That hasn't been released, and I doubt it's germane, but all the same.'

She held up both hands.

'My lips are sealed.'

'But,' he added, 'you weren't wrong, about much of anything, actually.'

'Except Il Spettro?'

She was teasing him but he declined to take the bait.

'Perhaps you shouldn't give up your book after all.' He glanced at the papers strewn around the room.

'Oh,' Eleanor Sachs said, 'I think perhaps I should. I checked, by the way. If I'd known what he looked like, Giovanni Trantemento – I mean once I'd met him, I'd have figured it out for myself. He's nothing like my Dad. For a start he was, what, six foot two? Nobody in our family even hits six foot.'

Pallioti looked at her. 'But you never met him.'

'No,' she said. 'I mean, once I saw the photo in the newspaper, I recognized him on the tape. It's pretty obvious he knew Roblino, too. They're practically hugging.'

'The tape?'

Eleanor nodded. 'Of the sixtieth celebrations. I told you. I used to study it. Late at night. My *Who's Eleanor's Real Grandfather Tonight Show.*'

Pallioti smiled.

'I don't suppose you have a copy of it with you? Here?'

Eleanor Sachs looked at him. 'Why?'

He shrugged.

She put her coffee mug down.

'You're looking for Massimo, aren't you?' she said.

Pallioti did not reply. Eleanor Sachs nodded.

'Yes, you are,' she said. 'That's why you wanted to know – if I could find anything out about the three men. You're looking for him because the other two are dead.' She was watching him. 'I thought you said the investigation was going in another direction? That it had nothing to do with the partisans?'

'I did. It is. And it probably doesn't.' Pallioti sipped his coffee. 'But it might be interesting to speak to him, nonetheless. If he's still alive.'

'Last one left standing, of the three of them, and the two women?'

Pallioti shrugged. 'Survivors are always interesting.'

'Maybe he could explain why they changed their names.'

'Maybe he could. If he wanted to. If he's still alive.'

Eleanor Sachs slipped off the stool and crossed her arms. 'One condition.'

Pallioti raised an eyebrow.

'If I show you this tape,' Eleanor Sachs said, 'and you find this Massimo, I want you to take me with you to meet him.'

Pallioti smiled. 'I can get a copy of it from the television station.'

She shrugged. 'True, you can. Of course, by the time they futz around and find it and then get it up here to you, it will take the better part of a week. And then, after that, you'll have the pleasure of watching the whole uncut four hours looking for something I can show you right now in five minutes.'

Pallioti thought about it for a moment. He eyed her.

'Two conditions.'

'Which are?'

'One. If I, we, find him, and you come with me, you can't harass him afterwards. No phone calls. No letters. No turning up unannounced insisting he's your grandfather – unless he invites you.'

Somewhat to his surprise, she nodded. 'OK,' she said. 'That's fair. What's the second one?'

'That you don't say a word – nothing about Il Spettro, or salt, or anything else, unless I let you.'

She rolled her eyes. 'You drive a hard bargain.'

Pallioti smiled. 'It's the only one on the table. As you say, I can wait until Monday and have the tape sent from Rome.'

'And view it without the benefit of my expert advice.'

He nodded.

'All right,' she said, throwing her hands up. 'All right. Uncle. You win. I'll get the tape.'

She disappeared into the bedroom, leaving Pallioti to wonder which uncle it was, exactly, that Americans always called on, and why?

❧

The video was grainy. Eleanor Sachs apologized repeatedly for the poor quality of the picture.

'I'm sorry,' she said. 'It's a copy of a copy. I left the original – well, the original copy – at home. This is my travelling edition.'

Pallioti leaned forward to get a better look at the TV.

'Here,' Eleanor said, jumping up, 'maybe this will help.'

She pulled the blinds down on the big windows. The definition improved immediately.

'I know it by heart,' she said, coming back and pushing papers aside as she perched on the edge of the sofa. 'Sorry. I forget it makes a difference to other people.'

The newscaster was a pretty woman in a blue dress who managed to mention medals and awards at least a dozen times in a minute and a half without ever actually saying what they were for, while a parade of surprisingly dapper and athletic-looking old men – and women – marched by behind her. Watching them, Pallioti felt a pang of sadness, then anger, for Isabella and Caterina. They should have been there. They should have been allowed to grow old.

The scene cut away from the parade itself to the ceremony. There were a few seconds of the President giving what sounded like an interminable speech. Rows of ageing partisans were seated behind him. Miraculously, none of them appeared to be asleep. Next were clips of individuals receiving their medals. Their names were called out. This would have been where Bruno Torricci got his information. A salute was given as each stepped forward, then the bright ribbon and gold medallion was finally pinned to their chest. Some remained resolutely stony faced. A few smiled. Others were moved to tears.

Eleanor picked up the remote and fast-forwarded.

'Honest,' she said, 'there's nothing here to miss.'

The camera sped through more people getting medals, then to something being sung – almost certainly the national anthem – then to a number of flags being raised and lowered, and finally to the President's reception at the Quirinale.

She put it back to regular speed. A minute later, Pallioti spotted Giovanni Trantemento. He was standing by himself. Neither Maria Valacci nor Antonio were in sight. Sensing the camera, Trantemento moved off, giving it a hunted glance. Then, a few seconds later, he appeared again, this time in a group.

'Here,' Eleanor said. 'Look.'

There were four old men, all linking arms. The woman in the blue dress bore down on them, as determined as a tidal wave. Brandishing her microphone, she asked inane questions about 'how they felt on this great day'.

Giovanni Trantemento looked as though he wanted to escape. He tried, but failed, thanks to a white-haired man in a tuxedo that strained across his bull-like chest who held him determinedly by the shoulder. Sensing the inevitable, Trantemento wilted. When the blue woman asked how they knew each other, the bull with the white mane gave a shout of laughter and declared into the microphone that they had been comrades.

'Brothers-in-arms!' he shouted. 'One for all! All for one!'

The man standing on the other side of him, Roberto Roblino, beamed and nodded in agreement. On the end, a small slightly hunchbacked figure, incongruously wearing a beret, as if he had confused Italy and France, scowled at the camera. Then he smiled a toothless smile.

'So, there's Roblino and Trantemento.'

Eleanor Sachs froze the frame, then rewound it, causing the anchorwoman to scuttle backwards like a demented crab.

'There.' She pointed at Roberto Roblino. 'See? I always thought there was kind of a resemblance, you know, to my dad, and maybe to me. But,' she added, laughing, 'I guess I think that about half these guys. At least he was handsome.'

She was right. Pallioti saw that in life, Roberto Roblino was handsome, and like his white-maned comrade, apparently vigorous. Unlike Trantemento and the little fellow on the end. Together, the four of them looked less like the ageing Musketeers than some kind of allegory – Bonhomie and Health framed by Ill-Humour and Shrunken Old Age.

'So,' she went on, 'if Nosferatu there is Giovanni Trantemento, alias Il Corvo, alias Giovanni Rossi, then my bet is that this guy has to be Massimo.' She jumped up and tapped at the white-haired shouter in the tuxedo. 'Unless, of course, he's someone else entirely.'

But already Pallioti knew he wasn't. Already he could feel something, stirring and shifting in his gut. Caterina had described Massimo as 'beefy'. She had also talked about his friend with a 'misshapen back'. It might be a coincidence. But he didn't believe in coincidences. He leaned forward, trying to get a look at the man's face.

'I showed this to Roberto Roblino, by the way,' Eleanor Sachs was saying. 'That's why I thought it was so weird, when you told me at the restaurant. Because he didn't point out Trantemento, although he eventually gave me his address, and he wouldn't tell me who this guy was. He's definitely a candidate,' she added, tapping the white-haired man in the tuxedo. 'Right height and everything. I couldn't tell if he looked like my dad enough without meeting him. But,' she added, making a face, 'Roblino claimed he couldn't remember his name. Can you believe it?'

Pallioti glanced at her. He thought of Giovanni Trantemento who never talked about the war, and of Roberto Roblino, who talked about it all the time – but said nothing. He thought of all the unopened plastic bags and Signor Cavicalli. *People collect for two reasons. Because there is something they want people to know. Or because there is something they don't.* He'd stake his reputation that in Giovanni Trantemento's case, it was the latter – and that Massimo knew all about it. So, yes, he thought. Yes, he could absolutely believe that Roberto Roblino had suddenly forgotten his comrade's name. What he didn't know, was why.

'Did Roblino say anything?' he asked. 'Anything about' – he gestured towards the screen, the shock of white hair, the beaming face, cheeks still red and weatherbeaten – 'that man? Anything at all?'

Eleanor rolled her eyes. 'Roblino said he didn't know him that well, never had. Which I didn't buy. Would you? But I definitely got the sense he didn't like him. When I pushed, Roblino stonewalled. Clammed up. Then when I asked about Il Spettro, he gave me Trantemento's name and address, so I thought I'd just ask Trantamento, and I dropped it. Not that that worked out,' she added. 'Now this guy—' She touched the troll-like creature in the beret. 'I do know who he is – not a grandfather candidate, I don't think. At least I hope not.'

'Oh?'

She nodded. 'Roblino said he was called Pecorella. Piccolo Pecorella, actually.'

Little Lamb. The same boy Caterina had seen with Massimo in the monastery's tool shed. Looking at the frozen image on the screen, Pallioti wondered if the choice of names was quite as random as Signora Grandolo thought. Il Corvo had certainly been fitting. Perhaps whoever chose the names for their particular GAP unit had a sense of humour. Or was clairvoyant. Piccolo Pecorella, the boy Massimo called his 'mascot', certainly seemed never to have grown much. Caterina had thought that he might have had a hunchback or an injury. But apparently he had survived the war despite it. Because as of eighteen months ago, he was alive and kicking.

'If Massimo's still with us,' Pallioti said, 'this Little Lamb, he'll know where to find him. If he's still alive himself, that is.'

'Oh, he is,' Eleanor Sachs said. 'Believe me. At least as of last week.'

Pallioti looked at her.

'Roberto Roblino gave me his name and address, after some arm-twisting,' she explained. 'I got the impression he did it because he thought it might shut me up.'

'And?' He tried to keep the impatience out of his voice.

Suddenly, he very much wanted to talk to Little Lamb. To ask him about Massimo. And how to find him.

'And,' she said, 'old Pecorello lives not too far from Siena. Right down the road, so to speak. I thought if I couldn't get Giovanni Trantemento to tell me who the fourth guy was, well, maybe the lamb would. I've tried a few times. Most recently just a few days ago. Silly me, thinking the death of his old friends might have softened him up.'

'It didn't?'

She shook her head.

'Just the opposite. He was pretty nasty. He yelled at me and hung up. When I called back, his daughter yelled at me. Said he was sick – and he didn't 'grant interviews'.'

Pallioti smiled.

'Oh,' he said, 'I think he'll grant an interview to me.'

Chapter Twenty-Nine

La Masseria Poggio Alta lay, perversely, in a valley some twenty miles east of Massa Marittima. In other words, Pallioti, thought, nowhere.

They had a fast drive down to Macereto before turning off the highway and driving into what could generously be called wilderness. Within a mile the road narrowed abruptly and began to climb, winding its way up a small mountain covered in beech and scrag oak and thickets of thorn. In these hills, last night's sleet had come down as snow. Drifts of white lay in the hollows. Below them, the Merse tumbled through a steep ravine, its brown current swirling past dead logs and boulders. Above the leafless arms of the trees, the sky was grey and heavy. It was twenty minutes before they saw another car. An ancient Fiat swerved around the corner, coming straight towards them, appearing to play chicken until it ducked back into its own lane and passed them with a long plaintive wail of its horn.

'Jesus.' Eleanor Sachs closed her eyes briefly, her small hands spread flat on the road atlas open in her lap. 'No wonder Italy's farms are in decline. The farmers are probably all killed in road accidents.'

Pallioti glanced at her. While he had pinpointed the Little Lamb's whereabouts, she had vanished into the cottage's bed-room, changing out of her leggings and sweat shirt into jeans and a denim jacket topped by marginally brushed hair. Now she looked a little pale, and as if she possibly regretted their mutual decision that although they had taken her car he should drive and she should navigate. Pallioti took his foot off the gas, tapped the brakes, and slowed down. He did not regret allowing her to come along – it was only fair after all – but it was not exactly kosher.

Eleanor Sachs shook her head, smiling. 'You're enjoying this, aren't you?' she said. 'You're like a kid who's run away from school. You're happy.'

'Yes,' Pallioti replied, because he was.

'Well, I hope, after coming all this way, that Little Lamb isn't a big old let-down.'

Pallioti shook his head. 'Don't worry. He won't be.'

'How do you know?'

'I have a feeling.'

'Ah.' She thought about that for a moment, then she asked, 'What if he yells on the phone because he's gone completely gaga?'

'Then we'll talk to the daughter.'

'I warn you, she's very scary.'

'Yes.' Pallioti smiled. 'So am I.'

Out of the corner of his eye, he saw Eleanor Sachs looking as if she was about to say she didn't believe him. Then she thought better of it and leaned back in her seat.

The Little Lamb, whose real name turned out to be Achilleo Venta, lived with his daughter, Agata, on what had probably been the family farm for generations. The road had finally deigned to come down out of the hills, and descended into a broad valley. The Masseria Poggio Alta, which appeared to be as grandly misnamed as its owner, lay down an unfinished gravel track, and if the tilted sign at the head of the drive sign was to be believed, was not only a *fattoria* dedicated to the production of 'artisan pork products', but also a B. & B.

Pallioti stopped in front of a fence and water trough and killed the engine. He opened his door. There was no sound at all in the farmyard. The same stillness that had infected Florence hung over the valley, pressing down on the tiled roofs, hushing the babble of a thin stream that ran along one side of the yard. Then Pallioti closed his door, and the silence exploded in a volley of high-pitched squeals. The noise erupted from the barn closest to them, and was followed by a frantic rustling that sounded like nothing more than a scurried stampede of rats.

'What the—?' Standing by the passenger door, Eleanor started.

Picking his way to the nearest shed, Pallioti looked over the gate. In the shadows at the back of the barn, he saw several dozen piglets huddled together in a bank of straw. They stared at him, blinking.

A faded *agriturismo* sign directed them along a path that ran from the end of the yard to the house. The bottom floor, which would undoubtedly once have been a barn itself, was now given over to a garage. The dented rear end of a white car poked out of it. A small tractor was pulled up alongside. Pallioti made out the shadow of a motorcycle leaning against the inner wall. Given the diversity of transport parked here, it was likely that someone was at home. A steep flight of stone steps ran up to the portico. He was contemplating whether to ring the large metal bell that was mounted on the wall beside them, or simply march up and hammer on the door, when a voice shouted, '*Chiuso!*'

Pallioti looked around. He could not immediately see where it was coming from.

'*Chiuso!*' the disembodied voice shouted again. 'Closed! Closed for the season! We only open in the summer.'

Eleanor plucked his sleeve. 'Up there,' she hissed.

Looking up, Pallioti could just make out a tiny wizened face peering over the balustrade. Pallioti mounted the steps, feeling

Eleanor right behind him. He suspected she was afraid she might vanish, be swallowed by pig muck, or the pigs themselves, if she strayed too far from his elbow.

'Signor Venta?'

It was not, Pallioti saw as he climbed the steps, that the old man had shrunk yet further. Instead, he was now in a wheelchair. A rug was tucked over his knees. A cane was propped against the wall beside the house door.

'I told you, we're closed!'

The old man was tussling with the brake on his chair.

'We're closed!' he said again as Pallioti reached the head of the stairs. 'What are you? Deaf?'

'No. A policeman.'

Pallioti leaned down and released the brake. The old man looked up at him. It was like being stared at by a tortoise. Milky eyes peered out of walnut wrinkles of skin.

'A what?'

'Policeman,' Pallioti said again.

Achilleo Venta grasped the wheels of his chair and turned it sharply towards the house door. There was certainly nothing wrong with the muscles in his arms.

'Well, she's not here,' he said. Pallioti presumed he was referring to his daughter. 'I don't know where she is. She does all the books. You'll have to talk to her.'

'I'm not interested in the books,' Pallioti said, mildly. 'I've come to talk to you.'

'Me?'

The old man had been reaching for the door handle. A pair of knitted mittens, secured by safety pins, just as his nephew Tommaso's often were, dangled from his cuffs. His naked fingers paused, claw-like, in mid-air.

'What have I done?' he asked, his voice suddenly plaintive. 'I haven't done anything.'

He twisted in the chair and squinted up at Pallioti.

'You don't look like a policeman.' Suspicion pinched

Achilleo Venta's face. His hand darted forward and closed over
the doorknob. The next thing they would see, Pallioti thought,
was probably a shotgun barrel sticking through the red-shut-
tered window. He took out his credentials.

Signor Venta let go of the doorknob and snatched them.
With palsied hands, he held them very close to his face, studying them. He looked several times from the photograph to Pallioti before he handed them back.

'Who's she?' he asked.

'She is my assistant,' Pallioti said quickly. 'Professor Sachs.
We've come a very long way to talk to you, Signor Venta,' he
added. 'I wonder if it might be at all possible that you could
give us a few moments of your time?'

For a moment, Achilleo Venta seemed to consider this, as if
his day were filled with things much more urgent than sitting
on his balcony in the cold looking over his empty pig yards and
waiting for his daughter to come back from wherever it was she
had gone. Finally, he nodded.

The inside of the farmhouse was not as bad as the outside suggested. A long front room was furnished with sofas and a
scrubbed pine table and chairs and backed by a wall of windows
that looked down onto a scraggy patchwork of fields. In the
closest, a number of giant sows rooted happily. The next was
dotted with the metallic humps of pig arcs.

'Those are my girls.' Achilleo Venta wheeled himself over to
the window. His face and voice softened as he looked down at
the huge black-and-white pigs. 'Finest mothers in the universe.'

He looked over his shoulder at Pallioti. 'You know anything
about pigs?' he asked. Then he started to laugh. 'No joke intended,' he chortled. 'Of course you don't know anything about
pigs. You don't know anything about any animals. Don't know
anything about anything that happens outside the walls of your
fancy cities. Where did you come from, Rome?'

'Florence.'

Pallioti thought he saw something flicker in the old man's face. A moment later, Achilleo Venta said, 'I almost died there. But I didn't.'

'What happened?'

It was Eleanor Sachs who had asked the question. As she stepped closer to the wheelchair, it occurred to Pallioti that the old man was not much bigger than she was. In her jeans and running shoes, with the jacket and no make-up, what vestiges of adulthood there were that hung about her seemed to have been peeled away. Standing between them, he felt as if he had tender old age on one hand, and vulnerable youth on the other.

Achilleo Venta looked up at her.

'Pneumonia,' he said after a moment.

He wheeled his chair in a slow half-circle. One of the mittens caught in a spoke. He tugged at it angrily.

'At least that's what they told me. You ask me' – his fingers worked at the safety pin – 'I think it was just death. Everyone was dying, that God-awful winter. They said it was pneumonia. But I know.' He peered at Pallioti. 'I saw. People just died. They just died because they wanted to. Because they couldn't stand it any more. Living like rats.'

Pallioti leaned down and unclasped the pin. He untangled the mitten and handed it to the old man.

'Pneumonia, despair.' Achilleo Venta looked at the mitten and dropped it on the floor. 'What's the difference?' he asked. 'In the end? Six months, I was in the hospital. I suppose they kept me alive. I was there then, too.' He pointed towards the wall. 'Over there, that's me. 11 August 1944. I got a medal for it. It wasn't over then,' he added, nodding, his jaw working, chewing on the memory. 'The fighting went on for days, but no one likes to remember that.'

Achilleo Venta stared at the mitten on the floor. He shrugged, his frail shoulders rising and falling inside the worn jacket that was too big for him.

'You had to go in,' he said. 'They sent us in, building after building. One by one, to clear them out. Like rats. Shooting the Fascisti, it was like shooting rats.'

Crossing to the wall, Pallioti peered at the black-and-white picture Achilleo Venta had pointed to. A row of young men, no older than boys, stood beaming in front of a wall of rubble. They were in shirtsleeves. Several wore shorts. Some shouldered rifles. Others held handguns. In a separate frame beside it, in a case identical to the one Maria Valacci had shown him, a medal nested on a bed of white satin, its ribbon bright beside the faded photograph.

'Is this Massimo?' Pallioti tapped vaguely at the glass.

Without looking up, the old man nodded. 'Second from the left,' he said.

It had been a guess, but now, peering at the picture, Pallioti picked out the square face, the bold, flat features and the broad shoulders that already suggested the barrel chest of the man on the video tape.

'Did you know him well?'

He asked the question quietly, hoping it was not a push too far, that it would not clamp down whatever trapdoor it was that had opened in Achilleo Venta's mind and made him decide to 'grant this interview' after all.

'Did,' he said, snorting. 'Still do. Always will. Not much choice.'

'Why is that?'

Pallioti turned around. The old man had wheeled himself close to the glass and was staring intently down into the field. One of the largest sows had given up rooting and was scratching her back, swaying in time to absent music as she rubbed against a muddy chain that had been looped between two posts.

'He's my cousin,' Achilleo Venta said finally. He looked up. 'Balestro. That was my mother's name. He's her brother's boy. My cousin, Piero.' He snorted again. 'Always bigger than life. Always better than anyone else. That's why we called him Massimo. I worshipped him.'

Pallioti could sense as much as see the look on Eleanor Sachs's face. Before he could stop her, she asked, 'Why didn't he change his name, like the others?'

The old man spun the chair towards her, wheels creaking. There was apparently nothing wrong with his hearing.

'Why would he?' he demanded, his voice heavy with sarcasm. 'Why would Piero Balestro change his name? He had nothing to hide! He was a hero! He had nothing to be ashamed of. Oh, no. Not Massimo!' He rolled the words on his tongue, making them sound obscene. Startled, Eleanor Sachs stepped backwards. The mitten scuffed under her shoe.

Achilleo Venta laughed. 'Massimo,' he said, 'always was better than all the rest of us.'

Pallioti bent and picked up the mitten. He placed it on the table. Achilleo Venta sat in his wheelchair, his chest heaving. His mouth worked. A thin line of saliva dribbled onto his chin. He wiped it away, shaking his head as if the anger had both embarrassed him and taken him by surprise. 'Peter Bales.' The words were not much more than a whisper. 'That's the name he used sometimes. Afterwards. When he felt like it. Peter Bales. If that's what you want to know.'

Pallioti waited a moment. Then he asked, 'Why did you say "ashamed"?'

'Huh.' The old man waved a hand, shooing the question away.

Pallioti persisted, gently.

'Signor Venta,' he asked again, 'why would Massimo be ashamed?'

Achilleo Venta looked down at his lap. He shrugged, trying to cover the bitterness that had erupted – shown itself, Pallioti suspected, after a lifetime of being tamped down, hidden away like a dirty black kernel in Little Lamb's heart.

'We all have something to hide,' Achilleo Venta muttered finally. 'Isn't that what they say? Even if you're a fancy doctor.'

'Piero Balestro was a doctor?'

'Was. Later.'

As he spoke, the old man's voice sank to something like a murmur. The words were stilted, muttered like a prayer, a secret catechism of resentment that Pallioti suspected he had recited to himself day after day, year after year, like a rosary.

'The rest of us get shot at. Find our houses in ruins, burnt, trampled, shat in. Have to beg for our bread. Starve. Dig fucking German mines out of our fields, if we live to get back to them. He goes to a fancy medical school. In America. Doctor Peter Bales.'

'How did that happen?'

Achilleo Venta stared at his hands, lying half useless in his lap. 'You want to know more, you'd better ask him.'

Pallioti nodded. 'I'd like to.'

'Well, it isn't difficult!' The old man's head snapped up. Anger made his voice tremble. 'He lives in Siena. Massimo, Massimo,' he muttered, turning his chair away. 'Biggest damn house on the damn block. Il Castello. Il Palazzo. Of course.'

Over the bent figure, the hunched shoulders and the faded wool of the blue beret, Pallioti met Eleanor Sachs's eyes. Her face was a combination of confusion and excitement. They had found Massimo, almost without having to look, but neither of them had any idea what it was, exactly, that had upset Achilleo Venta quite so much. Apparently just the fact of his cousin's existence. And perhaps that was enough. Perhaps it had always been like that, Pallioti thought, since they were little boys. Blood didn't take much account of subtleties – of once removed or twice. Cousins might as well be siblings. Love and hate, jealousy, devotion, it was all knotted into a lifetime. Throw in a war, a struggle for survival, and who knew what could happen.

'Signor Venta,' he asked gently, 'was your cousin Piero, Massimo, the leader of your GAP unit?'

Achilleo Venta looked up, his face momentarily blank, as if he was surprised to find Pallioti and Eleanor in the room. Then he shook his head and said, 'Of course. Massimo was always the leader of everything, wasn't he?'

'Did he give you your name?'

'Little Lamb.' Achilleo Venta smiled, but his hands moved fretfully in his lap. 'That's what my mother called me when I was a baby,' he said. 'It made Massimo laugh. He thought it was a big joke.'

'Not a very funny one.'

'Doesn't matter.'

Achilleo Venta fingered the remaining mitten that dangled from his jacket sleeve.

'I hated it,' he said after a moment. 'But he always had to be the boss. Or at least, he thought he did. Others thought different, but why would that matter?'

'Which others?' Pallioti bent down, trying to see the old man's face. 'Lilia?' he asked.

It had been a guess, but Achilleo Venta nodded. He was watching his hands, the gnarled fingers plucking at a hole in the thumb of the mitten. He found a loose thread and yanked it.

'Lilia,' he said. 'Lilia, and the other one. The boy. Not that they were ever apart.'

'They were each other,' Pallioti murmured, his eyes fastened on the old man's face.

Achilleo Venta nodded. His hands stilled. 'They were each other.' He looked up at Pallioti. 'Massimo couldn't stand that,' he said. 'But he didn't get everything, not everything he wanted.'

'Not Lilia?'

Achilleo Venta smiled. His cracked lips stretched over toothless gums. 'No,' he said. 'Not Lilia. And she was worth ten men.'

'Were you in the hospital, still, in June?'

The old man nodded. His eyes were fixed somewhere behind Pallioti, and far farther away than that.

'They took me to Fiesole. To the monastery where they kept

the crazy people, and the invalids. The weaklings, like me. They said there was something wrong with my lungs. In June, Massimo came. He took me away, found a doctor. He got me drugs. Then we went back to the city. To shoot rats.'

'And Lilia?'

The rheumy eyes looked back to Pallioti, fastened on his face.

'Gone,' the old man whispered. 'All gone.'

'Papa!'

Pallioti felt a rush of cold air and turned around to see a very large person standing in the open doorway. With her padded hunter's coat, overalls and boots, it was hard to tell if she was a woman or a man. Only the braid of long dark hair hanging over her shoulder gave her away.

'Signora Venta?' Pallioti straightened up as she strode into the room.

'Who the hell are you?' she said, ignoring his outstretched hand. 'And what the hell are you doing in my house?'

Pallioti regarded her for a moment, and decided *politesse* was pointless. He pulled his credentials out again.

'Your father has been kind enough to give us his time.' Pallioti caught Eleanor's eye. 'It was very gracious of him, and we are just going.'

'Now, wait. Wait a goddamn minute,' she exclaimed. 'My father's an old man, a hero. You can't just come in here and—'

Agata Venta made a snatch for the proffered credentials but was not fast enough. Her hand was still hanging in mid-air and she was still protesting as Pallioti took Eleanor's arm and propelled her quickly towards the door. He raised a hand to the old man, and was sure he saw Achilleo Venta smile.

A pair of dead pheasants lay across the top of the balustrade, their disjointed heads staring limply down into the yard. A broken shotgun had been dropped beside them. Pallioti could not see the dog; presumably it was chained up somewhere. As they emerged it let out a furious volley of barking. They had started down the steps, Eleanor just ahead of him, when a voice called out.

'Dottore!'

Pallioti turned around.

In his haste to wheel after them, the rug had slipped off Achilleo Venta's lap, revealing small bent legs encased in green woollen trousers that had seen better days. A red patch of sock showed through a hole in the slippers that were laced onto his feet like a child's. Under the jaunty tilt of the faded blue beret, the old man's face was lit up. His milky eyes blinked.

'Do you know what I called him?' he asked. 'Massimo? I was his Little Lamb. But do you know what I called that bastard behind his back?'

Pallioti shook his head.

Agata Venta had come out onto the portico behind her father. She loomed, towering over the back of his chair. Her mouth had opened. She was reaching for him, but something in the old man's voice stopped her.

'Jesus Christ,' Achilleo Venta said. He let out a bark of laughter. 'That was my joke.'

Grasping the wheels, he rolled towards the top of the steps.

'Jesus Christ.' He jerked the brake on the chair. 'That's what I called Massimo.' His bird-like chest rose and fell. His eyes fastened on Pallioti's. 'Do you want to know why?' he asked.

Pallioti nodded. He could feel Eleanor Sachs's hand, her fingers digging into his elbow.

'Why?'

'I called him Jesus Christ' – the tendons in the old man's neck strained as he leaned forward – 'because it was a miracle. Jesus Christ,' Achilleo Venta whispered. 'Because he went to hell. Then, after three days, he came back from the dead.'

Chapter Thirty

'What just happened back there?'

Neither of them had spoken since leaving the farm. Pallioti had reversed and turned quickly, driving down the rutted track, the sound of barking trailing after them like smoke. That had been five minutes ago. Now, Eleanor Sachs was staring out of the window. She ran a hand through her hair and shook her head.

'He called Massimo Jesus Christ,' she said, 'because after three days he came back from the dead. What does that mean? I'm telling you,' she added, 'he's lost it. Is this about Massimo being in the Villa Triste? Was it, what? Three days? Four? Why does it matter anyway? Who's counting?'

Achilleo Venta, Pallioti thought. Achilleo Venta was counting. He'd been counting for the better part of sixty years.

The old man's words bounced in his head – jumbled with pictures of a bright-blue mitten, stained woollen trousers, walnut skin creased and folded as a baby bird's.

They came around a corner. He focused on the ribbon of road. He had turned in the opposite direction coming away from the farm, suddenly sure of where he was.

'I have to think,' he said, and abruptly turned left.

Eleanor Sachs clutched at the dashboard as the car swung across the road. They slowed, pulling into the empty apron of a parking lot. She looked around.

'What is this place?' she asked.

Pallioti glanced up. Beyond the Renault's tinted glass, a damp field still littered with traces of last night's snow stretched to the slope of Monte Siepi. In the middle of it the skeleton of a ruined church rose up, its windows empty, arches naked against the leaden sky. It was every bit as forlorn and magnificent as he remembered. A flight of crows lifted from the broken wall of a cloister, spiralled like black kites and landed again. He killed the engine.

'San Galgano.'

Eleanor Sachs looked at him. 'San Galgano?'

Pallioti nodded. 'Built in the twelfth century, by the same monks who built Siena. Cistercians. They were excellent bookkeepers, among other things. It was abandoned by fifteen hundred. The campanile actually collapsed during Mass.'

'Oh.'

Eleanor leaned forward, her hands resting on the dashboard. 'I've heard about it,' she said. 'I've just never seen it before.'

In the grey light of the November day, the building seemed to float, its ruined walls melting into the whitening sky, the eye of its rose window staring, sightless, across centuries.

'Galgano met St Michael,' Pallioti said. 'On the hill, over there. Afterwards, he gave up being a knight and became a hermit. When his family came to try to talk him out of it, he thrust his sword into a stone and offered it up to the archangels.'

He was aware of Eleanor watching him. He turned to her and smiled.

'Later,' he said, 'three villains tried to steal it. But the stone cried out, and a wolf came and chewed their hands off. You can see them,' he added. 'There's a chapel on the hill. The stone and the sword are still in the floor. The hands are in a glass case.' He opened his door. 'I have some calls to make. There's a cafe, beyond the chapel. Let's meet in ten minutes for a cup of coffee.'

She nodded without speaking and got out of the car. A

minute later, Pallioti stood watching her over the roof of the Renault – a small dark figure, picking its way across a wet snowy field towards a ruin.

❧

'I don't believe that's a human hand,' Eleanor Sachs said. 'It looks more like a monkey's paw to me. And it certainly isn't eight hundred years old.'

She blew on the top of her coffee. Pallioti smiled.

'I don't suppose you believe Petrarch's cat is Petrarch's cat, either.'

'Certainly not.'

She rolled her eyes and reached for a packet of sugar. Apart from the two women behind the counter, they were the only people in the cafe. It was barely noon. Eleanor Sachs emptied the sugar into her coffee and stirred it with a small plastic stick. Then she looked at him.

'Did you make your phone calls?'

'Yes.'

'So,' she asked, 'will you tell me who Lilia is?'

'The GAP unit – the three men were arrested during an attempted assassination, outside the Pergola Theatre, on Valentine's Day. She was shot, but she got away.'

'And she was the woman the all-powerful Massimo couldn't have?'

Pallioti picked up his own cup and regarded her for a moment. The cold had put a blush of pink into her cheeks.

'That's right,' he said. 'At least, I think so.'

Eleanor eyed him.

'Worth ten men. She must have been something.'

'Yes, I think she was.'

'What happened to her?'

'She's dead.'

'I know that.' Eleanor Sachs stared at him. 'I told you that.

I mean before, what happened to her? It's important? Isn't it?' Her voice had a whine of insistence.

Pallioti put his cup down. The tone of her voice reminded him of Saffy at thirteen, of how utterly implacable she had been. As if she could read his mind, Eleanor leaned forward.

'You owe me,' she said. 'Without me, you wouldn't be here.' She looked at him for a moment, then sipped her coffee.

'Oh, I know,' she said. 'You're the police. You'd have got here. Eventually. But you wouldn't be here now. Not this fast. We had a deal.' She glared at him. The blush in her cheeks had heightened, making her eyes even brighter. 'You could at least tell me the truth.'

'I don't know what the truth is.' Pallioti shook his head. 'To be honest, I doubt we'll ever know.'

Cosimo Grandolo's warning to his wife ran in his head like a hamster on a wheel. *He said I could do more harm than good, seeing connections where they didn't exist.*

Finally, he looked up and said, 'Does the name Antenor mean anything to you?'

'Antenor?' Eleanor Sachs looked at him as if he had truly gone crazy. 'What does Antenor have to do with anything? And it's Antenora, by the way.'

'So you do know who he was?'

'I know what they are. They are two different things, a person and a place. Antenor was the person Antenora was named for. The guy who betrayed Troy.'

'Betrayed Troy?' Pallioti picked up his cup and put it down again. 'I thought he was one of the elders.'

Eleanor smirked.

'He was. That was the point. He was mad because they didn't do what he said, give Helen back. So he betrayed the city to the Greeks. And, incidentally, founded Padua.'

She sipped her coffee and shook her head.

'For what it's worth,' she added, 'Antenora is in Dante's ninth circle of hell. Canto thirty-two. It's reserved for traitors.'

'Traitors?'

Eleanor Sachs nodded. 'That's right,' she said. 'It's a particularly horrible place – not that much of the Inferno is a bargain. But Antenora is freezing cold, because Dante considered treason the coldest of human sins. It freezes the heart. And soul. Traitors are moral outcasts. Their lives may go on, but they're cut off from humanity. Forever.'

She took another sip of her coffee and went on, falling happily into the full flow of a lecture on Dante. But Pallioti wasn't listening. Instead, he was seeing the photograph Maria Valacci had given him, seeing the long, drawn features of her brother. The hero who had presented her with his medal. Who had told her she 'deserved it more than he did'. Whose hand had rested so awkwardly on her shoulder, and whose face had been filled with such sadness because he did not belong, for decades had not belonged, to a humanity that deserved rewards. Or, perhaps, in his mind, to humanity at all. No wonder he had put himself into exile, locked himself away at the top of his palazzo, condemned himself to gaze down on the city he could not be part of. How cold, Pallioti wondered, had his grand apartment been? The solitary rooms where he eked out his days alone, surrounded by drawings of the most intimate of human acts.

'Are you all right?'

Eleanor Sachs reached out and touched his hand.

Pallioti picked up his cup and nodded. She looked at him.

'Who was Antenor?' she asked. 'I mean, in this story?'

'I don't know.' He sipped his coffee. 'Probably no one.'

'It was Massimo, wasn't it?'

'No.'

'He was a traitor, wasn't he?' Her eyes searched his face. 'That's what you think, isn't it? It has to do with when he was at Villa Triste, doesn't it? That's what he meant, Achilleo Venta, about hell. What did Massimo do?' she asked.

Pallioti shook his head. 'I don't know,' he said.

But he had a horrible feeling he did. *Gone*, Little Lamb had whispered, *All gone*. Lilia and the boy she would not be parted from. And Caterina, and Enrico, and their parents. All of them whose names Issa had counted out on her fingers and repeated like a litany night after night after night. *Enrico is dead. Carlo is dead. Papa is dead.*

But how? That was what he didn't understand.

I called him Jesus Christ, because after three days he came back from the dead.

He could see the beginning of it: the arrest, the bargain that was made in return for an 'escape'. The fact that – what? – three, four days later, the safe house near the Pitti Palace, the one used after the weapons drop, had been raided. That would have been a valuable bargaining chip. *Too many people knew*, Issa said, and she was right. So, yes, he could see the beginning. But he couldn't see the end. Because no one knew where Radio Juliet was meeting. No one knew about the house off the Via dei Renai. Only those attending had been told, at the very last minute, and all of them were dead. Isabella had seen them. With her own eyes. She had seen where they had dug the trench, and knelt down. Unless Caterina had been right all along, and somehow she had been followed.

Pallioti put his cup down. He could feel the parts of the picture, sliding about as if they were on the inside of a kaleidoscope, but he couldn't make them come into focus. To do that, he would have to talk to Massimo.

His stomach felt sour, not just because he had slept badly, or because of the amount of coffee he had drunk, but because of what he was about to do. The treachery he had already begun to commit.

'Eleanor—'

She looked at him and saw what he was about to say in his face.

'No,' Eleanor Sachs said.

She jumped to her feet, almost knocking her chair over. 'No,' she said. 'If you're going to see him, I'm coming with you.'

Pallioti shook his head. 'You can't. A car is on its way. This is police business now. Part of an investigation into a murder, probably two. I can't possibly—'

'And this morning it wasn't? You sure could "possibly" when you needed me! You promised!'

The women behind the counter had stopped talking. There was no sound at all in the cafe except the low murmur of a radio somewhere in a back room and the anguished huff of Eleanor Sachs's breath. Pallioti stood up. He was a good head taller than she was.

'No. No!' Her voice rose in a wail of protest. 'You can't,' she said. 'You cannot leave me behind now. It is not fair!'

'A police driver is coming to pick you up. I'll wait here with you until he arrives and return your car this evening.'

He was determined to make sure she was returned to Florence. If he left her with her own car, she would simply follow him. Trail after him like a stray puppy he would be forced to kick.

'No!'

Looking at the angry hurt on her small upturned face, Pallioti saw the journey she had been on – the loneliness of it, mingled with hope – and felt an unwelcome wave of sympathy. Aware of how dangerous it was, he pushed it back. The effort was about as successful as closing the door on a flood.

'You can't,' Eleanor Sachs said again. 'You promised me.'

She bowed her head, and dug in the pocket of her jacket. Finding a tissue, she wiped her eyes and blew her nose. Then she crumpled it in her hand, speaking fast without looking at him and so low that the women had to lean over the counter to hear.

'You can't,' she said. 'You just can't do this to me.'

Painfully aware that he looked like a father bullying his teenage daughter, or worse, an ageing Lothario who, for some demented reason, had brought his child lover to the Abbey of San Galgano to abandon her in a sandwich bar, Pallioti took her shoulder and guided her to the far corner of the room. The women behind the counter did not even pretend not to be listening. The next time he came here there would probably be mouldy ham in his panini and salt in his coffee.

'Eleanor,' he said. 'Please. I'm grateful for your help, and I don't mean to be unkind, but you must understand—'

To his surprise, she nodded. Then she looked up at him. Her eyes were red-rimmed, but her lip was no longer trembling.

'I have been looking for almost three years,' she said. 'I know you probably think it's crazy, and maybe it is. It's damaged my career. It's trashed my marriage. But my father is dead. I never even knew the people who raised him. I don't know who I am, and I have nowhere else to look. I have turned over all the rocks. I have made an ass of myself chasing you. I've done everything I can.'

She paused and took a deep breath. Palioti could feel the flood gates giving way, the water tumbling in and rising around him.

'I have never been this close,' Eleanor Sachs said. 'I won't say anything. I swear to God. I'll do exactly what you tell me.'

She looked at him.

'But you have to let me come with you. I have to at least see this Massimo, or Piero, or whatever his name is. Please.' She reached out and took Palioti's arm. 'Because whatever else this man is – he might also be my grandfather.'

Chapter Thirty-One

The house was more than just a house. The block a lot bigger than a block. And neither, strictly speaking, were in Siena. But Achilleo Venta had got the size right. There was no question that Piero Balestro's estate, some ten miles south of the town, was large.

Chalky hills planted with what appeared to be wheat and topped by picturesque groves of cypress rolled out on either side of them in a landscape sent from central casting. The drive they were following had to wind through several hundred acres. At a best guess. The phone calls Pallioti had made had merely netted the man's current address. The exact specifics on the property – and anything else Guillermo could dig up on Piero Balestro, and/or Doctor Peter Bales, – would be waiting for him when he got back to the office.

He had made one last call before they left San Galgano, cancelling the car he had ordered to come and fetch Eleanor Sachs. The driver, who had already been cruising happily down the motorway, was probably not best pleased. Well, they would have that in common, Pallioti thought, because the truth was, he wasn't best pleased either. He hoped that allowing Eleanor to accompany him was not a decision he was going to come to regret. But he already knew – one way or another – that it probably was. He felt a flood of sympathy for everyone in the world who had children. This was what it must be like, he thought – forever allowing yourself to be backed into a corner against your better judgement.

Piero Balestro's home, when they finally reached it, sat on a knoll at the end of the drive. A mellow confection of stone and tile, it looked old on first glance, but on second glance, wasn't. A very shiny silver Alfa and some boxy red thing called a Jeep Wagoneer stood on the parking circle. Through the graceful line of cypresses that spread from the side portico, they could see the green slope of a lawn, and below it a paddock, backed by a line of stables.

Pallioti glanced at Eleanor.

'I know,' she said, as she opened the door. 'I remember. Not a word.'

The pale gravel crunched pleasingly underfoot. Four potted bay trees were lined up on either side of the wide front doors. An appropriately weathered pair of stone lions lay at the top of the steps, paws crossed, mouths open in a silent roar. The only discordant note was a security camera. Its round eye peered down from under the eaves of the house. Pallioti made a point of looking straight at it. He had noticed a similar one mounted on the electronic gates that had stood open at the head of the drive. Either Piero Balestro had become careless, which Pallioti somehow doubted, or he was expecting them.

Probably the only reason Agata Venta hadn't chased them down the drive with a pitchfork was because she had been too busy – first grilling her father, then alerting Dear, and obviously Very Rich, Cousin Piero.

Pallioti had never laid eyes on the man known as Massimo, had no proof that he had ever done anything wrong, and already he loathed him. He glanced around. At the perfectly manicured beds that edged the curve of the drive. At the newly painted shutters with their shiny brass fittings. At the blue glimpse of a swimming pool cover beyond a stand of camellia bushes. All traces of last night's snow had melted away. The sun was making a half-hearted attempt to break through the white sheet of cloud. It might yet be a nice afternoon. But this place smelled rotten. Underneath the shiny new veneer, it smelled as if something was dead.

For a second, Pallioti wished Enzo was not in Brindisi, but here, and that he had put his own long-held scruples aside and decided to carry a weapon. He was on the verge of taking Eleanor Sachs by the arm, marching her down the steps and back to the car, when the front door swung open.

The woman who faced them was even smaller than Eleanor. Her hair was so black it shone in the overhead lights from the hallway beyond. Her uniform, pale blue, looked as if it had been expertly tailored for a doll. The apron was newly starched, the cuffs and collar a pristine white.

'The Doctor is at the stables,' she said, looking at Pallioti and ignoring Eleanor. 'He said you should go down. Meet him there.'

Pallioti, who had reached automatically for his credentials as the door opened, slid them back into the inner pocket of his overcoat. He wouldn't be needing them. Massimo knew exactly who he was, and why he was here.

A paved path led around the opposite side of the house from the swimming pool and down a set of steps set into the lawn. Pallioti and Eleanor followed it. As they grew close, they saw that the stables were brick, a long low block fronted by a deep overhang. A weathervane, a galloping horse with its mane and tail flying, sat on the centre pitch of the roof. Eleanor opened her mouth, caught Pallioti's eye and closed it again. The steps led to the edge of the front paddock where three horses grazed lazily, their tails flicking, glossy bodies covered in red rugs.

Pallioti and Eleanor had barely passed the last gatepost when a man stepped out of the door in the centre of the stable block. He wore old-fashioned riding breeches, overly shined boots and a green loden hat with a feather in it.

'Dottore, Dottore! Such a pleasure.' Piero Balestro virtually threw his arms open. 'Welcome,' he cried. The gesture strained his tweed jacket, making the buttons look as if they would pop across his chest. 'This is an honour. I have heard so much about you.'

Pallioti wondered if that was actually true, and, if so, what the good doctor had heard. And from whom. He extended his hand.

'Doctor Bales. Or do you use Balestro now?'

'Ah, so you know about that, do you? My "Americanization"? But of course you do. Of course you are our all-powerful police.'

Piero Balestro smiled as if this was a great joke. Almost as funny as his knowing who Pallioti was before he introduced himself.

'Balestro, Bales. Legally, my name is Peter Bales. Use whichever you prefer, Dottore. And this is?' He dropped Pallioti's hand abruptly and turned to Eleanor.

'Professor Eleanor Sachs,' Pallioti said. 'She's been helping us with our enquiries.'

'Delighted. Delighted!'

Piero Balestro's voice was as loud and as full of bonhomie in person as it had been on the video tape. Pallioti wondered if it bothered the horses as much as it bothered him. Apparently not. The three in the paddock hadn't so much as looked up. A couple of others who had their heads stuck over their doors seemed to be asleep.

'Horses,' Balestro boomed, following Pallioti's gaze. 'Lawrence of Arabia said, "Somewhere in the pastures of the human soul, there are horses galloping." Do you like horses, Dottore?'

'No,' Pallioti said abruptly.

It wasn't, strictly speaking, true. But he was in no mood for a long-winded tour of Piero Balestro's equine empire.

'I don't want to take up much more of your time than I have

to,' he said. 'I'm sure you're a very busy man. But we would appreciate it if we could have a few words with you. Concerning an old friend.'

'An old friend?'

Piero Balestro smiled. He looked at Pallioti, his pale-blue eyes cold and sharp as ice in the broad genial features of his face.

'And who would that be?' he asked. 'Surely not my dear cousin Achilleo?'

'No,' Pallioti said. 'Not Achilleo. Another friend. Giovanni Trantemento.'

'Giovanni Trantemento?' Piero Balestro did a reasonable imitation of looking confused.

'Perhaps you knew him by another name,' Pallioti said. 'Giovanni Rossi. Il Corvo.'

'Ah!' He let out a guffaw. 'Il Corvo. Il Corvo, of course. My brother-in-arms! How is the old fellow?'

'Dead.'

Pallioti waited a moment, then he added, 'He was shot in the back of the head at the door of his apartment. About three weeks ago. The same thing happened to someone else you know. Roberto Roblino. Or perhaps you knew him as Beppe? Giancarlo Menucci.'

'Good heavens! Really? Both of them dead?' Piero Balestro did not look especially surprised.

Pallioti smiled. 'I was hoping,' he said, 'that you might be of some assistance.'

'Well, of course.' Piero Balestro spread his hands, embracing the world. 'Of course,' he said. 'Anything I can do to help the police.'

Above them, the weathervane clicked and rattled. The stillness of the day had broken. For the first time since the night before, the wind had risen. It had a cold northern tang. The horses stopped eating and pricked their ears. A handful of straw skittered down the concrete apron of the stable.

'I wonder,' Pallioti said, 'if there is somewhere where we might sit down?'

∽

The interior of the house looked as if it had been bought whole from a catalogue the week before. The only discordant note was a rather mangy ageing spaniel curled in a basket beside the sitting room's unlit fireplace. It opened one eye as they came in, then closed it again and began to snore.

Sinking down onto a chintz sofa so soft it was difficult to remain upright, Pallioti realized he'd mistaken the show at the stables. It was not meant to be Prussian Cavalry Officer, but English Country Gentleman. The picture was made complete by the appearance of the maid, who brought in tea in a china teapot. She placed the tray carefully on the table in front of Piero Balestro, and gave a small curtsey. As she left the room, Balestro winked at Pallioti.

'I brought her back from South Africa,' he said. 'Filipino. They learn languages like *that*.' He snapped his fingers. 'And they work much harder than blacks.'

Pallioti did not look at Eleanor Sachs. Instead, he leaned forward ignoring both the tea and the comment and said, 'I wonder, Doctor Balestro, if you could tell me where you were on the 1st of November?'

Balestro looked at him.

'Solely to eliminate you from our enquiries,' Pallioti added. 'Of course.'

'Of course.' Piero Balestro smiled. He fiddled with the teacups and saucers. His hands, as broad and strong as the rest of him, were the only things that gave him away. The fingers, like his cousin Achilleo's, were gnarled.

'Shall I?' Eleanor leaned forward and placed a cup carefully on a saucer for him. For a moment there was a trace of something that might have been warmth in Piero Balestro's face. He ran a hand through the thick mane of his white hair and said, 'November 1st, you say?'

Pallioti nodded.

Piero Balestro got up and crossed the sitting room. He opened a roll-top desk and made a display of flipping through a datebook.

'Well, it appears that I was here,' he said. 'I had the black-smith coming in the afternoon.' He closed the book and smiled at Pallioti. 'I like to be here when the girls get their new shoes. So exciting.'

'Did you say South Africa?' Pallioti threw the question in before he could launch into a soliloquy on equestrian footwear.

'Yes.' Piero Balestro snapped the datebook shut. 'Yes! By way of the United States. Not the most direct route, but there you are.' He smiled. 'Life is full of twists and turns.'

Obviously relieved not to be talking about his old comrade-in-arms, Il Corvo, Piero Balestro strode across the room, picked up a framed photo and handed it to Pallioti.

'After the war,' he said. 'I was lucky enough to go to medical school. On the GI Bill!'

He let out a guffaw. Across the room, Pallioti felt Eleanor Sachs stiffen. Before she could say anything, Piero Balestro added, 'Quite a joke, eh? But the Yanks, you can say what you like about them – they're generous. Reward the people who help them. That's when I changed my name. Used the Ameri-can version. It saved a lot of trouble.'

Pallioti glanced at the photo in his hand. In it, a young Piero Balestro stood, wearing a white coat and stethoscope, in front of a brick wall that might have been anywhere.

'I imagine,' he said, 'it must have saved you a world of trou-ble. Changing your name.'

'Well, it was the least I could do. To show my gratitude.' Piero Balestro either did not notice or chose to ignore Pallioti's expression and the tone of his voice.

Pallioti handed the picture to Eleanor. As he looked back to

Balestro, he saw her studying the photo, frowning as she searched for any clue, no matter how tiny, that might tell her where the wall might have been.

'I married a nurse,' Piero Balestro announced. 'From one of the field hospitals. Met her in Florence. Just after the war. Very romantic. Went back with her, on an American passport. They put me through medical school. Ann Arbor, Michigan. Coldest winters this side of hell. Marriage didn't last, of course.' He shrugged, as if it was both no surprise and of no account. 'So I went to South Africa. For the sunshine. Worked for a drug company. Opened a series of clinics. Clinics,' he said again.

Piero Balestro gestured, his wave taking in the French windows, the sitting room itself, the pool and lawn and stables and land beyond, as if the word explained it all.

'And there you have it,' he said. 'Until five years ago, when I started to get old.'

He sat back down in the armchair. 'A man gets old, he wants to come home.'

Out of the corner of his eye, Pallioti could see that Eleanor was still holding the photograph. Now, though, she was staring at Balestro. She started to open her mouth, but Pallioti cut her off.

'It must have been difficult for your children, their father moving to South Africa? Or did they go with you?'

Piero Balestro guffawed again as if the idea in and of itself was ludicrous.

'No. No,' he said. 'What would I have done with children? Women's work. They stayed with their mother. She married again. Good luck to her. Or I should say, him.'

'Daughters?'

'Boy and girl. I haven't seen or heard from them in fifty years,' he added.'

'And your old friends, from the war? From your time in the partisans?.Do you keep up with them?'

Piero Balestro spread his hands and laughed again. '*Certo*. I have no secrets, Dottore, from you. But you must stay quiet about them, my days in the partisans, or there'll be nothing left to put in my book.'

'Your book?'

'*Certo! Certo!*' Piero Balestro raised his eyebrows, as if it was common knowledge that he was penning the blockbuster of the century. 'It will be a revelation,' he said, 'I assure you.'

He reached for another photograph from a collection of heavy silver frames on the table beside his chair and handed it to Pallioti. It was a copy, or perhaps the original, of the photo that hung on Achilleo Venta's wall.

'Do you know what that is?' he demanded. 'The greatest day in our history! The liberation of the most beautiful city on earth.'

'Yes.' Pallioti handed it back to him. '11 August 1944. What did you do during the war?' he asked. 'Exactly?'

Piero Balestro propped the frame beside the still-empty teacups and tapped the side of his nose, winking.

'Very hush-hush,' he said. 'Though I suppose there's no harm in telling you. If you break the story, I'll know who to sue.' He looked from Pallioti to Eleanor. Then he asked, 'Have you ever heard of Il Spettro?'

'The Ghost?' Eleanor's voice was faint.

'Of course,' Piero Balestro said. 'Il Spettro. Well.' He leaned back in his chair and grinned. 'Let's just say, when my book is published, you'll know a great deal more.'

'And that would be what?' Pallioti asked, forcing himself to smile. 'His true identity, after all these years?'

Piero Balestro winked and tapped the side of his nose again.

'I'll send you an advance copy,' he said.

Eleanor Sachs leaned forward.

'Are you saying—'

'I'm not saying anything, young lady. Not until publication day!'

'But—'

'If we could return to Giovanni Trantemento—' Pallioti interjected, cutting Eleanor off. 'He's not in that photograph?'

He could feel Eleanor glaring at him.

'Giovanni? No.' Piero Balestro shook his head. 'No. He wasn't there for the final fight. Long gone by then, Il Corvo.'

'Long gone?'

'Yes. Yes, his mother was very sick, you see. He took excellent care of her. Took her to Switzerland.'

'And how did he do that?'

'How?'

Piero Balestro looked at Pallioti. For the first time, there was silence in the room. Pallioti leaned forward, battling the sofa.

'I would have thought,' he said, 'that travel passes, and money, were very hard to come by. In June 1944. So, how did he get them? A young man working with the partisans. And half Jewish. Bank accounts had been frozen, and I would have thought papers of that kind would be almost impossible to get hold of.'

The old man smiled.

'Nothing is impossible, Dottore.' The heartiness had gone out of his voice, replaced by a cold quiet. He spread his hands. 'I come from a family of farmers,' he said. 'And look at this house.'

Pallioti and Piero Balestro stared at one another.

'I repeat my question,' Pallioti said after a moment. 'How did a young man in the partisans come by three sets of papers and passes to get his family into Switzerland?'

'How would I know?' Piero Balestro shrugged. 'Il Corvo. He was always the cleverest of us all.'

'Really? Your leader, was he?'

'I didn't say that.'

'No. Achilleo Venta said that was you. Massimo.'

If the use of the name had startled him, he didn't show it. Instead, Piero Balestro said, 'A man did what he had to do, in those days, Dottore.' The words were clipped. He fixed Pallioti with his cold, pale eyes. 'People like you can't understand,' he said. 'All that mattered was to take care of your own. Nazis. Fascists. Partisans. It was every man for himself.'

Under the full head of white hair, Piero Balestro's eyes appeared colourless. Like the bottom of a clear glass that had nothing behind it.

Despite his padded jacket and the heated house, Pallioti felt cold.

'Tell me,' he said. 'What do you know about Radio Juliet?'

Piero Balestro didn't blink. For a moment he didn't move. Then he spread his hands again. 'Tragic,' he said. 'They were betrayed. All of them. Killed.'

'Betrayed by whom?'

'No one knows.'

'You must have been particularly sorry.'

'Me?' Piero Balestro smiled. 'Why would that be?'

'Because they were your comrades, your fellow GAP members.' Pallioti waited a moment. Then he added, 'And because of Lilia.'

For a second, he thought he saw something flicker across the old man's face. A memory? The shadow of a beautiful girl? The face of a woman 'worth ten men' who loved someone else, a pretty boy from the Veneto, a young officer who looked like an angel – exactly the sort of person a farmer's son, even a wealthy farmer's son like Piero Balestro, must have loathed?

'Lilia,' Balestro said finally. 'I don't remember her.'

Pallioti nodded. He toyed with the empty teacup. Then he said, 'She was shot. Lilia. Wounded, during the assassination attempt outside the Pergola Theatre. On 14 February 1944, Valentine's Day – when you and Roberto Roblino and Giovanni Trantemento were arrested. Before your miraculous escape.'

Piero Balestro smiled. His eyes didn't move from Pallioti's face.

'Yes,' he said. 'Yes, of course. Now I remember. That was lucky, wasn't it?'

Pallioti put the cup down. It rattled slightly in the saucer.

'For Lilia?' he asked. 'Or for you?'

'For all of us, Dottore. For all of us. Luck favours the fortunate.'

'So I've heard.'

Pallioti stood up abruptly.

'Lilia, however,' he said, 'was not so fortunate, was she? When Radio Juliet was betrayed, her whole family was killed. And the man she loved. She was pregnant. Did you know that? When she was deported.'

Piero Balestro did not get to his feet. Instead, he leaned back in his armchair and looked up at Pallioti. He smiled.

'Everyone's luck runs out, Dottore,' he said. 'I'm sure you can find your own way to the door.'

As Pallioti stepped out of the sitting room and into the hall, he took a deep breath. Pausing, he closed his eyes, trying to keep the anger that was boiling inside him from erupting. The maid appeared, the rubber soles of her shoes squeaking on the tiles as she scurried to the door and began struggling with an alarming number of locks. Finally, she stepped back, nearly tripping over a boot shelf that sat below a polished rack holding a shotgun and two rifles. Agata Venta's gun, dropped on her portico as casually as if it was an umbrella, popped into Pallioti's mind. Jesus, he thought, didn't anyone in this country lock up their weapons? He had started to say something when he felt Eleanor Sachs's hand on his elbow.

'Let's get out of here,' she whispered.

Five minutes later, the Renault turned out of the drive. This time, the electric gates swung closed behind it, all but clipping the fender. By the time Pallioti reached the motorway and turned the car towards Florence, it had started to rain. He settled into the fast lane and adjusted the wipers. Eleanor Sachs leaned back in the passenger seat.

'They're right,' she said.

'About what?'

She glanced at him. 'That you should be careful of what you wish for.'

Closing her eyes, she shook her head.

'If that man is my grandfather,' she said, 'I think I'll shoot myself.'

Chapter Thirty-Two

'Come! Come! I have your table ready. On a night like tonight—'

Bernardo threw up his hands as if the weather was a badly behaved child whom he had given up all hope of controlling. Shaking his head, he divested Pallioti of his wet coat and hustled him towards the sanctuary of his table in the back corner of Lupo.

With its low lights and flickering candles the restaurant was as dark and welcoming as a cave to a bedraggled wolf cub. Which was approximately how Pallioti felt. He was tired, hungry, bad-tempered, and wet. The rain that had started on Saturday afternoon had not let up. Now, twenty-four hours later on Sunday evening, it was still flinging itself at the city, pummelling the buildings and streets in a tantrum of icy gales and downpours that left the piazzas empty and sent what few tourists there were this late in the season running for cover.

As soon as he had got back to the city and into his office on Saturday afternoon, he had called Saffy and informed her that he would not be appearing for Sunday lunch. His sister had insisted that Maria Grandolo would be deeply upset, because she had wheedled an invitation solely in the hope of building on the new rapport the two of them had recently established. But Pallioti had not even laughed. He had been in no mood to be teased, and in the last twenty-four hours his temper had grown steadily worse. Even as he had driven up the motorway, Eleanor Sachs half asleep beside him, he had been piecing together the case against Piero Balestro in his head.

Everything he had found out only reinforced what he now believed – that sixty years ago Balestro, Roblino and Trantemento had betrayed Radio Juliet and God knew who else. That they had then fallen out, perhaps recently, perhaps a long time ago, and that Balestro had killed the other two – probably to shut them up. As far as he could see, it all fitted. The two men had opened the door to someone who, admittedly, they might not have liked, but whom they did not consider to be a threat. The gun used was exactly the sort of 'souvenir' old soldiers kept. The cash in Trantemento's safe pointed to blackmail. He was not entirely certain whether Trantemento had been the blackmailer or the victim, nor was he sure exactly what it was that had caused the rift between the three old 'brothers-in-arms'. He was certain, however, that Piero Balestro, or Peter Bales, or Massimo or whatever he wanted to call himself, would tell him. If he could get a chance to question him. Properly. Under caution. In an interview room.

The only problem was, no one else agreed.

Enzo Saenz, who had returned from Brindisi on Sunday without the confession he wanted but with what he called 'significant progress', had listened politely. He had even conceded that Pallioti might be well on his way to solving a crime that happened sixty years ago. However, despite the fact that the case against Bruno Torricci was looking a little less rosy than it had, that they had not yet been able to break his alibi for the day Roblino was murdered, or place him in Florence, or find the weapon; despite the fact that, other than the letters, the only other remotely interesting thing they had been able to come up with was the fact that Bruno's girlfriend worked for an IT firm that had installed a series of police software systems – not a crime in itself as far as anyone knew; despite all of that,

Enzo was not convinced that a series of events that might or might not have happened over six decades ago was the motive for two murders. He had heard Pallioti out. Then he pointed out calmly that the fact that Piero Balestro was not a very nice person did not, sadly, outweigh the fact that they had not one shred of evidence against him.

The investigating magistrate had concurred – and failed to be persuaded by the argument that turning over the Balestro property would undoubtedly yield such evidence, specifically the Sauer 38H that Pallioti could practically feel sitting smugly in an upstairs safe or gun locker. Feeling, the magistrate had pointed out acidly, was no longer a basis for charging people or ransacking their property. For charging and ransacking, one needed evidence. Otherwise one was on a fishing expedition. Which made one a sportsman, not a policeman. Having pointed this out, he had then gone so far as to inform Pallioti that he was 'surprised and disappointed'.

And the truth was, Pallioti was too. A good half of his disgust was with himself. Which, although admirably self-enlightened, did not alter the fact that, instead of sitting in Lupo and pointlessly reading the menu, he would rather be putting the fear of God into Piero Balestro before the murder weapon ended up in some river or pond or drainage ditch God knows where.

Where it probably was already. Where it had probably been within hours, if not minutes, of their leaving. If Balestro hadn't already been getting rid of it down at the stables when they arrived. Dismantling it and hiding the bits. Burying them, so to speak, in a heap of horse shit.

Pallioti sighed and put the menu down. Even his friend the Mayor was not his friend at the moment. After the investigating magistrate had called in a temper, demanding to know why the Mayor was allowing Pallioti to 'derail a perfectly good case' and in effect ratting him out, the Mayor had picked up the phone and thrown a fit. He had warned Pallioti that his new department was under scrutiny, that his budget was by no means guaranteed, that there were evil and dark forces who wouldn't mind seeing him and the Mayor taking permanent vacations and that everybody loved old partisans and hated neo-Nazis, so what was his problem?

Pallioti rubbed his hand across his eyes and told himself that it didn't matter what they said any more than it mattered what items he chose on the menu. Bernardo would bring whatever he felt like and it would be delicious, regardless. Much as the evidence against Piero Balestro would add up to a reasonable case, if he just kept picking away at it. Which was what he had been doing all day. Guillermo had been hauled back to his desk. Bales, Trantemento, Roberto Roblino – or Balestro, Rossi and Menucci, whoever they were – Pallioti had ordered that all of them, and anyone else Guillermo could think of, anyone even remotely connected with the case, be checked and double-checked.

So far, the great effort had not turned up a silver bullet. But doing it did make him feel better. And, as Guillermo had pointed out, he could afford to look on the bright side. At least there wasn't anyone else for Piero Balestro to kill. If he was going to do in Little Lamb, he'd have done it years ago. The only time-sensitive issue now was getting enough evidence on the old bastard to charge him before he dropped dead.

With that happy thought, Pallioti picked up the glass Bernardo had brought him and remembered to spare a moment for the good things in life, not least of which was the fact that Lupo was open on Sunday.

The foul weather guaranteed that the restaurant was quiet, the few occupied tables taken by regulars, old diehards, many of them alone. Usually sated, if not stuffed, after his family meals, Pallioti rarely came in on Sundays. Now, tucked into his dark corner, lulled by the soft hum of conversation and the wine, he paid little attention to the rest of the room. Bernardo removed the offending menu. A hot consommé was followed by veal

chops and mushrooms, and a small plate of spinach. A pear
with hard white slices of pecorino appeared. Pallioti had no
idea what the wine was, and didn't care. He was content to sip
it and let the events of the weekend slip away, show themselves
out like bothersome guests.

'Dottore?'

Pallioti looked up.

'This comes with compliments.'

Bernardo was holding a glass in one hand and a very expensive bottle of grappa in the other. Feeling suddenly uneasy, expecting to see the Mayor or the magistrate and wondering if
he'd have to apologize to them, Pallioti looked around.

'From the Signora,' Bernardo said, setting the glass on the
table.

Pallioti glanced beyond him.

Signora Grandolo was sitting alone, in the opposite corner.
She raised a hand. It was a slight, graceful motion. Beauty
knows no age. Pallioti did not know who had said it, but he
knew beyond a shadow of a doubt that it was true. Getting to
his feet, he crossed the room.

'I did not mean to disturb you.' She smiled up at him. 'It
was such a foul night. I couldn't bear the house alone. All those
windows rattling.' She gestured to the chair opposite. 'Will you
join me? Or are you too busy, keeping our world intact?'

'As long as I will not disturb you, Signora.'

'Never, my friend.'

Bernardo, who had been watching them, retrieved Pallioti's
glass and hurried across with the grappa bottle. At a nod, he
poured for Signora Grandolo as well. Pallioti sat down opposite
her.

She smiled.

'To the good fight,' she said, raising her glass. 'And to comrades. Fallen and living.'

'To comrades.' Pallioti joined her, tasting the faintly sweet,
sharp grappa on the back of his tongue.

She was wearing grey tonight, a soft colour. Smoke. A discreet pair of earrings, considerable diamonds, sparkled in the candlelight. As she reached up to adjust one, Pallioti noticed again that, in contrast, her wedding and engagement rings were simple. Seeing his eyes drawn to them, she smiled.

'Cosimo gave me some exceptionally beautiful things over the years,' she said. 'But nothing more valuable than this.' She twisted the plain gold band. 'Neither of my daughters wear one. They say they don't "need rings to prove their love". I don't know whether to admire them, or think they're frivolous. What is your opinion?'

'Is that what it is, a ring – proof?'

'No.' Signora Grandolo shook her head. 'It's just a ring. And some memories.'

She raised her hand to the light, letting the candle catch the dull gleam of the gold and the deep shine in the small cluster of stones that was her engagement ring.

'But,' she added, 'they're a testament too, I think. And a souvenir. A vow. A kind of promise that has nothing to do with proof. Would you agree?'

'Possibly,' Pallioti said.

'I don't know.' She regarded the rings, then looked at him. 'My daughters have great faith in the rightness of things,' she said. 'In the inevitability of the correct conclusion, without the assistance of things like vows and remembering. It's a belief in natural justice, I suppose. I'm glad they have it. But I'm not sure I share it. Perhaps that has something to do with the war.'

'Where did you spend it?'

Even as Pallioti asked the question, he wondered whether it was impolite, whether it sounded as if he were somehow angling to find out about her background, or her age, or any number of other things she would rather not tell him. He thought about Caterina Cammaccio's warning – that where the war was concerned it was sometimes better not to have an enquiring mind – and of her father who would apparently have found that horrific, and smiled, as if the memory was his own.

'What?' she asked.

Pallioti shook his head. 'Nothing,' he said, sipping his grappa. 'Just something I read. About the dangers of enquiring minds.'

'Better, on the whole, to have them than not, surely?' Signora Grandolo raised her own glass. Then she added, 'I was here, at the beginning. We moved about. Cosimo was in Rome, then in a POW camp. The bank is Florentine, of course. But his family has a house in Rome. You sit down to lunch and look out on the Palatine Hill. We lived there after we were married, for a few years, before he came back here to run the bank. I could never settle to it. Do you know Rome?'

'I know it. But not well.'

'No, don't tell me—' She smiled and sipped her grappa. 'A city is like a woman, you know her well only after living with her for a lifetime?'

Pallioti felt himself blush.

'Something like that, I suppose. Although you've managed to make it sound faintly ridiculous.'

'I didn't mean to.' She shook her head. 'I think it's true. About cities, and people. When you reach my age, a lifetime begins to feel short, to get to know anything. Which still surprises me. Surely, you must find that in your work?'

'Continually.'

The answer was more heartfelt than he had intended it to be. Pallioti laughed.

'The only thing I have found I can be certain of,' he said, 'is that I know very little, and I'm very likely to be wrong.'

'Then how do you ever solve anything?' She put her glass down, her face suddenly serious. 'How do you ever solve anything or convict anyone, if you can't know?'

'Oh, I didn't say you can't know. It was the amount of knowing I was talking about. It's a question of persistence, really,' he added, answering her question. 'Of putting together a picture.

Piece by piece. Until you see it. Until the story makes sense. Until all the pieces fit. With no cheating. No cutting and trimming. Then, you know. Not that it always helps you,' he added. 'In fact, a lot of the time it makes no difference at all.' He shrugged. 'But it doesn't matter, because most people simply tell you. If you wait long enough.'

'Confess?'

She smiled as if she found this hard to believe.

Pallioti nodded.

'Eventually. They don't always realize they're doing it. But they do.'

'So, it's true then – the lure of the confessional – that policemen are like priests.'

'I suppose so, Signora.' Pallioti smiled. 'In more ways than you would think.'

'That sounds rather sinister.'

Before Pallioti could consider this, Bernardo approached. Both of their glasses were nearly empty. He refilled them and turned back to the room. Tucked into the corner, their table was an island surrounded by flickering light and the warm lapping murmur of voices.

'Don't you think,' Signora Grandolo asked a moment later, 'that it's not so much people telling you things, as you knowing how to hear them? It seems to me,' she added, picking up her glass, 'that you policemen, good policemen – and I should think there are only very few of you – are rather more like hunting dogs than priests. I don't mean the sense of smell. I mean what you hear – the whistle. The rustle in the undergrowth that the rest of us are deaf to. It's a gift, I suspect.' She smiled. 'Like perfect pitch. Only a very few people have it. And it can't be taught.'

Pallioti shrugged. 'Perhaps.'

In fact, he was absolutely certain that she was right. He had been aware of it since he was a young man – the famous policeman's instinct – and always a little uncomfortable with it, partly because, like all 'gifts', it had little to do with logic and even less to do with being deserving. His career, he knew, to some extent had flourished through no merit of his own.

Signora Grandolo was watching him.

'You, for instance,' she said. 'You heard something, even through decades, didn't you? That caused you to come looking for those three men the other night?'

He looked at her, cradling his glass in his palm.

'Did you find them?' she asked.

The clear, thick liquid shimmered, clinging to the edges of the crystal.

'Yes.'

Pallioti could smell the faint trace of her perfume, mingling with the burning scent of the candle.

'Yes,' he said again. 'I found them.'

'And were they what you expected?'

'I think so.' He looked at her. 'Two of them are dead. The third—' He shook his head. 'The third, Signora, is the sort of man we fought the war to be rid of.'

'We'll never get rid of them. Those sort of men.' She reached out, her fingers touching the back of his hand. 'That's something else,' she said, 'that Cosimo taught me. That they're part of us, those kind of men. That the best we can ever do is contain them.'

Her fingertips were as light as a butterfly's wing.

When she smiled and took her hand away the memory of her touch lingered on his skin.

Chapter Thirty-Three

Pallioti swallowed his first espresso of the morning and put the cup down abruptly. It was Monday, the start of a new week and he had slept well, and woken to find that the rain had departed, leaving the air sharp and clear as crystal.

The barman raised an eyebrow. Pallioti nodded for another as he reached into the pocket where his mobile phone had begun to hop about like a cricket. He spent a few moments talking to Guillermo who, energized by his new fact-finding mission, had arrived at the office an hour earlier than anyone else. Having decided on their priorities for the day, and reiterated once more that it might be best not to share them with Enzo Saenz, or the magistrate, or, God forbid, the Mayor, should he for some reason appear in the office, Pallioti slid the phone closed and tried not to think of Don Quixote and Sancho Panza. He was putting it away when his fingers encountered a folded piece of paper. Pulling it out of his pocket, he saw the message left by the London Embassy giving him the personal contact number for Giovanni Trantemento's pen pal, Lord David Eppsy.

Pallioti smoothed it on the sleek zinc countertop of the bar, then downed the second espresso, left an overly generous tip, and pushed through the door and onto the street. A moment later he stood, like the rest of the city, on the pavement with his mobile phone clamped to his ear. It was not until he was listening to a burbling and then a ringing that it occurred to him to wonder what time it might be in Sri Lanka.

By the time David Eppsy answered his phone, Pallioti had stepped into the corner of a small piazza, sheltering from the road and the sound of traffic. He concentrated on a line of wheeled rubbish carts parked against the opposite wall as he apologized for the disturbance of calling and explained who he was. As it turned out, he did not have to ask about the time difference, because Lord Eppsy told him.

'Ha, ha,' he said, not sounding remotely disturbed. 'A voice from Florence! The past both literal and temporal! It's evening here, Inspector. And I can tell you with confidence that ahead of you lies a very good day.'

Pallioti wondered what he had been drinking. Probably gin.

'Thank you,' he said, and added, 'I am calling concerning a Signor Giovanni Trantemento. I believe you knew him?'

'Oh, yes. Oh, yes,' David Eppsy said quickly. 'Had a message about something. Was why I got back to you. Spot of bother, I gather?'

Large spot, Pallioti was tempted to say. But he confined himself to simply stating that the man was dead.

'Oh. Oh, dear. Dear me. How very sad. Poor old fellow. I am sorry to hear that.'

David Eppsy was either doing a very good imitation, or he was genuinely both surprised and unhappy to hear the news. He realized that, other than his sister, David Eppsy was about the only person who had even bothered to pretend to sound distressed on hearing the news that Giovanni Trantemento was dead.

David Eppsy swallowed. Pallioti thought he could hear the clink of ice cubes.

'He was,' the Englishman said, 'well, a gentleman. Dying breed. Rare as the auk. And of course, a connoisseur, in his field. Highly respected. A pleasure to do business with. He'll be a loss. Damn shame. Too rare, these days,' David Eppsy said again. 'A gentleman, of the old school. Too rare. I suppose,' he asked a second later, 'that it was a heart attack? Or—'

'I'm afraid not.'

Apparently the embassy had told David Eppsy nothing in the message they had left asking him to get in touch. Just as well. Being of the old school himself, Pallioti still put some stock in the value of surprise.

'I am afraid,' he said, 'that Signor Trantemento was murdered.'

'Good Lord!'

There was a pause.

'Good Lord!' David Eppsy said again. 'Murdered? How on earth did that happen?'

'I am afraid, in the most common way,' Pallioti said. 'With a gun. Someone shot him, in his apartment.'

'Good Lord. How horrible.'

'Yes.'

You don't know the half of it, Pallioti thought. He had a sudden vision of the terror on Giovanni Trantemento's face, of his broken glasses, his open mouth. Of Enzo, reaching down, dabbing his finger and pronouncing, 'salt'. He shoved it aside.

'The reason I am contacting you,' Pallioti went on, 'and I am sorry to take up your time, is that we found a letter from you to Signor Trantemento. It arrived the day he was killed. 1st November.'

'Ah.' There was a pause. 'Ah, yes,' David Eppsy said. 'Yes, of course.'

Pallioti had not really expected him to deny it, but he was glad, all the same, that he hadn't.

'I had just written to him, about our little – arrangement.'

For the first time a note of coyness crept into the Englishman's voice, a slight furtive edge. Pallioti ignored it.

'The letter,' he said. 'Can you tell me, exactly, what was in the envelope?'

There was a pause.

'Well, the note, of course. I assume you have that.'

'Yes. And what else?'

'Ummm.'

David Eppsy lowered his voice. Pallioti could hear him walking. There was the crunch of what might have been gravel, the creak of a wooden floor.

'The note, yes,' Pallioti prompted. 'And?'

David Eppsy cleared his throat.

'A money order,' he said. 'For three thousand pounds. Whatever that is in euros.'

'I see. A money order?'

'Well, two, actually. Bit more discreet, that way. They were issued—' David Eppsy laughed, and for the first time Pallioti felt sorry for him. 'Issued by Western Union,' he said. 'Rather good, actually.' His voice was suddenly overly jovial. 'Like book tokens. Saves you writing a cheque.'

'Yes,' Pallioti said. 'Exactly. Will you have a record of the numbers?'

'Oh, yes. Yes. Of course.'

David Eppsy sounded so pleased at the idea of being helpful that Pallioti wondered if he were a younger son.

'Of course,' he added. 'At least I should think so. Somewhere at home.' His voice fell again. 'Do you need them now?' he asked. 'I mean, I suppose it's possible. And I do want to help. I could arrange for someone – but it would be rather, well—'

'I don't need them now,' Pallioti said. 'I may not need them at all.'

'Well, if you do—' The relief in the man's voice was palpable. 'And if there's anything else I can do. Anything at all. Poor old fellow.'

'Yes,' Pallioti agreed. 'Poor old fellow. Forgive me,' he added, 'for interrupting your holiday. You have been most helpful.'

'Inspector!' David Eppsy broke in just as he was about to finish the call. 'Inspector,' he said. 'I wonder if – well, has there been a funeral yet?'

'No. No,' Pallioti said. 'We'll be releasing the body shortly. To his sister and nephew.'

'Well, when there is, a funeral, if you know – would it be possible for someone to contact me? I'd be grateful.' He gave a little laugh. It didn't sound very jolly. 'One likes to send flowers,' David Eppsy said. 'Gesture of respect, and all that.'

'I'll be certain to let you know. I'll call you myself.'

''Preciate it. Damn shame.'

Half a world away David Eppsy was still muttering when Pallioti closed his phone. He stood for a moment, watching a pair of pigeons as they squabbled over an orange peel beside one of the rubbish bins. They puffed their feathers, cooed and strutted, then lost interest and flew away. Pallioti opened his phone again. He made one brief call before he turned and walked quickly towards the river.

It was barely 9 a.m.; people were still scurrying to work. A bus turned into the street, somehow avoiding taking the corner with it, and lumbered up the pavement. The door to Giovanni Trantemento's building burst open just as it pulled away. A woman dashed out. She ran a few steps towards the bus stop, then stopped and swore. Pallioti caught the huge front door before it closed. As he slipped inside, he saw the woman step into the street. Shaking her head and buttoning her coat, she mounted the opposite pavement and started the now inevitable walk to work.

Letting his eyes adjust to the internal twilight, Pallioti looked around. He realized he had expected to see the solid little figure of Marta Buonifaccio standing in her usual spot beside the huge fireplace. But she was nowhere in sight. On the far side of the hearth, her door was closed.

He turned towards the cage of the tiny elevator. Its door was open, the coffin-like box waiting to be called into action. He considered it for a moment, then turned away towards the stairs.

It was like climbing out of a well. The building improved with height. At every landing, there was a little more light. Even so, it wasn't until he reached the landing above the third floor that he was actually able to look out of one of the windows. And then only if he stood on tiptoe. He craned upwards. All he could make out was the blank wall of the palazzo on the other side of the alley and a slice of sky above. Reaching up with both hands, he pushed on the leaded diamonds of glass. The frame did not give at all. Nor could he see a latch. As he suspected, it was welded shut. Satisfied, he turned and went back down to the hall.

He had knocked four times at the door on the far side of the fireplace, each time with a little more urgency, and was still getting no response, when he heard the voice behind him.

'You'll be bloody lucky.'

Pallioti spun around, expecting to see the squat Russian-doll shape of Marta herself. But it was not Marta. Instead, it was another old crone. 'She's gone,' she said.

'Gone?'

'Gone!' She shouted it at him, as if he were deaf. Pallioti tried not to flinch.

'Do you know where?' he asked.

'Not a clue,' she replied, eyeing him.

The woman, who might have come up to Pallioti's chest if she stood on her toes, swung the shopping bag she was carrying as if she were considering using it as a dangerous weapon.

'I'll tell you though, it's bloody inconvenient,' she added. 'You should have seen the mail. All over the floor when I came in. Them up there' – she nodded towards the upper storeys of the building as though she were talking about the gods on Olympus – 'having kittens. Why they couldn't pick it up

473

themselves, don't ask me. I had to spend a bloody hour sorting it. Chinese food, taxis—' She leaned forward and hissed between her teeth. 'Blue movies.' She looked at Pallioti and nodded. 'You name it, they put it through the door. Although,' she said, 'I'd lay money, someone asked for the films.' She nodded as if she was imparting the wisdom of the ages. 'They don't waste flyers where there isn't any business.'

'No,' Pallioti said. 'No, I'm sure you're right, Signora—?'

'Who wants to know?'

He started to reach for his credentials, then thought better of it. If he wanted Marta to talk to him, which he did, he probably wouldn't persuade her by causing gossip about visits from the police.

'I'm a friend,' he said, smiling. 'Severino Cavicalli,' Pallioti added quickly, extending his hand. He hoped the proprietor of Patria Memorabilia would forgive him, but it was the first name that came to mind.

'Cara,' she said. She considered his outstretched hand for a moment before extending her own. Enclosed in a red mitten, it looked like a small paw. 'Cara Fratto. I clean for them.' She nodded at the stairs again. 'Three days a week, fifty-two weeks of the year, including Easter. They're babies, can't even cook a meal for themselves. I leave their dinner with a note telling them how to put it in the oven. *Nati con la camicia.*' The unliteral translation of *Born with a silver spoon in the mouth*. Cara Fratto rolled her eyes. 'But they pay well.'

'Do you have any idea,' Pallioti asked, 'when Marta might be back?'

She shrugged in a way that suggested that perhaps she did, and perhaps she didn't. Pallioti tried another tack.

'Do you know how long she's been gone?'

This time the shrug came with an answer.

'Well, I haven't been for three days and there was certainly that much mail. All over the floor. What is it? People get a university degree and they can't bend down? Not only that, they see me and they walk right past. Not a word of thanks. Nothing.' She leaned towards him. 'You wait,' she added. 'You just wait. You get old you become invisible. Poof!'

Pallioti started slightly. Which apparently gave Cara Fratto some satisfaction. She treated him to a grin that creased her wizened-apple face.

Pallioti nodded sympathetically. Feeling that they had formed some kind of bond, he decided to push his luck.

'Well,' he said. 'I guess Marta's probably visiting family.'

Cara gave a sharp snort.

'If so, it's the first time in ten years.' She raised the shopping bag. 'They can't cook,' she said, jerking her head towards the stairs, 'but there's nothing they don't know. According to them, Marta doesn't have any family. Also according to them, I don't get this in the refrigerator, the spinach will wilt, the pears will rot, and the cheese will sweat. After that, the world will probably come to an end.'

She turned towards the elevator. Pallioti watched as she pulled back the metal grille and dumped the shopping bag on the floor. Cara Fratto closed the door, pushed a button, stepped back and watched as the gears started to grind. She gave a nod of satisfaction, then turned towards the stairs.

'You find her, you tell her the mail's her job,' she said over her shoulder.

She gripped the banister, looked up, sighed, and started to climb.

Pallioti waited until the small shape had disappeared, plodding its way towards the heights of Olympus. Then he crossed the room quietly, lifted the waste-paper basket parked under the lamp, and upended it onto the mail table.

℗

Eleanor Sachs had every intention of breaking the promise she had made to Pallioti. And doing so sooner rather than later. In fact, she had considered turning around and driving straight back down to Siena on Saturday evening. Then she had thought better of it. Not because she was afraid of him, but because she was afraid of Piero Balestro. Everything about him, to put it bluntly, gave her the creeps.

The fact didn't lessen her determination to talk to him, to find out who his children were, and whether their stepfather's name had been Faber. But it did persuade her that forewarned might include being forearmed. Or something like that. The long and the short was, if she was going to venture back to cross-question the Minotaur – and that was exactly what he'd reminded her of, a cold-eyed randy old bull – then she ought to be prepared. Finding out something – anything – she could about him, might come in handy. Even Theseus had taken a ball of string.

So she'd given up the idea of making the excursion on Sunday, and instead spent the day online. There, she had found information on four Bales Clinics, all in what appeared to be poor, remote townships in South Africa. Doctor Peter Bales had also had a private practice, considerably more stylish, if the website was anything to go by, in Johannesburg. The accompanying picture showed a much younger Piero Balestro. The biography agreed that he'd graduated from the University of Michigan Medical School in 1950. There was no mention of his wife, or of any children. No mention of a family at all, or even of the fact that he was Italian. From his photograph and biographical notes, Peter Bales looked to be an all-American boy.

It was the hope that she might find some record of his marriage to the American nurse he claimed to have married in Florence, and with any luck his wife's name – or even better, an address – that had driven her to the city archives early on Monday morning.

By eleven, Eleanor had trawled through marriage records, and Red Cross records, and records concerning hospitals and come up with nothing. She was about to quit, had about decided that it didn't matter, that she'd just get in the car and drive down to Siena and confront the old creep, when she thought about the Pergola Theatre, and Radio Juliet – and what Pallioti had told her. And Piero Balestro's reaction when he had brought it up. It was the only time Balestro had faltered, the only time anything Pallioti had said had seemed to have any impact on him. Admittedly, it hadn't been much. A prick in his bull's hide. But it had been something. And if she was going to break one promise to Pallioti, the least she could do was keep another.

Eleanor filled out a search slip and put in two more requests, for material covering the dates a week on either side of the Pergola shooting in February and the Radio Juliet arrests in June of 1944. The library was not terribly busy. She got up, stretched her legs, went outside and checked her mobile phone. There were no messages. Her husband had stopped calling since the disaster of a weekend they had spent in Positano. She came back twenty minutes later to find two document boxes deposited at her work station.

The material was almost all copies, the original documents either being elsewhere, or deemed too fragile to be handled by researchers. Some of it – the copies of news sheets and testimonials, reports of GAP actions – she'd seen before. She glanced at her watch. It would take her an hour and a half, at least, to reach Balestro's estate, and she wanted to eat something before she left. She was hungry and pretty much losing interest when she came across the papers at the bottom of the second box.

Eleanor recognized them at once. She'd seen some of them before. They were records from the Villa Triste. She lifted them out and set them on the desk. They always made her feel slightly queasy, these meticulous records of death, so neatly kept. So carefully noted. They were only photocopied sheets, but she ran her fingers along the lined entries anyway. It was an exercise she made herself carry out – to remember that these neat letters represented, not just names, but lives, hopes, dreams, and ambitions that had been beaten, broken, and snuffed out.

She closed her eyes and willed herself to think of the small, insignificant pieces of lives that had been lost. The memory of a birthday party. The joy of sunlight, or rain. The sound of a voice. The taste of a favourite food. A glass of wine. Of bread and salt. Nothing to anyone, except those who had lost them. Then she looked down at the page, and blinked.

Eleanor Sachs felt her pulse quicken. She looked, and looked again. What she saw was wrong. It had to be. But it was there, under her fingers. She moved them slowly along the words, along the neat copperplate writing, like a child learning to read, just to be sure she wasn't making a mistake. But she wasn't. She checked the date at the top of the page. *15 June 1944*. She looked again. But the words still said what they said.

Eleanor glanced around the room. There hadn't been many other readers to start with, and most of those had left, either for lunch, or for the day. The girl at the front desk was reading something. Occasionally licking her finger, flipping through pages. Without taking her eyes off her, Eleanor reached down into her shoulder bag.

The thing was too big, cavernous. She should get a neat little purse so she would have no trouble finding things. Like her mobile phone. She was lifting it out, when she realized it was stupid. The phone would make a chirping sound when she turned it on and another when she took a picture. There was no way, in the silent room, that she wouldn't be noticed – and promptly thrown out. And even if she managed to get a picture of the page, the screen was so tiny it would hardly do any good. Something told her she didn't have time to mess around linking the phone up to a computer. Pallioti needed to see what was in front of her and he needed to see it now.

Eleanor looked around again. Her mouth was dry. She licked her lips. Then in one swift motion she reached out, slid the page onto her lap, and into the open mouth of her bag.

❧

Pallioti had finished his sandwich and was on his way back to the office when his phone rang. Without breaking his stride, he pulled it out of his pocket. When he saw that the caller was Eleanor Sachs and not the Mayor calling to shout at him again, he stopped and flipped it open.

'Good morning, Dottoressa,' he said. 'Or should I say afternoon?'

The results of his hunt through the waste bin had been most satisfactory. The sun was still out. His sandwich had been better than usual. All in all he was feeling remarkably chipper.

'Where are you?' Eleanor Sachs sounded strained. Worse than strained. She sounded frantic.

'Where am I? I'm in the piazza—' Pallioti looked at the phone and frowned. He could hear traffic, the honking of a horn. 'Where are you?' he asked. 'What's the matter? Are you driving?'

'Yes. No,' she said. 'I'm on the Lungarno. I'm pulled over. Near the Excelsior. Can you come?'

'Eleanor?' Had she been arrested? Pulled over and wanted him to bail her out? 'What's—'

'I've found something,' she said, cutting him off. 'You have to see. It doesn't make any sense. But it's important. It's from the Villa Triste.'

Five minutes later, Eleanor Sachs looked up and saw Pallioti coming towards her down the pavement. He wove past a couple of window-gazers, held up his hand and stepped into the traffic to avoid a woman with a baby buggy. When he opened the passenger door, she felt a pang of relief. She had been sitting with the bag on her lap, her hand inside it, holding the paper as if it might vaporize before she could show it to him.

'Here.' Without saying anything else, she handed him the flimsy photocopy, glad to be rid of it, as if it were explosive, or somehow incriminating.

She watched as his face creased with concern.

'What—'

'It's from the Villa Triste,' she said. 'Thursday, 15 June 1944.'

He looked up.

'Where did you get this?'

'I stole it, about an hour ago, from the archives.'

Pallioti frowned.

'It's just a copy!' she said. 'For God's sake, it's not the end of the earth. Halfway down – just read it!'

Pallioti pulled out his glasses. He lifted the sheet up so he could see it better. Under the date, there was a list of names.

Aurelio Enrico Cammaccio, B. Florence, 1885, 59 yrs, Professor. 11 a.m. Removed – Executed.

Enrico Bernardo Cammaccio, B. Florence, 1921, 23 yrs, Deserter. 11 a.m. Removed – Executed.

Carlo Francesco Peralta, B. Venice, 1921, 23 yrs, Deserter. 11 a.m. Removed – Executed.

The next three names on the list he did not recognize.

Mario Tommaso Benelli, 19. Porfirio Rodrigo Andarri, 18. Romolo Teodoro DellaChiesa, 19.

All listed as deserters, they too had all been 'removed' at 11 a.m. on 15 June, and executed.

Strong arms, lopsided smiles. No more than boys, they had dug a trench and knelt down. Pallioti felt his chest tighten. He looked at the last three names on the list.

Piero Balestro, B. Siena, 1921, 23 yrs.
Giancarlo Menucci, B. Siena, 1924, 20 yrs.

Giovanni Rossi, B. Pisa, 1921, 23 yrs.

After each were written the words, 11 a.m. *Removed*. And then the final word. *Executed*.

Chapter Thirty-Four

He had not bothered to call Enzo Saenz, or even Guillermo. Instead, he had stared at the paper in his hand, then opened the door and ordered Eleanor Sachs out of the driver's seat. When she had insisted on sliding over to the passenger side instead of getting out of the car, he hadn't even bothered to argue, just barked at her to fasten her seat belt.

They were past San Casciano before she said anything.

'They did it, didn't they? They betrayed that Radio group, Juliet? That's what this is about?'

Without taking his eyes off the road, Pallioti nodded. He came shockingly close to the car in front, flashed his lights and leaned on the horn until the driver swung over, gesturing obscenely.

'What happened?' Her voice was tight.

'They were arrested. In February. After the shooting at the theatre. The three men, Massimo, Il Corvo, Beppe.' Pallioti had a straight empty stretch of road ahead, but still didn't look at her.

'But not Lilia?'

'No. She got away.'

'And they were taken to the Villa Triste, and kept for three days, and then they escaped. Except' – Eleanor glanced at him – 'They didn't. Not really.'

'No.'

Pallioti heard Signora Grandolo's voice in his head. *No one ever walked out of the Villa Triste.* They didn't escape from there, either. Isabella had told Caterina as much. One guard in the front of the truck. One in the back. For three men. Both too injured to prevent all three escaping. It was nonsense, and Giovanni Trantemento had all but laid it out. Antenor. He must have half hoped, consciously or not, that someone would figure it out. That someone would take the burden away. Absolve him before it was too late. *You deserve this medal more than I do.* He had all but underlined it in red. No wonder Massimo had cause for concern, had decided to close Trantemento's mouth before he could finally spit out the sin.

'So, it was a set-up,' Eleanor said. 'They were allowed to escape, get away, and the price was Radio Juliet.'

Pallioti nodded. And what else, he wondered? The safe house used after the weapons drop, almost certainly. In which case, they must have been Mario Carita's golden boys. A cache of weapons, ammunition, explosives – and how many arrests? How many lives smashed? Then Juliet.

No wonder they had been able to ask for anything – new identities. Sets of papers to get a Jewish family to Switzerland. Safe passage into Spain. Money for doctors and drugs. *All that mattered*, Piero Balestro had said, *was to take care of your own*. But Issa had thought GAP was her own. *GAP will take of me*, she had told Caterina. *We have a sacred bond of trust.* It was that belief, not her sister's carelessness, that had cost them their lives. One of them must have contacted Carita that morning, as soon as they were told the address of the meeting place, the house off the Via dei Renai.

Pallioti tried to tamp down the rage he could feel growing inside.

'But how did he do it?' Eleanor asked. 'How did Balestro come back and fight at the liberation, how was he there in August? Wouldn't people have guessed, known he was arrested with the rest of Juliet?'

'Maybe not.' Pallioti glanced at her. 'That was in June. He got his cousin out of Fiesole, got him to a doctor somewhere. They must have lain low for at least a month or a few weeks for Achilleo to recover.'

'And by August, in Florence, things were chaotic.' She nodded. 'If they just showed up at the end, in time for the glory, spun some story or other—'

'Il Corvo and Beppe were long gone.' Pallioti finished the thought for her. 'There was no one from Juliet left alive to contradict anything Massimo said.'

'And his cousin would have lied for him. Corroborated anything he said.'

Pallioti nodded. He suspected that Achilleo Venta was luckier than he knew to be alive – lucky he'd been useful to his beloved Massimo.

'And those two women.' Eleanor glanced at him. 'The sisters?'

Pallioti nodded.

'They were arrested, and transported. But they escaped. They ended up in Milan. And, well, you know.'

'What was her name? Lilia? You said she was pregnant?'

'Yes,' Pallioti said. 'She was pregnant.' He pushed another car out of the fast lane. 'The father was executed. He was part of Radio Juliet. She never really recovered. It broke her heart.'

'And the baby?'

Pallioti shrugged.

'I don't know,' he said. 'He was born in Milan. He probably died.'

Eleanor lapsed into silence. She stared out of the window. Pallioti concentrated on the road. It should have been a relief, or at least some kind of vindication, to know that he was right, that his much-vaunted sixth sense, his 'hearing' as Signora Grandolo called it, had not deserted him. But it wasn't. The moment he had seen those names on the Villa Triste ledger, understood that they had been made officially dead, and why, he'd felt like a fool. The worst kind of amateur.

He'd been played, and what was worse, played by the dead – just as Isabella had been, all those years ago.

He had wondered, briefly, about the escape, then put it down to luck, which he didn't believe in. But the second part of the trick he had missed completely. It had been right in front of his face, but he hadn't seen it. The fact that Issa had been chosen, taken to the clearing in the woods – not by chance, or because she had made a lot of noise in the cells, but because of who she was. A hero. Someone people owed their lives to. Someone whose word amongst her comrades was unimpeachable.

Whoever arranged for her to be taken to that clearing knew that. And knew that if she survived and reported that all the members of her GAP unit had been executed – as she had, at the very first opportunity in Verona – she would be believed without question. Because she had seen the bodies with her own eyes.

Except she hadn't.

Instead, what she had seen was exactly what she had been shown. Her father, her brother, her lover. And below them a tangle of arms and legs. Arms and legs that she expected to belong to Il Corvo and Beppe and Massimo. But that in fact had belonged to three boys. Three strangers who, for all Pallioti knew, had been arrested and shot for just that purpose.

There was an efficiency to it – a wit, even – that made Pallioti wonder if it had been thought of by Carita himself. Or had Massimo come up with the idea – that she should look down on Carlo's dead face, and provide the men who had betrayed him with an alibi? If she died in the camps, there would be no witnesses. If she lived to tell the story, her word would set him free forever. Guarantee that Massimo and Beppe and Il Corvo were dead. Because Issa said so. And no one comes looking for dead men.

Pallioti blinked. The road was unwinding ahead of him, spooling out fast in a thin grey ribbon.

But someone had. That was exactly what had happened.

His foot hit the accelerator.

Everyone's luck runs out, Dottore.

✑

The sky was a sharp noontime blue. Once again, Piero Balestro's electric gates stood open, their railings glinting silver against the packed white earth of the drive. There could be a thousand reasons for that, all of them innocent. Or not. Pallioti glanced at the security camera. Its tiny red eye blinked in a steady rhythm.

They turned in and started down the drive. It had not been forty-eight hours since their first visit, and already the place felt strange. The dun mounds of the hills, their crowns of cypress, and the soft sage scrub that grew in the drainage ditches, were absolutely still. There was not a breath of wind. Earlier, mist would have pooled in the valleys. Pallioti could see the glisten of a small pond in a hollow. Dots of white spattered across the hillside beyond. Sheep. If he rolled his window down he was sure he would be able to hear the faint, monotonous tinkle of bells.

He glanced at Eleanor. She was staring through the windscreen as if hypnotized.

'When we get there,' Pallioti said, 'I want you to stay in the car. Lock the door. Don't get out unless I tell you. If anything happens, leave. Drive out of the gates, and call the police.'

She nodded.

'What do you think we're going to find?' she asked a moment later.

He shook his head.

'Honestly,' he said, 'I have no idea.'

The first sign that anything was wrong was the jeep. It wasn't there. The silver Alfa sat exactly where it had before, its nose facing the line of cypresses. Pallioti could see a sharp mark in the gravel, a skid where the jeep had reversed, quickly. There was no sign of life around the house. Through the trees they could see the horses still grazing in front of the stables.

He got out of the car and stood for a moment. Something about the stillness made him inclined to be quiet. The leaves of the bay trees were almost black against the soft stone of the house. The brass latches of the shutters sparkled in the sun. The lions, their paws crossed, looked implacably out over the steps. There was a faint hum in the camellias, possibly the buzz of an out-of-season bumblebee, still hunting for pollen, unaware that come nightfall it would not survive the frost.

Pallioti was not aware that Eleanor had opened her door until she spoke.

'What's that?'

She was half in, half out of the passenger seat, her head cocked like a dog's. Before Pallioti could admonish her, tell her to do as she was told and not be so stupid, he heard it too.

At first it was nothing but a distant echo of sound. Then it rose, hit a high note, and died. If the wind had been blowing it would not have been possible to hear it at all.

Pallioti had turned towards it, was about to step around the front of the car, when the front door of the house burst open.

'Oh! Papa, I—' At the last moment, just as she put her foot on the top step, the maid looked up. 'Oh!' she exclaimed. 'You're – I thought you were—'

She tried to stop on the second step, but lost her balance. Her arms flailed, the small doll-like hands reaching towards Pallioti, who managed to grab her and steady her down onto the gravel, stop her from falling flat on her face.

'I'm sorry! I'm so sorry.' Embarrassed, the maid tried to step away, but Pallioti hung onto her.

'Are you all right?'

'Yes. Yes.' She nodded, a blush rising from under the collar of her uniform and creeping upwards, deepening the coffee-coloured skin of her cheeks. 'I'm so sorry,' she said again. 'I thought you were—'

Her accent became thicker as she became more agitated, making her Italian almost incomprehensible.

'You thought I was who?'

The tiny woman's eyes pooled with tears.

'Thought I was who, Signorina?' He asked more gently this time, and the maid began to cry. Her face crumpled. She shook her head.

'Papa Balestro,' she said. 'I thought when I heard the car – Papa Balestro.'

'Papa?'

Pallioti could hear Eleanor behind him

The maid's hair had come loose, escaping from the plastic clip that held it. Dark silky strands swung across her face, catching on her damp cheeks.

'I'm sorry,' she wept. 'I'm sorry. I'm sorry. I've been so worried. I didn't know what to do. I thought, when I heard the car—'

Pallioti was looking towards the house. Through the open door he could see the hallway. The brass chandelier of countrified design shone on the too-new terracotta tiles. Letting go of the woman's arm, he mounted the steps and pushed the door open wider. A single pair of hunting boots rested upside down on the rack. Above them, the rifles hung where he had seen them the day before. The shotgun was missing.

He turned around.

'Where is Doctor Balestro?'

The maid wiped her eyes. Tears stained the cuff of her pale-blue uniform.

'I don't know, Dottore. I don't know.'

'What do you mean?'

She shook her head, looking at Pallioti as if he might somehow have the answer.

'When did you last see him?' The question came out as a bark, making her jump.

'Last night,' she said. 'Late. I always check on him, to see if he needs anything.'

'And did he?'

She shook her head. 'No. He was on the telephone. He waved at me – to go away. So I went. Then, this morning, I heard the car.'

'When?'

'Early.' She began to cry in earnest. 'Very early. He goes hunting, at this time of year. He takes Pepe, the dog. But—'

'But?'

'He's always back. For breakfast. By nine, before he goes down to the stables. I cook him—'

Pallioti did not care what she cooked him.

'Where's the dog?' Eleanor asked. 'The dog.' She glanced at Pallioti.

Before anyone could say anything, they heard it again. Echoing in the still November air was the faint wail of an animal in pain.

'Stay here.' Pallioti waved towards the house. 'Go inside and lock the door. Don't open it for anyone but me.'

The maid nodded, scuttling up the steps like a small animal seeking sanctuary. The door swung closed. There was a clicking as the battery of locks began to turn. Pallioti ducked through the line of trees and stepped out onto the lawn. Below, in the paddock, the horses raised their heads.

'There,' Eleanor said.

The sound came again. From where they stood, it seemed a little louder.

He glared at her.

'You should stay here.'

Ignoring him, Eleanor started down the steps that led to the stables. As he followed, Pallioti glanced back. Under the noon sun, the house was a pale block of stone. Between the deep-red shutters of the sitting-room window, he saw a small face. As he watched, the maid raised a hand and pressed it to the glass.

The track that skirted behind the stable led past several paddocks, all of them empty. After the last one, the gravel gave way to compacted chalky earth. Pallioti took it at a trot, Eleanor fell in behind him. The wailing had become regular now, rising and falling like a siren. The track wound around the small lump of a hill. Ahead, Pallioti saw a pond and a strip of wood. Naked branches of chestnut and beech filled a small valley, winding through it like a river. They had almost reached the treeline when he saw the flash of red. Pallioti raised a hand. Eleanor stopped. The dog's cries had lessened, wound down into whimpering, as if it sensed them coming. Slowly, they walked forward together.

The jeep had been parked in a stand of trees, nose in. Pallioti had not looked, but he realized when he thought about it that, of course, there would be a service drive for the stables opening off the road – an access for feed deliveries and horse vans. Piero Balestro would have taken it this morning, as he probably took it every morning during the hunting season. He would drive this far, then park and unload the guns and the dog. The wood would provide attractive cover. The pond was probably a winter home for ducks. Looking to the far side of it, Pallioti spotted what looked like a hide, several segments of wattle behind a stand of bulrushes.

The old spaniel had fallen silent. Its leash was tied around a sapling some twenty feet away, in a stand of thin, newly planted alder. Seeing them, it sat, and started to whine.

Wary of the jeep, Pallioti circled away from it, meaning to approach the dog from the side. Then he saw Piero Balestro.

The old man was lying some two or three yards from the passenger door, which was open. He was wearing the same tweed jacket, this time with a green down vest of the kind hunters favoured over it. His brown boots were still shiny. No dust had settled on them. The soles were clean. It looked as if he had got out of the car, crossed to the passenger side, opened the door, then turned and walked no more than ten or a dozen steps.

One arm was pinned underneath him, the other flung out, gloved hand palm up.

'Alessandro?'

Eleanor pointed at the ground. Just beyond Piero Balestro's outstretched hand, lying in the short dead grass, was a small gun.

Pallioti nodded. He squatted down on his haunches. Piero Balestro's head was twisted, his eyes open. They stared, colour-less, almost white, against his livid cheeks. Some people believed that the last thing you saw was imprinted on your eye, locked into your soul. Looking into Massimo's soul, Pallioti saw nothing.

He had been shot, once, in the forehead. The hole was not big. Surprisingly little blood dribbled out of it. His mouth was open, as if in protest, or surprise. There were white crystals on his lips. Beside his chin was a pile of salt.

Chapter Thirty-Five

Tape was strung through the trees like garlands. It looped round trunks and hung from bare branches. The entire distance of the track, from the stables to the scene, had been closed off. The medical examiner and scene of crime officers had walked like strange white-suited aliens over the yellowing brow of the hill.

Now Carla Nanno, the same ME who had handled Giovanni Trantemento, knelt over Piero Balestro. Her gloved fingers poked and probed. She glanced up.

'Approximately eight hours,' she said. 'As a best guess. Right after sunrise. It's not an uncommon time for people to kill themselves.'

'You think that's what this is?'

She shrugged, looked from Piero Balestro's hand to the gun that had already been photographed and measured ad nauseam.

'Well, it certainly could be self-inflicted,' she said. 'No question. Maybe I'll find something that says different, when I get him on the table. But I doubt it. Of course,' she added, 'that doesn't mean it was. Self-inflicted. I'm just telling you that, as of now, it could have been. That's my best guess.' She nodded towards his outstretched hand. 'I'll test, obviously. But it looks like there's a powder burn on the glove.'

Pallioti nodded.

'What about the salt?'

She looked down. Took a finger and ran it under the old man's lip. There was something obscene about it. Pallioti tried not to flinch. Carla Nanno frowned.

'Well, it's in his mouth. But not nearly as much as the other one. That would make sense. I mean, you wouldn't eat it if someone didn't make you. Like I said, we'll have to see when we open him up.' She looked up at Pallioti. 'It's in his pockets, too,' she said. 'Did you know?'

He didn't. Having found that he could not get a signal, and having given Eleanor his phone, and instructions to go back to the car and drive as far as she had to to call Enzo Saenz, Pallioti had not touched Piero Balestro's body. He had not even touched the dog. He wanted the leash photographed and checked for prints. He had explained this, speaking in a low murmuring tone to the spaniel, who had eventually stopped whining and lay down, its head resting on its paws as it regarded him solemnly. After that, he had walked carefully in widening circles until he had found what he was looking for. It was nothing, really. A couple of broken twigs. Ten more minutes' walking, winding through the trees in the strip of wood, had brought him to a small paved road. He had stood in the middle of it, then walked fifty yards up and down either side. Where, exactly as he'd expected, he'd found nothing.

Now he watched as Carla Nanno bent over the prone figure, proprietorial and protective as a nurse with a critical patient. She lifted the slit of one of Piero Balestro's vest pockets. Sure enough, a thin white dribble escaped.

'Where is the bag?' Pallioti asked.

She looked up at him.

'What?'

'The bag. For the salt. How did the salt get here?'

She shrugged.

'I don't know. Is it in the car?'

Pallioti glanced towards the jeep. The forensics team had

finished with the outside. Now two officers were crawling around inside it,photographing and swabbing and measuring. When they had finished that, it would be towed away to be analysed for fibres and hairs and bits of skin and anything else that might have come from whoever it was who had met Piero Balestro here just after dawn this morning and shot him in the head.

The forensics labs could strip and eat it, if they wanted, Pallioti thought. It was a pointless exercise. This killer didn't leave prints, and wouldn't leave tracks. He just came and went, like Eleanor's Ghost, sowing his bodies with salt.

Eleanor herself had been put in a police car and driven back to Florence. Pallioti had asked if he could borrow her car for the rest of the day, and for once she hadn't argued. Had just reached out and squeezed his hand.

'What about his wallet?'

Carla Nanno looked up. 'Inner left jacket pocket,' she said. 'Over two hundred euros in notes. And four credit cards. All present and accounted for.'

Pallioti nodded.

The medical examiner was saying something.

'His jacket pockets. Maybe he just filled them, up at the house.' She shrugged. 'You know, why bother with anything else? Bringing a bag or anything. If all he was going to do was put a handful in his mouth and put the gun to his head. Like I said,' she added, standing up, 'I'm not saying that's it, for definite. It just looks like it probably was. I mean, it would be my bet. If that is a powder burn on the glove, I don't know how else to explain it.' She shrugged. 'We'll see how much he swallowed. Maybe you'll pull prints off the gun.'

Pallioti glanced at it and nodded. He didn't tell her that he also thought pigs might fly. And possibly sooner. From where he was standing, he could see the Bakelite handle. The bottom of the grip was crumbling. It had been left for them, like a gift, precisely because it would tell them nothing.

*

One of the crime team was backing out of the jeep. She put a foot down, her white bootee testing for the ground, then stood up, clutching a handful of plastic evidence bags. As Pallioti approached, she looked up and smiled nervously. The girl looked barely old enough to be out of school. He'd noticed that was happening more and more often these days. Peering through the door she had just emerged from, he saw a shotgun case resting across the back seat. It appeared to be still zipped up.

He nodded towards it.

'Is the gun inside?'

'Yes,' the girl nodded. 'It was zipped when we found it.'

'Ammunition?'

'A box of cartridges. In the glove compartment.'

Pallioti nodded. He didn't bother to ask what kind they were. At least one of Balestro's rifles, he was sure, would take .22s, the most common ammunition in the world. The same that would be found in the gun beside his outstretched hand, and in his head. They would discover that he bought them all the time. There would be at least one box, probably more, somewhere in the house. His gloves would probably come from the same place, if it was a decent hunting shop.

'Salt,' he said, looking back at the girl.

'Dottore?'

'I'd like you to look for salt.' He nodded at the jeep. 'Any traces at all you might find. In the mats, the seats. Anywhere in the car. It's especially important.'

She nodded, trying not to appear confused. 'Salt?'

'That's right,' Pallioti said. 'Salt.' Then he walked away.

∽

In the house, Enzo Saenz was going through Piero Balestro's desk. He was back in jeans, the suit he had taken to wearing apparently a thing of the past. At least for today. Frowning, head bowed, his ponytail tucked into the collar of a leather jacket under which a shoulder holster was plainly visible, he looked less like a police inspector than a thoughtful and rather meticulous criminal. Only his hands, encased in the standard white latex gloves, gave him away.

Pallioti stepped into the room. Again, he had the same sensation he had had upon entering the driveway this afternoon. The place looked exactly the same, but was different. He had noticed this before in the homes of the recently dead. A sudden change in the air. A shifting of molecules. Demoted from the status of possession to mere object, things became denser, duller, colder.

'Have you found anything?'

Enzo shrugged.

'Hard to tell. About this? I would say, no. About some strange transfers of significant sums from Cape Town to a bank in the Cayman Islands, probably.'

Pallioti thought of the winking eye of the security camera, the shine of the electric gates and the battery of locks on the front door.

'He was afraid of something. Or someone.'

Enzo glanced up.

'Well, my gut instinct, looking at this lot, is that he might have had reason to be.'

'He said something about "clinics" in South Africa. He worked for a drug company there. At least initially.'

Enzo picked up another sheaf of papers from the rolltop desk and flicked through them.

'Well,' he said, 'couple that with the fact that when I asked the maid why, if she was so worried, she didn't go looking for "Papa Balestro" or call the police, she told me that she's not allowed to go out of the house or use the telephone, and' – he shrugged – 'we'll see. I'll want the Finanza to take a look at all this. It may not do us much good. But at least they'll owe us a favour.'

'Ammunition?'

Enzo nodded. He put the papers down.

'Four boxes upstairs in a locked drawer. There's also a safe. Set into the floor under a wardrobe. Very professional. I'll have it open by evening. But frankly, I doubt there's going to be anything in it for us. I found the gun licences, too,' he added. He turned to face Pallioti. 'They're all in order,' he said. 'For the shotgun and the rifles. No small arms. On the other hand, if it was a souvenir, he probably wouldn't have registered it. Would have just kept it in a box somewhere, to remind him of his glory days. Which might be why he used it this morning.'

'So you think that's what happened?'

Enzo waited for a moment. He looked down at his white-gloved hands, then at Pallioti. In the late sun that streamed through the big windows his eyes were not brown, but tawny, almost golden, like a bird of prey's or a cat's.

'Honestly,' he said. 'After what you told me the other night, and what Guillermo told me before I came down here, yes I do. I owe you an apology, Maestro. I think you were right all along. When the theatre thing went wrong, the three of them were arrested and someone, probably Massimo, saw a way out. He seems to have been the ringleader. They did a deal and were allowed to escape. The price was the radio network. I think they thought they'd got away with it, and to be fair' – Enzo shrugged and looked around the room – 'it looks like, for a long time, they did. But things catch up with people. I don't know if it was the medals, or before – but they fell out. Maybe someone wanted to come clean, developed a conscience, even if it was late in the day. More likely, I think it was the medals. We know Trantemento didn't want anything to do with them, but I'll bet the other two did. Maybe that explains the money in the safe, at least some of it. We know Trantemento wrote Roblino's letter. I'll bet he wrote Balestro's, too. For a price. Maybe someone was blackmailing somebody. Or maybe they were all blackmailing each other. Or there was something in this book Massimo was talking about that caused a stink. Getting the medal certainly would have helped publicize that, by the way.'

'Any sign of it? A book manuscript?'

'None,' Enzo said. 'It might turn up, or, like most books, it might have got no farther than his head. The truth is,' he added, 'we'll probably never know what happened between these three. But yes. Yes. I think you had the bones of it right. Massimo killed the other two. It explains why they didn't fight. Why they let him in. Then on Saturday when you came calling, he knew it was over. From everything you've told me, he doesn't sound like the type to let anyone else take control. So he decided to do the honourable thing. Or the easy thing. Or whatever you want to call it. I'm open to suggestion,' Enzo said. He looked at Pallioti. 'Of course,' he added, 'I'll wait until after the medical examiner is done. But if you're asking me what I think—' He nodded. 'That's what I think.'

'And Bruno Torricci?'

'A bigoted scumbag who can't spell and probably makes his living pouring cement for the Camorra, but for once, about this, he was telling the truth. He didn't kill anyone.'

Pallioti nodded.

'And the salt?'

Enzo shrugged.

'The ME thinks he just put it in his pocket. She's probably right. The others? Making them eat it?' He shook his head. 'Who knows? He was a savage bastard? Something they did sixty years ago, some supposed "betrayal" that's been bugging him? They were probably up a mountain somewhere and the others wouldn't let him salt his sausage and he's never forgotten it. That's what these guys are like,' he added. 'If they were you and me,' Enzo said, 'if their minds worked the same way ours do, they wouldn't go around shooting people.' He shook his head. 'But honestly?' he added. 'Why the salt? The chances are, we'll never know.' He smiled. 'One of the first things you taught me, Lorenzo. We can't know everything.'

Pallioti nodded. His undercover officers had taken to calling him Lorenzo at about the same time he'd started calling them the Angels.

Someone shouted from upstairs. Enzo shouted back, then excused himself.

From the sitting-room doorway Pallioti watched Enzo Saenz take the stairs two at a time. Then he walked down the hall and into the kitchen.

The maid was sitting at the table. A uniformed policewoman was making tea, using the same pot and cups that had been on the tray on Saturday. She was murmuring into a radio clipped to her shoulder as she reached for a sugar pot, opened a drawer and found teaspoons – something about a social worker and immigration. The dog, who had been untied some time ago and returned to the house, slumped in front of the huge stove. All of them looked up as Pallioti came into the room.

The maid's face was tear streaked. Looking at her, Pallioti could not decide if she was fifteen or thirty-five. The police-woman offered him tea, but he shook his head. A row of canisters stood beside the stove. Methodically, he opened each one.

'Salt,' he said, when he had finished. 'Where do you keep the salt?'

The maid looked at him.

'No,' she shook her head.

'No?'

'No. No salt. Only a little.'

She got to her feet, opened a cabinet, and handed him a small cardboard shaker that looked as if it might have been stolen from a fast food restaurant. Full, it could only have held a few tablespoons.

'There isn't any more in the house?' Pallioti asked.

'No.'

She took the shaker out of his hand and replaced in it the cabinet.

'Papa had blood pressure,' she said. 'Salt not good for you.'

Chapter Thirty-Six

'*Bravissimo! Bravissimo*, my friend!'

All rancour forgotten, the Mayor was apparently Pallioti's best friend again. In fact, Pallioti had not heard him sound so ebullient in years. If he was not careful, he might rise straight out of his chair and begin to bounce around the ceiling. Or at least drop the phone.

They had just received news from the Finanza that the haul of papers taken a week ago from Piero Balestro's desk and safe had indeed led back to a major drug company which had been a focus of attention for some time concerning the illegal sale of tainted drugs for the treatment of HIV in several African countries.

The safe had also coughed up quite a lot that was of significant interest to Immigration. Piero Balestro's clinics apparently ran a lucrative sideline in the sale of babies for adoption. The maid, who, it turned out, at a best guess was only seventeen, had probably been one of them. Immigration and the social services were still trying to sort that out. In the meantime, Interpol, Europol, the FDA and FBI in the United States, and several other Pols, Feds and tax agencies were all equally delighted.

In addition, if all that were not enough, Cesare D'Aletto was riding high in the mezzogiorno. The journalist who had first come up with the neo-Nazi angle and whom Enzo had talked to early in the investigation had turned out not to be blowing hot air after all. Closer examination of Bruno Torricci's girlfriend had revealed that she had once worked for the IT company supposedly implicated in messing up ageing partisans' benefits. Having come to an agreement with them to leave quietly in return for a hefty cheque, she had moved on to her present job freelancing as a 'software specialist' for the company that had installed systems not only for Brindisi, but also several other southern policing divisions. There, she had used her not-inconsiderable skills again, most notably to install several 'back doors' through which various operators, including herself, had been able to access the systems and information databases concerning pending and ongoing operations and investigations.

That was how Bruno Torricci had known about Cesare D'Aletto's suspicions concerning the gun that had killed Roberto Roblino. He'd merely used the information to taunt D'Aletto and Enzo Saenz and waste their time and patience. And as far as anyone could tell, that was about all that had happened so far. The police in the south had been embarrassed, sent on wild goose chases and plagued by leaks to the media. But the scope for more dangerous mischief was obvious.

Having put a stop to it had made Cesare D'Aletto a hero. Rumour said he'd been offered a significant promotion and agreed to accept it only on the grounds that he could stay in the south and 'finish the job he'd started', which only made him more of a poster boy. In his most recent press conference, he'd made a point of publicly thanking Enzo Saenz and Pallioti, both for their help and for 'providing an extraordinary example of exemplary policing'.

The upshot of all this, according to the Mayor, was that Florence had banked enough favours to last for several decades, Pallioti's new division was being spoken of as 'an Inspirational Model of Cooperative Law Enforcement for the Twenty-First Century', and his own critics had been kicked so far into the long grass that they would have to mount a safari to find their way out.

'*Bravissimo!*'

He dropped the phone. There was a shuffling of papers, then another, '*Bravissimo!*'

'Anything you want, my friend,' the mayor said, finally taking time to draw breath. 'Now is the time to ask!'

Pallioti looked out of his window. From where he was sitting behind his desk he could see a bright early December sky and the grey top of the palazzo on the opposite side of the piazza. What could he say? That he would like Enzo and the magistrate to revise their opinions concerning the death of Piero Balestro, which had now been definitively listed as a suicide?

Without a shred of evidence to the contrary, that was hardly likely to happen. And even if it did, the Mayor would doubtless argue that it was deeply undesirable. Two homicides had been solved, wrapped up and tied with a bow. And if what had finally been given to the media was a little vague – well, that was deemed to be, if not preferable, at least more palatable, than the unpleasant truth – that three ageing and decorated heroes were in fact brutal traitors who had caused countless deaths and unknown suffering and then lived long, and by most measures fruitful, lives before they finally fell out and killed each other. For a start, the families, and not just Maria Valacci and Roberto Roblino's housekeeper, would go demented.

Since receiving the news of his cousin's death, Little Lamb had suddenly become Massimo's greatest defender. Pallioti had broken the news himself to the old man, driving straight there after leaving the Balestro house. Agata, who had been tending the pigs at the time, had seemed slightly stunned. Her thoughts had rather obviously flown straight to the bank account and the property. Achilleo Venta, on the other hand, had burst into tears, his fragile shoulders shaking as his gnarled hands had gripped Pallioti's.

An hour later, as he drove down the rutted drive and turned towards Florence, Pallioti had thought that it was not the first time his job had given him cause to reflect on the very strange nature of love. He doubted it would be the last.

'It is sad, my friend, this squabble between our Holy Children. I know you are not happy.'

The Mayor knew him too well. They had been friends for a long time.

'Sometimes,' the Mayor went on, 'sometimes we compromise for the greater good.'

'Yes,' Pallioti said. 'Sometimes we do.'

After agreeing to have lunch, at the Mayor's expense, and saying goodbye, Pallioti picked up his pen and began to drum it against the edge of his blotter. His mind ran over the conversation he had had with Saffy the night before. So far, she was the only person who seemed as troubled as he did by the idea that Piero Balestro had suddenly, after all these years, been so unhinged by Pallioti's visit that he had waited twenty-four hours before having a violent, and apparently unique, attack of conscience that left him moved to fill his pockets with salt and drive out and shoot himself at dawn with a gun no one could remember him owning.

Of course, she had agreed, it was possible. Anything under the sun was possible. Massimo might also be revealed as a private but dedicated family man, and a model altruistic doctor committed to healing the poor.

Except he hadn't been.

His will left nothing to charity. The young woman who kept his house had been little better than a slave. He had left a wife and two children in the States without speaking to them for years, and spent his time – first in Zimbabwe and then in South Africa – not selflessly healing the sick, but instead selling them black-market drugs at ridiculous rates and possibly in exchange for babies. She had no problem, Saffy had said, in believing that he might have killed the other two, especially if they were going to ruin his little book debut. But it would be a cold day in hell before she would believe that a man like that performed a hundred-and-eighty-degree turn in the space of two days and took a gun to himself. For a start, she insisted, his ego was too big.

Pallioti, of course, agreed. But they had also agreed that there was no evidence that pointed to much of anything else. A track through the woods and a few broken twigs that led, metaphorically and otherwise, only to an empty road – where someone might have parked, and someone might not have. The fact that a pair of gloves had been found in the driver's side pocket of the jeep and that the ones he had been wearing – which did indeed have a powder burn – did not match the brand he usually bought. No trace of salt in the fabric of the seats or the carpet, or anywhere else in the jeep. Even Pallioti had to admit it didn't add up to the proverbial smoking gun.

Still, the conversation had left him feeling better. They had poured the last of the wine and changed the subject. To the sales from this show and the subject matter of Saffy's next one. To the apparently fabulous hotel Maria Grandolo's family had co-opted for their autumn break. To whether or not Saffy and Leo would finally rent a villa by the sea for next August, and if so, whether they should opt for Agrigento, which was closer and would allow Pallioti to come for weekends, or Sardinia which was reliable, or somewhere in Apulia, which, since her holiday, Maria was now championing vigorously. Secretly, Pallioti hoped they would nix the last option. The idea of having Maria Grandolo stalking him down the beach and turning up half naked in the swimming pool was enough to make him volunteer for August overtime.

He considered the papers on his desk. There were the final details of the fraud case that needed to be cleared up, and the pile of information Guillermo had amassed on Roberto Roblino, Giovanni Trantemento, and Piero Balestro. It included copies of property deeds and tax forms and, in the case of Roblino, even import and export licences. There was also a copy of the original Red Cross report Eleanor Sachs had dug up. She'd faxed it, with a note promising that it had been legitimately copied and not stolen. Pallioti slid it out and stared at it. Eleanor had been right the first time, it was hardly worth it, just a few sentences.

Cammaccio, Caterina. Presumed dead. Personal effects registered Allied Military Field Station #44871, Bologna, 21 April 1945. Forwarded – Red Cross Personal Property Reclamation Office, Florence, June 1945.

Pallioti took off his glasses. He rubbed the bridge of his nose. He picked up his pen and sat for a moment, tapping it again on the edge of the blotter. Then he put it down and turned on his computer. He was never going to be a whizz, but he had mastered Google.

Fifteen minutes told him what he wanted to know. The Allied offensive had begun on schedule on 9 April. The first wave was eight hundred and twenty-five Liberators and Flying Fortresses. By late afternoon they had dropped 175,000 bombs. And that was just the beginning. The fighting was particularly intense just south of Bologna as the American Fifth Army fought its way down to the Po. Almost a week later, on 15 April, Allied bombers dropped 1,500 tons of explosives – three times more than the Luftwaffe had dropped on the British city of Coventry – on the Monte Sole massif. And still the Germans held out. It was another six days before Bologna was liberated by Polish troops on 21 April.

Pallioti took his glasses off. He stared, unseeing, out of his window, across the tops of the palazzos and the beautiful red roofs. He could not imagine what it would have been like, in that particular cauldron of hell where Isabella and Caterina had finally died. What truly amazed him was that there was any Italy, any Europe, left to liberate at all.

Pallioti had finally shut the computer down. He had put the papers into his drawer, when Guillermo buzzed him.

'*Pronto.*' He hit the button on his intercom without even looking up.

'I have someone here to see you. A Professor Sachs,' Guillermo said, as if he didn't know exactly who she was.

'Eleanor Sachs,' Pallioti heard Eleanor say.

He smiled.

'Send her in.'

Pallioti had not seen her since the day they had found Piero Balestro. She was wearing jeans and her denim jacket. She looked at her watch.

'Sun's over the yardarm,' she said. 'Or something like that. I was thinking maybe I could take you to lunch?'

They decided to walk, and had crossed the Ponte alla Carraia and turned towards the Carmine, looking in windows and enjoying the brightness of the afternoon without the burden of conversation, before Eleanor finally spoke.

'I'm going home.'

Pallioti looked down at her.

'No, I mean really home,' she said. 'To the States. I'm not going back to England. Don't say anything,' she added. Her small shoulders gave a jump under her jacket. Her hands were dug into her pockets. 'My marriage is over and I hate Exeter anyway. It's best.'

When they arrived a few minutes later, he held the door of the restaurant for her. It was a small and pleasantly noisy trattoria where anonymity was more than possible because no one cared about anything other than the food. They wound their way through a crowded babble, successfully avoided a hurtling waiter, and claimed a small table against the wall in a back room which was thick with the fug of conversation and steam rising from plates of the daily special.

Eleanor Sachs shrugged her jacket off, shedding it onto the back of her chair in one neat gesture. She laced her hands above the thick white plate as Pallioti poured her a glass of wine from the carafe that had been half hurled at them.

'I should have gone a long time ago,' she said. 'In fact, as has been pointed out to me more than once, I should have given this up after the first try.' She raised her glass and smiled. 'Then at least I could still fantasize about who I was. Imagine some big romantic story. I'm just glad I didn't discover all this before my Dad died.'

Pallioti thought again of Caterina's caution about the war and enquiring minds. He was still not altogether certain he agreed with her. Probably, given a choice, he would side with Signora Grandolo and Professor Cammaccio; insist that, like things that went bump in the night, the truth was best known and faced.

'Piero Balestro wasn't your grandfather,' he said.

The wine was thick and inky, a concoction from the family vineyards near Castellina. She put her glass down and looked at him.

'Are you certain?'

Pallioti nodded.

'If you are certain that your father was, in fact, born in Italy,' he said, 'then yes. Both of Piero Balestro's children, a boy and a girl, were born in the United States. In Ann Arbor, Michigan. His wife did remarry. But she didn't put either child up for adoption. She married again and they took their stepfather's name. They've since married and have families of their own.'

He reached into his pocket and placed a folded piece of paper on the table.

'Those are their names and addresses. If you care to contact them and double-check, I see no reason why it would be difficult.'

'Thank you,' she said. Her small face opened into a smile. 'I would have lived with it – but I'm glad I don't have to.'

'Will you go on looking?'

She looked at him for a moment.

'For Il Spettro? If he exists? You promised—' – she smiled – 'remember? That if you found him you'd tell me?'

Pallioti nodded. Eleanor picked up her glass and chinked it against his.

'Promise?' she said.

Pallioti smiled. 'Cross my heart.'

'Maybe I won't.' Her face grew serious. 'Not right now, anyway. Maybe I'll just leave it where it is. Take all this as a cautionary tale and be happy with my fantasies. You know, sort of, "it's better to journey than arrive"? I don't know,' she added. 'I've spent so much time in the last few years, racing around trying to untangle the past, I think I've missed the present. I'm not even sure what it was all for any more. I mean, if it matters. Even who your parents are. Much less your grandparents. It doesn't make us any more or less who we are, knowing that – does it?'

She looked at Pallioti as if she actually expected him to be able to answer this, to give her some kind of absolution that would, once and for all, set her free. He was relieved when the waiter swooped down on them, more pausing than stopping at their table and essentially telling rather than asking them what they were going to have for lunch.

By the time he had gone, Eleanor was distracted enough to begin playing with her knife and fork, arranging and rearranging them across her empty plate.

'You know,' she said finally, 'I watched that stupid video about a million times. I was convinced that if I looked at it long enough, or just one more time, I'd see what I was looking for, just because I wanted to.'

'And did you?'

She looked up and laughed.

'Yes! Oh God, yes. I was looking for a man who looked like my father, even a little. I had myself convinced that that was what I would see – it was what I expected, so I saw it. My grandfather was this big partisan hero, so every old man who had been a partisan and was the right height, or smiled a certain way, was going to be him. Isn't that always the problem?'

She leaned back as the waiter smacked two white bowls of something thick and steaming down in front of them.

'With eyewitnesses?' she asked, picking up her spoon. 'I mean, that they're either trying to please you, so they see what they think you want them to see. Or they just see what they expect to see, which isn't necessarily what's there.' She shrugged. 'That's what I've heard, anyway.'

'Yes.' The Bollito Misto, if that's what it was, was delicious. Pallioti thought of Isabella, the bodies, the arms and legs. 'Yes,' he said. 'You're absolutely right.'

Eleanor shrugged and reached for a piece of bread.

'Human beings aren't as inquisitive as they like to think they are,' she said. 'We're basically delusional. We think we're all smart and energetic, but most of us are bone lazy and kind of dumb. Take my students. No,' she added, breaking the bread in half, 'actually, don't. Anyway' – she picked up her glass and raised it – 'I should thank you, for opening my eyes.'

'I don't think I did that,' Pallioti said. 'But if I did, you're welcome.'

He took another sip of wine and put his glass down.

'So,' he said. 'Where will you go?'

'Go?' She looked up. 'Oh, right. In the States. Well, my Dad had a house. In Pittsburgh. Don't laugh,' she added. 'Pittsburgh has a lot going for it. Well, maybe not. But I own it. And it's vacant and there's a university and the usual assortment of colleges there. So.'

'So, you'll keep teaching.'

'I guess.' She reached for more bread. 'I'm not bad at it. I don't know that I'm that good at it, either,' she added. 'To be honest. But I do have a PhD, and there's such a demand for specialists on Petrarch.' She smiled. 'Actually, you know, I wasn't going to teach when I got to Exeter. We just needed the money. I was going to stay home in my perfect little thatched cottage with perfect little flowers by the door and have three perfect children and a perfect dog.' She picked up the spoon again. 'That strikes me as so weird now. I can't imagine what I was thinking. Crazy, I guess.'

'Perhaps you were in love?'

She shook her head.

'I'm afraid not. Not that I don't think it's possible,' she added quickly. 'I'm not that type, one of those, "there's no such thing" people. This just wasn't the right thing. That's all. What about you?' she asked suddenly. 'Have you ever been married?'

Pallioti shook his head. She smiled.

'Just to your work, right?'

'Something like that.'

'But that was your family I saw you with? That afternoon? You do have a family?'

'Oh yes,' Pallioti said. 'A sister, and a nephew, and a brother-in-law.'

'And all those friends.' For a moment she looked wistful.

'I suppose,' he said, remembering the large noisy table. 'Yes.'

'Then you're lucky.'

Pallioti picked up his glass. He was lucky. And he knew it.

'The one thing,' Eleanor said suddenly, 'you know, that I really miss, is that I never knew my grandmother. My Dad talked about her, a lot. But I never knew her. I always thought, if I had a daughter, I'd name her after her. Catherine.'

Pallioti glanced up from his bowl.

'I thought you said her name was Maria?'

'Oh, it was. Catherine Maria. Caterina Maria, actually. She used the Maria. But I prefer Catherine. Or Caterina. Caterina,

Catherine. I know it's not unusual or anything,' she added. 'But I think it's beautiful. Don't you think it's a beautiful name?'

Pallioti nodded.

'Yes,' he said. 'Yes, it's a very beautiful name.'

∽

After they had parted, Eleanor insisting that she was finally going to make the effort and actually go and see the Brancacci chapel, Pallioti took his time walking back towards the river – winding down alleys, turning away once, and then again, from the direct routes. He supposed, in the back of his mind, that he knew perfectly well where he was going, and had, in fact, been meaning to come here for weeks, but for some reason had to tease himself, pretend he was just strolling, just happening to pass, rather than walking directly. Eventually, he turned into what was now a fashionable shopping street lined with clothing boutiques and shoe shops. Then he looked up at the plaque.

Like the one at the house near the Via dei Renai, it was beside the door. On the upper storeys of the building, above the shop's display, there were ranks of stone-mullioned windows. Some of them might still even be flats. One had been the apartment where, in February 1944, containers of grenades and rifles, of sidearms and Allied ammunition dropped in a snowy field near Greve, had been stored.

He looked up and down the fashionable street. It had been here that the trucks had come. Through this door that Mario Carita's men had run, weapons drawn, boots pounding, certain of exactly what they would find – because someone had told them. And it was through this door, too, that the precious arms, all stockpiled for the liberation, had been carried, and those arrested had been marched or dragged. This street had been the last thing those people had seen on that February morning. Their last stop before the Villa Triste.

The plaque said simply,

*To Those Who Gave Their Lives
In the Fight Against Nazi-Fascism
20 February 1944
They Died for Justice and for Liberty*

Beside it, just like the Via dei Renai, there was a metal bracket that held a small glass vase. The bouquet in this one was made up of mixed blue and pink blossoms, a handful of each. The flowers were fresh. A crisp blue ribbon fluttered gently in the breeze. The card hung from a raffia cord. Pallioti did not have to turn it over to know that it was embossed with the words, Remember The Fallen.

He stood for a few more moments, studying the ribbon and the flowers. Then he reached into his pocket and pulled out his wallet. There, nestled among the euro notes, was the card from the florist that Signora Grandolo had handed him as they walked back from the monument to Radio Juliet. He noted the address, then turned on his heel and walked quickly away.

Chapter Thirty-Seven

The flowers were white. Forced hot-house lilacs. And roses. Even in the generous confines of Pallioti's new office, their scent was almost overwhelming, a mixture of sweet and sharp perfumes, as if winter and summer had been shaken into a heady cocktail.

'*Bellissima.* Someone's lucky.'

Guillermo eyed the large white box whose lid had been removed, as the florist advised, to allow the bouquet to breathe. 'A dozen blooms,' Pallioti had said. 'No, twenty-four.' It had taken her almost half an hour to select and arrange them, to sprig the centre and edges with the soft dove-green eucalyptus, and bind the stems with a thick satin ribbon. He did not even know how much they had cost. He had handed over his credit card and signed the receipt without looking.

Now he ignored Guillermo's comment and handed him a piece of paper.

'I want you to check this,' he said. 'Now. Use whatever authorization you need. Don't tell anyone.'

Guillermo's eyebrows went up, causing a wrinkle that reached above his forehead and onto the polished dome of his skull.

'*Si*, Dottore.'

He folded the paper and strode from the room, suddenly all business.

Through the open door, Pallioti could hear the frantic tapping of computer keys. He could have done the search himself, at a pinch. But Guillermo would do it in half the time, and suddenly he felt that time was of the essence. Like Caterina, he sensed it sliding away, grains going faster and faster through an hourglass.

It was dusk. The lights came on, illuminating the palazzo opposite, the loggia, and the fountain. The first snow had begun to fall. Fat, languid flakes drifted from the darkening sky. By the time Guillermo came back into the room they had piled into a small drift on the outside ledge. He handed Pallioti the paper. Pallioti looked down at it, then back at his secretary.

'Are you sure?' he asked. 'Absolutely certain?'

'*Si*, Dottore. *Certo*. Absolutely certain.'

Pallioti nodded. He made some notes on the paper, then put it in his pocket and stood up.

'Call the garage,' he said. 'I need a car.'

As he spoke, he lifted the white lid with the gold lettering and fitted it carefully on top of the box.

The journey took no more than twenty minutes, yet seemed timeless, as if they were flying and might land anywhere. When they finally reached the house, climbing up the steep hill and turning in at the gates, the driver glanced over his shoulder.

'Shall I wait?' he asked.

Pallioti shook his head as the car came to a halt.

'No,' he said. 'Go home.' He slid the box across the back seat, gathering it in his arms, and opened the door.

Standing on the gravelled drive, Pallioti watched as the car drew away. The red tail lights flicked and vanished through the gate. Around him, snow carpeted the world in silence. His shoes left dark prints as he climbed the steps and walked across the terrace.

Light glittered through the chinks in the closed shutters,

catching the rims of the empty lemon pots that lined up like soldiers, guarding the front of the villa. When he reached the door, Pallioti stood for a moment, breathing in the cold air and the scent of the flowers. He knew that if he turned around, he would see the city below, a carpet of winking lights, punctuated by the rising ark of Santa Croce, the jagged honey-coloured tower of the Palazzo Vecchio, and the soft swelling mound of the Duomo. Finally, he reached out a gloved hand to pull the bell. It wasn't necessary. She was waiting for him.

'My friend!'

The hall Pallioti stepped into was both austere and beautiful. The hand that decorated it, whether that of the 'small ugly man' or of Signora Grandolo herself, had had the deft, sure touch that comes not with money, but with the absolute confidence of belonging.

The marble floor had been left bare, the grain of the stone adorned only by polish. A few small tables held lamps that cast warm orbs of light against the plastered walls. The graceful curve of a stone staircase led up to what would once have been the *piano nobile* and was now most likely bedrooms, perhaps a study and personal parlour. It was a pure product of the Renaissance, as Florentine as the woman who stood before him. Like her, it did not need embellishment, but could rest on the hard, perfect beauty of its bones.

He handed her the box. Setting it on a table beside the stairs, she lifted the lid carefully. A cloud of scent escaped and drifted into the hallway. Signora Grandolo let out a small exhalation of pleasure.

'They're beautiful.' She looked at him, her hands hovering above the blooms. 'But why?' she asked. 'Why?'

'Because,' Pallioti said. 'I wanted to thank you.'

She shook her head.

'I didn't do much.'

'Yes,' he said. 'I think you did.'

Signora Grandolo regarded him for a moment. Then she

reached up. The shawl she was wearing had slipped. She pulled it tighter around her shoulders. The material shimmered in the light. There was a slithering sound. Apparently of its own volition, the satin ribbon spilled out of the white box. Slipping over the ivory petals, it uncoiled itself across the polished wood of the table.

'Why have you come?' she asked.

'Because you asked me to,' Pallioti replied. 'When I decided if the story I was chasing was important, or when it was over – you asked me to come and tell you about it.'

'Ah.' She nodded. 'And is it?'

'Important?' Pallioti was pulling his gloves off. He folded them and put them into the pocket of his overcoat. 'Yes,' he said. 'At least to me. And over?' He considered this for a moment. 'Yes,' he said again finally. 'Yes. I think now that the story is finally over.'

Signora Grandolo smiled. She picked up the heavy satin ribbon, coiled it and placed it next to the box of flowers. 'In that case,' she said. 'Perhaps we had better sit down?'

In less sure hands, the room she led him into might have been intimidating, or worse, merely pretentious. It ran half the length of the front of the villa. There were three groupings of sofas and chairs, one at either end and one in the middle. The floor was scattered with carpets. Piles of books sat on long low tables between the tall shuttered windows whose lines had not been disturbed by curtains. A grand piano sat at the far end of the room, this one open, used as an instrument for music rather than a platform for the display of family photographs.

Those were present as well. Dotted about, most in plain silver frames, many black and white, they showed the Grandolos, and their daughters, and later sons-in-law, and grandchildren. Pallioti noticed several photographs that, by virtue of his height, or lack of it, and the distinctiveness of his features, which indeed were not handsome, had to be Cosimo Grandolo as a young man. There were no corresponding portraits of Signora Grandolo as a girl. The first in which she appeared was an engagement picture. She was sitting, so she would not tower over her husband-to-be. Cosimo Grandolo stood behind her chair, a protective hand on her shoulder. The date engraved on the frame was August 1948.

Pallioti leaned down. Her dark hair was parted on the side, as was fashionable at the time. Curled under, it fell to her shoulders. Her folded hands displayed the small engagement ring. A bracelet of some kind of deep-coloured stones, probably sapphires and doubtless a family piece that was rapidly returned to a safe in the bank, ringed her elegant wrist. She was smiling. But underneath, he thought he detected something else in her face. Sadness. Or perhaps just memory.

He straightened up and turned around. Signora Grandolo was standing beside the hearth, where a fire had been lit. Shadows caught the side of her face.

'I didn't realize it at first,' he said. 'But this story – it's about what we see and what we believe we see. They're two separate things, both real and not, at the same time. Don't you find?'

When she didn't answer, he shrugged.

'It seems contradictory, but it isn't – it's something every cheap magician working in the piazzas, pulling rabbits out of hats and doves out of sleeves, understands. All too well. And yet, in the normal course of things we refuse to accept it, again and again. A friend of mine reminded me of that today.'

He had unbuttoned his overcoat. Now he shrugged out of it, folding the soft dark cashmere so the damp shoulders were turned inwards.

'Please.' She gestured towards the sofa.

Pallioti folded the coat across the arm. He had already turned down her offer of a drink. For a moment he watched the lick of the flames, the quick dance their shadows threw on the hearthstone. He opened his mouth and closed it, as if he did not know where to begin, or as if he were reluctant to speak the words. Finally, he said, 'It all began a long time ago.'

Signora Grandolo smiled. 'Like all the best stories.'

'Like all the best stories,' Pallioti agreed. Then he said, 'Once there were two sisters.'

He waited for her to sit, but she shook her head.

'I've been sitting all day. Desk, reading. But please—' She gestured to the sofa.

He sat. This time the cushions were reassuringly firm. On the table in front of him a book lay open. The biography of a general. A pair of Signora Grandolo's glasses were propped beside it.

'Their names, these sisters,' he said, 'were Isabella and Caterina. One was blonde and one was dark, and they lived here, in Florence, with an older brother and their parents. Their father was a university professor.' He glanced at her. 'A gentle, literate man who hated the Fascists. Quietly, the way most people did, if they wanted to stay alive and keep their jobs. Their mother,' he went on, 'had money, so they were comfortable. By the time the armistice came, the elder sister, Caterina, was a nurse. She was engaged to be married, to a naval officer, a doctor. The other sister was at the university. Their brother, Enrico, was in the army, a junior officer. Rather than be deported to a German labour camp, as so many were' – he nodded towards a photograph of Cosimo Grandolo that sat on a side table – 'Enrico and a friend of his, a young man called Carlo, deserted. They made their way back to Florence, where Enrico's father put them in touch with a group in the university, part of the CLN for Tuscany that was organizing resistance. They went into the mountains. The family had been enthusiastic hikers, especially the youngest daughter, Isabella, and quite quickly she joined them. Before long, she and Carlo were running an escape route, from Fiesole up through the high passes, along the route of the Via degli Dei and down to Bologna. They took mostly POWs, Allied airmen, at first. Then, when the crackdown came, when the occupation started to turn ugly, Jews as well. Whole families sometimes. Children.'

Pallioti paused.

'I've met some of them, the survivors,' he said. 'As I'm sure you have. Well, I've met at least one. A Signor Cavicalli. Perhaps you know him?'

Pallioti could sense as much as see her eyes on his face.

'He and his son run a shop called Patria Memorabilia, in Santa Croce,' he said. 'I believe the sisters got their family out – the other sister, Caterina, was helping by this time, too, on the ground here in Florence. They saved their lives, the Cavicalli family. Got them to Switzerland. Signor Cavicalli has never forgotten it.' He shook his head. 'But then again, people don't, do they? Not about things like that. Not about the war.'

Signora Grandolo was still standing by the fireplace, her back as straight and strong as a ballerina's. Pallioti took a breath and went on.

'By the winter of 1943 to '44,' he said, 'as you know, things got difficult. The family became involved with Radio Juliet. In fact, they were running it. Caterina was still nursing – the influenza was very bad and people were dying. She used information she obtained at the hospital. They managed to keep transmitting, but it was dangerous. Isabella was working with GAP by this time. On Valentine's Day 1944 she was caught up in an assassination attempt. She was wounded, but got away. The three men with her, whose code names were Il Corvo, Beppe, and Massimo, didn't. They were arrested and taken to the Villa Triste.'

Pallioti leaned forward.

'Three nights later,' he said, 'they escaped. Or rather, it looked as if they did. In fact, they had done a deal with Mario Carita. Effectively, they'd been "turned". They were set loose, welcomed back to GAP as heroes for having saved Isabella then escaped themselves – but in fact they were traitors. They'd made a bargain with the devil. If GAP found out what they'd done, they'd have killed them. So they began to pass information. The location of a safe house where weapons were stored. Names of people involved. And finally, the jewel in the crown, the thing Carita really wanted. Radio Juliet. But you know about that.' He shrugged. 'Everyone does. How the whole network was grabbed, all at once.'

Signora Grandolo nodded. It was only the faintest movement of her head.

'That was their final act, the betrayal of Radio Juliet,' Pallioti said. 'Beppe, Il Corvo, and Massimo, and they extracted a price for it. They were all paid. Probably well.'

Pallioti smiled, his features suddenly sharp in the shadows from the fire.

'And not in salt,' he added. 'That came later. Then, in June '44, in addition to money, Beppe got safe passage into Spain. Il Corvo was given papers and travel passes to get his mother and sister, who were Jews, to Switzerland. Those two, I think,' he said, 'were probably trapped. Terrified of what GAP would do to them if they found out and more terrified of what Carita would do if they didn't cooperate. They probably at least had a conscience. Even guilt. I like to think so, anyway. The third, Massimo.' He looked up at Signora Grandolo. 'I think he was the ringleader. I suspect the whole thing was his idea.'

Pallioti leaned back on the sofa.

'As I said the other night,' he continued, 'Massimo was the kind of man we fought the war to get rid of. But they don't go so easily, do they? In the end, they had to hunt Mario Carita down and shoot him like vermin. He was hiding in the Val d'Aosta, more or less in plain sight, unrepentant. Massimo was the same kind. Cruel. Sly. So much so, that he – or perhaps Carita, but I suspect Massimo himself, came up with the perfect alibi for all of them. And he used Isabella to do it. He had particular reason to hate her. He was jealous. I think he'd been in love with her. He made her believe they were all dead, the three traitors. She was shown bodies she expected to be theirs. So that's what she saw. The men on the top of the pile were her father, and her brother, and Carlo, her lover, whose child she was carrying at the time. It broke her heart.'

Pallioti paused. 'But this is where it gets interesting,' he said a moment later. 'Because it taught her something, too. About being dead.'

He leaned forward, picked up the book on the general and put it down.

'You see,' he went on, 'Isabella was an extraordinary woman.' He glanced up and smiled. 'Although Caterina was equally extraordinary in her own way. Ordinary people who did extraordinary things. They escaped, by the way,' he added, 'the sisters. They got to Milan, where GAP gave them new identities. They kept on fighting. But at the same time, they both kept on thinking about what had happened to Radio Juliet. And how it had happened. Neither of them could let it go. Neither of them could forget. Isabella had her baby, a little boy. And then, in March 1945, Caterina had a chance to take him and go to Naples. Her fiancé, it turned out, was still alive, and he'd arranged to get her out. This part, I admit,' Pallioti said, 'I'm not too certain about. I don't know the details. All I know is that Isabella convinced Caterina to take the baby, and planned to join them later. But something went wrong. I don't know what. By April 1945, they were both dead. Within days of the liberation they'd fought so hard for. Caterina in a field hospital in Bologna, and Isabella just west of the city, hit by an Allied bomb.' He looked up at her. 'Or that's what everyone believed, anyway.'

Firelight flickered against Signora Grandolo's face, and rippled the fine soft wool of the shawl. She stood as still as a statue, one hand resting on the mantel.

'You see, I don't know which one of them it was,' Pallioti said. 'I'm not sure. But one of them survived. She got back here to Florence, somehow, and when she got here, she realized that everyone thought she was dead, and also that being dead might have its advantages. I think she learnt that from what happened to Radio Juliet. So she took another woman's name, and built a life for herself. But all the while, she remembered.'

He ran his finger along the edge of the book, feeling the sharp edge of its dust jacket.

'She remembered everything she had talked about with her sister,' he said. 'In the prison they were thrown into, and later in the apartment they shared in Milan, about what had happened. About who it could have been who betrayed them. Who was responsible for the deaths of their father and brother, mother and comrades, and the death of the man Isabella loved.' Pallioti shook his head. 'I suspect she looked. I suspect she did everything she could to try to work it out. Went through records, searched out people like the Cavicallis – did you know, by the way,' Pallioti asked, looking up at her, 'that Signor Cavicalli had a twin? A twin brother. And a little sister. The little girl was just a tot, not more than three or four, when they escaped. It must have been an extraordinary walk. At night. In the snow. In any case' – he shook his head – 'she was never able to find anything. The records said all the men from Radio Juliet had been executed. Everyone who had known anything was accounted for. So, although she never forgot, I suspect she might have given up looking. Until one night almost two years ago. During the celebrations for the sixtieth anniversary, when she turned on the television, and saw three dead men. Can you imagine? Right there in front of her, with medals on their chests. Il Corvo, and Beppe, and Massimo.'

The names fell into the room, smooth and fast as stones falling through water. Pallioti was sure he could feel the ripples lapping outwards, into the silence and the night and the snow.

'After that,' he said, 'it was easy.'

A log shifted on the fire, sending up a small shower of sparks. Both of them looked at it. Then Signora Grandolo reached for the poker, bent and pushed the charred piece of wood back into the flames.

'Go on,' she said.

'Well.' Pallioti shrugged. 'Finding them wasn't difficult, once she knew they were alive. There are records everywhere. Organizations like Remember The Fallen, more than willing to help.'

Pallioti watched her back, supple and strong for a woman of her age, as she replaced the poker carefully in the brass bracket, straightened up, and looked at him.

'What I did wonder, though,' he said, 'was why she waited so long. A year and a half. But I think I know.'

He leaned back on the sofa again and looked up at her.

'You see,' he said, 'these sisters, they were terribly brave, rash even, when it came to themselves. But where lives were at stake, other people's lives, they were very, very careful. In all those ambulance runs, all those trips in 1943 and 1944, they never lost a parcel. They were known for it, among the partisans. So, it was a point of pride. Being careful, not making mistakes. And given her history,' he went on, 'I imagine she understood that this one last job had to be perfect, or she wouldn't be able to finish it. And she wanted that, very badly. After all, she'd been waiting a long time. Decades. So she planned extremely carefully. And that takes time. My guess is that she'd had the gun for some years,' he added. 'Sixty, possibly. It was probably a souvenir. As for the salt,' he said, 'well, I suspect she'd thought about that for a long time, too. Don't you think?'

The question hung in the room, unanswered.

'In that warehouse in Verona, when she lay down on the floor with those women dying around her, I wonder,' Pallioti said, 'if that was what she dreamed of? That someday she'd find whoever betrayed Radio Juliet, whoever killed all the people she loved, and get them on their knees, and make them eat their reward?'

He took a deep breath, suddenly confronted with the vision of Giovanni Trantemento's face, and forced himself on.

'Roblino, Beppe,' Pallioti said. 'I think he was the easiest. The stupidest, the most gullible. A windbag. All she had to do was ring him up and pretend she was the widow of some partisan, or even just interested in his collection of memorabilia. Possibly she just turned up at the door. Women are almost never threatening. No offence, Signora, but especially when they reach a certain age.'

He was not sure, but he thought he saw her smile.

'Now Trantemento,' he continued. 'He was a bit more tricky. He was shy, and very clever. But still, I doubt it was too difficult. The building isn't hard to get into. Of course,' he added, 'he had to be killed first. As I've said, Giovanni Trantemento was clever and quite wary, so Roblino's death might have alerted him. And Roblino needed to be killed quite quickly afterwards, just in case he became alarmed. Strike hard and fast. Use the advantage of surprise.' Pallioti smiled. 'That's how she did it. Il Corvo first, and then Beppe. Which only left Massimo.'

Pallioti waited for a moment. Then he said, 'He was the most difficult, wasn't he? Massimo. He had security. The maid was always in the house. No.' Pallioti shook his head. 'Massimo certainly wasn't as easy as the other two. But,' he added, 'not insurmountable, either. No problem is insurmountable for someone so determined. And clever. And by that time, of course,' he added, 'you had help. Because you had me.'

Pallioti could feel as much as see her eyes on his face, feel the beautiful, deep, cerulean blue of them.

Silence pulsed through the room. Finally, he leaned forward, his elbows on his knees.

'It was the only mistake you made,' he said. 'Lying to me. Telling me that you didn't have the complete records for the Villa Triste because they had been destroyed. I can see that you were in a spot – that you were afraid, once I saw those records, from 12 June and 15 June – who had been arrested and who had supposedly been executed – that once I saw that, I would understand, and get to Massimo before you could. So, it was a gamble, wasn't it? Either you showed me, and potentially deprived yourself of Massimo. Or you lied to me, and hoped I wouldn't find them. But,' he smiled, 'of course I did. As you knew I would. It wasn't even very difficult. It was just too late. You'd made sure of that, too.'

Signora Grandolo didn't move. In the light from the fire her shawl, an iridescent blue-green the colour of a peacock's tail or a dragonfly's wing, shimmered like water. Pallioti couldn't read the expression on her face.

'When you heard from Maria—' he said. 'Using her was very clever, by the way,' he added. 'I'd like to think you were just a bit concerned, when you read in the paper that I'd been seen at Trantemento's building, that I was obviously involved. I imagine you raised the topic, of how dreadful it was, what had happened – and perhaps also wondered aloud if your great-niece Maria's friend wasn't the sister of that policeman?'

He shook his head. 'Saffy wouldn't have told Maria much, of course,' he said. 'She didn't know anything, and if she did, she would have known better than to mention it to anyone. But it was a useful way of keeping tabs on me, wasn't it? And at some point, you must have seen how you could positively turn it to your advantage. I'd noticed the enthusiasm before, but not to that degree,' Pallioti added, raising an eyebrow. 'What did you have to do?' he asked. 'Point out that I was very eligible, that Seraphina would be delightful to be related to? Maria's desperate to please you, so it can't have been hard. Although,' he added, 'I'm sure you'd have found another way if she'd been uncooperative. Perhaps just offered Remember The Fallen's services, if I hadn't been so obliging and delivered myself into your office. In any case,' he went on, waving aside the problem, the memory of how easily she had made it seem that she was the one being generous, the one doing him a favour.

'That Sunday,' he said, 'when you heard from Maria that I hadn't come to lunch, you must have worried. You had to find out what was going on. What did you do?' Pallioti asked. 'Have Bernardo call you, let you know when I came into Lupo again? Don't worry,' he added. 'I won't mention it to him. It's not his fault. I did enjoy the grappa.' He looked at her. 'And the company. Very much. But I also told you all about Massimo, didn't I? That's how you knew you'd have to do it fast. That you couldn't wait, or I'd get there first.'

They studied one another, their eyes meeting across the shadows that flickered from the hearth.

'Dropping the gun was exactly right,' Pallioti said. 'The perfect way to get rid of it. But I should have known you'd know that. And about the powder burns. The gloves. That was clever.'

He thought he saw something move, the echo of a smile, acknowledging the compliment. But the light was so low and it passed across her features so quickly that it was impossible to be sure.

'Do you want to know how I knew?' he asked finally. 'What made me certain?'

He waited for a moment. Then he said, 'It was the flowers. I talked to the florist this afternoon. Just a chat. She told me that you have standing orders, and that she's allowed to use whatever she has extra for most of the bouquets. All of them, in fact. Except two. She says you are very, very particular about it. Always have been. There must be two white arrangements. The first is primarily roses, and larger than the rest. You collect it personally, every two weeks. The other is not as extravagant, but you are, if anything, more definite about it. It's for the Via dei Renai. She knows, because although you always place them yourself, and always on a Monday, once, when your husband was dying, you asked her to do it for you. Five white roses. Only her best. She offered once simply to give you a half dozen for the same price – it makes her bookkeeping easier. But you said no. It had to be five. She thought that was strange,' Pallioti said. 'But she didn't understand, did she?'

He looked up at her.

'That six would be wrong. That it had to be five. One each – for your mother, your father, your brother, your sister, and Carlo. And that they had to be taken on Monday – because 12

June 1944 was a Monday – to the last place where you were all
together.'

If Signora Grandolo blinked, he did not see it. He took a
breath.

'After that, I checked,' he said. 'It wasn't difficult. It never is,
when you know what you're looking for.'

He pulled out of his pocket the piece of paper Guillermo
had handed him, unfolded it and placed it on the low table in
front of the sofa. She made no effort to reach for it, or look at
the words that were written on it.

'It's a name. The name you used when you applied for the
job at your husband's bank. That you lived under for the next
two years, until you married and became a Grandolo. Ration
cards. Identity passes. They were all issued to you. And not to
you. Because the woman Cosimo Grandolo married was called
Donata Leone.' He smiled. 'And the only problem with that,'
he said, 'as you know, is that Donata Leone died. Of pneumonia. In January 1944.'

He paused.

'What I don't know,' he added, 'what I suppose I am hoping
you might tell me, is whether you knew that because you were
with her – because you nursed her, and sat with her, and held
her hand? Or because you heard about it from your sister?'

If she was going to say something, he thought, it would be
now. He looked at her, at the perfect bones, the extraordinary
eyes. The way she stood, the elegant lines of her hands with
their two simple rings.

'I wasn't sure, at first,' he said, 'exactly how you managed not
to be recognized. But once you put your mind to it, you managed. And of course,' he added, remembering what Eleanor
Sachs had said earlier, 'circumstances were with you. We see
what we expect to see. And no one expected to see you back
here because you were dead. A little hair dye, different clothes.
A shorter step. The same thing, more or less, that Isabella did
after the shooting at the Pergola. Did you suspect them then?'

He leaned forward, fixing her with the gaze that had worked so often in interrogation rooms. 'Was there something strange about it? About their stories? The escape. Was there a smell, something not quite right? Something you never forgot but could never prove? Until you saw them that night on television.'

He didn't know if he actually expected her to answer. He supposed, in some vastly exaggerated part of his ego, that he did. That age, loneliness, the desire to confess – the desire, if nothing else, to share the story – perhaps even to boast about it, would kick in.

But even as he thought it, he realized he should have known better. With lesser adversaries, it might have happened. Not with this woman.

Pallioti looked around the room. At the soft pools of light and hollows of shadow. At the dense carpets and the polished furniture. He wondered whether, if he listened, he could hear the echoes of conversations that had taken place here, the running of children's feet, the whispers of discontent, the old jokes and repeated refrains that made up a family. There was no television. Probably, it was upstairs, in a study or a library, where it could not disturb the perfect symmetry of this house. She had been watching, he thought, perhaps with her sick husband beside her, or perhaps alone, probably considering turning it off – possibly only half paying attention. Until the woman in the blue dress squawked out another question, and shoved the microphone into Massimo's face.

The silence in the room deepened and thickened until Pallioti thought he could hear the snow falling outside, drifting against the walls, fingering its way into the slats of the shutters. In the fire, a flame cracked and guttered. He reached out and fingered the edge of the paper that lay on the table. The black characters of Guillermo's neat, even hand flickered in the firelight, as though they might come alive and jump off the page.

'I may have found your son,' he said. 'Or your nephew. But

probably I haven't. Probably,' he said, smiling sadly, 'I just wanted to help someone.'

Pallioti got to his feet, feeling old, as if time had defeated him. He picked up his coat.

'He lived in Cleveland, Ohio. In the United States. And then in Pittsburgh, Pennsylvania. He died a year ago of lung cancer. His parents were Italian, Victor and Catherine. Their last name was Faber. Shortened from Fabbionocci. I don't know if that means anything to you. But if it does, he had a daughter. Her name is Eleanor Sachs. She taught at Exeter University, in England. She's going back to America.' Pallioti nodded at the paper on the table. 'It's all written down there.'

He finished buttoning his coat. Then he looked into Signora Grandolo's face, knowing that this was the last time he would see her. He realized that he would have liked to have touched her again, to have felt the warm firmness of her hand, and smelled just once more the exotic sharp note of her perfume.

He reached into his pocket. His fingers curled around the worn cover of the little red book. Giving it up was like giving up a lover. He leaned over and gently placed it on the table.

'I believe,' Pallioti said, 'that this is yours.'

PART SIX

Chapter Thirty-Eight

It was only a few days later that Pallioti heard that Marta Buonifaccio had returned to her apartment in the palazzo where Giovanni Trantemento had been killed. He was busy at the time, and his first instinct was to forget about her. He had already started the process of checking Signora Grandolo's whereabouts. Not that it mattered. He knew he would find that she had been in Apulia, staying with her family in the hotel Maria had been so enthusiastic about. Possibly he would find that she had had reason to be in the countryside south of Siena from time to time as well, and that no one had seen her on the afternoon Roberto Roblino died, or the morning when Piero Balestro was killed. He would look, but he would not see her car on the security tapes from the garage near Giovanni Trantemento's apartment, or on Balestro's cameras. Nor would he find a licence for a Sauer 38H, or a purchase receipt for a box of ammunition, or any record of her buying men's gloves.

And in the end, he would not apply for a warrant. Because there was no point. The winking eye of a security camera could not capture her any more than he could. She had come and gone leaving no evidence, nothing at all. Except one black crumbling piece of Bakelite. That was it. The rest was nothing but a story. And Signora Grandolo was just an old lady.

Like salt, the case left a dry taste in his mouth.

So, his first instinct was to forget about Marta Buonifaccio. To put the past behind him and, in the dreaded parlance of the day, 'move on'. But he had agreed to have dinner with Enzo, to talk over the constraints of the budget, and the prioritization of cases for the new year, and the palazzo was only a minor detour, a few blocks from the new restaurant where he had had Guillermo book a table. For some reason he could not quite put his finger on, he no longer gravitated to Lupo.

It was 6.30 when they arrived at Giovanni Trantemento's building. The street lamps glowed a sulphurous yellow, throwing shadows upwards onto the rusticated surface of the facade. If anything the canyon between the palazzos seemed steeper, the doorways darker. Enzo, having usurped Pallioti's driver yet again, scanned the entrances of the alleys as if any number of hazards might be lurking in them. Then he pulled up in front of the door.

'Shall I come with you?'

Pallioti shook his head and opened the car door.

'I'll be five minutes,' he said. 'Well, perhaps ten.'

He could not envision that his conversation with Marta would be anything but short and to the point. Looking back on it, he realized he should have known better.

The entrance hall was unchanged. Stepping into it still felt like diving into dirty water. The light was not only low, it seemed to be actually murky, as if the centuries had collected and blossomed like algae. The lamp cast the same halo of light onto the mail table, where Marta's presence was immediately evident. There was not a stray envelope or flyer in sight. Those that were present were stacked in neat little piles, their corners perfectly aligned at ninety-degree angles. One of them would be from the taxi firm Pallioti had used as an informant. Taking Cara Fratto's advice to heart – that flyers would not be wasted on houses where there was no business – he had dropped by the office of First Class Taxis and confirmed that they had, indeed, delivered Marta Buonifaccio to Peretola Airport at four o'clock in the afternoon exactly three days before he made his last visit. This lunchtime they had called to inform him that they had just collected her and delivered her home. She had, apparently, been in Rimini.

At first, it had struck Pallioti as a strange place for an out-of-season visit. Then he had realized that the once-grand seaside resort still had two distinctive draws. Prices – it was 'once grand', and thus cheap, especially at the end of November. And a casino.

Marta's apartment door did not have a bell. He knocked, his knuckles rapping the polished wood. The door opened before he could lift his hand again.

'Ispettore.'

The greeting, if you could call it that, was issued with something less than enthusiasm.

'Signora Buonifaccio. Welcome home. Do you mind if I come in for a moment?'

She looked as if she would have liked to have said yes, she did mind, very much, but couldn't summon the courage to do it. Instead, she simply nodded and stepped back. Entering the tiny sitting room, Pallioti felt like a bully. He told himself not to be stupid, that he was just doing his job. He turned to her and smiled in an attempt to make up for it.

The effect was the complete opposite of what he had intended. Marta Buonifaccio paled visibly. When he added, in what he thought was his kindest voice, 'I am so sorry to disturb you, but I wondered if I could ask you a few questions?' her small, solid figure became still.

'Please,' she said, when she finally remembered to breathe. 'Sit. What can I get you, Dottore?'

Pallioti sat, in the same chair he had occupied before, not because he wanted to, but because he hoped it would put her at ease. He didn't approve of what she'd done. But he didn't want her to drop dead of fright.

'Nothing, thank you. Nothing,' he said again. 'I just have a couple of questions.'

Marta nodded. She did not sit down, but stood before him playing the Russian doll again, disappearing inside herself, again and again and again, hands folded, eyes dropped to her feet.

Pallioti shifted uncomfortably, almost wishing he had not come, that he was not compelled, like a bitch in heat, to seek out the answer to every question – to know beyond the shadow of a doubt that he was right.

'Signora Buonifaccio,' he said, now wanting to get this over as quickly as possible, 'I am afraid that you took Signor Trantemento's wallet, when you found his body.'

She looked at him, expression draining out of her face.

'I suspect that it was on the desk, beside his keys,' Pallioti said. 'Probably where he had placed it the last time he came in, the afternoon before, just after he had cashed a cheque for five hundred euros.'

She neither agreed nor disagreed with him.

'I don't think you went through his pockets,' Pallioti added, trying to make this sound better, as if merely stealing from the dead was somehow more acceptable than fleecing them.

'I suspect you just saw the wallet and took it. Then, once you had called the police, you realized that you didn't want to be found with it. So you removed the cash and went outside and threw the wallet into the alley. That's why you were wearing a headscarf inside, so we wouldn't see that your hair was wet. And that's when the letter got wet, too, wasn't it? The mail had arrived earlier, before it started to rain. But the letter was still in your apron pocket when you went out to get rid of the wallet.'

He looked at her for a moment.

'I don't think you meant to steal the letter,' he said. 'And you didn't. You gave it to me, which was entirely proper. But you did that after you had opened it. After you had removed the money orders for three thousand British pounds' worth of euros. It must have felt thick. The paper for those money orders is quite stiff. And perhaps you knew, or understood, that given the nature of Signor Trantemento's business, he sometimes received money orders, perhaps even cash, in the mail?'

He looked at her, waiting for at least some acknowledgement. Or even a sign that he had spoken. None was forthcoming. Marta Buonifaccio just stood there, in the middle of her sitting room, facing him like a statue.

Pallioti was beginning to have an unfortunate sense of déjà vu. Signora Grandolo, at least, had been listening to him. He was quite sure of that. He had had the sense, even if she had not replied, that they were in a sort of silent conversation, that the tension in the air could have been plucked like a finely tuned string.

Here, however, the air was dead. If he did not know better, he might have thought that the woman standing in front of him, in her flowered apron and olive-green cardigan, with her cap of curled hair and new felt slippers, was stone deaf.

'Signora Buonifaccio,' Pallioti said. 'Is there anything you would like to tell me?'

Nothing had been stolen from either Roblino or Balestro. It was the anomaly that had driven him here. Now he wished that it hadn't.

The news came on the television. The talking head of a newsreader, who might have been the blue-dress lady, yammered silently.

'Anything at all you would like to say?' Pallioti asked.

This time, at least, she shook her head. Then she looked down at her feet again.

Pallioti began to feel ridiculous. Finally, he pulled the cuffs of his shirt, aligned his cufflinks – little ovals of shiny black onyx set in a thin gold rim – and got to his feet. With the two of them standing in it, the little space felt like a cell. In his black suit and black overcoat, Pallioti towered over her. Marta Buonifaccio did not look up.

'Thank you for seeing me,' he said, finally. 'I'll let myself out.'

ᴄᴏ

'Holy Mother of God! What is it with me and old women?'

Enzo raised his eyebrows as Pallioti slid into the passenger seat of the car.

'She wouldn't speak to me,' Pallioti said. 'Not a word. She let me in, all right. She didn't really want to, but she did – invited me to sit. Then stood there and didn't say a word.'

'She didn't deny taking the wallet? Or the money?'

'No. She didn't say anything. Nothing.'

Pallioti raised his hands and dropped them on his knees.

'I don't know,' he said. 'I was so sure I was right. But who knows? Who knows? Perhaps Giovanni Trantemento was burgled and robbed and just happened to be gobbling a pound of salt for lunch! It doesn't matter now, anyway,' he muttered, aware that he was sounding like a sulky teenager. 'I just would have liked to have known,' he added. 'I wasn't going to throw the lonely old woman in jail.'

Enzo, who had listed to this outburst without saying anything, looked at him.

'What's her history?'

'Her history?'

'Yes. Do you know?'

Pallioti threw his hands in the air. In fact he did know. Marta Buonifaccio had turned up, like everyone else, in the trawl Guillermo had made at the end of the investigation.

'I mean, during the war?' Enzo said.

'She was – I don't see what this has to do with anything – she was a chambermaid, at the Excelsior. She was, I don't know, booted out, fired. Accused of stealing. That's what made me so sure of this.'

'And afterwards?'

'She – she went to join her aunt. On a farm.' Pallioti stopped talking suddenly, aware of what he was about to say. 'On the Monte Sole massif,' he added. 'They were killed, all of them. Everyone but her. In the massacre.'

'September 1944.'

Pallioti nodded, wondering when, exactly, he had become such an insensitive clod. He'd never even asked the poor woman about her family.

'Afterwards,' he said, 'she got back to Florence. Somehow. She got married. Had a life.' He thought for a moment. 'I still don't see what that has to do with any of this?'

Enzo shrugged.

'Neither do I, exactly.' He opened his door.

'Where are you going?' Pallioti asked.

'Five minutes.' Enzo ducked his head in and smiled. 'The engine's running. Turn the heat on if you get cold.'

He slammed the door, turned down the collar of his leather jacket, then caught the door of the palazzo as a couple stepped out. They looked at him, slightly alarmed. Whatever he said reassured them. A moment later they smiled broadly and nodded, starting down the street arm in arm.

Pallioti drummed his fingers on the dashboard. He decided to count backwards from a hundred, betting himself that Enzo would reappear before he got to fifty. At thirty-two, he gave up, and played with the radio until he got a re-broadcast of *Turandot* made some years ago at La Scala.

He had just about decided that in fact he had been wrong all along, and that Marta Buonifaccio had killed everyone, including Enzo; and was wondering how long he ought to wait before he called for back-up, when the palazzo door swung open and Enzo Saenz reappeared. The street light caught his profile, making him hawkish and sinister. He slipped into the front seat of the car, quick and quiet as an eel.

'The five hundred euros from the wallet,' he said, 'she took that. And the money orders. She cashed it down the street, no problem. There's a *tabaccaio* guy who does it under the table. She was going to throw the wallet out of the window, on her way down the stairs. But she wasn't tall enough to reach and the windows don't open anyway. She didn't want to go back into Trantemento's apartment, have to step over the body and all, and she was worried about fingerprints. So she took it out and threw it in the alley. Then she called the police. She thought he'd been burgled, so she didn't think it would matter. She's sorry,' Enzo said. 'She didn't mean to cause any trouble. And she had a couple of big wins in Rimini so she's going to write to Maria Valacci, apologize and pay her the money back. I said we'd leave it there.'

Pallioti looked at him slack jawed.

'How on earth—' he asked. 'Why wouldn't she talk to me?'

'Because she's terrified of you.'

Enzo tried to say it gently, but the words still stung.

'Dottore,' Enzo said. He pulled his ponytail. 'What do I look like? A kid. A bum. You?'

'What's wrong with me?'

'Nothing,' Enzo said. 'Nothing. The Sexiest Cop In Europe.'

'Italy,' Pallioti snapped.

'Whatever.' Enzo smiled. 'The point is, there's nothing wrong with you. With the way you look. Nothing. Unless you worked in the Excelsior in 1943. As a maid. The lowest of the low. Someone completely powerless. And then were accused of stealing.'

Pallioti stared at him.

'Think about it,' Enzo said gently. 'They didn't call that winter the Terror for nothing. What do you think the Gestapo looked like? Me?'

Pallioti looked down at his black cashmere overcoat, his impeccable black suit. Being, at least in theory, undercover police, the Gestapo had not worn uniforms. Nonetheless, they had prided themselves on their appearance. Accused of being a dandy, Himmler had had his clothes tailored at great expense. His officers had been known for their manners. Their politeness. They were not mere thugs. It had been a point of honour that they never raised their voices.

'She can't help it,' Enzo said quietly. 'It's not her fault. Or yours.'

Pallioti shook his head. He didn't know what to say.

'Dinner.' Enzo slapped the steering wheel. 'What we need is dinner.'

He turned the engine over and put the car into gear. As they slid out onto the street, the city sucked them in, moving and shifting around them. In the beams of the headlights, Pallioti saw shadows – of other black cars. Of men in black suits. Of uniforms, grey as dust, and flags with a tilted and broken-armed cross. It had been over six decades ago. Sometimes that didn't seem very long.

Chapter Thirty-Nine

Winter unfurled slowly into spring. At Easter, Saffy launched a new show and announced that, for the first time next August, the Benvoglio family, who usually preferred to take their holidays in the mountains during September, would indeed be going to the seaside. They had rented a villa in Sardinia, something far bigger than they needed. She planned on photographing in the mountains, and thought it would be a good idea if Pallioti joined them. For at least a whole week. If not the month. When he objected that he didn't think he'd be 'much good' at the seaside, she told him not to be ridiculous. When he said that he thought he might have forgotten what to do, exactly, on a holiday, she pointed out gently that that was the point.

They finally declared a truce. But he did find himself, as the days grew warmer, stopping at windows filled with especially beguiling things to be used by little boys at the beach.

He had just finished one such browsing session and was on his way into the office when he passed a newspaper kiosk and came to a dead halt. Containing, along with football schedules and movie reviews, both celebrity gossip and a running commentary on who was last seen wearing what, the city weekly had been published the night before. A stack of the papers lay in bundles on the pavement. Donata Grandolo's face stared up at him. There was a black rim around the photograph. Above it, in bold letters, the headline read, *Philanthropist in Her Own Right, Beloved Widow of City Banker Dies Peacefully at Home.*

The street stopped around him. It fell away, disintegrating like a picture made of iced sugar. In its place was the beautiful room, the crack and snap of flames, the shimmer of a shawl the colour of a dragonfly's wing. Around it all, the scent of flowers, warm and sharp at once, rose in a cloud of whispers.

Pallioti swallowed. He took some coins out of his pocket, watched while the paper seller snapped the string and handed him a copy. Then he walked on, clutching the sheets of newsprint. But he did not read, or even look at them. He was too busy following the figure of a girl as she vanished ahead of him, weaving through the crowd in her men's clothes and heavy sweater, or hurrying around the corner, coat open over her nurse's uniform, white band with a red cross stitched around her arm.

In his office, he read the piece. It didn't say much. Her family had announced her death yesterday. Her heart had stopped beating sometime during the previous night. She was eighty-two years old, survived by two daughters, two sons-in-law, three grandchildren and many great-nieces and great-nephews. The funeral would be held at San Miniato.

Pallioti folded the paper and put it in the bottom drawer of his desk. He had two meetings that morning. Enzo was investigating what looked to be a major new fraud case. And he was scheduled to have lunch with the Mayor.

It wasn't until he came back, stepped into his office at just past three o'clock, that he found the letter. It was lying squarely in the centre of his blotter. The envelope bore simply his name, no address. He did not recognize the handwriting, but he knew immediately who it was from.

*

Picking up the thick, creamy envelope, Pallioti stood, weighing it in his hand. He looked out of the window. It was a clear, perfect May afternoon. Small white clouds formed, then puffed away. When he was a child, he had been told that clouds like that were moved by the beating of angels' wings.

He stepped out of his office. Guillermo looked up. When he saw the envelope, he frowned.

'I don't know how that got here, Dottore. I assume Security cleared it. It was here when I came back from lunch.'

Pallioti nodded.

'I hope it's not – perhaps you shouldn't open it. I'll take it down and have it scanned. Or call Security. Morons.'

Guillermo was reaching for his phone, but Pallioti shook his head.

'Don't worry, Guillermo,' he said. 'It's fine.'

'Well, how do you know? Dottore, it could be—'

'It's nothing,' Pallioti said. 'Nothing. Just a letter from a ghost.'

In the piazza, tourists and pigeons flocked. The flower seller had set out a new row of bright tin buckets. Red, yellow, and the deep purple of the first irises splashed against the paving stones. Under the loggia a mime artist, dressed in a white bed sheet and wearing a crown of laurels, stood on a plinth. As Pallioti walked by, he turned, Dante with a hand outstretched.

The bench was in the far corner. People rarely found it, because it was in the shade and almost behind a not-very-good statue of someone from the Middle Ages whose name, if it had ever been known in the first place, was now forgotten. Pallioti brushed a few crumbs away. Then he sat down and opened the envelope. The small red book slid into his hand. He slipped it into his pocket, and extracted the letter. It was several pages. The paper was from Pineider, engraved in discreet grey with her initials. This time the ink was dark blue. The letters were firm, and did not waver.

My Dear Friend, she had written.

I hope I can still call you that. I believe I can, despite our differences – which were not so much differences really, were they? – as the fact that, in this instance, we were cast as adversaries. I can't think of a more worthy one. In another time we would have been the best of comrades. Perhaps more. But time deals capricious hands. We play what lies before us.

If you are reading this, it is because I am gone. And you will have guessed by now, I think, who I am. Or rather, who I was.

You were right, of course, about almost everything – and certainly about the important things. I wanted to tell you. Truly, I did. And I wouldn't have minded, if it was just myself – how much can an old woman mind spending time in jail? And I am sure they are far nicer now than the Villa Triste. But, you see, it isn't just me. I have my daughters. Sons in law. Grandchildren. My family. They are the jewels of my life. Cosimo left them in my care, and it would not do to have their mother and grandmother behind your bars. Forgive me that.

As for the rest, as I said, you were almost completely right. I thought you would like to know the whole story – something tells me that you don't negotiate well around the blank spaces – and to be honest, I would like, for once, to tell it. So I'll start, as all the best storytellers recommend, at the beginning. Or rather, where you left off.

The knock came only a few minutes after Caterina wrote those last words. She was barely in time. She ducked into the bedroom, saying she had forgotten something, and did not do a very good job of hiding her little red book. Not that it mattered. I would have found it anyway. I always did. Caterina was never much good at concealing things. I was the great liar in the family.

You must understand though, and this is important – my sister was wrong. She was not careless or a coward. She was one of the most careful, bravest people I have ever known. Enrico and me, there was something the matter with us. Some sort of genetic flaw. We never felt fear. About anything – whether it was falling out of a tree, or being caught on the loggia roof, or dying of cold in the mountains. Physical danger annoyed us, but it didn't frighten us.

There's no courage in that. There's no courage in facing things that do not scare you.

Cati, on the other hand, was afraid of everything. Of the dark. Of mice. Of Papa driving his car off the road in a rainstorm. Of Mama slipping on the ice in winter. Of breaking her wrist, or ankle. She would never use skates or go skiing when we went to the mountains for Christmas. Mostly, she was afraid of losing things – places, homes, people. I think that's why she became a nurse, to keep us all in one piece. Fix us if we broke. So her courage – her courage was extraordinary. I never thought twice about entrusting my son to her. I believed in my sister absolutely. I still do.

And that is one of the reasons I had to do what I did. It wasn't just Mama and Papa and Rico and Carlo and those other boys who died. It was Cati, too – all the years, her whole lifetime, knowing her, that she spent believing it was all her fault. Blaming herself for what happened. But, as you would say, I am getting ahead of myself.

Watching her walk out of that door, running to the window to see Cati and my son getting smaller and smaller and finally turning the corner and vanishing – I have done difficult things, but I believe that was the most difficult. Harder than looking down at dead faces in a trench, no matter how beloved, because they were dead. I could join them, but I could not get them back. Cati, on the other hand – I could have knocked on the glass, leaned out and shouted. I could have run after her. I could have just lifted a hand, breathed a word, and she would have stayed. So, finding her book. You can imagine. And how can I ever thank you, my dearest friend, for returning it to me?

I left Milan only days after Cati left. There was no point in my staying. They had some use for my special skills in Bologna, and I wanted to be in place when the storm hit. We all knew the fight would be coming over the mountains, and I felt closer to home there. Or at least, I knew I could get home. Cati was right. Back *then, I could walk the Via degli Dei blindfold. Perhaps I could still do it now. It saddens me that I'll never have the chance to try again.*

If you've seen the Red Cross and the CLN reports, you've probably sorted out what happened that April. They were right in so far as they went. I was on a sabotage unit – I just didn't die. And Cati's book was turned in to a field hospital – she just wasn't with it. Word had been passed to me by then that she was safely in Naples. This is how it happened.

We had been sent to Anzola, six of us. I did not know the people I was working with very well, not like Florence – for all the good that did me. Units had formed and re-formed, so many were getting killed. Our job that week was to make absolutely certain that the railway line to Modena was destroyed. The Allies had finally broken through the Gothic Line. But for all their bombing, it was not going quite as planned. They didn't just roll down to the Po sweeping the Germans before them. The fighting was hard. You back rabid dogs against a wall and they have nothing left to do but bite. Our job was to be certain that the train line could not be used either to evacuate or to reinforce the Germans. Of course there was air support. Like you cannot imagine. That, my friend, is hell. But still someone had to be certain the targets were actually hit – and that they were beyond repair. And to do something about it if they weren't.

There were a lot of abandoned farms and houses by then; anyone who could had run. In any case, we had found a house not far from the railway line – which looking back on it was stupid, but we were so tired. We had been working flat out for five days. There were still Fascisti around, a few, enough to be dangerous. And Germans, of course. A whole retreating army of them. And deserters. They were all angry, and defeated, and terrified. They'd shoot anything that moved.

The house we found was locked. Pathetic. And human. The key was outside in the barn, under the edge of a trough, wrapped in oilskin. We used it instead of breaking a window.

We got there just after daybreak. We intended to wait until dusk, then make our way west, destroying signal points, sabotaging track, bridges, anything we could find. There was no cellar. We stayed downstairs, and fell asleep immediately.

It must have been just after noon when I woke up. It was very still, but I could hear something. I thought at first it was a baby crying – perhaps in my dreams it had been – then I realized it was a dog, whining. It's amazing how universal that sound is – the sound of fear and loneliness. I thought it had to be the family's and that it had been left behind. I got up and went into the kitchen, and I saw it at the window. It had jumped up on an old trough that was against the wall in the yard, and was looking through the glass. It had white front paws and they were very dirty. I don't think I'll ever forget that.

I couldn't get the window open, so I went through the pantry, and out into the yard, and I had just picked it up. I was standing there, holding this little dog, petting it, trying to make it stop shaking, when I heard it – the noise of the first plane. I looked up, but I couldn't see anything. And then it was there, all of a sudden, right above me.

I didn't run, I dived. Afterwards, I thought I was dead.

My head was ringing. I couldn't hear, and I couldn't really see. There was rubble everywhere: stones, beams, earth. Plates – I remember a blue tin plate. And the dog. The dog was there. It was huddled against my stomach, as close as it could get, as if feeling me could somehow keep it alive. Then there was nothing. I must have blacked out. I'm sure I did, because the next thing I knew it was night.

The stillness was exquisite. There were stars. The dog was still next to me. It's amazing how comforting the presence of another living creature can be, how much you want to know there's any other heart that beats.

I lay there, feeling almost happy. I know that sounds strange, but I was watching the stars. I could hear Papa pointing them out to me, showing me Orion's Belt. The Pleiades. Making me spot the

Pole Star, so I would never be lost. Then the dog licked my face, and began to whine again. The noise was like a reel, pulling me in – and in that moment, I knew that if I did not do something, I would die.

I knew I was hurt, but I did not know how. I could hear Caterina's voice quite clearly, telling me not to move until I knew what was wrong. So I began testing myself, every bit – asking it if it still existed. Hand. Finger. Foot. Toes. Knee. Then, one arm – but not the other. I tried to roll over. It felt as if my left arm was being ripped off. I must have screamed. I'm sure I did. It probably terrified the dog. Thank God, there was no one else to hear. After that it took me a while to understand. Then I did. My arm was pinned under what had been, I suppose, a beam from the pantry ceiling. I couldn't move it at all, and I knew quite quickly – my brain knew – that I had to. My brain understood that if I lay there, either someone would find me – someone who would kill me – or I would die slowly and very horribly of thirst and exhaustion and gangrene.

I reached over and tried to pull it. That was a mistake. But there was a little motion, just a bit. After my head stopped reeling I remembered that I had been wearing a jacket, a man's hunting jacket, and at some point, I'm not sure when, it occurred to me that if I could get out of it, I might get free. I might be able to slip my arm through the sleeve like a casing. So that's what I did. It must have taken me an hour, but I managed.

After I was up, I knew I had to keep moving. So I walked. The dog came with me. We crossed the tracks, what was left of them, and headed straight for the mountains. But we didn't get far. I collapsed in a barn. And this is when the second of my nine lives – third, if you count the shooting at the Pergola – was saved.

The family was still there, at the farm the barn belonged to. They had lost their son in the Monte Sole debacle, so they took one look at me, and knew. For a month those kind people kept me and the dog. They splinted and bandaged my arm. They fed me by hand, like a baby with a spoon. They moved me once, the day after I arrived, when the remnants of the Jäeger division came staggering through. That was when they gave me the gun. The Sauer. Their son had given it to them. He had taken it from a dead German officer. In the end, it didn't save his life, but it might have saved mine. They came into the barn once, sat and rested there for an hour or so. We could hear them speaking German right below us, the dog and I. I hung onto him, but he didn't make a squeak. If they heard us, heard the straw move, they must have thought we were rats, or been too tired to care. We huddled in that loft two days and nights – listening to the sound of broken men and whining engines, the endless tramp of defeat.

By the time I was well enough and ready to start walking, it was June. When I left, the family insisted I take the gun. The dog and I walked at night. The Degli Dei is beautiful under the moon – if you have never walked even a piece of it, you really should. It was summer. We slept in the huts, or in the woods. Those kind people had given me a satchel and food. It took me six days to get to Fiesole. It was dawn when I stood there and looked down on Florence.

The rest, you more or less know. Or guessed. I didn't plan it, incidentally. I didn't plan to be dead or to become Donata Leone. I was going to go to San Verdiana and find my mother. Then I was going to take her to Naples, and join Caterina. It wasn't until I got to the town hall – I needed papers: everything, you see, had been in the jacket – that I realized what had happened.

I had a string leash for the dog – I had given him a name by then, Piri – and we were standing in a line like everyone else, all refugees with nothing, and there were lists, posted on the walls, of the dead. I saw Mama's name first. She had died in San Verdiana in the winter of 1944. Then I saw Caterina's name, Caterina Cammaccio. And mine – Laura Bevanelli.

At first, I panicked. I thought something must have happened in Naples. Then I looked again, and it said that Cati had been in Bologna, and that's when I understood. She wasn't Caterina Cammaccio by then anyway – Caterina and Isabella Cammaccio had been vaporized, transported to Ravensbrück. (If you escaped, as I *told you, they still put you down as 'transported'. They weren't about to admit that people got away.) So I knew at once what it was. The CLN had listed me as dead because someone had come looking for our group, and been to the farmhouse, and found the jacket. The red book had been found in the inner pocket where I kept it, and whoever found it had turned it in to the Red Cross in case my family came looking for it. But it was Cati's name in the front. That's why she was listed as dead, too.*

I stood there in the line, and I thought about it.

I'd thought and thought, of course – in Verona, in Milan, in that barn – about what had happened on Via dei Renai. And I suppose if I am honest, you are right – part of me did go back to find out. But I had no idea who it was who had betrayed us, or what they might do. And as I thought about it, with Mama gone and Cati safe, suddenly it seemed better, safer, to be dead.

They say your life does not change in a split second. But mine did, then.

I was only a few people from the table where they were taking names. A few moments later, I stepped forward, and when I did, I said 'Donata Leone'.

And that was it. Everything was over. And everything else began.

I know what you will ask. My son. I did love him, I assure you. More than anything. But I also wanted him to be safe. And free. And believe me, I knew Caterina was the best mother anyone could ever have. I understood that she had probably already heard that I was dead. Lodovico would have used all his contacts with the Allies and the Red Cross, and they would have found that I had been killed on 17 April. And I knew Cati and Lodo wanted to go to America. He had been told they could – that was the other reason he sent for her. So I understood that the chances were good by then, in late June, that they were already gone. (Cosimo found out later. They sailed for the United States on a hospital ship at the end of May.) Try to understand this: I wanted them all to have a life. The best life they could have. And I knew, always – but especially by the time I could have done it, after I married Cosimo – that if I went to find them, if I even contacted them, Caterina would insist that I take my baby back. She would give him up. After everything else she had lost, she would lose her child. And he would lose his mother. I would take the one thing I had given both of them.

I couldn't do it. It wasn't right. So I let them go. I know my son had a wonderful father, and an even more wonderful mother. One who never, even for a moment, gave him up.

I found a flat. A garret, really. And I got a job quite quickly, in the kitchen of a restaurant, such as it was. Florence, remember, had been liberated for almost a year. I peeled vegetables. I washed dishes. Mostly, I stayed out of sight. But you were right, I was worried about being recognized. And so I changed. I had kept my hair short. It was easier. I kept it dyed, dark. Again, I practised walking differently. I chose clothes I would have hated. I changed the way I spoke. I stayed away from the places I had known as a student and away from my parents' house – that was the hardest thing, and I confess, a few times at night, the dog and I climbed up the hill and watched. And then we became thieves.

I remembered that Cati had written about Mama burying their jewellery in the garden. I knew the house was empty, because I had been watching it. So, finally, one night, I climbed in through the hedge. My friend, how you would have laughed. I didn't know exactly where the things had been buried, so I was like a demented mole, digging under every special bush I could remember while Piri, bless him, stood guard. It took me three nights, three journeys back to find it, but finally I unearthed the oilskin packet. Over the next year, I sold almost everything. Even Mama's aquamarine. I kept Papa's watch. I gave it to Cosimo. He was wearing it the day he died. And Caterina's engagement ring. I used it as my own. You saw it a dozen times on my hand, and commented on it at least once, I remember.

In the end, I didn't get much money for the pieces. I had to pawn them, and you can imagine, in those first years after the war, how that market was flooded! But what I got made things better for

Piri and me. Mainly because we found a safer place to live. I spent some of it on having my hair properly done – I completely changed how I looked. And I bought some proper clothes.

I only ever met two people who recognized me. The first was Signor Cavicalli – although, I confess, I do not know which one! You were right, of course. He and his brother were the twins of the family Carlo and I took through the mountains on the last run we made in the winter of 1943. The one Caterina paid so dearly for. It was a hard slog, that trip. And dangerous because our parcels were so ill-equipped and cold and tired. Carlo carried the little girl much of the way on his back, and I was afraid for the young woman, who was not well. But they survived. All of them. And as you said, you don't forget that. Signor Cavicalli certainly didn't. He spotted me, in the marketplace, one afternoon. He was a young man by then. Probably starting at the University, and thin and stringy as a bean. But I recognized him at once, as he recognized me. Our eyes met. We said nothing. Just stood for a moment in the crowd, remembering, until his friends called to him, and he gave a little bow, and turned away.

The other person who recognized me was Emmelina's niece. It was some years later, when my oldest daughter was a baby. I was carrying her, stepping out of a shop, and I looked across the street and saw a woman watching me. At first, I couldn't place her. But she knew me. I understood that at once. Both of us had changed so much. Both of us had seen each other last as young women. Then I realized – it was Emmelina's niece. We stared at each other for a moment, then we smiled, and went our separate ways. All I can say to you is that I knew, absolutely, that any secret I had would always be safe with both of them.

I listened, and I learned, and when I found out what Cosimo was doing, I applied for a job at the bank. I got one, eventually, as a secretary. And then I heard that Cosimo was asking for volunteers, for employees to give their spare time to help with paperwork, and with tracing people for Remember The Fallen. So I volunteered. I didn't throw myself at him. But I made myself useful, and

I got into the papers. Reams and reams and boxes and boxes of them.

At first, I didn't care all that much about the work – about re-housing, and buying books and clothes and tracing families. That came later. At that time, in the beginning, I had only one thing in mind. I was hunting. I didn't know for what. I just knew that there was a smell. You were completely right about that. When I finally saw those pages from the Villa Triste, the entries that 'proved' everyone had been executed, I was disappointed. Not because of the other two – but because of Massimo. I knew, I had always known, that there was something wrong about him. He was a bastard. A pompous, vain, bullying bastard. I enjoyed killing him. I'm sorry, but I did. But that was yet to come.

Cosimo and I fell in love. Not like I had loved Carlo. There is no love like that first great love – and of course it never lasts long enough to be difficult. With Cosimo it was different. He was a wonderful man. And in case you are wondering, I told him the truth. About everything. Before we were married.

We were happy for almost fifty years. More than anyone deserves. Perhaps some part of me never stopped looking, never stopped checking papers, names that might have been connected to JULIET. But it wasn't an obsession. It was just there, like the stiff-ness in my arm – something I lived with. I had two beautiful daughters. I had a beautiful life. Even Piri lived to be a very old dog. He is buried in our garden. When Cosimo died, I was very sad. But that was natural. He was ten years older than me. Our time comes. And we had been so blessed.

And then, one night, two years ago, I was watching television. I don't usually. But this was the sixtieth celebrations, and we had been invited, because of Remember The Fallen. We would never have thought of going – you'll understand why – but I was curious. So I poured myself a glass of wine, and was looking through a book my daughter had sent me, and I had the television on, when I heard that voice. I heard Massimo.

There's a bray he has. A laugh. It's hateful.

I looked up. I almost spilled the wine. And there they were. Right in front of me. Massimo, Beppe and Il Corvo. Three dead men with medals on their chests.

The strange thing was, I didn't even have to think about it. It was as if it had been waiting inside me for all those years. I knew exactly what I had to do.

I suppose I had kept the Sauer for just something like this. Perhaps even for this. Funny, how your mind works when you're not even aware of it.

I thought about it, through the autumn and winter – you were right about that too – not because I was wondering whether I was going to do it, but because I knew I had to get it right. There was something else as well, another reason. I couldn't think of doing anything until Cosimo died. I couldn't risk getting caught and being taken away. He was very ill by then. He couldn't have managed without me. I owed him that – to be certain I was with him at the last.

In the meantime, though, I began to plan. I studied maps, paying special attention to back roads. I swam more, exercised my shoulder and my hand. I even went hunting once or twice with my son-in-law. He won't have missed a box of ammunition.

I killed Trantemento first. I watched the building for a while. As you said, no one ever notices old women, and it gave me a chance to get used to wearing my old coat and carrying a dreadful huge old bag. Then, on 1 November – I was happy about the rain – rain is good cover, people do not look at other people when they are hurrying in the rain – I slipped into the house and went straight upstairs.

All I had to do was knock on his door. And do you know the strange thing? He recognized me. At once. I think he even knew why I'd come. I would simply have shot him if he made a noise. But he didn't. He didn't say a word. When I told him to get down on his knees he looked almost relieved.

As for Beppe, I had done my homework. I knew when he was

likely to be home and alone. It was me who suggested the hotel in Apulia for our family holiday, and with so many people it was easy to get away for a few hours. I rang him from a bar earlier that day. I didn't want any record on my own phone, of course, and I was careful not to give a name, just to say I thought my husband had known him in the partisans. That was enough. Plenty, actually. He didn't just invite me in, the poor fool had set up a pretty table in the garden.

I didn't even try anything like that with Massimo. I always knew he would be the most difficult, the one most likely to fight. He had no conscience, you see. He was an arrogant, bullish man. Nothing in him but righteousness.

You had pushed me a bit, but it was hunting season, and I thought he would go out. He usually did. I was prepared, if I had to – if he hadn't gone hunting that morning – simply to go to the house or the stables and shoot him. I had to finish it, you see – before you did. But in the end, that wasn't necessary. My daughter has a country house not too far from Siena, and last autumn I started watching him. For all his security cameras, he made the most basic of mistakes. He became a creature of routine. I knew the back roads around the property and I had found a place to watch the front gates. I left just after dawn and got down there at first light. After I saw him leave it only took me a few moments to circle to the back of the woods. I was waiting for him when he got out of the car. I called his name, and when he came towards me, I shot him. I couldn't fuss with the salt, make him kneel or eat any of it. There was too much of a risk that he might have got to his gun, so I had to compromise, be content with putting a bit in his mouth and his pockets. Thank you, incidentally, for the compliment about the gloves. They were my son-in-law's, an old pair that went missing over a year ago. I wore them over my own and even practised firing in them. I couldn't afford to miss. After he was dead, I simply slipped them off and put them on him, and arranged the body.

I tied up the dog. Then, finally, I dropped the gun. And it was over.

*There is one more thing. Your Eleanor Sachs. Or Faber, as I be-
lieve she now calls herself. Fabbianocci did, indeed, mean something to me. It was Lodovico's last name.*

*I thought long and hard, but in the end, I did not contact her.
It's selfish, I suppose, but I wanted what time I had left with my
own daughters, undisturbed. Although Cosimo knew everything
about me, my daughters know nothing. Cosimo always said it was
my choice as to what and when I told them. I never did. We fought
the war to end the past, not to live in it forever.*

*You will see that I have not left Cati's book for them to come
across, or burnt it – as I admit I considered doing. Instead, I am
returning it to you, along with two other souvenirs. I trust your
judgement, my friend. Do with them what you think best.*

*I have never been able to find out where Mama was buried,
but I did go to see Carlo, and Papa, and Rico one more time after
that morning in Siena. I wanted to tell them what I had done,
and that, finally, they were free.*

*I took them a last bouquet. All roses. If you visit, you will find
a card there – probably a bit worse for wear by now. But if you
can still read it, you will see that this time it was not from Remember The Fallen, but from me – Issa.*

Or if you prefer, Il Spettro.

Pallioti sat for a moment, staring at nothing. The letter lay in
his hands, the envelope on the bench beside him. He reached
down to pick it up, to slip it into his pocket beside the little
red book, and realized that there was something else inside.
Two other souvenirs.

Turning it up, he tapped the bottom. A ring fell into his
hand, a small familiar cluster of rubies, and a photograph.

The photo's paper was brittle with age. Pallioti held it up
gently, grasping the corner between his finger and thumb. On
the back, in faded ink, were the words *Issa and Carlo, 10 May
1944*.

Turning it over, he saw that the figures had faded. They

appeared slightly ghostly, as if they, too, were finally leaving. But he could still make them out. A girl with cropped hair wearing a man's trousers and shirt stood in front of a tall, fair boy. His bare arms, sleeves rolled up, were looped around her shoulders. Looking up at him, she was laughing. A meadow stretched around them. Behind them, mountain peaks rose into what must once have been a bright blue sky.

EPILOGUE

—◦◦◦—

PITTSBURGH, PENNSYLVANIA

August 2007

The street was tree lined. Branches spread over it, dropping little green propeller-like seeds onto the tarmac. Roots pushed up, buckling the concrete sidewalk. The houses were not large. Each of them sat on a small patch of lawn. Each had a front walk. Some had a garage. Eleanor Sachs's did not.

A new-looking Volkswagen Beetle was parked in her driveway. Pallioti could not decide if this was a good or a bad sign. He had suddenly been gripped by the idea that she was away. At best, the car might mean she had not gone on a driving vacation. But she might still have taken a taxi to the airport. As he had. Enzo had offered to drive him, but he had hemmed and hawed, and finally said 'no'. This was a trip he wanted to take, from start to finish, alone.

Sunlight the colour of honey dripped through the canopy of leaves. A woman came by, walking a dog. Two joggers ran down the centre of the street, their feet falling in tandem. He had been waiting for an hour, and the shadows were lengthening when he finally saw her, a small figure with the same dark hair, and the too-big bag over her shoulder. She was wearing a T-shirt and a flowered skirt and sandals, and seemed to be either talking or singing to herself, head bent, watching the sidewalk and hopping occasionally. He smiled when he realized what she was doing. Not stepping on cracks.

Eleanor Sachs checked her mailbox. He had already noted a utility bill, two magazines and a copy of today's newspaper – the fact that there was mail had been one of the things that convinced him to wait. She continued up the front walk. On the porch, she dug in her bag for a key.

His plane had been delayed due to a thunderstorm early in the day. As he opened the car door, he could feel the close muggy embrace of late summer. He crossed the street, fingering the envelope he had folded the ring into. The small red book was in his pocket, the worn photograph tucked inside the front cover. Somewhere down the block, he could hear the rattle of a kid on a skateboard.

He rang the bell. The top of Eleanor's front door was heavy bevelled glass, so he saw her legs first, coming down the stairs. Then the rest of her. She was running her hand through her hair, saying something to a large grey cat that scuttled in front of her. Then she looked up.

Eleanor Sachs stopped, frozen, one hand on the banister, her mouth opening in a small, soundless 'oh'. Pallioti took a breath. He could feel everything going wrong, crumbling. Then she smiled. And stepped across the foyer and opened the door.

For a moment, neither of them said anything. Eleanor took in his blue jeans. His summer shirt. The fact that he wasn't wearing a tie.

'What,' she said finally – the smile, which was rapidly turning into a grin, creased her face, lit the deep, deep blue of her eyes – 'what on earth,' she asked, 'are you doing here?'

Pallioti took the red book out of his pocket. He held it out to her. The faint stamp of the gold lily caught the evening sun. Eleanor looked from the book to him.

'I've come,' he said, 'to keep a promise.'

Acknowledgements

With very special thanks:

To my husband, for all the hours he spent listening and traipsing about the Italian countryside hunting down ghosts of the Partisans.

To Jane Gregory, and to all of the wonderful people at Gregory and Co. for their kindness, expertise and endless patience.

To Maria Rejt and Sophie Orme for their sound judgement, excellent advice and generous support.

And to the faculty of the Paris American Academy, and in particular John and Marsha Biguenet, for their inspirational teaching, wise counsel and for helping me to believe I could.

Thank you.